W9-CPB-637

Acclaim for David Kent's novels of Department Thirty

THE MESA CONSPIRACY

"Adjust the lights and make a big pot of tea: this one will keep you going all night! Makes you want to go back and read the beginnings of Department Thirty."

—*New York Times* bestselling author John J. Nance

DEPARTMENT THIRTY

"One heckuva good ride. . . . A page-turner until the end, it is hard to put down. . . . A truly great read. If you're a fan of thrillers, pick up this book!"

—*Oklahoma Gazette*

"Compellingly mysterious and gripping . . . a fascinating adventure."

—*Edmond Life & Leisure* (Edmond, OK)

"A thrill-a-minute ride . . . a classic man-on-the-run thriller."

—*Mystery Scene*

"Wow! Terrific . . . engrossing from first page to last."

—*Madill Record* (Madill, OK)

"A tangled web is woven . . . the author knows how to write a compelling mystery."

—*The Daily Oklahoman*

"A satisfying read. . . . Kent does an excellent job of keeping the level of suspense high and, most importantly, the reader turning pages. . . . A promising debut."

—Thebookreporter.com

THE MESA
CONSPIRACY

DAVID
KENT

POCKET STAR BOOKS
New York   London   Toronto   Sydney

This book is a work of fiction. Names, characters, places and incidents are products of the author's imagination or are used fictitiously. Any resemblance to actual events or locales or persons, living or dead, is entirely coincidental.

An *Original* Publication of POCKET BOOKS

A Pocket Star Book published by
POCKET BOOKS, a division of Simon & Schuster, Inc.
1230 Avenue of the Americas, New York, NY 10020

Copyright © 2005 by Kent Anderson

ISBN: 0-7434-6999-2

First Pocket Books printing January 2005

10 9 8 7 6 5 4 3 2 1

POCKET STAR BOOKS and colophon are registered trademarks of Simon & Schuster, Inc.

Cover design by Jae Song

Manufactured in the United States of America

For information regarding special discounts for bulk purchases, please contact Simon & Schuster Special Sales at 1-800-456-6798 or business@simonandschuster.com.

For Benjamin, William, and Samuel,
who tamed the wind and planted the jewel tree

ACKNOWLEDGMENTS

Family first: My wife Martha has been steadfast and strong through darkness and light, and I could not do this without her. My sons, Ben, Will, and Sam, bless me with joy and wonder, intelligence and integrity. They are amazing.

My spiritual family at Northwest Christian Church (Disciples of Christ) provides a haven of love and acceptance. Within this faith community, I am especially grateful to The Next Generation. You have done more than I can even understand, much less express.

My parents, Bill and Audrey Anderson, my sister Teresa Anderson, and my in-laws, Harold and Mary Watson, have been enthusiastic and supportive throughout this process.

My colleagues at KCSC, past and present, have been patient and understanding through the years, and continue to be some of my closest friends in the world.

For specific assistance in the writing of this book, I would like to thank the following:

Keeli Pfeiffer, for insight on being a surviving twin; and Ryan Pfeiffer, on being the spouse of one.

Lawyer and friend M. C. Smothermon, for clarifying the legal issues involved in exhumation.

The ever-knowledgeable Lane Whitesell, and my colleagues with the Association of Music Personnel in Public Radio, for helping with Drew's choice of opera.

My good friend of twenty-plus years, Charles Newcomb, who served as aviation consultant as well as offered general feedback on the manuscript. Any aviation facts I got right are directly attributable to him; any mistakes are my own fault. Charles, in turn, also consulted aviation mechanic Jeff Bright, who gave additional technical advice.

Teri Anderson, Christy Breedlove, LeeAnn Bauermeister, and Melanie Coldren, for their work with deaf and developmentally delayed children, and for teaching me the beauty of sign language.

The writings of Allison Weir, for making the Tudor era come alive.

My indispensable critique group: Sami Nepa, Dave Stanton, Judy Tillinghast, and Mike Miller, who also helped with various computer crises. Susan "Ms. B" Bumgarner offered valuable feedback as well, with a great eye for detail.

My literary agent, John Talbot, works with faith and patience to help move me in the right direction and then makes sure I get there in one piece.

Kevin Smith, my editor at Pocket Books, has once again proven that it is possible to have remarkable insight and be an incredibly nice guy at the same time. He also sets speed records for responding to e-mails from nervous authors.

I would like to thank the rest of the Pocket team, especially Erica Feldon, Hillary Schupf, Alexandre Su, David Chesanow, Johanna Farrand, and the incredible sales and marketing staff. Finally, many thanks to the booksellers who opened their stores to me and promoted my work to readers.

David Kent
Oklahoma City, Oklahoma

Tell me not, in mournful numbers,
Life is but an empty dream!—
For the soul is dead that slumbers,
And things are not what they seem.

—Henry Wadsworth Longfellow,
"A Psalm of Life"

THE MESA
CONSPIRACY

PROLOGUE

July 27, 1965

DEATH AND LIFE. LIFE AND DEATH.

It was almost funny, Maggie thought. She was about to give birth, and yet she longed for death.

She had sinned, and her sins were so great that she deserved to die. She had betrayed Terry, betrayed her own soul, betrayed the lives that grew inside her. Death would be a relief, even a blessing.

But first there was the pain, and the pain meant that before she could slip away into oblivion, she had to get on with the business of giving birth.

The doctor—gowned, masked, and gloved—sat on a low stool between her legs, shouting at her with what sounded like the voice of God. But this wasn't the loving God Maggie had always believed in. This sounded like the Old Testament God of Noah's flood, the God who destroyed Sodom and Gomorrah, the God who turned Lot's wife into a pillar of salt.

"Push, woman!" the voice thundered. "Come on, now, don't you know this is almost over? Push, push! Don't just lie there, Maggie—*push, I said!*"

Maggie trembled all over as another contraction washed over her. For nearly a year she and Terry had lived in this desolate place, far from family and friends—far from everything, it seemed. Everything except the mesa. Black Mesa towered over the harsh landscape like an unforgiving parent, stern and forever expectant. There were times over the last year when she'd looked out the windows of The Center, fantasizing that she and Terry could walk away. They would escape to the mesa and no one would follow them there.

But it was just a fantasy. She'd known this day would come, somewhere in the unbearable heat of the high-plains summer, and that she would have to face it. She would have to face the living, breathing proof of what she had done.

Terry had given up his mechanic's job, and she'd left waiting tables at Eva's, to come to this place, to do this thing. But then, in her confusion, in her despair, she had committed the most horrible sin of all, and there was no turning back. The contractions proved it.

Maggie squeezed her eyes closed and bit her lip, tasting blood. Almost against her will, she pushed, trying to think of Terry and the plans they had made. Terry had said everything was in place, that it was all ready. It would be all right. *Trust me, Mags,* he'd said a few days ago.

But I deserve to die, she thought.

"Push!" the doctor shouted at her.

She pushed, and all she could feel was the pressure. A relentless assault of mind-numbing, body-wracking pressure that made her grip the rails of the bed so hard, her hands ached. She raised her head a couple of inches, just far enough to see the pale little form, awash in blood and fluid, passing into the doctor's hands.

Life.

As she saw her first child, everything else began to fade away. Her own mistakes, the doctor's thundering voice, the desolation of this place . . . it all blurred into nothingness, and she felt her own heart beating. The pendulum began its swing back toward life.

"I want to see . . ." Maggie muttered.

"No." The doctor shook his head. "It's better if you don't. Remember, we have a special place for them. We'll take care of everything." He turned to the nurse: "Go, will you? Go now! Take him out of here."

Him. Oh Lord, a boy child. Terry had wanted sons so much. Sons he could teach to throw footballs, to take deer hunting in the fall, to share his love of machinery and tinkering. A boy. Now it seemed her betrayal was complete, all-encompassing, suffocating.

Maggie's eyes filled and she pushed again. Then her second baby was outside her, the doctor snipping the cord. He swaddled the little form tightly and yelled for the nurse to come back.

Maggie pulled herself up slowly. Dizziness curled around her, and the pain was still so intense, it felt like her insides were being ripped from her. *In a way*, she thought, *they are. They are.*

"My babies," she whispered.

Maggie raised herself up farther, watching as the doctor shifted the bundle around. A flap of the blanket fell away and she saw the tiny face.

The baby's eyes were open.

Maggie screamed.

The doctor whirled on her. "Maggie, listen to me! Don't look! It serves no purpose for you to look. Just lie back and relax."

"No!" Maggie screamed.

She heard voices from the hallway. She couldn't make out the words, but she heard Terry's voice. *Terry!* He was here, after all.

The doctor grabbed her by the shoulders. "It's over, Maggie. They're gone. We've already made the arrangements."

She heard Terry's voice outside again, closer and angry now. Then another voice, one that chilled her, despite the night heat. The voice of sin and pain and death.

The door flew open and *he* stood in the doorway, light spilling in behind him. "Maggie, my dear, your husband is proving difficult. A stubborn young buck. He doesn't seem to understand what's going on here."

Maggie gazed at him with silent hate. *Oh, you evil, evil man. You tricked us, you tricked me. . . .*

"Maggie!" Terry shouted from the hall.

"It's finished," the man said, and Maggie felt as if she were falling away, falling into his dark eyes. "Nothing's going to change it, not the mindless ranting of your foolish husband, nor your tears and hysteria. Understood?"

Maggie squeezed her eyes closed.

"Understood?" the man shouted.

Tears spilled out and streaked down Maggie's face. She nodded once.

"Good," the man said, nodded toward the doctor, and slammed the door.

She could hear Terry in the hall, then running feet, two sets. Another door slammed far away.

Maggie realized she and the doctor were alone in the room now, and she began to feel a creeping coldness up her back.

The doctor carefully placed the squirming baby in a little bassinet beside the bed. He turned his back to Maggie and fussed with his tray of instruments. When he faced her again, he was holding a syringe of amber liquid.

"Let me give you something to relax," he said.

Maggie whipped her head from side to side. "Terry—the babies . . ."

"Forget them, Maggie," the doctor said, thumping the syringe.

The door to the room flew open again.

Terry!

This time he was holding something in his hands, but Maggie's senses, frayed like old electrical wire, couldn't make it out. Whatever it was, he looked like an avenging angel from heaven. *Oh, Terry, I'm so sorry for what I've done! Please forgive me!* But then, Terry didn't know of her sin, which was even worse. She carried it alone, inside her like a cancer. She couldn't even speak the words. There were only formless, random thoughts in her mind.

The doctor looked over his shoulder. "Get out of here," he snarled.

"Get away from her," Terry said, his voice calm.

Maggie heard a little cry, tiny and struggling but as clear to her as church bells ringing on Sunday mornings back home. She thought of the top of the huge mesa that looked down on this place, running for miles and miles through the sparse countryside. She remembered her fantasy, she and Terry leaving The Center, climbing to the top of it where no one would find them.

Then there was an explosion that set her ears to ringing and a brilliant flash of white light.

Then nothing.

December 24, 1970

Art Dorian walked through the door and into another world.

Somehow, before he opened the door to the small, ordinary room with its folding table and metal chairs, still smelling of fresh paint, he might have been able to go back. He could have dropped off all the paperwork, gotten into his car, and been back on campus within a few hours. He could have spent Christmas walking through the new snow on the college common, lost in solitude and quiet contemplation of the coming semester.

But he walked through the door, smelling the paint, thinking that his country had called him, and he had no choice but to answer.

Not quite true: He could have politely refused and gone back to life as a scholar and teacher. It wasn't his country that convinced him, but his oldest and closest friend in the world.

Dorian sighed and crossed the threshold.

The man sitting at the folding table was in his early forties, a few years older than Dorian, very tall, broadshouldered, with an angular face full of shifting planes. His hair was nut-brown, already shot through with gray, his eyes a deeper brown and very alert. Dorian noted that the man's prison clothes had been discarded. They'd given him a navy blue T-shirt and pants, and brown work shoes.

"Mr. Brandon," Dorian said, and swept a hand toward the metal chair across from the man. "May I sit?"

Charles Brandon shrugged and leaned back in his chair. It teetered on its back legs.

"How was your trip?" Dorian asked, sitting and centering the file folder in front of him.

Brandon thumped the chair back to the floor. "Since it involved leaving the Englewood Federal Correctional Facility, it was the best trip I've ever taken. Who are you?"

"Art Dorian. I'd like to—"

"You're a spook of some sort?"

Dorian flinched at the slang. "No. I'm with a new unit of the U.S. government, and we'd like to talk to you."

The planes of Brandon's face shifted. "A new unit? My, aren't we formal? This new *unit* have a name? I'd like to know who had the pull to whisk me out of Englewood that way."

"Department Thirty."

Brandon raised his eyebrows. "How refreshing. At least it's not another set of alphabet soup."

Dorian brushed a finger across his thin line of a mustache. "No doubt you're wondering why you've been brought here."

Brandon leaned back again. "Tell me, Art Dorian of Department Thirty. Why aren't you with your family on Christmas Eve?"

"I have no family, Mr. Brandon."

"Pity. You don't look like law enforcement to me."

Dorian shrugged. "My background is academic. An assistant professor of history."

"Don't tell me. American political history."

"Actually, the English Renaissance."

Brandon's eyes widened. "Oh, how wonderful. Then you must know about my namesake."

"Charles Brandon, Duke of Suffolk. Childhood friend of Henry VIII, later his brother-in-law."

"Oh, come now, Art Dorian of Department Thirty. That's not the best part and you know it. He married Henry's sister in secret after her husband the king of France died. The Brandons' granddaughter was the ill-fated Lady Jane Grey, the infamous 'nine-days queen.' The Brandons were right in the middle of all that era's political intrigue, deal-making, backstabbing, manipulations."

"You seem to have studied a bit yourself."

"How could I help it, given the name?" Brandon's eyes locked onto Dorian's. "So you've come to do some deal-making of your own, is that right? A Tudor scholar comes to make a deal, to do some backroom politics."

Dorian smiled. "We can discuss the Tudors another time, Mr. Brandon. Let me tell you about Department Thirty. We were created by Congress at the same time as another new program called Witness Security, which is administered by the United States Marshals Service. It gives new identities— new lives, basically—to people who have witnessed federal crimes and can provide information, yet are frightened of testifying. Department Thirty, on the other hand, lives in something of a parallel universe. We were created to work with those who have *committed* crimes. We make a judgment about whether certain individuals have knowledge or information the government believes would be beneficial to our national objectives, and if those individuals decide to cooperate, the slate is wiped clean. Their old lives cease to exist. We will create the paper trail, set you up in a new community in a new profession. . . ."

"And ignore the crimes that got me here?"

Dorian took a deep breath and thought about his words very carefully. This had formed his own moral objection to the idea of joining Department Thirty. "It's a question of what people do versus what they know. We make a judgment call. It's a matter of greater good."

"Greater good. You know what I did, then."

Dorian patted the file folder. "I do."

"And you know how long I did it before I was caught?"

Dorian nodded.

Brandon snapped his chair back again. "So let me make sure I have this all straight. You want me to talk about everything I did before you caught me, and in return you give me the new identity and whatever protection I might need."

"No," Dorian said.

Brandon looked up sharply. "No?"

Dorian took a deep breath and shook his head slowly. "Mr. Brandon, Department Thirty doesn't care about the crimes for which you've been convicted. I have no comment on them whatsoever. We're interested in the job you held before your conviction."

Brandon leaned forward.

"You were the general counsel to the House Intelligence Committee. You worked for the committee itself, not an individual member. Our feeling is that you can provide valuable information, untainted by any political bias."

The planes of Brandon's face shifted, and Dorian saw the hardness he hadn't noticed before. For the first time he felt the man's malevolence. For the first time he let himself think about why this man had been sent to federal prison, and he thought he understood. Dorian decided that Charles Brandon could probably have convinced anyone to do just about anything.

Brandon leaned back, the malevolence melted, and he began to laugh.

Dorian waited patiently, then said, "Is that funny?"

Brandon slapped his hands on his legs. "You want to know where the bodies are buried. You want to know what the CIA and DIA and FBI told the committee about who's running what agents and levels of penetration. You want to know about secret funding. You want all the dirty laundry of the intelligence forces so your new little Department Thirty can build up its own power."

Dorian kept his voice even. "Are you interested?"

Brandon's smile vanished like chalk being wiped off a blackboard. "How many others have you recruited into this little program?"

"Witness Security has already worked with dozens of people. For Department Thirty, you're the first." Dorian allowed himself a thin smile. "Case number one."

"Even better. So I talk about all the secret testimony before the committee, names and dates and amounts and locations, and I'm finished with jail?"

Now Dorian leaned forward. "If you go into this program, Charles Brandon never leaves this room. He disappears off the face of the earth, and a new man walks out the door."

Dorian watched him. The man's mind was racing through the possibilities. Dorian knew he was brilliant, both as counsel to the committee and in the planning and execution of the crimes that had eventually landed him in prison.

"What about my family?" Brandon finally asked.

Dorian shook his head. "No connection with your old life. It's all or nothing, I'm afraid."

Brandon smiled his slow, malevolent smile again. "Then that seals it. I'm in."

Dorian blinked.

"Do I get to choose where I live?" Brandon asked.

"Within reason."

"Oklahoma," Brandon said immediately.

Dorian's eyebrows went up. "Unless I'm mistaken, some of your crimes were committed in that state. That would not be advisable."

"If you'll double-check, my 'crimes' were actually 'committed' in Colorado and New Mexico, Professor Dorian."

"Why Oklahoma?"

Brandon shrugged. "Clean air, nice people. Lots of space. A low cost of living. My family isn't well known there, unlike some other parts of the country. I'd think that would be a bonus for you."

Dorian hesitated, then nodded. "I'll look into it."

"My money was frozen when I was convicted. I want my assets back, transferred to the new identity."

Dorian looked at him and rubbed an index finger across his mustache. It was his call. He could turn around and leave this room with its fresh paint smell and tell the federal marshals outside to take the prisoner back to Englewood. No one would ever know the difference. Or he could do what Department Thirty and his boyhood friend had sent him here to do: make a deal with this man.

"I'm waiting, Professor," Brandon said.

God forgive me if I'm wrong, Dorian thought, then nodded.

He reached into his battered brown briefcase and took out a small cassette recorder. He attached a microphone and checked the cassette inside it.

Then he extended his hand across the table. "Welcome to Department Thirty," Dorian said.

PART ONE

1

Present Day

BEFORE HE EVEN ANSWERED THE PHONE, ERIC ANTHONY knew that Colleen must either be dead or very close to it.

He squinted at the caller ID readout and recognized Colleen's number. He knew she was too weak to reach the phone, and the hospice nurse would only call him in a real emergency.

He looked away from the computer in his home office, where he was parked eight to ten hours every weekday. He'd just been researching the voting record of Oklahoma's senior U.S. senator, as it related to transportation issues. Highway funding, mass transit, gasoline taxes . . . mind-numbing boredom punctuated by the occasional revelation. The advertising agency and political consulting firm that employed Eric had identified transportation as a key issue to Oklahoma voters, and its client, who was challenging the incumbent, was paying big bucks for the opposition research.

Of course, keeping his mind numb was part of the reason Eric Anthony did this job. He could work at home, only going into the agency's office twice a month or so for meetings. He didn't have to face the stares of the people in the halls, the mutterings, and the occasional bold one who would ask him a question outright. In a firm populated by political junkies, they all knew who he was.

Eric spoke quietly to the hospice nurse for a moment, then bookmarked the Web site he was using for reference, saved the report he was writing, and made a quick call to Laura's office. He couldn't get through to her, of course, but he told her secretary that Laura would need to pick up

Patrick today. Laura would complain, because that's what Laura did, but this couldn't wait. Colleen was dying today, this afternoon, *right now.*

He walked away from the clutter of the office and into the bathroom. He splashed a little cold water on his face and let it drip down his chin. Looking at the face in the mirror, he understood the confusion of some of the others at the firm. They couldn't believe the eternally rumpled Eric Anthony could have done what he did. At nearly forty years old, he was thirty pounds overweight and wore glasses that always seemed to slip down his nose. In those infrequent staff meetings, he would gaze over them when he wanted to make a point, looking faintly ridiculous in the process. His eyes were a vague hazel that no one had ever called piercing, and he never seemed to know what to do with his hands, spending most of his time with them in his pockets, jingling keys and coins.

He stepped outside the house, his face still damp. An hour earlier it was sunny and eighty degrees. Now the temperature had dropped to the sixties and clouds were rolling across the prairie sky. *Springtime in Oklahoma,* Eric thought. Thunder cracked somewhere far to the west.

It was funny, and somehow just like one of the bad movies Colleen had been in when Eric was a kid, that she was dying on a day like this. She was always as unpredictable as the Oklahoma weather, and now she was slipping out of this life on a day where an unexpected thunderstorm was brewing. Even at the close of her life, she couldn't escape melodrama, like a badly written movie script.

Colleen, he thought. *Poor, tragic Colleen.* The closest thing to a mother he'd ever had.

The thunder rolled. Halfway to his car, Eric broke into a run.

It only took Eric seven minutes to reach the house in which he'd spent his teenage years, in Oklahoma City's Gatewood neighborhood. Northwest of downtown, the homes dated from the 1920s, old for this young city. Towering oaks and elms lined the streets, sometimes with branches touching from opposite sides of the street.

Colleen Cunningham's house was the one in various states of being painted, with torn storm windows and cracks between the bricks. It had looked the same for as long as Eric could remember. Colleen would say, "We need to paint the house," and would start on it, only to get distracted by something else and leave it partially done—for years. That was essentially the story of Colleen's life, Eric thought, told in the peeling paint of the old house.

The rain started as he pulled into the driveway. In true Oklahoma springtime fashion, it didn't begin sprinkling and gradually build; instead, the skies opened into a major downpour in seconds.

Eric left his Honda Civic behind Colleen's burgundy '68 Cadillac and let himself in with his key. The inside of the house was the same as outside: cracks in the plaster walls, dust on the mantel, books and newspapers in every corner, dirty plates and glasses on top of the ancient television set.

Eric paused, as he always did, his eyes inevitably drawn to the framed poster over the mantel. Colleen's best film role had been in a 1972 thriller called *Angels Cry*. She'd played the socialite wife of a wealthy banker who turned out to be a serial killer. It could have been so much B-movie fodder, but Colleen's performance had an understated intensity, especially in the film's final scene, when she confronted and ultimately killed her husband. Eric had been seven the year *Angels Cry* came out, and Colleen, with no thought as to what was appropriate for a seven-year-old and what wasn't, had taken him to the premiere. He'd had nightmares for nearly a month after seeing his guardian on a huge screen blowing a hole in a man's chest. When he wrote Colleen's obituary, sometime in the next few days, it would mention *Angels Cry*, even though she had left Hollywood and hadn't acted in more than twenty years.

Eric had always hated the poster with a passion, and he especially disliked the prominent place it had in their home. It was dark and foreboding, with a shattered-glass effect slashing across the images of Colleen and her screen husband. Every time he saw the poster, it reminded him of the nightmares he'd suffered as a child. As a teenager, he'd asked Colleen dozens of times to take it down, or at least put it in her own room, but she'd always shaken him off, insisting it was her best work and deserved to be where anyone could see it. As an adult, after he'd moved out, he'd stopped pestering her about it, but it still bothered him, a grim reminder of his strange boyhood.

Eric thought about his own career, of what he had done in self-defense five years ago, of the whispers in hallways. *Funny how things come around, isn't it?*

The hospice nurse came in from the kitchen. "Eric, you're here. I thought I heard the door."

Eric looked away from *Angels Cry.* "How is she?" He waited a second. "That's a stupid thing to say, isn't it? She's dying. That's how she is."

The nurse nodded with an I've-heard-this-all-before sort of wisdom. "She'll be glad you're here. Why don't you go on back?"

Eric nodded back to her, making his way through the messy dining room and the narrow hallway to Colleen's bedroom at the rear of the house.

Over the course of the cancer's advance through her body, he had ceased to be amazed at her appearance. But Colleen Cunningham, once known to moviegoers as Colleen Fox, was only sixty-three years old, and now looked twenty years older. The chemo had taken her once luxurious dark hair. A gray frizz covered her head. Her skin was so loose that it looked as if it needed to be reeled in to take up the slack. She was propped up in bed in her old pink nightgown, looking angry.

"Sit your butt down. Don't just stand there," she said, and her voice had only a fraction of its old power. When he was a kid, her voice could make him cower in a corner of his room. Now it was a papery rustle.

Eric eased into the wooden chair beside her. "How do you feel?"

"Don't. Don't even try that. I'm going to be gone pretty

damned soon, a few hours, a day, whatever. I feel like shit, and I'm ready to get this over with."

Despite himself, Eric felt his eyes begin to fill.

Colleen clamped a hand on his wrist. Her fingers felt to him like an assortment of twigs wrapped loosely in plastic. "Don't start that. Time for that's over." She went into a coughing fit and spat a wad of blood-streaked phlegm into the wastebasket by the bed. "Come on, we've got business to talk about."

Eric blinked. "We've already made the funeral arrangements. Everything's set, Colleen."

She shook her head, and he watched her eyes. Throughout the illness he'd always counted on her eyes still being bright, a fierce, smoldering brown. Now they looked dull, as if someone had pulled a filmy sheet over them.

"Not talking about the damn funeral." She let go of his wrist and patted it in an almost motherly way. "I don't know how the hell you turned out as good as you did. God knows I didn't do a very good job with you. I had too many other things to think about. Movies, men, booze, dope, then more booze and dope."

Eric shrugged and looked at the walls. "I don't know how well I turned out, but thanks for trying."

Colleen made a noise in the back of her throat. When she spoke again, her voice was even raspier. "Don't pull that self-deprecating bullshit on me. It might fool those people you work for now, but not old Colleen. You're smart, you're honest, and you give a damn. Not too many like that. Where's the boy?"

"I had Laura pick him up."

"Good. Don't want him to see this. He's a damn good kid, and you're a damn sight better with him than I was with you." She tapped his leg. "You and Laura ought to try again."

"We've had this conversation before. She didn't want to be married anymore, and she didn't want Patrick, either. She's married to her career and that's the way she likes it."

Colleen pursed her lips. "I suppose. Now listen: one piece of advice and then I've got to tell you something important.

The advice is: Forget about everything that happened before. It's gone, and it doesn't matter. Not a damn bit of it. Forget your old job—forget it! You beating yourself up every day over something that you couldn't control won't help you or Patrick or anyone else."

Eric was silent a moment. "It's not like that," he finally said.

"Yes, it *is* like that, you idiot. Forget it and it doesn't have any damn power over you. Now the important stuff. I was supposed to tell you this after you were an adult, when you asked about your parents." She fixed him with one dull eye. "But, dammit, you never asked."

Eric said nothing.

"See, you're doing it again. You've got it all backwards. You remember stuff best forgotten, and won't even consider the things you should be remembering."

"What's the point?"

Colleen poked his leg again. "The point is, I'm a dead woman, and if I don't tell you this now, you'll never know." She went into another coughing spasm, not quite as violent as the last one. "You see," she rasped as it passed, "now or never. After you were about ten years old, you never once asked me a thing about your parents, about how you wound up with me . . . nothing. Why?"

"No point, I already said. You were raising me. You were my family. End of story."

She poked him harder, making him flinch. "No, no, and no. Beginning of story. For someone who's smart, you're awfully stupid sometimes."

Eric swallowed back a response, reminding himself again that she *was* his only family, and she would likely be dead before the sun went down. He turned at the rain on the window. "It's blowing up quite a storm."

The poke turned into a slap on his knee. "Stop that shit! Don't you change the subject on me. Now listen: I don't have time to do this more than once, and I may have forgotten part of it. Dope can do that to you, make you forget things. You never did any dope, did you?"

"No, Colleen," Eric said. "Not even once."

"Not even in college?"

"Not even once," he repeated.

"You were always so damn straitlaced."

Eric shrugged.

Colleen sighed, and her body seemed to shrink into itself. "First things first. Your name isn't Eric Anthony."

She said it so matter-of-factly, for a moment it didn't register with Eric. He looked down at her.

"Did you hear what I said?"

"Colleen, I think you—"

Colleen flapped an angry hand. "Dammit, you listen to me! My body may be worn out, but my mind's fine!"

"But, Colleen—"

"Will you shut up for a minute and listen? I mean, your name is Eric Anthony, but that's not your *full* name. I had to drop part of it—you know, to help keep you safe."

Eric twitched.

Colleen sighed again. "Doesn't make a damn bit of sense, does it? No, of course it doesn't. It never has. Your full name is Eric Anthony Miles. Got that. Miles, just like miles that you travel."

Eric blinked. He thought he detected the room beginning to spin a bit. He leaned over the bed. "What do you mean, keep me safe? Who's Miles? Why did you—"

"Use the name if you want, don't if you don't. But that's who you are. What, who, why—wish you'd asked me these questions a few years ago." She brushed a hand across her face, fingertips brushing against the sallow skin. "I was living in the loft in Venice. First place I had when I went to L.A. I'd been there nearly two years. Remember that apartment?"

Eric nodded. "I remember. I liked the stairs. I used to roll my cars down them, carry them back up, and roll them down again."

"Damn little plastic cars all over the place. Good apartment, though. I'd had a couple of commercials by then, and one line in a bad TV police drama. I was 'Woman in Bar.' My first paying dramatic job, 'Woman in Bar.' It was summer, and I just remember thinking how glad I was to be in California with the breezes off the ocean, and not back here in Oklahoma, with nothing to do but sweat. It was late at night, and for once I was alone. I'd been chasing after this assistant director, but he went home to his wife and I was alone in the loft. And here's this knock on the door at nearly midnight."

Colleen stopped and Eric looked at her. The cloudy film over her eyes had lessened somewhat, and they were far away now.

"So I went downstairs and opened the door and here's this guy I've never seen before. He's about my age, maybe a year or two younger, good-looking in a sort of working-class way. He hasn't shaved in a few days, and his eyes are all red and his clothes are all wrinkled, and he's holding a baby."

"Colleen, I really don't think—"

"I'm the one who's dying, and if I *think*, then you're going to sit there and listen until I finish, or until I kick off, whichever comes first. Are we clear?"

Her voice was still papery, but Eric imagined there was a little of the old power in it. He held up his hands. "All right, all right. Go on."

"Well, here's a guy holding a baby, and even I could tell that the baby was really young, like just a few days young. The guy says, 'Hello, Colleen. I'm Terry.' And I say, 'Hello, Terry. I'm Colleen. What the hell are you doing here?' See, I was a smart-ass even then. And he says, 'Colleen, meet my son. This is Eric.' "

Eric stared down at her. When he was very young, he remembered asking Colleen if she was his mother, and when she said she wasn't, she said something about cousins twice removed. Then he'd asked about his mother and father and she said, "Ask me when you're older." But by then he'd washed his hands of his parents and resolved never to think about them again. They weren't a part of his life.

Eric nodded at her to continue. Rain thumped the bedroom window as if asking to be let in. Thunder cracked overhead.

Colleen turned her head toward the window. " 'It was a dark and stormy night,' " she quoted. "Nice stage dressing:

Remember to thank the production designer." She shook her head and tapped Eric's leg again, this time more softly. "I didn't let him in. I thought, *Here's some nut holding a newborn baby standing on my doorstep, I've got an audition in the morning, and what can I do to get rid of this guy?* I asked him if he wanted money and told him I didn't have any, barely able to pay the rent on the loft. He just sort of smiled and told me to reach in the pocket of his shirt and pull out the photos there. The baby was beginning to squirm, and so I did. There were two pictures. The first one had been taken at a family reunion about ten years before, back when I still cared about hanging out with any of the family. I was about thirteen when the picture was taken, and it was of me with this cousin of mine, actually my second cousin. Her name was Maggie. Her mom was my cousin, and Maggie was about my age. She lived in some little town and I only saw her about once every two or three years, but I always liked her. I hadn't seen her or talked to her since a couple of years before I moved to L.A., but here was this picture. Then I looked at the other one, and it was a wedding picture of this guy who's standing in front of me, and he's with Maggie."

Colleen coughed again, still less violently. It seemed to Eric that the closer she came to death, even her coughs were weaker. "Water," she said.

Eric poured her a cup of water from the pitcher by the bed and handed it to her. A few drops dribbled out of her mouth and ran down the front of the cotton nightgown. She dabbed at the front halfheartedly, then leaned back against the pillow in exhaustion.

"Dammit," Colleen whispered.

"What?" Eric said, taking the cup from her.

"Light-headed. Dammit, I can't go yet. I've got to tell you this." She blinked her eyes several times, turning slowly back to him. "This is your damned fault, you know, and thank you so much for making a dying woman work so hard."

"What do you mean, my fault?"

"If you'd asked me when you were eighteen or twenty-five or thirty or something, we could have gone over it then."

"But I didn't—"

Colleen let out a big breath. Eric caught the sickly smell coming from her. "Save it. We've had *that* conversation before too. Now, remember when you write the obit, make sure and say that Colleen Cunningham of Oklahoma City, Oklahoma, was also Colleen Fox, acclaimed star of films such as *Angels Cry*. They better mention *Angels Cry* and not some of the shit work I did."

"I'll make sure."

"You better, or I'll come back and kick your ass. You need to lose weight, by the way. Get that gut off. Now where was I? Did I tell about the pictures yet?"

"Yes."

"Okay, so this guy Terry had married my distant cousin Maggie, and now he was on my front porch. I let him come in and he was shifting you around on his shoulder, and I asked him where Maggie was. He got all nervous and fidgety and said something had happened. That's all, just that something had happened. Then he dropped the bomb on me: He asked if I would take you and raise you. Keep you safe, he said."

Eric leaned forward. Suddenly everything else had fallen away. What he'd done five years ago was gone. His ruined marriage was gone. The weary boredom of his job was gone. Almost against his will, he wanted to *know*. "What did you tell him?"

"I told him he was crazy. I couldn't take a newborn baby! What do you think I told him? And then I asked him . . . I asked him why me. If they didn't want the kid, there was other family. Maggie's parents were still relatively young and healthy, and there were Maggie's brothers, and all kinds of aunts and uncles who still had contact with the family. *Why me?* And he looked at me . . ."

Colleen looked up at Eric, and he was surprised to see tears streaking her bone-dry face. Colleen never cried. He couldn't remember having seen her cry even once when she wasn't acting. In her real life Colleen Cunningham had no tears.

Eric took her hand again, and it hung limply in his. Colleen wiped her tears, and once again, the simple motion seemed to exhaust her. She lay back, her breathing ragged. "He said . . . I swear I'll never forget this . . . he said that if you stayed with me, that they wouldn't find you."

A chill ran up Eric's spine, tickling the hairs on the back of his neck. "Who wouldn't find me?" he whispered.

Colleen shook her head. "He wouldn't tell me. He just said you had to be hidden or someone would come after you. That's why they looked me up, because I was so far removed from the family that no one would think they'd leave you with me." Another slow head shake. "He told me to be sure and tell you all this when you were grown, that he knew someday you'd want to know. He told me to give you a different name but that someday you should know your real name: Eric Anthony Miles. Well, that was just too much for me. It was starting to sound real cloak-and-dagger, and I didn't know this guy, just that he was married to Maggie. I went in the kitchen and pulled back a shot of Jack Daniel's to steady my nerves. Maybe it was three or four shots. When I came back, he was gone. You were all wrapped up in the blanket on the couch and he was just gone."

"Just like that?"

Colleen nodded. "I ran outside just in time to see tail-lights disappearing around the corner. So here I am with a baby. I didn't know what to do with a damn baby. I had better things to do than change diapers." She bowed her head.

"But you kept me."

"So I did. I almost called the child welfare people twenty times in the next week. But I never could do it. It's like this: The family had always been so disappointed in me, my whole life. 'You want to be an actress? Shit, girl, might as well be a whore.' That's what my dad told me. No one ever thought I could do anything, and most of the time they were right. But here, right here, was proof that someone in my family—even a distant relative—was trusting me, and trusting me with something important." Colleen shrugged into herself. "So I kept you. When you were older, I had to get you a birth certificate, and I just made sure to give them the date Terry told me. Told the Vital Records people that you were my cousin's baby and had been dropped on my doorstep. They didn't care. I just dropped the last name and made you Eric Anthony."

"Did you ever see him, or my mother, again?"

"No. Not a letter, not a phone call. It was like your parents had dropped off the face of the earth." Another coughing spasm wracked Colleen's body, and she hacked up more phlegm. When it subsided, she couldn't do more than whisper. "I'm feeling light-headed. Eric, are you still here?"

"I'm here."

Colleen blinked, looking confused. "I've got to rest. Stay here. You hear me? Stay here . . . I'm not . . . done."

She sank back on the pillows. For a moment Eric thought she was gone, but her chest rose and fell very slowly. He stood up and ran a hand through his hair. In the hall he told the nurse she was just asleep, then walked back into the bedroom. *Death room*, he thought.

Eric sat back down in the chair beside Colleen and watched her slow, halting breaths. The hospice nurse drifted in and out, taking Colleen's pulse, fluffing pillows, emptying the wastebasket. The whole business had a hypnotic effect on Eric and he finally dozed, listening to the rain and thinking of his father—the very idea that he *had* a father seemed foreign to him—saying, "They won't find him."

Miles.

The power of a name. The most basic way a person defines himself, Eric thought. The single point of reference everyone can understand: a person's name.

Colleen seemed lucid. Weak, but definitely not out of her head.

Then my name is not my name, Eric thought. It sounded like a riddle.

Eric Anthony.

Eric Anthony Miles.

Who were "they"? And why would they want me? he thought as he fell asleep.

It was twilight, the rain still pounding the window, when Eric woke to Colleen's hand on his leg.

"Come on," she whispered.

"I'm here," he said, snapping forward. "I'm awake. What is it?"

She coughed. "I'm dying, that's what it is." Colleen splayed out her fingers, reaching.

Eric folded her hand into his.

"You . . ." She coughed again. "You still go to that church? Baby in the manger, Jesus on the cross? You really believe all that?"

"I do."

"Put in a good word for me, boy. I'm probably bound for whatever hell there is."

Eric squeezed her hand. "Don't be so sure. I'll miss you, old woman."

"Not so damned old." She squeezed back. "You were a good boy, and you're a good man." She blinked rapidly several times. "I'm dizzy, Eric. I didn't know that you got dizzy at the end. No bright lights or anything, but . . . dizzy. Like a . . . like a staircase. You know, one of those circular staircases, like I'm climbing one. Damn."

Eric let one tear fall.

"Don't," she rasped. "Look . . . reach in the pocket of my nightgown, this side. Envelope. Read it. Your . . . Terry left it with you, tucked into the blanket that night he left you with me. Directions."

"Directions for what?" Eric reached under the sheet, found her pocket, and pulled out the yellowed envelope.

"Get me off this damn staircase," Colleen whispered, and Eric felt her hand relax in his.

He waited a moment, watching her chest. No movement this time. Her eyes fluttered closed, and something like a sigh escaped her. He kept holding her hand, looking at her face in the glow of the little lamp beside the bed.

Eric blinked and said a silent, clumsy prayer. "God bless you," he whispered aloud. "You were better than you thought you were, Colleen."

He folded her hand across her chest and looked down at the envelope in his hand. He opened the flap and shook out the single sheet of white paper. Small, masculine printing filled the page. He read over it: It was a set of directions that began at the town of Boise City, in the farthest county of Oklahoma's remote panhandle. He read how the directions led northwest to the far corner of the panhandle, where Oklahoma met New Mexico and Colorado. The directions culminated at the point where all three states touched.

Eric's eyes fell onto the bottom of the page:

From the marker, there's a trail leading into Colorado. Walk up into Colorado a hundred steps or so. Turn and look back toward New Mexico. Look for the twins and stones. I hope you will understand.

"What?" Eric said aloud.

He looked back to the bed and almost spoke again, then realized he couldn't ask Colleen.

She didn't look at peace. She only looked dead, the one person who'd ever tried to be a family to him. All the men and the drugs and the alcohol aside, she had tried. She'd done the best she could—just as he was trying now, with Patrick.

But it's so hard sometimes, he wanted to tell her.

He could almost hear her voice: *Quit your damn whining— I don't want to hear that shit! Get busy!*

Eric looked at the paper in his hand, again coming to the bottom of the page and that firm printing.

Look for the twins and stones.

Words written by a man who'd left his newborn son with a near stranger.

. . . twins and stones.

Colleen had thought this was important enough to give to him before she died, but what was it all about? What could he possibly find in the remote country of the far Oklahoma Panhandle?

"Colleen, I wish you'd told me about this before," he said.

You never asked, she'd said.

"I guess I'm asking now," he said, then went to find the nurse and tell her that Colleen was dead.

2

THE CITY OF HARRISONBURG, VIRGINIA, LIES IN THE Shenandoah Valley, in the crevice between the Blue Ridge and Allegheny Mountains. Around one hundred miles from Washington, D.C., it is a small college town centered around the campus of James Madison University. Across the street from the university stood an unobtrusive gray stone building made from the same stone as the campus buildings. In fact, it was often mistaken for an extension of JMU. There was no insignia on the building, no sign or logo, just a single glass door and few windows.

Inside the national headquarters of Department Thirty, past the empty reception area, was the only real office in the building. It held three computers side by side, six phone lines—one direct line to each of the regional offices—and dozens of piles of paper. On the wall was a picture of the current president of the United States. A single man sat behind the desk, finishing his morning coffee and bagel.

Daniel Winter had been the administrative director of Department Thirty since its inception. He was an unobtrusive man of sixty, medium height and build, calm features, given to wearing gray middle-of-the-road suits, neither Armani nor Sears. He was never noticed in crowds. But then, Daniel Winter rarely had the opportunity to be in a crowd.

It had been his old friend Arthur Dorian's idea to house Department Thirty here, away from Washington, yet close enough to D.C. for convenience purposes. Likewise, Dorian had suggested that the department's "regional" offices be in smaller cities, places like Oklahoma City and Sacramento and Charlotte, rather than Dallas and Los Angeles and Atlanta. He'd felt it was in keeping with Department Thirty's behind-the-scenes mission, staying away from the spotlight of the major metropolitan areas.

Poor Arthur, Winter thought. It had been more than a year since Arthur Dorian was killed. Art Dorian, Department

Thirty's first officer, whom Winter had recruited himself when the department was created. Art Dorian, who had served so long and so well, slowly fading from his desire to be the preeminent English Renaissance scholar in America. Art Dorian, who had been shot to death at a national historic site near the tiny town of Cheyenne, Oklahoma, while trying to bring closure to one of the department's earliest and biggest cases.

He turned at a sound in the hall and watched as a big man came through the door. Winter smiled unconsciously. He'd often said that the man who'd been known as Dean Yorkton for most of his adult life lacked only a plastic pocket protector full of pens to look the part of the ultimate technician. And in truth, the man had a scientific background and had lived a cover as a civil engineer for some twenty years, the longest-running field assignment in Department Thirty's history. He'd been assigned as the next-door neighbor and department liaison to a husband-and-wife team of professional assassins who had sought the department's protection in the mid-seventies. Winter sighed, thinking again of his old friend Arthur Dorian. It had been a strange twist in that very case that had gotten Arthur killed last January.

Winter knew the man's real name, and knew his current cover, but he was more comfortable thinking of him as Yorkton. The field man was of indeterminate late middle age, with a paunch that made him look like he'd swallowed a basketball. His hair was cropped short, almost military-style, and, like Winter, he was balding. His black work pants were a size too large, giving him a baggy, fluttery sort of look, and his shirt didn't quite tuck into his waist evenly. His eyes were magnified by thick round glasses.

"Morning," Yorkton said.

Winter stood to shake his hand. "Good morning." His voice, like the rest of him, was calm and even, with no regional inflection. The big man sat down across from Winter. "How's Indiana?"

Yorkton shrugged. "Boring assignment. Very low-maintenance."

"Coffee?"

"Not that instant swill you drink," Yorkton said. "Only real coffee with real caffeine."

"It'll kill you dead," Winter said.

"Better that than what happened to Art Dorian."

Winter stared at him.

"Come on, Daniel," Yorkton said. "Neither of us has time to waste. Let's get down to business. We need to fill Art's position. No one could replace him, but we need someone managing his cases." He looked thoughtfully at Winter. "I know you went back even further with Art than I did."

Winter nodded. "We were boys together. I was a couple of years older than he, and neither of us had a brother. We each had a sister, so we . . . used each other for brothers, I suppose is the best way to put it."

"It was a damn shame what happened. Art was a good man. He used to say his whole career was about making up fish stories. He had a big catfish stuffed and mounted on the wall in his office, just to remind both of us of that." Yorkton leaned over, snapped open a battered gray briefcase, and took out a file folder. He handed it across the desk. "Daniel, let's not dance around each other. We both know I have no real authority in the hierarchy of this department. All the decisions belong to you. I'm just a field officer. But my job is observation, and based on my observation this is the right person to take over Art Dorian's cases."

Winter flipped open the folder and almost groaned. Clipped to the front of a thick group of papers was a photograph of a striking young woman. She was very tall and slender, with brick-red hair and fierce green eyes. Her cheekbones were a little too sharp to qualify her as a classic beauty, and the eyes a bit too direct, but otherwise she could have passed for a fashion model. She was dressed simply—a khaki turtleneck, black pleated slacks, low-heeled shoes—but she wore the clothes beautifully, as if they'd been made just for her. She was leaning against a gold sports car, arms folded across her chest, wearing a look that wasn't quite a smile but wasn't quite somber, either.

"Deputy United States Marshal Faith Siobhan Kelly," Yorkton said.

Winter thumped the photo. "A six-foot-tall redhead with a gold sports car. This would seem a little contradictory to what we're all about, wouldn't it?"

"The surface features won't count for much, and she's only five ten. Would she stand out any more than Art Dorian did with that little antique mustache, wearing three-piece suits to baseball games and barbecues?"

Winter waited a moment. Yorkton was a smart-ass, but he was also very good at what he did. "Point taken."

"She brought in the Adam and Eve case last year, found Dorian's killer, and brought down his coconspirator."

Winter flipped pages in the file. "Twenty-six years old. Master's degree in criminal justice. Second in her class at the Academy. Grandfather was born in Ireland, immigrated to Chicago, beat cop for forty years. Father is a captain of detectives in Evanston. Brother is a Customs agent stationed in Tucson." He looked up. "She's not right for us. She's going to look at everything through a law enforcement perspective. You know we don't—"

Yorkton held up a hand. "If I may . . ."

Winter waited a moment, then waved his own hand: *All right, go ahead.*

"Thank you," Yorkton said. "You're right, her background is law enforcement to the bone. I don't dispute that. But she's not your typical deputy U.S. marshal. You see, she looked on Art Dorian as a mentor, even as a bit of a substitute father. Her relationship with her own father, the captain of detectives, is strained at best. So here was Art, just down the hall from her office." He spread his hands wide.

"So it was personal for her when Art was murdered," Winter said.

Yorkton pointed at him. "Exactly right, Daniel. She stepped outside her law enforcement detachment and started to think in different ways. She started to ask the right kinds of questions and, even more impressive, she started to get answers. She almost got herself killed. Remember the chief deputy in the Oklahoma City office, Phillip Clarke?"

Winter shook his head. "Hell of a mess."

"Hell of a mess is right. Corrupt as he could be for thirty years. He tried to strangle our Deputy Kelly, right in her own bedroom. She fought him off, wound up shooting him in the shoulder. He's locked up now, and she's changed. Don't tell me an experience like that wouldn't change a person."

Winter nodded. "I'll grant that."

"She's bright, she's ambitious, still wants to prove herself to everyone around her. What intelligent twenty-six-year-old doesn't? But now she's had a tiny exposure to our world, even though you might say it was forced on her. She has an excellent attention to detail. I think she can do this job."

Winter looked at him thoughtfully, picked up his bagel, chewed, swallowed, wiped cream cheese off his lip. "What's your interest here? If I didn't know better, I'd say you were all hot and bothered for this girl."

Yorkton laughed outright. "Look at me. Now look at her picture. Do you know how ridiculous a statement like that is?" He sobered quickly. "My interest, as it has been for all these years, is in Department Thirty and continuing our mission. By the way, there's one other thing you should know about Faith Kelly."

"And that is?" Winter said.

"She's seen some of Art's case files."

Winter nearly came out of his chair. "What?"

Yorkton shrugged, beginning to tap out a rhythm on the arm of his chair. "Art gave her a key to his office. After he was killed, she used it. How do you think she was able to do what she did last year? I don't know if she's seen files on the other cases in his jurisdiction, but . . ." He shrugged again.

Winter's well-honed composure began to slip. "Those files are absolutely classified! What the hell was Arthur thinking, giving some rookie deputy marshal a key to his office?"

Winter gathered himself: It wasn't good form to let a field officer see him lose his patience. He looked at the photo of Faith Kelly again and he began to understand what Arthur had been thinking. Arthur had been married to Department

Thirty for a long, long time, but still liked to think of himself as an historian, a professor, a normal person. He'd seen in this bright and attractive young woman a daughter that he might have had. Winter shook his head. *Poor Arthur, trying to be normal to the very last.*

He finally looked up at Yorkton again. "I think the case is made," he said slowly. "The fact that she's been exposed to departmental case files ends the debate. Deputy Kelly will take over Art Dorian's position." He closed Kelly's file and handed it back to Yorkton. "And she'll do it whether she wants to or not."

3

FAITH KELLY WRAPPED BOTH HANDS AROUND THE BUTT of the Glock nine-millimeter automatic and pointed it toward the sky. Her body was on full alert, and she knew all hell was about to break loose.

She stood on the back deck of a modest ranch-style home in the working-class suburb of Harrah, Oklahoma, just east of Oklahoma City. Considering the man who lived in the house had once manufactured nearly twenty million counterfeit dollars, the home was exceptionally unremarkable.

The counterfeiter was a New Yorker named Timothy Corelli, allegedly with ties to one of the big crime families. He'd very painstakingly fashioned the plates, imported exactly the right kind of paper, and made his twenty million in the basement of his nice suburban home in Mamaroneck. It all happened in 1986, and Corelli vanished off the face of the earth. After a while he had gone into the unsolved bin: Television programs did features on him, comparing him to D. B. Cooper.

One of the chief mandates of the United States Marshals Service is tracking down fugitives, and Faith Kelly had inherited the cold case after there were several Corelli "sightings" in Oklahoma. Before the events of a year ago January, she would never have even been considered for such a case. Up until then she'd been a green rookie and, worse yet, a girl crashing the boys' club.

Cop's kid, trying to prove a point, Phillip Clarke had said as he tried to strangle her.

The scars on her neck had faded, and there was only a two-inch line scar on her face, running diagonally downward from the crease beside her nose. She'd acquired it when shards of glass from her dining room table embedded themselves in her face as she fired her weapon through the glass table at Clarke when he came after her for the last time. Her friend Scott Hendler, an FBI agent who wanted to be more than a friend, had told her the scar was "alluring."

Alluring or not, the Corelli case came to her, and after exhaustively reviewing the man's biography, she thought she had something that would hang him. Timothy Corelli had one weakness: He was a wine connoisseur, and he had a passion for a certain wine from a tiny, obscure vineyard in the south of Spain. It was imported into the States by only one company, and sold at only one wine shop in the entire state of Oklahoma. After Faith obtained their records, she found one Timothy Carter, who lived in this modest suburban home.

Faith was perfectly content to be at Carter/Corelli's back door. She knew that when faced with an unexpected visit at the front door, a nonviolent suspect such as Corelli would more than likely do the obvious: try to get out the back. If and when he did, she would have him. If she had trouble with him, Deputy Marshal Derek Mayfield, the best marksman in the office, was positioned in the trees beyond the yard with a high-powered rifle.

She steadied the tiny earpiece and boom microphone at her mouth. As she did, a burst of static sounded in her ear. Faith winced.

"Bravo One, base," Scott Hendler's voice said in her ear. He was a block away in the mobile command post.

"Base, Bravo One," said one of the Secret Service boys at the front of the house.

"You have a green light, Bravo One."

"Roger that."

Faith breathed quietly through her mouth. Over her ear-piece she heard the guys in the front ringing the doorbell, then knocking.

There was another sound, something being knocked over inside the house. She imagined Corelli looking out his window and seeing the unknown men standing there. She took a silent step toward the back kitchen window.

In a burst of activity she saw Timothy Corelli run into the kitchen. He was a small, dark man, and he was carrying a brown leather satchel.

"Base, Bravo Two," she said quietly, keeping her eyes on the window. "I have a visual of the suspect. He's in the kitchen."

"Bravo Two, Bravo One," said the Secret Service man in the front. "We're going in. We'll just make sure he keeps heading your way." She heard the sound of the door splinter-ing open.

Corelli jumped at the sound. He disappeared from Faith's view around a corner. Five seconds later she heard the back door.

Faith grinned. This was why most law enforcement offi-cers never complained about backdoor duty on raids.

Corelli burst onto the porch. Faith leveled the Glock at him. "Federal marshal, Mr. Corelli! Stop right there! Put the bag on the deck."

Corelli spun toward her, and she saw him struggling with the decision.

"You wouldn't shoot me," he finally said in a whispery voice.

Faith didn't move a muscle. The gun didn't waver. She kept it trained on a spot just above his heart. She met his eyes.

Corelli frowned. He shuffled his feet.

"Now, Mr. Corelli," Faith said.

Fear flickered across Corelli's bland features. He dropped the satchel.

"Step away from it."

Corelli took two steps back. Faith followed him with the barrel of the gun. He could still run.

"Lie down on the deck, facedown, arms out above you."

"Oh, hell," Timothy Corelli said, and complied.

Still covering him with the Glock, Faith cuffed him. She patted him down, then said into her mic, "I have the suspect. He is unarmed, and he is under my control."

There were whoops and applause in her earpiece.

"One thing," Corelli mumbled into the deck. "How? After all this time, how'd you find me?"

Faith smiled. "Next time, try a nice California chardonnay."

"Ah, Faith . . ." Hendler said in her ear. She heard him clear his throat. "You're being ordered to stand down."

Faith wrinkled her brow. A droplet of sweat stung her eye. "What?"

"Orders have come in for you to stand down. Leneski's going to move up into your position. He's on his way now."

"What?"

"Orders from on high, Faith."

"I've got the suspect, Scott, and we're taking him in."

"The orders are from Department Thirty."

Dammit, she thought. *What the hell is this?*

But her stomach began to tighten, and she knew it could only be one thing: The whole mess from last year was finally coming home to haunt her. *Well, eighteen months of respect is better than nothing.* Then: *No, dammit, I'm not going that easily.*

She holstered her weapon and silently backed off the porch. Leneski, a burly man in his mid-thirties, was already moving up behind her. Their eyes met. He shrugged. She nodded to him and watched as he moved onto the back porch and took control of Corelli.

Faith began to jog, then scaled the low fence at the back of the yard. She passed Derek Mayfield in his tree and, three minutes later, emerged onto a blacktop road. The mobile command post was a white Ford van, parked on the gravel shoulder. She yanked open the back doors, climbed in, and said, "What the hell's going on?"

The command post was under the direction of Owen

Riggs, the assistant special agent in charge of the Oklahoma City FBI office. Two of the Secret Service agents were still inside, as was Scott Hendler, who sat under a pair of headphones at the communications console.

Hendler was only three or four years older than Faith, and three or four inches shorter. He was slim and wiry and going prematurely, self-consciously bald. He had a perpetually tired look about him, earning him the Bureau nickname of Sleepy Scott, but Faith knew he was sharp and was on his way up in the FBI.

Owen Riggs, a big man in his fifties who'd worked the New York field office for fifteen years, turned to Faith. "Who'd you piss off now, Kelly?" He smiled, but there was little humor in it. Riggs liked operations to run smoothly, and rightfully so.

Faith shrugged and looked at Hendler. "Talk to me, Scott."

"Wrong," Hendler said, not unkindly.

Faith glared at him.

"Nope," he said. "I'm not the one who's going to talk to you." He punched a button on the console and lifted a phone receiver.

Faith took it. "This is Faith Kelly. Who am I talking to?"

A nondescript male voice said, "Deputy Kelly, please forgive the poor timing."

"Who is this?"

"Daniel Winter, calling from Virginia. I called your office and they told me you were in the field. Sorry for the high drama, but we have important business to discuss."

Winter. Winter. Faith knew the name. But from where?

"What I'd like you to do is go to the Department Thirty office—Arthur Dorian's office, if you will—and wait there."

Oh, shit. Now she knew: She'd heard Art mention the name. Daniel Winter was the ultimate boss over Department Thirty. Presidential administrations of both parties came and went, but Winter retained his position year after year. He and Art had been longtime friends, she recalled, but Art had once jokingly—or at least she thought it was jokingly—compared him to J. Edgar Hoover.

"What's this about, sir?"

"Someone you know is on the way there now, Deputy Kelly. I just wanted to call you personally and tell you how important it is that we speak with you. I understand you have a key to the office. Let yourself in and wait there. It may be a while, but please wait."

Faith wanted to scream. "Sir, I—"

"If it helps you any, the officer who's coming to talk with you is the man you know as Dean Yorkton."

Faith flashed on an image of the big man sitting at her dining room table, drinking coffee and tapping out an irritating rhythm with his fingers.

"He's on a plane now," Winter said. "It'll be a few hours, but above all, wait for him, Deputy. Do you understand that?"

Faith noticed that Winter's voice was friendly, carefully moderated, but with an undercurrent of steel. This man wasn't used to being questioned. "Yes, sir, I understand that. If you could give me some idea—"

"Thank you for your cooperation, Deputy Kelly. I'm sure we'll talk again."

The phone clicked in her ear.

The Secret Service agents turned away. Scott Hendler looked up at her with concern on his bland face. Owen Riggs coughed into his hand.

"Well, Kelly," Riggs finally said. "Don't tell me. It's Department Thirty shadow stuff."

Faith nodded slowly, unsure whether to be angry or confused. Anger was starting to gain the upper hand, though.

"Those guys are damned spooky," Riggs said. "CIA, NSA—those guys have nothing on Thirty. Too spooky for this old cop. Well, it's been nice knowing you, Kelly. See you down the road somewhere."

Faith hadn't been in the Oklahoma City Department Thirty office—she still thought of it as Art's office—since last January. She still had the key, and no one had asked her about it, but she'd purposely stayed away. First it was out of grief over all that had happened, and later she'd simply been too busy to think about it.

It was on the second floor of the U.S. Courthouse, on Robert S. Kerr Avenue in the heart of downtown Oklahoma City. The Marshals Service office was just down the hall, and this tiny room in the corner had been where Art Dorian quietly went about his work for so many years. When she put the key in the lock and opened the door, her first thought was: *It smells like my house.* Faith smiled: her own modest home in The Village section of Oklahoma City smelled this musty all the time. She didn't do house-keeping.

The blinds were drawn, morning sunlight shafting down through them. The desk was old-fashioned and institutional. *Just like Art,* she thought. There was a single telephone, a computer covered with a thin layer of dust, a gray three-drawer filing cabinet, a desk blotter with a few stray papers tucked into it.

The most commanding feature of the office, partially because it seemed so out of place, was the large stuffed cat-fish mounted on a wooden plaque on the side wall.

My whole career is about making up fish stories, Art had told her.

Closing the door softly behind her, she walked to the fish and ran a hand over the rough exterior. She lifted the plaque from its hooks on the wall and turned it over, reading the inscription on the back: LAKE TEXOMA, JULY 4, 1981.

Of course Art hadn't really caught the fish in Lake Texoma, or anywhere else. It was all part of his immersion in Department Thirty and his wry humor to remind himself and anyone else who came in the office what his life was all about. Faith thought the idea of Art Dorian standing on a lakeshore fishing was very nearly the most ridiculous thing she'd ever heard. Reciting Elizabethan poetry, perhaps, but not fishing.

She replaced the fish on the wall and walked to the desk. She settled into the chair, unconsciously running her finger across the scar beside her nose. It was a grim, permanent reminder of her first—and, she hoped, last—exposure to Department Thirty.

She leaned back in the chair and closed her eyes.

Three and a half hours passed with Faith alternately dozing and pacing the little office, slowly simmering at having been pulled off the Carter/Corelli bust. When the phone rang, she grabbed it almost before it had finished ringing.

"Kelly," she barked into it.

"I guess you've forgotten Department Thirty protocol," Yorkton said. "Never identify yourself when you answer the phone."

"What the hell's going on with you people? Your man Winter actually pulled me off an important operation to sit here and wait for you for nearly four hours."

There was a sigh on the phone. "A pleasure to talk to you, as always, Deputy. You need some fresh air. Get out of that stuffy little office and stop staring at the fish on the wall. Come downstairs, across the street to the memorial. The east side, by the Survivors' Tree."

"What's this about?"

"I want to talk to you. More to the point, Daniel Winter wants me to talk to you. Don't dawdle, now." The line went dead.

"Dammit," she muttered.

Faith stood up and left the office, took the stairs to street level, and walked through the high-ceilinged lobby of the federal courthouse to the revolving door. Outside she saw thunderheads building, and the temperature had dropped. She crossed Robert S. Kerr Avenue in the middle of the block and walked east to Robinson. Half a block south, she turned and entered the Oklahoma City National Memorial.

It was like stepping into a library or a church, only quieter. Here there were no whisperers, no toddlers squealing. People came here at all hours of the day, all times of the year, from all over the nation, and they simply walked quietly around the place where the Alfred P. Murrah Federal Building had once stood.

Faith passed through the golden Gates of Time on the east side with 9:01 carved above it. Looking down the length of the reflecting pool in the center, she saw the western wall with its 9:03. In the center the time seemed to stand still, forever at 9:02 A.M. on April 19, 1995. She hadn't been in Oklahoma City then, was still in high school in Illinois, but like the rest of the world she'd watched and listened and waited, and later grew enraged when she learned of the day care center on the Murrah Building's second floor.

The reflecting pool was only an inch or so deep, and off to the left were the 168 empty chairs representing those who had died. The chairs were all arranged in nine rows, according to the floor of the building the person had been on when the bomb exploded. Nineteen chairs, smaller than the others, stood in the second row.

Faith turned away and walked up a set of concrete steps to the plaza where the Survivors' Tree stood. A slightly listing American elm, it had stood in a parking lot surrounded by burning vehicles on April 19. But the tree itself withstood the assault, and in a few days had gained its nickname. A few feet opposite the tree was a curved waist-high wall overlooking the rest of the memorial. Beside it stood the form of a big man.

Faith made a noise in her throat. It seemed somehow sacrilegious to curse in a place like this, but she felt like it anyway. She walked in long strides to where the man stood. Below them, half a dozen or so tourists walked along the reflecting pool.

Neither of them spoke for a moment, then Yorkton said, "Well, Deputy Kelly."

Faith sighed. "What do you want?"

Yorkton didn't turn. "Remember the first time we met?"

"You mean when I was out on my run and you stalked me, then broke into my house? How could I forget? You really know how to show a girl a good time."

"Slightly acerbic as always, I see. How have you been the last year or so?"

"Fine. What do you want?"

"Fine? That's it? Come now, just *fine?* How boring." For the first time he turned toward her. He raised a hand toward her face and she backed up instinctively. "Forgive me. It's a small scar, not too noticeable."

Faith kept looking out at the pool. A bearded man with three young boys—one blond, one brown-haired, one black-haired—had entered the memorial. The little blond boy nudged his foot toward the edge of the pool, drawing a stern reprimand from the man. Faith shook her head. *I'm losing my mind.*

"The docs did a fair job," she finally said.

"And your throat?"

"Those scars faded. I had to do some speech therapy to get used to talking again." She shrugged.

"Why are you so uncomfortable talking about yourself, Deputy Kelly?"

"I have other things to think about," she said. "Why are you here, and what does Winter want?"

Yorkton drummed his fingers on the top of the granite wall but said nothing.

"All this melodrama is fun," Faith said, "but I have work to do." She turned around and started to walk back toward the tree.

Yorkton watched her walk a few steps, then said, "Don't you want to know how I spoke up on your behalf?"

"No." Faith kept walking.

"You don't even want to know why I came all the way across the country to see you, nearly a year and a half after your last connection to Department Thirty?"

Faith was almost to the corner of the plaza. "No, I really don't. It's over. Let's leave it that way."

"No, Kelly. It isn't over."

Something in his voice made Faith stop and turn around. He was staring her down now, not drumming his fingers, barely moving at all. She recognized the difference: This was the serious Yorkton. The game-playing was finished.

"What?" she said.

He waited a moment. Below them, the man with the boys

had moved around the edge of the pool. A park ranger had appeared at the far end and was talking to an elderly black woman.

Yorkton looked all around the memorial and moved a few steps closer to Faith. "Come to work for us," he finally said.

Faith's instinct was to laugh in his face, but she knew instantly it was no laughing matter. Her first thought was of the photos of Art Dorian with his chest blown open, lying in a field.

She reached out and steadied a hand against the rock wall.

"I won't insult your intelligence with a bunch of patriotic talk," Yorkton said. "But I will say that you are very talented, and we need talented people."

Faith shook her head. "I don't think so. You guys are a little too far out there for me. I did what I did last year because I had to."

Yorkton cocked his head toward the memorial. "Oh? And why was that? Why did you have to?"

Faith felt the little shiver of anger run through her again. "Don't be a smart-ass. You know why."

"Why?"

Faith waited a moment, then leveled an index finger at the big man. "To hell with you, and Winter, and everything else associated with Department Thirty. Go back to whatever identity you're using and leave me alone."

She turned and started down the steps. By the time she reached the bottom, she was jogging. She turned the corner and ran into one of the three boys with the bearded man, knocking the boy to the concrete.

"Whoa!" said the man.

The little brown-haired, blue-eyed boy, who looked to be around six, sat on the ground crying, more from surprise than pain. Faith knelt beside him. "I'm sorry," she muttered.

The boy recoiled, crying harder.

Yorkton appeared at the base of the steps. "Here, here, what's happened?" he said in full voice, the concerned bystander.

The man helped his son up and hefted him onto his shoulder. "Shh, it's okay," he said softly. He looked at Faith, not unkindly. "It pays to be careful when there are kids around." He walked away, the other two boys glaring at Faith.

Yorkton tsk-tsked. "Now I've gotten you all out of sorts. This isn't the cool, ambitious Deputy Faith Kelly I know, running in inappropriate places, knocking over children. . . ."

"Oh, fuck you," Faith spat.

Yorkton flinched. "I know—"

"You don't *know* anything," Faith said. "Don't try to use Art to get me to come do your dirty work."

"Department Thirty is not dirty work," Yorkton said. "Let's be clear on that. Just because we deal with people who have broken the law, that doesn't mean the information they provide doesn't uphold and enforce the law. Yes, it's a trade-off. You would take over the Oklahoma City office, manage the six existing cases, and any new ones that might come in to this region."

"I'm going back to work. You go crawl back under your rock."

In long strides Faith started walking alongside the reflecting pool.

Without raising his voice, Yorkton said, "You don't have a job to go back to."

Faith turned on him. "What did you say?"

Yorkton put out his hands in a Let's-all-be-reasonable-about-this gesture. "You no longer have a job with the Marshals Service. Winter has already seen to it."

"You bastard. How did you—"

"When Winter wants something, he gets it. Now, you have a very serious decision to make. You can come in as a Department Thirty regional officer. We'll double your Marshals Service pay, with full government benefits. The work is challenging, important, and it does make a difference, even if the difference isn't visible to you. Believe me, it's visible to others. Or . . . you're out of a job. I suppose you could pack up and move back to Evanston. You could work for your father's department. You'd probably have to start out as a patrol officer, though. Or do you think he'd allow you on the force at all?"

"You bastard," Faith said again. Somewhere far away, thunder rolled.

"Call me all the names you want, but the choice seems clear." Yorkton smiled.

Faith had an urge to reach out and punch Yorkton in his soft gut. Her stomach churned, her head felt heavy. She put her hand in the pocket of her blazer and grabbed the inner lining, twisting it between her fingers.

If only Art hadn't been killed, none of this would have happened.

If only I'd left it all alone last year . . .

She swallowed. She suddenly wanted a drink of water more than anything in the world. She met Yorkton's hooded eyes. "You know, it doesn't make sense to me."

"What's that?"

"Why you would want someone like me, someone who doesn't even want to be a part of Department Thirty, to manage some of its cases?"

Yorkton smiled. "Oh, people rarely *want* to join us. They have to be convinced. I've been told Arthur was that way. Winter had to work and work on him to get him to give up his professorship. You? You're different. You, shall we say, backed into it by opening that case file last year."

"I had no choice! Art was—"

She stopped. In the weeks before Art Dorian was murdered, he had slipped the word *retirement* into some of his conversations with her. He'd begun to think seriously about it and had expressed his concern about how difficult it was to find people with both talent and conscience to work in Department Thirty.

Had Art been hinting to her even then that she might succeed him?

"Dammit," she muttered, walking a few steps away from Yorkton. This time he didn't follow, instead watching her.

The scar beside her nose began to itch, as it seemed to do

when she was stressed. She knew it was an illusion but couldn't seem to help it. She took one red nail and scratched it reflexively, then walked a few more steps. *Damn you, Art.*

She surprised herself at the thought. *Were you setting me up for this? Were you trying to bring me into Department Thirty, but got killed before you could retire?*

She pulled her hair back from her face. The thunder rumbled again, closer this time. Faith looked up; clouds were moving across the sky. While she liked Oklahoma, the openness of both the land and its people, she missed the seasons in Illinois. Here the seasons seemed to be all jumbled up: It could be warm in winter, stormy in spring, sun and thunderstorms and wind and snow, all within a week of each other. At least in Chicago you knew what to expect.

Oklahoma was the equivalent of Department Thirty, and Chicago was the Marshals Service. Unpredictable, sometimes volatile, versus clearly defined lines and boundaries.

She'd met Art Dorian the week she arrived in Oklahoma City, at a gathering of federal law enforcement officers from all the agencies with offices in the city. FBI, ATF, Customs, DEA, the Marshals Service, even the Secret Service—it was an annual event, a barbecue at an acreage north of Edmond. Good food, free beer, lots of war stories. As both a woman and a new arrival, Faith had found herself in the minority. She'd just been edging over to talk to one of the few female FBI agents when she'd spotted the little man in the outdated, ridiculously formal three-piece suit, smoothing his little mustache with an index finger. He'd been standing by himself under a tree, looking as out of place as she did.

"Feel like you're playing a game and no one told you the rules?" he'd said in a dry voice, then smiled.

That was her introduction to Art Dorian's world. She'd begun paying weekly visits to his little office, and he gave her tidbits of investigative information, little nuggets paid out here and there, case studies he recommended she read. She'd realized in a fairly short time that she gained more insight from Dorian in a few minutes a week than six years of college and a year at the Federal Law Enforcement Academy. Even more, he'd never once talked down to her, never once made her feel like a little girl trying to play a big boys' game. He'd accepted her for who and what she was and didn't seem to find her to be a curiosity—as every "boyfriend" she'd ever had did—or a fool, as her own father did. By the time of his murder, she'd come to view Art Dorian as the father she never had. Cruel to Captain Joe Kelly, perhaps, but that was how she'd felt.

She was almost to the west wall of the memorial, with its 9:03 carved high above her head. Yorkton was quite a ways from her now, still looking at her, still drumming his fingers on his leg.

Did you think I could do this, Art?

She looked up and made eye contact with Yorkton. The man started toward her as if she'd beckoned to him.

"Eerie place, this," he said when he reached her. "Skews your perspective."

"Oh, shut up. I've heard enough of your silly stage dressing."

Yorkton gave a mock bow. "There's the observant Faith Kelly at work. Attention to detail. I told Winter this morning—"

"Just shut up." Faith pressed her hands to her temples. "This is crazy."

"Yes," Yorkton said.

"So glad you agree."

"No point in denying facts. It *is* crazy. But the information we've gained from people now under our protection has saved a lot of lives over the years and put a lot of bad people away."

"But the people you protect *are* the bad people. Remember?"

"I remember. Didn't Arthur ever give you his little lecture about making a judgment call, and the greater good, and all that? He was as good as anyone at explaining what we do."

Faith nodded. "He did. I didn't even know what Department Thirty was. The other deputies kind of whisper about it and shake their heads and tiptoe past the door, that sort of thing. But yes, Art explained it to me."

Yorkton reached inside his jacket and pulled out a computer disk. "There are files on here outlining some of your procedures, contact information, and such. There are also updates of the paper files in Arthur's office—*your* office, I should say. You have six cases in your region. You'll need to familiarize yourself with them as quickly as you can, and pay a visit to each of them to introduce yourself as their case officer. Remember, you're the sole point of contact for these cases. We keep things very tightly compartmentalized, for everyone's sake."

Faith took the disk. *Art, you were really good,* she thought. *I'll give it my best shot for you.*

"All right," she said. "Damn it all, Yorkton. I'll get started."

"There's also a contact number on there for me, where you can reach me anytime, day or night. Just in case."

"Just in case."

"Good-bye, Officer Kelly."

"Officer? Is that my title?"

"That's what we all are: simple officers. The department's not big on titles." He turned and started walking away from her along the reflecting pool.

Okay, Art, you've got me, she thought. *I'm not sure why, but you've got me.*

Faith slipped the disk into her pocket, walked through the "wall of time," and started back up the street toward the federal courthouse.

4

AT THE POINT WHERE THE TWO LARGEST RIVERS IN North America converged, a man in his thirties, with curly blond collar-length hair and icy blue eyes, sat quietly, unmoving, three steps away from the rivers' confluence.

As he watched the pale blue ribbon of the Ohio River merge with the darker current of the Mississippi, Drew thought about borders and boundaries as they were represented by the two great rivers. Off to his left, across the Ohio, was Kentucky. To the right, on the other side of the Mississippi, were the oaks of Missouri. He sat on a log at the muddy edge of the rivers, between the two, on a tiny patch of Illinois.

Borders and boundaries. He was fascinated by the concept that arbitrarily drawn lines, and even natural occurrences like the rivers, sectioned people off into one jurisdiction or another. He'd never felt such boundaries himself. Since Drew did not exist in the eyes of the world, he felt a freedom from such things. He was a citizen not of any state or country but of the world at large. He could move from one place to another more easily than anyone he knew. His name did not appear on a birth certificate or Social Security card, his fingerprints were in no database: He was unhampered by artificial boundaries.

He sighed. He still had work to do, and little time for ruminations. He heard steps coming down the trail behind him and, without visibly moving, tensed his body. A police officer appeared, a slim middle-aged black man with gun, handcuffs, and stick riding on his hips. He wore the uniform of the Alexander County Sheriff's Department. A gold name tag identified him as Haliday.

He walked to the water's edge, three feet or so away from Drew, poking at some driftwood and frowning at a couple of plastic bottles on the ground. He stood without speaking for a long time. He and Drew watched together as a coal barge, pushed by a red and white tug, motored down the Mississippi to their right. At the confluence it performed an elaborate turn, so smoothly that it might have been choreographed. It turned into the Ohio and started upriver, the tug now on the other end of its load, pulling instead of pushing. The two men watched the operation until the barge was out of sight.

"Really gets your attention, doesn't it?" the deputy finally said.

"Sure does," Drew said.

Haliday gestured toward the rivers. "It's like the old Ohio doesn't want to give it up. It keeps a little of that color out in the middle of the current, even after it merges. Little splash of color in with the Mississippi mud."

Drew looked off to the right, eyes trailing the Mississippi. The deputy was right: He could see the spot, not far from where he sat, where the color of the water actually changed, as if the Ohio had refused to die. He nodded, then turned to look at the man.

Haliday met his glance. "Been here before?"

Drew shook his head. "First time."

"Where you from?"

"Memphis," Drew lied.

"Wondered if that was your Dodge with the Tennessee plates."

Drew heard a scraping, something being dragged across concrete somewhere back up the trail. "What's going on up there?"

"Oh, don't mind that," Haliday said. "We're having a little event here today."

Drew smiled. He already knew all about the "event." He leaned over and picked up his battered blue backpack from the ground beside him, slinging it over one shoulder. "Well, I should get back on the road anyway."

"Nice talking to you," the deputy said. "You take care, now."

With one last glance back toward the two great rivers' confluence, Drew walked up the trail. Before him was a memorial made of wrought iron and concrete, the Boatmen's Memorial, constructed to honor those who had died on the rivers. He wondered if those who were about to die here would be accorded the same sort of honor.

On the lower level of the boat-shaped memorial, men and a few women, some in uniform, were moving around, setting up tables and chairs. Drew counted three different kinds of uniforms. A few children ran around the nearby playground. As he came out of the memorial, two men finished attaching a banner to the edge of it:

SOUTHERNMOST ILLINOIS PEACE OFFICERS' ASSOCIATION ANNUAL PICNIC. WELCOME!

Drew read the banner, then walked on. He knew that within an hour, there would be as many as two hundred people here, at the tip of Fort Defiance State Park, overlooking the rivers. He smiled at the irony of the park's name. He hadn't chosen the location, but the name was part of it. The symbolism of defiance would be very important within the next few hours.

He went into a park bathroom, listened for footsteps, then unzipped his backpack. The bundle of TNT was already wrapped together, the fuse wires connected to a five-dollar kitchen timer. Drew's employer had construction interests, and it had been easy to obtain. In an era when C-4 was readily available and the military used "smart" bombs, this job would be accomplished using old-fashioned, unglamorous dynamite. There was enough power here to level the Boatmen's Memorial and probably blast several of the lawmen right into the river.

Homeland security, indeed. Drew was amazed at the foolishness of society's "official" structures. The world would view this as an act of terrorism: In fact, that was the idea. Drew found himself in a strange situation, a professional pretending to be a terrorist. He did not hate. He had no opinion whatsoever of the members of the Southernmost Illinois Peace Officers' Association, or law enforcement as a whole, or the government in general. There was only the job. His employer looked at big pictures, at consequences, at chains of events, at reactions. Drew looked only at details, and how and when and where. Never what or why.

Still, he couldn't help but wonder at the way the world would react. Just as they had after Oklahoma City and September 11, they would ask the same questions, and there would still be no answers. No matter how many young Arab men were detained at airports, no matter how much luggage was opened, no matter how many personal e-mails were intercepted, the terrorist would always find a way. The world had yet to learn that lesson. He, as an outsider, saw it with great clarity.

Drew placed the explosives in the bathroom's trash can,

turned the timer to fifty-five minutes, and stuffed a wad of paper towels on top of it. He took his backpack, left the bathroom, and walked back into the spring sunlight. More people filled Fort Defiance State Park: sheriff's officers from a six-county region, police from every town in the area, Illinois State Police troopers.

Drew got into the red Dodge Neon with the Tennessee plates and drove northward out of the park, back toward the small town of Cairo, two miles away. There he checked out of his motel, then lingered for a while in the parking lot, reading a St. Louis newspaper.

When the explosion came, Drew's first impression was of something very heavy being dropped on a tile floor. There was a reverberation, and the car under him shook ever so slightly. He got out of the car and stood beside it, looking south. Thick black smoke thundered into the sky.

He watched until he heard the first sirens. Then he started the car and pulled away from the motel. In a few minutes he crossed the Mississippi River back into Missouri. He turned south on Interstate 55.

Two hours later, he exited the interstate between bottom-land fields of cotton and soybeans and pulled into a truck stop in Blytheville, Arkansas, just across the Missouri line. *More borders and boundaries,* he thought vaguely. He pulled to the side of the truck stop, took his small overnight bag and a manila envelope, and went to a row of pay phones.

Tearing open the envelope, he read the script several times before calling the first number on his list. When the call was answered, he said, "Record this call. You'll want to have it on tape." He waited ten seconds, then said, "The Sons of Madison United are responsible for the action at Fort Defiance, where the Ohio and Mississippi Rivers come together. The location is no accident. This is an act of defiance against your so-called government law enforcers. There will be more to come. The defiance has begun. We are the Sons of Madison United."

He hung up, then made the same call to two other numbers. When the calls were finished, he drove to the motel next door, unlocked a room, and went inside. He stripped off his clothes, pulled off the curly blond wig and mussed his own short, straight brown hair, then pulled out the deep-blue contact lenses and threw them in the trash can. He washed off the stage makeup that had given him a much fairer complexion than his own.

He dressed in loose-fitting blue jeans, a plain white T-shirt, and baseball cap. He reached under the bed and pulled out a laptop computer. He plugged the modem cord into the motel's data port and connected to his e-mail program, composing a three-word message:

IT IS DONE.

He did not sign the message. The recipient would know who had sent it. He disconnected the computer and put it, along with his old clothes, in the trunk of the Neon. He then checked out of the motel and walked back to the truck stop. On the far side of the parking lot, behind a line of semis, was a black Nissan Sentra.

In less than five minutes he was back on the interstate. Drew still had far to go.

More than six hundred miles away from the place where the two rivers joined and Fort Defiance burned, Nathan Grant sat in the study of his gated mansion a few miles from another border, the Oklahoma-Texas state line. He looked out onto his private pier and past it to the choppy waters of Lake Texoma.

The mansion was in the tiny community of Caney Creek, a resort area—Grant wouldn't call it a town—which boasted equal numbers of high-dollar mansions like his, side by side with blue-collar trailer homes. Grant appreciated the irony.

He alternated his gaze between the pier, his computer, and the big-screen TV playing CNN with the sound off. The network had broken away from their regular political program to provide continuous coverage of the "terrorist attack." Grant was vaguely irritated: He already knew about the bombing and wanted to know more about the political landscape. Speculation was rampant as to who would be opposing the president in his reelection bid next year, and CNN's pundits had thrown their spotlight on two: a longtime senator from Michigan, and the charismatic governor of Oklahoma, Angela Archer.

The media were agog over Archer, Grant thought, as the first woman to be considered a serious contender, one who could run a real race. She was from one of the nation's most powerful families—"a prairie version of the Kennedys," one of the pundits had said.

Grant smiled, then his smile faded as an UPDATE graphic scrolled across the screen. He grabbed the TV remote and unmuted the sound.

The news anchor, a young Asian woman whom a graphic identified as Andrea Chin, said, "We've just had an update on the death toll from the horrific blast this afternoon near the small town of Cairo, Illinois. The bombing, which took place at Fort Defiance State Park at the southernmost tip of Illinois, was at an annual picnic of area law enforcement officers. We can now confirm sixty-three dead. That includes not only police officers but family members as well. At this point eight children are listed among the dead." The young woman paused unsteadily. "More than fifty others have been taken to area hospitals, and at least half of those are reported in critical condition."

The camera shot widened to show a gray-haired, academic-looking man in a poorly fitting navy blue suit, seated beside the anchor. "Joining us now," Chin said, "is Dr. Gerald Wood, professor of political science at Texas Christian University, and a leading scholar on extremism in America." She turned to face the man. "First, Dr. Wood, let's listen once again to the tape recording of the call CNN received this afternoon, about two hours after the bombing."

Grant listened to the scratchy recording, watching as the transcribed text scrolled across the screen. His pulse quickened. He leaned forward, increasing the volume with the remote.

The recording ended and the camera came back to the man and woman in the studio. "Dr. Wood," Chin said, "who are the Sons of Madison United, and why haven't we heard from them in the past?"

Wood cleared his throat. "They're a relatively small cell, centered mostly in the areas of Kentucky, Tennessee, Missouri, and Arkansas. We've never been able to get an accurate feel for how many there are, since they're dispersed pretty widely. Also, up until today they've never broken any laws, so law enforcement has no record of them. All we have are a few public meetings, some letters to the editor, and their own Web site."

"Where does the name come from?"

"Well, they seem to have surfaced sometime in the eighties, when their founder, a former newspaper editor named Wayne Devine, claimed to have unearthed an obscure letter that James Madison had written. In it Madison supposedly claimed that the Constitution should never be changed further after the original ten amendments, the Bill of Rights. The quote that Devine liked to use was that further amendments would 'offend the cause of justice and liberty to all men.' The letter was a phony, of course: Madison never wrote any such thing, and it was later proven that Devine had written it himself."

"And the group's beliefs?" Chin asked, leaning forward.

"Simply stated, they believe that every amendment after the Bill of Rights is invalid. Emancipation of slaves, women's suffrage, income tax—all invalid, in their view. They are particularly obsessed with the Second Amendment. In their interpretation this not only gives Americans the *right* to keep and bear arms but *requires* them to do so. As an extension of this, they believe that the 'well-regulated' citizen militia eliminates the need for what they call 'government-based' law enforcement."

Chin sat back. "Let's make sure we have this straight: This group believes that police are unconstitutional?"

Wood smiled uncomfortably. "That's pretty much it. Their letters to the editor and the information on their Web site bear this out. And of course it explains why they would attack a gathering of police officers."

Chin nodded. "Thank you, Dr. Wood. I'm sure we'll be checking in with you in the days to come." The camera panned back to Chin alone. "Recapping what we've learned, the death toll . . ."

Grant snapped off the sound. He nodded toward the TV. It had begun. For more than thirty years the coals had been growing hot, and now they had exploded into flame.

He rubbed his hands together, turning back toward his computer. The message was still on the screen.

IT IS DONE, he read.

He nodded to the machine, as if expecting it to acknowledge him, then deleted the message. No reply was necessary.

He sat down at the desk and composed an e-mail of his own, addressing it to CNN, National Public Radio, and *The Washington Post*, the same three outlets Drew had called. If Drew's call had caused a storm, he imagined a hurricane in the newsrooms when they received his message. He pressed Send.

The message could never be traced back to him. He had arranged for several highly secure e-mail accounts, and this one went first to a network server in Toronto, where it then bounced to a "remailer" somewhere in Denmark. It then filtered through ISPs in California and Delaware before reaching its destination.

When one of his two phones rang, he simply stared at it for a moment. That phone hadn't rung in nearly two years. Out of the corner of his eye, he saw Governor Archer back on CNN, making a speech somewhere in New Hampshire. He looked back at the phone: Only a tiny handful of people had the number to the direct, secure line, and he couldn't imagine why any of them would be calling him tonight.

He picked up the receiver. "Grant," he said into it.

"Good evening, Mr. Grant," said a young female voice. "I'm sorry to bother you, but I wanted to touch base with you and—"

"Who is this?"

"Oh, I'm sorry, sir. My name is Faith Kelly. I'm your new Department Thirty case officer."

5

WHEN FAITH HUNG UP THE PHONE AFTER THE LAST
call was finished, she stared at the fish on the wall for a
moment. "What do *you* think?" she asked it.

When it didn't reply, she swiveled around in the chair and
looked out the window. The rain had pounded for an hour
and a half, then stopped as abruptly as it had started. Now
the street below was rain-slick, and people were again
milling around the memorial, even in the dark.

Faith had called each of the six Department Thirty cases
assigned to her jurisdiction. *My jurisdiction,* she thought. It
felt strange to think that way. This was still Art's office, wasn't
it?

She'd quickly learned that she would likely soon have
only five cases. A former CIA analyst who'd had a big drug
problem in the late eighties had been diagnosed with AIDS.
Department Thirty had relocated him to Las Cruces, New
Mexico, his new identity that of a mid-level university
administrator. His doctors had given him less than six
months to live.

Faith swiveled back around to the computer screen and
reviewed the updated files Yorkton had given her. Her other
cases included a big-time Washington lawyer and fund-raiser
who had shot and killed her husband's mistress; an accoun-
tant who had engaged in some Enron-type shenanigans but
was relocated because some of his firm's clients had included
the fronts for various terrorist networks; a former U.S. congressman from Wisconsin whose lobbying firm had gotten
tangled up in illegal arms sales; and a carpenter who'd sold
weapons underground to a number of domestic militia
groups.

And then there was case number one.

The computer file was no use to her in learning much
about Nathan Grant of Caney Creek, Oklahoma, formerly
Charles Brandon, eldest son of one of the old East Coast

publishing families and general counsel to the House Select Committee on Intelligence.

Grant/Brandon was the first case Department Thirty had ever processed. Art Dorian had done it himself, right down to the man's name and getting him started in real estate in rural Oklahoma. But there was precious little information about what Brandon had done that turned him into Grant.

Faith stood up and stretched. Grant had been polite, if a bit distracted, on the phone. She'd asked if he needed anything from the department, and he'd said he didn't. They'd made a tentative plan to meet in person to do an annual review in a couple of weeks' time.

But she still didn't have a feel for him, the way she did for the other five. Their files were exhaustively detailed, with sections on the crimes they had committed and on the information they had provided to Department Thirty in exchange for their new identities. The Grant file told about operations that had resulted from his information, but about his crimes, there was nothing. The only reference was a notation in Art's hard copy file saying that Brandon's family was told he had died of a heart attack at the federal prison in Englewood, Colorado on Christmas Eve, 1970.

She paced the office, beginning to feel a little claustrophobic. "That's not like you, Art," she said to the room. Art Dorian had been the most meticulous individual she'd ever met. No detail escaped him. His keen attention to detail had made him jot a note to himself nearly thirty years ago on the Adam and Eve/Elder case, which had eventually led her to his murderer.

Faith sat back down and looked at the paper file again. She flipped pages and began to notice a pattern. Many of the official departmental papers had been signed by Daniel Winter. She compared that to the others. The paperwork for the other five had all been signed by Art as case officer.

She remembered what Yorkton had told her at the memorial: *Remember, you're the sole point of contact for these cases.*

So why was Daniel Winter's signature on this case's paperwork?

Faith tapped a nail on the desk. She rubbed her eyes and flipped her hair back away from her face. What she needed was food. It was nearly eight o'clock and she hadn't eaten since morning—not since before she'd left on the Carter/Corelli raid. That seemed like a very long time ago now.

She was reaching for the light switch when a tap sounded on the door. She opened it and saw Scott Hendler in the hall. His white shirt was open at the collar, his FBI-standard red tie was loosened, and he looked tired.

"Hey," Scott said.

"Now, that's a clever opening line," Faith said.

Hendler smiled. "I thought I might find you here."

Faith turned off the light, closed and locked the door. "You must be with the FBI."

"Can't get anything past me."

Faith pulled her hair back again. "How'd the rest of Corelli go?"

"Faith . . . I'm sorry you weren't there. I know you put it all together."

Faith nodded. Scott at least knew how much the case had meant to her.

"It went well," Hendler said. "We just finished processing him. Leneski brought him in. Corelli actually started to cry, showed us where everything was. He had the plates and quite a bit of the money itself in his attic, just stacked up everywhere. It was right next to his wine rack, that wine that you nailed him on. But he blurted everything out, confessed everything, wants to throw himself on the mercy of the court. That's actually the way he said it: 'the mercy of the court.' I didn't know anyone really talked that way."

They walked a few steps down the empty courthouse hallway. Faith said nothing but nodded.

"How are you?" Hendler said. "I mean, really. Mayfield in your office called and told me the word was you'd gone over into Thirty. I guess it's for real."

"I guess."

"You thinking about old Dorian?"

"A little. But I'm thinking about all these cases, people who broke the law—I mean, broke it big time—and we're protecting them in exchange for information." More to herself than Hendler, she added, "I have to start thinking in a different way."

"You want to get a beer? We can go over to Chelino's. Grilled jalapeños on me."

Faith looked at him. She knew he wanted to be more than colleagues and friends, and she had dealt with that ever since she'd met him. For the most part it had been all right, and he'd actually been a good friend. After all, he was the one who'd found her last year on her dining-room floor with glass embedded in her face, and Phillip Clarke across the room with a bullet in his shoulder. It occurred to her that almost all her real friends here in Oklahoma were male. Other women she'd met seemed a little hesitant around her, as if they weren't quite sure what to make of her.

"You know what, Scott?" she said, smiling a little. She looked down at his balding head. "That sounds great. You buy the peppers, I'll buy the beer."

Chelino's was in the Bricktown warehouse district, just east of downtown. The transformation of Bricktown from empty warehouses into more or less trendy restaurants and clubs had gone a long way in helping revitalize downtown Oklahoma City after decades of a downward spiral.

Hendler had grown up in Oklahoma City and, after short tours in Utah and Pennsylvania, somehow managed to get the Bureau to assign him to his hometown field office. He'd told her about Chelino's, how it had started in a converted Dairy Queen on the south side of town and had grown into a major player in the competitive Tex-Mex restaurant business.

They sat at a table in the big, open, noisy front room and ordered two bottles of Dos Equis. When the beer came, Hendler ordered a plate of grilled jalapeños to go with their chips and red salsa.

"So, what's it like?" Hendler finally asked. "Thirty, I mean."

Faith waited before answering. "I don't think I'm supposed to talk about it." She shook her head. "Strange. It's very damned strange, Scott. I just have to unlearn all the real rules of law enforcement." She shrugged and took a swallow of the amber liquid. "I'll get used to it."

Hendler shifted on his seat and took a drink of his own beer. "You're different."

She snapped her eyes to him. "What's that supposed to mean?"

"Don't get defensive. You're just . . . different over this last year. You're . . ." He drank again.

"I'm waiting."

"Harder, maybe? I'm not sure that's the right word. Definitely more confident. You used to second-guess everything you did."

"Maybe I still do, and just hide it better."

"Maybe so, but that's still different."

Faith raised her bottle in salute. The grilled peppers came, in a steaming pile on a hot plate. Faith plucked one off and ate it. She squeezed her eyes closed against the heat. When she opened them, Hendler was smiling at her.

"My point exactly," he said.

"Oh?"

"The first time you came here, you literally cried when you ate one of those."

"Give me a break. I'm Irish from Chicago. We don't get these in Illinois, trust me. Then again, Oklahoma doesn't get real pizza, either." She ate another pepper, chasing it with a few chips. Somewhere back in the bowels of the restaurant, someone whooped and yelled something in Spanish. A burst of applause went up.

"Scott," she said, then thought, *Careful, Faith. Don't screw it up on your first day.* "Tell me something."

Hendler leaned forward conspiratorially. "Anything."

"You've been with the Bureau how long now? Five or six years?"

"Six years in September, but who's counting?"

"So you're pretty plugged in to the world of DOJ by now."

"Not really, but go ahead and ask anyway."

Faith crumbled a corn chip into several small pieces. "What do you know about a guy named Daniel Winter? He's a . . ."

"He's a legend, or something like it. Director of Thirty, appointed by Nixon, but he's lasted through presidents of both parties ever since. Carter supposedly hated him, and Reagan never even met him once."

"You know a lot about Winter for someone who's not plugged in."

Hendler shrugged. "He lectured to a couple of my classes at Quantico—weird topics, like 'Thinking outside the Investigative Box.' Strange stuff like that. I don't think anyone paid much attention to him, but you can't help but be impressed by how long he's lasted." He signaled for another beer. "He's the one who called you this morning at the command post."

Faith nodded.

"And he's the one who said you wouldn't have a job with the Marshals Service if you turned down Thirty."

"Yep."

"Pleasant man."

"Yep." Faith crushed another chip. She thought again of the file on Charles Brandon, bare of details about his crime and conviction, and about all the paperwork signed by Daniel Winter. She wondered about how distracted Brandon/Grant had sounded when she'd called him.

"You think something's up with Winter?" Hendler asked.

Faith smiled. "You're right, nothing gets by you." She almost said, *You ever hear the name Charles Brandon?* but caught herself, just as she'd seen Art Dorian do so many times.

". . . of your cases?" Hendler had said.

Faith looked at him. She'd lost his words in the restaurant noise and her own thoughts. "What? What did you say?"

"I said, do you think Winter is personally tied in to one of your cases?"

Faith opened her mouth, closed it, opened it again. "Can't talk about the cases, Scott. You know that."

"I know that. But why are we having this conversation, then?"

Faith thumped her beer bottle on the table and ate another pepper. She reached across the table and covered Hendler's hand with hers. "Thanks for caring, Scott. I appreciate you. I really do." She patted his hand. "But I can't tell you anything. First day on the damned job and I can't tell you or anyone else a damned thing. And if I did"—she leaned forward—"then I would have to kill you."

Hendler recoiled in mock fear. "Killed by a tall redhead with a big gun. But what an epitaph!"

Faith drew her hand back, laughing. "You got it. So watch your step, Special Agent Hendler." The smile faded. "But if you run across anything about Mr. Winter, I'd love to know."

"So I can give you information but you can't give me any?"

"Yes, sir. Sweet deal, don't you think?"

"Hell of a deal. Nice work if you can get it."

Faith leaned back. She thought back to the Brandon/Grant file, about how careful Art Dorian was in his record-keeping, almost to the point of obsessiveness. As she ordered another beer, she began to think that there was something very, very wrong about the man whom Art Dorian had renamed Nathan Grant.

6

ERIC DID A LONG VISUAL SWEEP OF THE FLAT, TREELESS landscape thousands of feet below him, checked his Global Positioning System unit to make sure he was where he was supposed to be, and thought, *What the hell am I doing?*

As soon as he had the thought, he instinctively looked around the airplane. *I didn't say that out loud, did I? Got to watch the language, old man.* Then: *At least right now it doesn't matter.*

He glanced at Patrick. The boy was big for five, taller than many kids two years older than he. When he was born, full term but critically ill with a bacterial infection in one of his lungs, the nurses in the neonatal intensive care unit had pointed out that Patrick was the biggest baby in the unit at nearly nine pounds, side by side with preemies who weighed less than two.

He was definitely Laura's child, at least physically. He had her fair skin and always seemed to have high color in his cheeks. His eyes were cornflower-blue and very large. His hands had her long, slender fingers—fingers made for the piano, Colleen had once said. That was another hard one for Eric to swallow. He would never play the piano. He had never heard music.

But what about Beethoven? Colleen used to say. *He wrote that Ninth Symphony when he was stone cold deaf.*

Yes, Colleen, but he went deaf as an adult. At least he had heard music for most of his life. He could still hear it in his head: He knew what it should *sound like.*

Patrick had been profoundly deaf since infancy. No one had an explanation. He had been on oxygen for nearly two weeks at birth, and for some reason children on oxygen as newborns were highly likely to develop hearing impairments. Eric had become an expert on possible scenarios over the last five years.

Eric's heart ached. With Colleen in the ground for three days now, Patrick was all he had left. Laura was just an acquaintance now, someone with whom he had more or less civil, polite conversations from time to time. She didn't seem like someone whom he'd once loved to distraction, who'd given birth to this little boy and then announced she didn't want either Eric or Patrick. She was just another cog in a past he couldn't seem to shake.

Eric adjusted the microphone at his chin and spoke into it. "Boise City traffic, Cherokee two-eight-one-one Bravo, five southeast, descending out of seven thousand, landing Boise City."

The airplane was a 1969 Cherokee Arrow, and he'd put a down payment on it with his government severance package. He had been toying with the idea of learning to fly before his career and his marriage imploded, and those events simply pushed him the last step. He'd taken the lessons, acquired his license, and a year later bought his Cherokee. He'd discovered that flying was therapeutic in a lot of ways, a melding of relaxation and mental gymnastics. Everything was different up here. Colleen could still live up here. Patrick wouldn't be deaf up here. He wouldn't be just a home-based "research associate" making barely twenty thousand dollars a year up here. The past would fall away with every foot he climbed into the air. Up here there were no bad choices, no old screwups, and up here he hadn't killed a man.

Eric shook his head. *Stop the daydreaming, idiot,* he told himself. *We're out here for a reason.*

Folded in his shirt pocket was the yellowed sheet of paper that ended with the words *Look for the twins and stones. I hope you will understand.* Words written by a man who said he was his father, yet had left his mother and taken him to a woman he'd never even met before. A man who'd insisted his son have a different name.

Eric was nearly forty years old and had never known his full name. And it was thanks to the man who'd carefully scripted those words on the yellowed paper.

The implications reverberated everywhere he turned. Would he have to change Patrick's birth certificate to read Patrick Miles instead of Patrick Anthony? Laura still used Anthony as part of a hyphenated last name. He could just imagine *her* response.

But then, perhaps Colleen had truly been out of her head at the end. She'd seemed lucid, but . . .

No. Eric remembered when he was a kid: No matter how drunk or stoned, Colleen had always been rational, could always form thoughts and articulate them. The booze and dope hadn't robbed her of that, and neither could the cancer.

Boise City Municipal Airport was in visual range now, and Eric spoke into the radio again: "Boise City traffic, Cherokee two-eight-one-one Bravo, left downwind for full stop, runway two-two, Boise City."

He came into the single runway from the southeast, landing easily and taxiing into the area where he could tie down the plane. Patrick looked over and gave him a thumbs-up. Eric smiled: He'd taught Patrick that one.

When the plane was secure, Eric took a moment to look around. At least, he thought, Patrick wasn't missing anything here. It was so quiet, Eric could swear he heard his own heartbeat.

Patrick caught his eye. *Are you okay?* he signed, using Signing Exact English. He'd begun learning SEE before he was two years old, after his deafness was confirmed.

Eric smiled at him. The boy's long, slender fingers were also perfect for sign language, and his teachers had told Eric that Patrick's sign vocabulary was extraordinary for a five-year-old. Eric spread his own arms apart, then signed, *Strange place. I'm a city boy.*

Patrick frowned, then signed, *City dad.*

Eric looked down at him. *You're right. City dad.*

He put an arm around Patrick's shoulders and they walked a few steps, and Eric had to again wonder what his parents might have had to do with *this* place. The panhandle had always been an abstraction to Eric, an urban dweller from Oklahoma City. He knew its history as "No Man's Land," unclaimed by either Kansas or Texas and later attached to Oklahoma Territory. That was the extent of his knowledge.

Unlike some states that use the term *panhandle* to describe a long thin, strip of land, the state of Oklahoma is indeed shaped like a pan, albeit one with a jagged bottom. The panhandle, 160 miles long and thirty miles wide, protrudes from the far northwest corner of the state, gradually rising in elevation to meet New Mexico and Colorado at Black Mesa in the far northwest corner of Cimarron County, thirty-some miles from where Eric now stood.

Eric had read on the Internet in the last few days that Cimarron County did not have a single traffic light, that it was the only county in the United States to touch four other states and was more than 120 miles from the nearest inter-state highway.

And they're proud of that? Eric wondered to himself.

His was the only plane at Boise City Municipal Airport. There were half a dozen or so buildings of corrugated metal, and a couple that were just frames. Holding Patrick's hand, they walked to a tiny squarish building at the end of the runway, white with peeling green trim. A sign above the single window read ELEV. 4180.

Using the wall phone inside the little building, Eric called the Cimarron County Sheriff's Department and the dispatcher gave him the combination to a lock that held the key to the airport's courtesy car. Once he had the key in hand, he walked back outside, around the little building, and stopped in front of a seventies-vintage black and silver Chevy Suburban sitting on a patch of tall grass. The top of the cab was solid rust.

Patrick tugged at his father's sleeve. *Does it work?* he signed.

I don't know, he signed back. *Let's find out.*

He checked the tires of the Suburban, unlocked the door, and slid in, leaning across to open the other door for Patrick. He hooked a thumb at the backseat, indicating where the boy should go. Patrick frowned: He was forever trying to get his father to let him ride in the front seat, but Eric never gave in.

You know the rule, he signed. "Safer back there."

Patrick gave an exaggerated eye roll—he looked just like Laura when he did that, Eric thought—and climbed into the back, buckling his own seat belt.

Eric took stock. It was dusty and there were a few papers and potato-chip bags on the floor, plus a flap of the ceiling cover was hanging down over the front passenger seat. "Let's hope you run better than you look," he said.

To his surprise, the big engine roared quickly to life and sounded well tuned. *Ready?* he signed back over his shoulder, then watched the mirror as Patrick nodded. The boy was smiling, the smile Laura had had when they first met each other. Everything in life was a grand adventure.

Let's go, Eric signed, saying it out loud as well.

There wasn't much to the town of Boise City. Highways converged from four different directions at an old-fashioned courthouse square. According to the directions his father had scribbled thirty-nine years ago, he was to take the western road toward Kenton. Eric did, and was out of Boise City and back onto the high plains within two minutes.

His mind played over Colleen's dying hours as he drove through the flat, treeless plain that stretched away to the endless horizon. Colleen had seemed genuinely distressed that Eric had never, as an adult, asked her about his parents. It troubled her enough to make it the last thing on her mind before she died. He thought of Colleen as a vivacious, ambitious young woman, out to prove herself, suddenly faced with the child of a distant relative she barely knew. And why?

So they wouldn't find you.

They.

Who were *they*? And what did *they* have to do with this harsh, isolated plains country?

"And why do I care?" Eric said aloud, a bit angrily. He'd once had a purpose, a driving ambition to help society and its institutions. That had ended in a rain of gunfire five years earlier. Never mind that Weldon Hawthorne had fired at him first, and it was clearly self-defense. Patrick was born twenty-seven days later and his marriage had ended a year after that, back home in Oklahoma, far from the power of D.C., the power Laura had craved.

He glanced over his shoulder. Patrick was looking out the window, enraptured with this strange landscape.

Twenty miles west, the road bent sharply north, and it was as if that single turn brought them out of Oklahoma and into the foothills of the Rockies. Mesas and buttes began to appear amid the scrub of the shortgrass prairie. At one point Patrick tapped excitedly on the window and they saw four pronghorn antelope galloping parallel to the highway.

"This is Oklahoma?" Eric said.

A few miles farther on, they rolled down a hill into the tiny community of Kenton. Eric had read online that it was the only town in Oklahoma that operated in the mountain time zone.

As far as Eric could tell, Kenton consisted of only two businesses, a general store/diner and a tiny little building that served as a tourist center. Other than that, there were only a dozen or so scattered houses and two churches. He pulled the Suburban into the little white building with KENTON, OK VISITOR CENTER in black above the door.

Postcards and various curios lined the single counter inside, and behind it sat an old man, shaven bald on top but with a magnificently full white beard. His face was lined nearly as hard as the landscape that surrounded this area.

"Morning," he said.

"Good morning," Eric said softly, then cleared his throat.

"Here, sign our guest book," the old man said in a resonant baritone with just a hint of an Oklahoma drawl. "I'm Good Mattingly."

Eric looked at him quizzically as he took the pen.

"It's really Thorogood," the man said, "but who would want to call a kid that? My parents just called me Good. Made it tough whenever I did something wrong. Who ever heard of Good doing something bad?" He laughed deep in his throat.

Eric started to sign his name the way he'd signed it his entire life, then stopped for a moment. He finally wrote *Eric Anthony Miles and Patrick, Oklahoma City* in the book. Looking at it, he thought, *Why did I do that? That doesn't look right.*

Mattingly leaned over the counter. "What do you do down there in the City? No, let me guess: I can always guess a man's occupation right after I meet him."

Eric raised a hand. "Oh, it's—"

"Don't tell me, now." He made a show of looking Eric up

and down. "You're in sales. Computers, office supplies. How'd I do?"

Eric smiled slightly. "Sorry, not even close. I'm a researcher for an advertising agency and consulting firm."

Mattingly laughed out loud. "I must be slipping." He leaned over the counter and looked at Patrick. "What's your name, young man?"

Patrick looked quickly at Eric. Eric signed, *He asked your name.*

Mattingly's eyebrows went up.

Patrick put both hands over his ears and shook his head forcefully. Then he made a sign-language *P*—thumb tucked between the downward-pointing index and middle fingers—and placed it over his heart, making his "sign name." Then he smiled.

"He's telling you he's deaf and that his name is Patrick."

Mattingly looked startled for a moment, then reached down and across the counter, extending his hand. Patrick put his small fair hand in the old man's and they shook.

"Tell him that's a good handshake," Mattingly said.

Eric repeated it in sign, and Patrick signed, *Thank you.*

Mattingly nodded. "Y'all drive up this morning?"

Eric shook his head. "Flew into the airport in Boise City. We're using the airport's courtesy car."

Mattingly laughed. "Well, that ain't exactly LAX over in Boise City, is it? You here to hike up the mesa? The young 'un's probably too small to go. Parts of it are pretty steep."

"Actually, I'm looking for the three-state marker. The directions I have were kind of vague."

"Well, of course they were. It's way out in the middle of nowhere."

And we're not already? Eric wondered.

The old man pointed a gnarled finger back the way they had come. "Go back out of town until you see the sign that points toward Colorado. Take that road north. It'll be about five miles to the mesa trail, but stay on that road past the mesa. You keep going until the paved road ends, another three or four miles or so. You'll get a gravel road that forks off. Go to the left. Then you get off the gravel road, and there's a little trail that'll lead you to it. It's not very big, but you can see it a few feet away."

Eric nodded. "Thanks." He took Patrick's hand and they turned to go, then he turned back around. "Have you lived around here long?"

Mattingly smiled. "I'm eighty-one next month, seventy of them spent within an hour's drive of this very spot."

Eric smiled back. "This probably sounds crazy, but does the phrase 'twins and stones' mean anything to you?"

"What?"

" 'Twins and stones.' Does that ring a bell?"

Mattingly blinked. "Got me on that one, son."

"Doesn't make sense to me, either. Well, thanks."

"You're welcome. Enjoy your visit."

Good Mattingly watched Eric and Patrick climb back in the Suburban, and as soon as they were out of sight, he turned the guest book around to face him. "Eric Anthony Miles and Patrick, Oklahoma City," he said aloud. Then a moment of recognition clouded his face and Mattingly stumbled against the counter, knocking over a rack of Black Mesa postcards.

"Well, I'll be damned," he said.

7

THE BLACKTOP COUNTY ROAD WOUND AND TWISTED ITS way between the mesas and buttes, and Eric had to slow down every hundred yards or so for metal cattle guards across the road, the rural equivalent of speed bumps. Cattle grazed off to their right, some dangerously close to the road.

He passed no more than two or three houses set well back from the road, then saw the turnoff for the parking lot to the Black Mesa trailhead. Somewhere out there on top of the mesa was the highest point in the state of Oklahoma. Eric kept driving.

Five miles farther on, the blacktop ended and the Suburban bounced onto gravel. At the road fork Eric saw a wrought-iron sign on the right reading BACA COUNTY, COLORADO. He bore left, then took a tiny turnout toward the little granite monument. Mattingly was right: There wasn't much to it.

Eric and Patrick got out of the Suburban and stood for a moment in the high-plains sun. If Eric had thought it was quiet at the Boise City airport, the silence here was chilling. Even the famous Oklahoma wind was calm. They stood and simply looked around, at the absolute bigness of the landscape. There were few trees except those that climbed the sides of the mesas. Eric wiped his forehead: It was warm for May, and nearly noon by now, the sun high.

Patrick tugged his father's sleeve and signed, *Wow.*

Wow indeed, Eric signed back. "This gives me the creeps," he said aloud.

They walked to the little monument, about three feet tall on a concrete base. It was fashioned out of gray granite, with the names of the states engraved in black. Facing them was OKLAHOMA. Eric walked around it to the side that faced west.

He beckoned to Patrick. Eric didn't know the sign language for NEW MEXICO, but he pointed to the marker. Patrick was a good reader, and Eric had shown him the spot on the map before they'd left home this morning.

Eric gazed off toward the west. He was facing a barbed-wire fence that came to a point just beyond the monument, then turned at a ninety-degree angle, running as far as he could see.

They walked around the marker to the side that read COLORADO. Patrick's eyes grew wide: He'd heard of Colorado. There were mountains there, an endless source of fascination to an Oklahoma flatlander.

Eric pulled the yellowed paper out of his pocket and unfolded it, looking at his father's handwriting: *From the marker, there's a trail leading into Colorado. Walk up into Colorado a hundred steps or so. Turn and look back toward New Mexico. Look for the twins and stones. I hope you will understand.*

The "trail" was a couple of ruts bisected by a line of grass. Eric took a few steps into Colorado.

He stopped, hearing nothing, feeling nothing but the awesome openness of the land. He closed his eyes and said a short prayer.

Colleen hadn't raised him in church, but she hadn't stopped him when he wanted to go with friends as a teenager, either. She'd seemed more amused than anything by his interest in religion. He'd tried every imaginable Christian denomination, finally settling as an adult on a "mainline," moderately liberal church. No hellfire and damnation, no slavish devotion to doctrine, just the simple message of love and forgiveness and redemption. They'd also accepted Patrick without question, never once telling Eric they weren't set up to deal with a special-needs child.

"Please, Lord," Eric muttered, although he wasn't sure for what he was asking. *"Please."*

Patrick, dancing merrily from state to state around the marker, stopped what he was doing and went to his father. He pointed at the paper. *What's that?*

Always observant, Eric thought. *Something Colleen gave me,* he signed.

Patrick wrinkled his brow, lines slashing across his little forehead.

Looks even more like Laura when he does that, Eric thought.

What are we doing here? he signed. *Really.*

Eric smiled. *You are too smart for my own good. I'm not sure. Let's walk this way.*

Eric took Patrick's hand and they walked up the trail, going up a slight rise farther into Colorado. Eric kept his eyes on the ground. There were tiny cacti with a red tint to them, and an abundance of a small, roundish plant with long, thin spiky leaves.

After a while they stopped and Eric looked back toward the monument. He was no good at estimating distances, but the Suburban was a speck behind and below them.

He looked back toward New Mexico. The fence line was

now parallel to where they stood, running toward the far horizon.

He put his hand in his pocket and jingled his keys. He tapped his foot.

Look for the twins and stones. I hope you will understand.

He whistled a couple of notes and jingled some more. He could feel his heartbeat in his head.

He squinted toward the fence. Nothing but grass, cactus, and the little round spiky plants.

"This is crazy," he said.

He took a step back down the trail.

Patrick scuffed his feet and Eric turned back. Patrick was pointing toward the fence.

What? Eric signed.

Patrick waited a moment, furrowing his brow again. Eric knew he was searching for the right word.

Shiny, he finally signed. *In the grass.*

Eric sharpened his gaze on the fence line, the border between Colorado and New Mexico.

"I don't . . ." he said, then let the sentence die.

He squinted. He trusted Patrick's senses: The boy was a classic example of other senses making up for the one that didn't function. His eyesight and sense of smell were remarkable.

Where?

Patrick pointed. He pulled his father's arm and turned him at a slight angle from where he'd been.

Eric shaded his eyes, staring hard into the distance of the stark, strange landscape. He kept staring, and was about to turn around and sign to Patrick that there was nothing out there, when he saw a tiny glint in the grass by the fence line.

See it? Patrick signed.

Eric nodded and took a step forward. There it was again, what looked like a sliver of gold on the ground.

He started to walk forward, off the trail and cross-country. He began to jog, growing winded quickly, realizing how out of shape he was. His breathing already ragged, he turned it into a run, not quite sure why. Patrick loped beside him, trying to keep up on shorter legs. The boy was grinning: To him it was a race.

Eric stumbled on a rock but managed to stay on his feet, fairly leaping over a little cactus in his path. There was the glint again. He looked skyward. If they'd come at any other time of day when the sun wasn't so high, they might never have seen it.

They reached the fence and Eric placed a hand between barbs on the wire, steadying himself. Patrick pulled up beside him.

The boy's fingers flew. *Daddy, are you okay?*

Hell no, I'm not okay, Eric wanted to say but didn't. *I don't know what my name is anymore, and I'm a hundred miles from nowhere, chasing shadows.* But he nodded, trying to concentrate on his breathing.

He couldn't see the glint now, the little finger of golden light that had reflected off the hard ground. Eric started working his way along the fence, actually walking the boundary between New Mexico and Colorado.

Twenty steps later he found it and his heart somersaulted into his throat.

It was a flat granite grave marker, the same color as the three-state monument back behind him. It was outlined with a shiny gold border, which had reflected the high sunlight.

Eric squatted next to the fence and brushed grass off the stone. His pulse began to roar in his ears.

An intricate carving of a lamb was at the top of the stone, right under the gold border. Under it were the two names: LINDA AND BRENDA O'DELL. Beneath that: BORN & DIED MARCH 31, 1955. Beneath the dates, in smaller print was GOD'S ANGELS.

Newborn twins, buried far out in this remote country.

But why? And what did Linda and Brenda O'Dell, whoever they were, have to do with him?

Eric felt an urgent tug, which turned into a slap on his arm. He looked up. Patrick was pointing excitedly.

Another one! he signed.

A few feet away, on the other side of the fence in New

Mexico, was a rose-colored marker, similarly buried in the grass.

MANUEL FELIX RAMIREZ. HECTOR FELIX RAMIREZ. JANUARY 2, 1961. ASLEEP WITH JESUS.

"What the hell?" Eric said aloud.

He began to look on both sides of the fence, and continued walking beside Patrick.

LEE AND LEAH PORTER. SEPTEMBER 29, 1964.

SEAN HAMPTON. STEVEN HAMPTON. OCTOBER 15, 1964.

MICHAEL W. GOLDMAN. JONATHAN W. GOLDMAN. MAY 11, 1957.

What is it? Patrick signed frantically.

Eric shook his head.

Twins and stones. I hope you will understand.

"Twins and stones," Eric said. "What are they doing out here?"

The names began to blur, but in a relatively small area Eric counted more than a dozen sets of twins, born and died on the same day. The earliest date was 1955. The latest was 1965.

Eric stopped and straightened, looking back toward the trail. He could see why the directions said to walk up the trail and look down, rather than going straight toward the fence. The stones were deeply flush with the ground, and many were partially covered with grass or dirt. The only chance to really see them was to catch the light just right. Terry Miles—*his father*—had known that. His father had been here, right here, and knew about all these children.

Eric counted eight more stones, all with sets of twins, all with a single date engraved on them.

This is insane. What does this mean? Why didn't Colleen give me this years ago?

Because I never asked.

He continued walking along the fence line, then his foot brushed one final marker, which lay directly beneath the last wire of the fence, half in one state, half in the other. This marker was rose-colored.

He brushed some dirt off and stumbled against the fence, ripping his shirtsleeve and gashing his arm on the barbed wire. Blood started to dribble from the cut.

Eric ignored it, riveted to the stone.

The first thing that caught his attention was the date: JULY 27, 1965. Then, two chilling words: GONE HOME.

His eyes strayed upward and read the names:

EDWARD A. MILES.

ERIC A. MILES.

8

FOR SEVERAL LONG MOMENTS NO THOUGHTS WOULD form. He simply saw the date—his birthday—the words GONE HOME carved below it, and the names.

His name. The name Colleen had told him before she died.

And beside it, another name: EDWARD A. MILES.

He blinked at the stone.

Patrick pointed down at the rose-colored marker. He was still a few feet away, not quite close enough to read the names. Eric shifted so he blocked Patrick's view.

It's a mistake, Eric signed. *I thought it was something else.*

Boy, that sounds lame, he thought, looking at the grave again.

EDWARD A. MILES.

ERIC A. MILES.

Eric shivered in the midday sun. He stood up, steering Patrick away from the stone. They started to walk back toward the Suburban. Eric pulled out his pocket notebook, and as they passed each of the other graves he copied down the names and dates. Twenty pairs of infant twins buried in hidden graves.

Where are we going? Patrick signed as they approached the car.

Home. Let's go home.

Eric thought of the other two words carved on the stone: GONE HOME. He reached into his pants pocket and began to twist the inner lining. Instead of jingling his keys this time, he wrapped them up in his fist, feeling the metal digging against his palm.

Five minutes later he and Patrick were in the Suburban, bouncing back up the road into Oklahoma. Eric tried to keep his mind focused elsewhere: on the landscape, on his driving, on Patrick, on anything but what he'd seen. Finally he gave up. His entire concept of his own life had just been turned upside down.

"Who's buried there?" he said aloud.

He thumped the steering wheel, passing the Black Mesa trailhead parking lot. Eric shook his head. He couldn't think straight.

Five miles later he turned onto the state highway that would take them back to Boise City.

"Edward," he whispered. "Edward A. Miles. Who are you?"

Thorogood Mattingly had the distinction of owning the westernmost residential dwelling in the state of Oklahoma, less than a mile from the three-state marker. After he'd seen the old Suburban turn up the highway and drive away from Kenton, he'd locked up the tourist center, leaving the postcards scattered all over the floor. He climbed in his old Ford pickup truck and drove out the way the Suburban had come.

By the time he turned into his long gravel driveway, far beyond all the other houses in western Cimarron County, Mattingly's hands were shaking on the steering wheel. On top of that, he felt the arthritis acutely. Shaking, aching hands.

Damn good thing I can't operate anymore, he thought. *Might slip a scalpel and lose someone. These hands are no damn good for anything but selling tourist trash.*

The pain was so bad that by the time he'd let himself into the frame house in which he'd lived most of his life, he had to take three extra-strength aspirin. That didn't stop the shaking, though.

Mattingly fluttered around the house, sitting for a moment on his 1950s vintage couch, sweeping dust off the mantel, running water into a glass under the kitchen tap, then pouring out all the water. He moved like a nervous bird, unsure of which way to fly.

He remembered them all, of course. All of the babies. Some of the mothers had been panicked, some had a quiet resignation, some were determined just to get it over with. Then there had been Maggie Miles.

"Bad, bad," Mattingly said, shaking his bald head, pulling at his beard.

That had been a bad scene. The last one—it was all over after that. All those babies . . .

"Oh, bad," Mattingly said, his mind spinning in two different directions. He had to talk to someone. He had to let someone know. He had to . . . *what?*

What the hell are you thinking, old man?

He whirled around as if someone had actually spoken.

Stupid old man. Now you're hearing voices. But you still have to . . . to make it right?

No, can't do that. I've paid enough already. God knows I've paid enough. Lost my license to practice, lost everything I ever wanted. I've paid, dammit!

Then he thought of Eric Miles and his beautiful little deaf son.

Mattingly clapped his hands over his ears in unconscious imitation of the boy.

He fluttered to the stairs and gripped the rail, going up step by painful step. A wooden kitchen chair sat at the top. He'd put it there when his arthritic knees began to grow worse, so that he could sit and rest after climbing the stairs. This time he ignored the chair and walked into the room he'd once used as an office.

He stared out the window. A hundred yards away, beyond his property line, was the building they'd called The Center. Low and square, with few windows, no wonder Maggie Miles had felt claustrophobic. All the deliveries had been done in The Center. The deliveries . . . and everything else. Mattingly tried to remember all the little rooms inside; he hadn't been in the building since 1965, and more than once had thought about venturing over there with a full can of gasoline. But it wasn't his to burn, and in some ways it was a grim reminder of what he'd done, of what his own weakness had wrought.

Mattingly turned away from the window and opened his old metal filing cabinet. At the very back, alone in a file folder, was a sheet of plain white paper on which he'd scrawled a phone number. A phone number and the word *Brandon*.

He winced just at the sight of the name. He'd had to give up his medical license and sign a gag order for his part in the project. Then all the records were sealed and buried as deep as the U.S. government could bury them. He'd later heard that Charles Brandon died of a heart attack in prison in Colorado. He hadn't believed it: The man was a healthy specimen, no hints of heart disease. He'd given him his annual physical for nine years running. Brandon had even joked about that. He could have had any number of high-flying government doctors do his physical, yet he always let the old country GP, Good Mattingly, do it for him. *Since he was in the neighborhood anyway,* he'd joked.

Then, in early 1972, Brandon—or whatever his new name was—had appeared on Good Mattingly's doorstep. *Write down this phone number,* he'd said. *If there's anything I need to know, if the past comes knocking, you'll let me know, won't you, Dr. Mattingly? Of course you will.*

Mattingly had never called the number, not even once. Not until today.

His hands shaking, he made the call. He punched in all the digits except one, his finger hovering above the phone. "What do I say?" he said to the empty office. "What do I tell him?"

Was this wrong? Should he just leave Eric Miles and his son alone?

Almost against his will, his hand jabbed at the last digit and the phone began to ring.

I don't know what to say!

There was a click and a mechanized voice told him to leave his message after the tone. The tone sounded in his ear, and Mattingly stood for a moment, crushing the receiver against his ear.

"I don't . . ." he said. Why had he called this number? *Stupid old man, you're losing it. You've finally gone over the edge.* He looked out the window and caught sight of The Center again.

Eric Miles. That was it.

"This is Good Mattingly," he said in a rush. "I . . . you remember me? Well, I guess you do. Eric Miles came to Kenton today. You remember, don't you? You remember which one he was? He came and he asked directions to the three-state marker. He's . . . what did he say he was? A researcher for a . . . what was it? . . . an advertising agency. He lives in Oklahoma City. He has a little boy, and the boy's deaf. I don't know . . . I don't know why I'm telling you this now. I better go."

He practically threw the phone back on its receiver. What the hell was he doing, babbling like that? That wasn't like Thorogood Mattingly, M.D., who had once been the most respected physician in the Oklahoma Panhandle and who people thought had gone crazy when he came back from a trip and announced he wasn't practicing medicine anymore.

Guilt, Good. That's guilt you're feeling. You just sold out that boy Miles. It's not his fault what happened all those years ago. It's not his doing. It's your doing, and Brandon's.

Mattingly found himself wondering what kind of a life Eric Miles had had to this point. "No, now stop thinking that way," he said aloud, his voice cracking. He finally sat down, his knees and hands both feeling achy and swollen. "Rest," he said, and leaned his head back in his chair, his old office chair, his doctor's chair.

It was late afternoon when he jerked awake again. He'd been dreaming, which he did more and more lately. There had been an army of young women, young pregnant women. They marched up the road, not from The Center, but from the marker. From the location of the gravestones. They'd marched in his house and up his stairs and into his office, twenty young women with swollen bellies. The one in front was Maggie Miles, with her honey-colored hair and her fresh-scrubbed small-town good looks, and she opened her mouth and said, "First, do no harm."

Mattingly shot out of the chair, his joints screaming for mercy.

First, do no harm.

Even though it wasn't spelled out in so many words, every physician knew the sentiment expressed in the Hippocratic oath.

"But I took care of you," he said to the office. "I didn't hurt you, any of you. I gave you the best care possible."

He remembered the last vestige of the dream, Maggie Miles's accusing eyes. They said, *How could you? You're a doctor, I trusted you. He was something else,* he made me sin, but you . . . *you're a doctor.*

Mattingly tripped over his chair and fell squarely on his butt. He held his breath: *That's all I need now, to break a hip like old men do.* But he simply got up again; everything seemed intact.

He sat in the chair and fumbled for the switch on the computer that sat there. He knew what he needed to do. He'd seen early that computers were the future, and he swore he'd had the first PC in the panhandle. *Crazy old Doc Mattingly,* they'd said back then. *Living a sci-fi fantasy out there at the edge of the world.*

He'd laugh last about that, wouldn't he? Mattingly logged onto the Internet and put in Eric Miles's name in a search box, then waited a moment. He typed *advertising* after it and pressed enter.

No matches.

Mattingly frowned. That would have been too easy. He thought for a moment, then tried *Eric Miles* and *Oklahoma City* for his search. He found two references, one to a high school social studies teacher, the other an obituary for a World War II veteran.

Mattingly pressed his fingertips to his temples. "All right, we'll attack it a different way," he said to the computer monitor.

He entered *Oklahoma City* and *advertising agency.* That got him dozens of matches. He started down the list, pulling up Web sites of ad agencies located in the city. On their Contact pages he looked for Miles's name.

Ninety minutes later he still hadn't found the man, after going through all the sites. "He's there," the man said to the empty room. *Everything* was on the Internet. He'd even found references to himself on there before, and he'd been quietly fading from sight for more than thirty years.

Think, old man! Think!

He recalled Miles and the little boy standing in front of his counter in the little tourist center. He'd turned the guest book around. Miles had taken the pen . . . and he had *hesitated.*

Mattingly shot out of his chair.

Miles had hesitated before signing his own name. Then he'd signed all three names. How many adults signed casual documents with their first, middle, and last names?

What if . . .

Mattingly went back to the computer. He could try various combinations of the name. Maybe, just maybe . . .

He went back to the list of Oklahoma City advertising agencies. Another hour passed. The only Miles listed with any of them was a woman named Johanna, a copywriter. Strike the last name.

Mattingly got up, his joints complaining. He wandered around the office, pausing by the window, catching sight of The Center again. He flinched as if he'd been poked in the gut with something sharp.

"Find him," he muttered.

Back at the computer, he tried looking for Anthony.

On the Contact page of Solomon and Associates, with an address on North Broadway in Oklahoma City, he found *Eric Anthony, Sr. Research Associate.*

"Found you," Mattingly whispered.

He blinked at the screen, at Eric Anthony's name and the highlighted area below it, showing his e-mail address.

He tried to conjure a picture of the man but couldn't. The

image he got was of the little boy, that beautiful fair-skinned little boy putting his hands over his ears and shaking his head forcefully, then signing his name and smiling up at Mattingly.

Mattingly pounded the desk. "Oh God," he said, and Good Mattingly began to cry. He couldn't even remember the last time he'd cried. It had been that long. All his screwups, his foolishness, his greed . . . there they were, all gathered together in the person of Eric Miles's little boy.

And Mattingly had screwed up again. He was still intimidated by the man who had once been Charles Brandon: the man who had taken advantage of his weakness, the man who took advantage of everyone's weakness. So he'd, figuratively speaking, run first to Brandon, calling that number. Maybe Brandon had forgotten about the number. Maybe he never checked the messages. It had been so long. . . .

He straightened slowly. But he hadn't told Brandon that Eric Miles had been living under the name Eric Anthony. His pulse quickened. There might be hope yet. Good Mattingly clicked on Eric Anthony's name and began to write a message. He would make it right. For the first time since he met Charles Brandon, he would do right. He would talk to Eric before Brandon—or whoever he was now—could. He would get Miles back up here. He would show him The Center. He would tell him . . . he would tell him everything he knew.

Mattingly nodded at the computer and slowly pressed *Send*.

9

FAITH KELLY'S NEW RUNNING SHOES SLAPPED THE PAVE-ment of The Village, her middle-class Oklahoma City suburb. The eastern horizon was just beginning its faint glow toward sunrise, and she still had three miles to go.

Faith had been pushing herself harder and harder on the

daily run. She wasn't in her marathon shape, though that really didn't matter. It didn't look as though she'd have the time to run in any marathons anytime soon, now that she belonged to Department Thirty. But she used the five miles every morning to sweat out the things that flooded her body and mind, to cleanse herself.

Better than going to mass, she thought, then blanched at the thought. *Good old Irish Catholic guilt.*

She loped around a corner and onto Britton Road, a main thoroughfare, though it was almost deserted before dawn on Sunday morning. She passed a brightly lighted donut shop just as two middle-aged men came out the door. One whistled. The other shouted, "Who says Amazons are extinct?"

Faith grinned without breaking stride. She was used to it, of course. A nearly six-foot-tall redhead in spandex running gear did tend to attract attention.

There it was again, that Department Thirty thought that peeked at her from around corners these last few days. She should have been the last person Department Thirty would want. Her background was all wrong, and she was not an unobtrusive presence, intentional or not.

"Crazy," she muttered, letting her thought turn to the one case that still occupied her mind.

Case number one.

Charles Brandon. Nathan Grant.

How was she supposed to understand him if she didn't know what he had done that brought him to Thirty's attention in the first place?

This was what she didn't like about programs like Witness Security and, on another scale, Department Thirty itself. Too many gray areas, not enough clear boundaries. For all her life there was the law, and you stayed on either one side of it or the other. No gray areas. She'd been at this less than a week and she wanted to take someone's head off. But by the same token she was intrigued by it all, by the idea that lurking around somewhere in all those shadows was the truth. And in the truth, the guilty would get punished and . . . the rest of the guilty would get new identities.

Fifteen minutes later she stopped on the front porch of her two-bedroom brick house. She did a few leg stretches and pulled off the bright green bandanna she always wore as a headband when she ran. She shook it out and wiped the sweat off her face, then pulled her hair out of its runner's ponytail.

She stepped into the house, avoiding as much of her clutter as possible—*Have to remember to clean house tomorrow*—then showered and dressed in jeans and a casual, loose-fitting cotton shirt and drove downtown to the office.

The federal courthouse was deserted on an early Sunday morning as well, as was most of downtown Oklahoma City. She left the Miata in the underground parking garage and rode to the second floor in the elevator reserved for law enforcement personnel.

In the office she said good morning to the catfish, then sat in the chair and turned on the computer. She inserted the disk Yorkton had given her and reviewed case number one again.

Maybe she was looking for things that weren't there. Maybe she was overreacting. Maybe the whole business of becoming part of Department Thirty had her seeing conspiracies everywhere.

The hell she was. Her father had told her last year that all a good cop really had going for them was instinct. Even though she wasn't really a cop anymore, her instincts fairly screamed that she needed to know more about this case.

One of the files on Department Thirty's internal policies and procedures had clearly stated that the departmental director was available to case officers twenty-four hours a day, seven days a week. Faith decided to test the policy. She picked up the phone and called the Department Thirty main number in Virginia.

After four rings Daniel Winter said, "Working extra hours already, Officer Kelly?"

Faith waited a moment. She had no idea what kind of man Daniel Winter was. "Director Winter, I guess you're working early as well."

"Not really. When I'm not in the office, the phone forwards automatically to my home and then to my cell. We'll need to arrange that for you too. You need to be immediately available if any of your cases needs you. You should also have a small travel bag packed and be ready to move if there's a crisis." Winter paused. He sounded as if he was chewing something. "Pardon me. You certainly didn't call me on a Sunday morning for more procedures, now, did you?"

"No, sir. I am sorry to bother you, but I've been doing some reading on the cases."

"Questions?"

"Just on case number one. There doesn't seem to be any information, either on disk or hard copy, about what Grant's crimes were, about why he was imprisoned in the first place. I mean, Brandon. He was Brandon then."

Winter chuckled. "Confusing, isn't it? Of course it is." The humor in his voice faded. "Everything you need is in your case files."

"Well, sir, it's just that I don't really have a feel for him. I mean, all the other cases have court transcripts, police reports, and such. There's nothing on Brandon. Also, I thought it was kind of curious that so many of these reports are signed by you, instead of Art Dorian. The other cases—"

"All I can say, Officer Kelly, is that you have all the material you need there."

"Sir, I—"

"I really can't tell you anything else. Besides, that case is pretty much self-sustaining as far as I can tell. He's a low-maintenance identity. I understand he's done quite well for himself in real estate. Has a bit of a tendency to go through wives, but otherwise we haven't had to do much except the annual review for many years now."

"Director Winter—"

"I'm glad you have an eye for detail, Kelly. Yorkton told us you did. If that's all, I hope you'll excuse me: I'm late for church."

"But—"

The phone clicked in Faith's ear. "Well, thank you for your

support," she said to the dial tone, then hung up and began leafing through Dorian's hard copy file again. Even in a case that had been active for more than thirty years, it was much slimmer than any of the others.

Forget it. I have better things to do.

She started to go through the other case files, reading things Yorkton and Winter had flagged for her attention. Her case in New Mexico, the former CIA analyst with AIDS, was having trouble with his health insurance paying for his medication and had requested the department's assistance.

While each Department Thirty case was expected, after a one-year adjustment period, to be financially self-sufficient in his or her new life, the department maintained an account of discretionary funds for each one, just in case. While Faith had no problem okaying a release of funds for the man's medicine, she had to wonder at the morality of it. People across the country went without medication they needed in order to buy food, and elected officials in the pockets of pharmaceutical companies refused to enact meaningful health care reform. At the same time Department Thirty, with just Faith Kelly's signature on a form, could release almost unlimited funds to get medication for a man who had committed a series of felony drug-related crimes, just because he'd once possessed information that was deemed important to . . . who? Daniel Winter? Art Dorian?

Art, did you struggle with these issues? she wondered, then signed the form authorizing the funds for the man's medication.

She was an hour into some of her own personnel paperwork when the phone rang.

"Officer Kelly, it's Nathan Grant," said the deep voice on the other end of the line.

Faith closed her personnel file and sat up a little straighter. "Good morning, Mr. Grant."

"I'm sorry, I didn't catch your first name when we talked the other night. I was . . . preoccupied."

"Faith. Faith Kelly."

"Good. May I call you Faith?"

"If you like. What can I do for you, Mr. Grant?"

"I'm afraid something's come up since you and I talked, and we may need to move up our meeting."

Faith opened her datebook. She was scheduled to drive to Overland Park, Kansas, on Tuesday to meet her case there, the lawyer who'd shot her husband's mistress. "How about late next week? I think—"

"Well, Faith, I was actually thinking of today."

"Excuse me?"

There was a pause. "I know the department's phones are safe, but I'd rather talk face-to-face. It seems . . . well, I have it on good authority that an issue from my former life is about to crop up."

"Your former life."

"Yes. You're up to speed on my case, aren't you?"

"I've read what's here, but there's—"

"I'm taking this . . . this 'issue' very seriously, Faith. Why don't you drive down here today? You should be back in the city before nightfall. Tell me, do you like catfish?"

Faith's eyes strayed to the fish mounted on the wall. *Fish stories*, Art had always said. Now she was talking to one of those fish stories. "In what way?"

"Fried, usually."

"What?"

"Fried catfish. It's delicious, and the best little catfish place in America is the Catfish Platter, right here in Marshall County. I'll order us lunch. When you get here, my wife will probably come to the door. Tell her you're here about the Moore property."

Faith quickly opened the Brandon/Grant file. His current wife was his third since entering the department's protection. "All right."

He gave her directions to his home in Caney Creek on Lake Texoma, then hung up. Faith read quickly through the file again. She'd wanted to know more about the man now known as Nathan Grant. It looked as though she'd get her wish, much sooner than she'd thought.

10

FAITH DROVE THE MIATA SOUTH ON INTERSTATE 35 OUT of Oklahoma City and into the green, gently rolling horse country of south-central Oklahoma. After two hours she exited at Ardmore, drove east through the pleasant courthouse town of Madill, and bent south again, fast approaching Lake Texoma and the Texas state line.

Kingston was a town with one traffic light. Grant had told her to turn right at the light and follow the winding road. She did so and was soon out of Kingston again. A green sign on the narrow two-lane road announced that Caney Creek was five miles away. Faith pulled the Miata to the shoulder of the road and let it idle for a moment. She took the Brandon/Grant file from her briefcase and skimmed over it again, memorizing what little she knew about the man.

Charles Brandon was the adopted son of one the old-line East Coast newspaper families. His biological parents were unknown, in a classic, almost stereotypical case of an infant being dropped off at the door to a Providence hospital in the middle of the night. He'd grown up with great wealth, spending summers in Maine and occasionally Europe. He went to Harvard for college and then applied to law school, which angered Willis Brandon. He'd wanted young Charles to assume control of the family publishing empire.

Charles wanted to get involved in government and politics. By this time the Brandons had other sons—natural, biological sons—and the old man had pretty much dispensed with Charles altogether. Even so, within a few years in Washington, Charles Brandon was the general counsel to the House Select Committee on Intelligence. It was the McCarthy era, the Cold War frigid. A heady time for a sharp young man involved in government intelligence oversight.

He remained in D.C. with the committee until 1965, and there the file abruptly ended. There was a typed notation, initialed by "A.D."—Faith recognized Art Dorian's precise printing—of Brandon's conviction in federal court of "crimes unrelated to his governmental duties."

Another page signaled that all court records pertaining to Charles Brandon had been sealed. The signature was a scrawl that Faith took to be Daniel Winter. From there the file proceeded to Brandon's processing into Department Thirty in the early seventies. There were several pages regarding his statements and testimony to the department, and the results of that testimony. A suspected Soviet mole in the State Department had been tracked down. A rogue CIA operation in East Germany was exposed. The true nuclear capabilities of the Soviet submarine fleet had been learned, not the sanitized numbers that were known to the public. Covert operations interested in "regime change" in obscure places like Nicaragua and Iran were examined.

Faith shook her head. None of this had ever been made public. It all went into Department Thirty's "information archives." She'd learned that there were two kinds of Department Thirty information that was gained from their cases. There was the information that was used to bring civil or criminal cases in open court. For example, when the infamous assassins Adam and Eve had sought protection, they'd provided reams of names and dates and places and account numbers, which kept the Justice Department busy for years in investigations and prosecutions, all highly public.

Then there was "archive" material. This was information that never saw the light of day, never reached public or media scrutiny. Art had never gone further than this in his talks with Faith, but she presumed it was filed away for a rainy day, a sort of informational savings account. Someone, somewhere up the line in Department Thirty, could use the information as a bargaining chip, as barter, perhaps for other information.

Gray areas, Faith thought. Her professional life had turned to one big shade of gray.

The file then went into Brandon's life as Nathan Grant. He had been wildly successful in Oklahoma real estate, even making money through the "oil bust" of the mid-eighties that had devastated the state's economy. As Grant, he sat on numerous civic committees and advisory boards. He had commissioned works of art, was well known in the state capital, and had even donated money for the construction of a new children's wing of the regional medical center in Durant.

A dusty pickup truck rattled past her, and Faith dropped the Miata back into gear. *It's right on the road,* Grant had told her when giving directions. *You can't miss it. Just look for the gate.*

Five miles later she could see the blue water of Lake Texoma shimmering under the sunlight through the trees. To her right were small, neatly kept trailer homes. She passed a little convenience store and a couple of larger houses. Then she saw it, at another road junction: a curving wrought-iron gate with GRANT above it.

She pulled up to the gate and pressed the button on the little box mounted there. A moment later the gate slid open. Faith took a deep breath and prepared to meet her first Department Thirty case.

Nathan Grant was in his office at the rear of the house, alternating his gaze between the deck and private pier that stretched out into the lake, and the big-screen TV with CNN blazing away its Sunday talk show.

On the screen Wolf Blitzer was asking pointed questions of the president's chief of staff, who appeared defensive and restless. The opposition leader in the Senate, a fatherly-looking man, responded with subtle attacks on the administration's integrity and trustworthiness.

It was all working just as Grant had hoped and planned. Timed to hit the Sunday talk shows and big newspaper editions, the e-mail he'd sent had reverberated throughout Washington. It had been a simple message, but the political fallout was beginning.

Someone should ask the President about his own ties to Sons of Madison United.

That one sentence had translated into shouted questions at press briefings, reporters thrusting cameras as the president toured the damaged areas of Fort Defiance State Park. There were denials, indignity, outrage, from the president's camp. The president of the United States connected to extremists, to cop-killers, child-killers, *terrorists*?

Of course, there was no evidence to back up the e-mail, and the administration's vehement denials would stand unchallenged.

For now.

"Lovely, lovely," Grant said to Wolf Blitzer on the screen. He pressed the Mute button on his remote and tossed it onto his leather couch.

Grant let his thoughts wander down a different road: Good Mattingly.

At first, listening to Mattingly's rambling message, he hadn't been sure of what the old man had said. But he replayed it three times, and each time the name was there.

Eric Miles.

An interesting development. Grant wasn't sure how he felt about it. But he'd decided to attack the problem—if indeed it was a problem—on more than one front. He hadn't come this far to be undone by carelessness.

The intercom on his desk buzzed and his wife said, "Nathan, honey, Faith Kelly is here to see you about the Moore property."

Grant crossed to his desk. "Thank you, Rachel. Have her come on back."

Then he clasped his hands behind his back and turned to stare through the window at the choppy waters of the lake.

The first thing Faith thought of when she met Rachel Grant was "trophy wife," followed by "ex–rodeo queen."

She was only in her early thirties, five years or so older than Faith. She knew from the file that Grant himself would turn seventy-eight this year. The third Mrs. Grant was platinum blond, fair-skinned, and slender. She wore designer jeans, an intricate leather belt with her name stitched on it, a tight blouse that accentuated her figure, and gray boots. She had a "Little Dixie" drawl that wouldn't quit, and as she led Faith through the huge house she kept up a running commentary about the beauty of the lake area, the friendliness of the people, and what a steal the "Moore place" would be, whether as a primary residence or a weekend getaway.

After myriad turns and hallways filled with a strange combination of art that ranged from black-and-white photographs of rural railroad stations to French impressionists, they came to a tall set of wooden double doors.

Who has double doors in their house? Faith thought. But then, she was a cop's kid, forever middle-class. The behavior of the wealthy was foreign to her. She felt a slight tide of resentment: *He has all this because we set him up and got him started. Even after he broke the law.*

Rachel Grant rapped lightly on the doors, then said sweetly, "Go on in, honey. He's ready for you. I hope you're able to work out a deal."

When Faith walked into the study/office, she first saw the big picture window and the tall man standing there with his back to her. *Classic ploy,* she thought. *Try to establish superiority by showing them your back.* She stifled a sigh, then her eyes were drawn by a huge painting that commanded the wall to her left. It depicted a young red-haired girl in a flowing white gown, blindfolded, kneeling before a wooden block while a priest stood beside her. In the background two other women wept. To the young girl's right stood the headsman, leaning on his ax.

Staring at the painting with its breathtaking color and detail, Faith didn't notice that Grant had turned around.

"Captivates you, doesn't it?" said the deep voice.

Faith nodded. "It does. Who's the girl?" She looked away from the picture and into Grant's face. The man had none of the stooped shoulders or gnarled limbs of age. The lines on his face only added mystery to it, and his eyes were so dark that the irises were almost indistinguishable from the retinas. He was tall and slim but broad-shouldered. Faith remembered from the file that he had a private gym somewhere in this house and still worked out every day.

Grant's dark eyes had widened. "You don't know *The Execution of Lady Jane Grey*?"

Faith shook her head.

"Ah. You'll have to forgive me. Art Dorian and I talked quite a bit about Tudor history over the years. Tell me, Faith, did you know your predecessor in the job?"

"Yes."

"Fine man, Professor Dorian. His original ambition was to be the top Tudor historian in America. Funny how things get derailed." He walked to the wall with the painting, running a hand along the base of it. "Do you know the story of Jane Grey at all?"

Faith shook her head, wondering if she had the patience to listen to this man prattle on about his obscure interests.

"Oh, you should study the English Renaissance era," Grant said. "Not all the pomp and pageants. I mean the politics, the intrigue." He tapped the base of the painting's frame again. "Jane Grey was the granddaughter of my namesake, Charles Brandon."

Faith looked around quickly.

"Don't worry. Rachel vanishes to parts unknown when I'm discussing 'business' in here. No danger to Department Thirty security there. Anyway, Brandon had married Henry VIII's sister. Their daughter Frances married a lazy sot named Henry Grey, who later became duke of Suffolk. Now, you know that when King Henry died, his only son inherited the crown."

"Edward, wasn't it?" Faith said, trying to remember world history from high school. "Edward V?"

"Close. Edward VI. But Edward was only nine years old, so England was ruled by advisors. Six years later, when Edward was dying of tuberculosis, the advisor was John Dudley, the duke of Northumberland. It was plain Edward was dying, and equally plain that the next in line for the crown was Mary Tudor, Henry's eldest daughter." Grant spread his hands apart. "Edward was a passionate reformist, a Protestant. Mary was an old-fashioned Catholic. Dudley knew he'd be out of power if Mary ascended the throne, so he concocted a wild scheme to keep a Protestant puppet under his thumb. He played to Edward's fears of the Great Judgment and convinced the boy to write a new will, leaving the crown to his teenage cousin . . . Lady Jane Grey."

Faith's eyes flickered back to the painting. "I don't remember ever hearing of a Queen Jane. Didn't Mary come next? Wasn't she the one they called Bloody Mary?"

Grant nodded, eyes gleaming like sharpened knives. "See, you know more than you think you do. You couldn't be around Professor Dorian for long and not have some of this rub off on you. No, Faith, Jane is a footnote to history. Dudley married her off to one of his sons, and then Edward died a few weeks later. He revealed Edward's new will and had Jane crowned in secret. She was an amazing intellectual and a fanatical Protestant. She never wanted the crown but took it out of obedience to her parents, who were hugely ambitious." He took his hand off the painting and let it fall.

"And what happened?" Faith said after a moment.

"Nine days."

"What?"

"Jane was queen for nine days. You see, Dudley didn't count on Mary being as popular as she was. No one really knew who Jane was, but they all knew the princess Mary. The people rose on her behalf, all the councilors deserted Dudley, and Jane fell after nine days."

Faith stared at the painting, the young girl in virginal white leaning toward the block. "And she was executed."

Grant followed her glance. "The painting isn't historically accurate, of course. Headsmen were always hooded, executions were held outdoors, and Jane didn't wear white. But Monsieur Delaroche did a fine painting, didn't he? Yes, she was executed. In fact, Mary wanted to spare her because she understood Jane had just been a pawn manipulated by powerful men. But politics was politics and it became a necessity."

Grant sat down behind his expansive desk and motioned Faith to a chair. "The moral of this story?" he said.

Faith raised her eyebrows.

"If you're going to do a daring yet illegal power grab, make sure you have the support of the people." Grant smiled, but it faded quickly. "And so to business."

Faith took out her pen and legal pad. "You mentioned something about your former life."

Grant looked squarely at her, and she thought for a moment she was falling into the cold, dark eyes. But she didn't look away. She'd learned a long time ago that most men weren't prepared for a woman to meet their gaze directly, and it disarmed them when one did.

Grant didn't look disarmed, but after a moment he leaned back in his chair. "Forgive me, Faith. I've spent more than thirty years looking across this desk at Art Dorian. It seems strange to talk to someone else about anything related to Brandon."

Faith noted how he spoke of Brandon as if he were a different person. But then, wasn't he? *This is crazy*, she thought for the thousandth time.

"I've read your file," Faith said carefully.

Grant nodded. "I have it from a good source that an issue from Brandon's life may be about to give us some trouble. There's a man named Eric Miles."

Faith wrote down the name.

"I don't have a lot of information," Grant said. "He'd be in his late thirties, and he's a researcher for an advertising agency in Oklahoma City. He has a young son, who is deaf." He stopped, looking across the desk at Faith.

"And what exactly is the problem with this Miles?" Faith said.

"Well, it's obvious. We—or you, I should say—need to make sure he doesn't find out who I am."

Faith waited. She stared down at her legal pad, where she'd written Eric Miles's name in block letters. She underlined the words three times each, then doodled a square, a circle, and a triangle. She drew a face inside the triangle, then looked up again.

"Mr. Grant," she said slowly. She noticed he didn't ask her

to call him by his first name. "There are a couple of things I should tell you. Your file . . ."

Grant leaned forward.

"Your file," she continued, "is not very complete."

She stopped, listening to her heart beating. She had no idea how to handle this, but plowing relentlessly forward was all she could do.

"As a matter of fact," Faith said, "your file doesn't tell me anything about the crimes that led you into Department Thirty. I have your testimony and statements once you were under the department's protection, but I have no idea what you did to get here. Are you telling me that this Eric Miles is related to those crimes?"

Grant rubbed a hand across his face. "I don't think in terms of crimes."

"I'm sure you don't," Faith said without thinking, then sat silently, her gaze locked on Grant. Physically the man wasn't intimidating, just an old man with white hair and a lined face, but he radiated menace. He radiated cunning and power. On some level she understood why so many women had been attracted to him. Back in college she'd disdainfully called such girls and women "power fuckers."

Grant smiled malevolently. Faith's blood chilled. "Eric Miles is connected to the chain of events that put me in reach of your department. We should know what he intends to do, don't you think, Officer Kelly?"

"Aren't we on a first-name basis anymore?"

"Sarcasm is not a pleasant quality in a young woman—or anyone else, for that matter. Professor Dorian was never sarcastic with me. Not once in more than thirty years. You could take lessons from the way he did things. Now, unless I'm mistaken, *Officer*, your job is to protect me. If protecting me means getting information on this man, then so be it."

Faith leaned forward herself, letting her legal pad tumble off her lap to the expensive hand-woven Persian rug on the floor. "So be it, Mr. Grant. But let me ask you: If I don't have all the facts, how can I investigate anything? How can I find out about someone from your former life when I don't know all the details? This isn't some fill-in-the-blank quiz. I need answers before I can ask the right questions."

"Do your job, Officer. Or do I need to go a little further up the food chain?"

"I'll do my job, Mr. Grant." She stood up. "Anything else I need to know? I should be getting back to the city."

"Too bad you won't be staying for lunch. Our catfish plates should be delivered anytime."

Faith wondered at the way Nathan Grant swung between courtly manners and searing malevolence, all in a matter of seconds. "No, thanks. I've had enough fish stories for today. I'll let myself out, Mr. Grant. I'm sure you'll be hearing from me."

With a final look at the painting of the doomed teenage queen Jane Grey, Faith hauled open one of the huge double doors. Five minutes later she was back in the Miata, on the twisting road toward Kingston.

I'll do my job, all right, Mr. Brandon/Grant, she thought as she nudged the car up to seventy. *I'll do it so well, you may just regret it.*

When Faith Kelly was gone, Grant paced the room, tracing a path between the Jane Grey painting and the big-screen TV on the other wall.

He didn't know if he could count on Kelly to do what he needed her to do without tipping his hand. He would have to deal with Eric Miles, though he wasn't sure yet in what way. He would have to be very, very careful. There were too many complicating factors to take it lightly—factors no one else knew.

Then there was Dr. Mattingly. There was nothing complicated about that one. The old fool could be a real embarrassment if he wasn't handled now.

Grant stopped in mid-pace and picked up the phone on his desk, punching in the number of the groundskeeper's house here on his estate. A moment later he said, "Come up to the house, please, Drew. I have another job for you. Maybe a couple of jobs."

While he waited for Drew to come up to the house, he picked up the remote and turned on the television again. He channel-hopped until he found what he was looking for: CNBC was interviewing Governor Angela Archer about the rise of homegrown domestic terrorism and the current administration's response to it.

She sounded all the right notes, every inch the stateswoman. When the interviewer tried to goad Archer into openly criticizing the president, Archer simply smiled that famous down-home Oklahoma smile, giving no hint that she'd attended Wellesley, Oxford, and Stanford. "There'll be plenty of time for that later," she drawled. "Right now we need leadership, not rhetoric."

Grant muted the sound as the topic moved to the economy. He knew Archer could handle the issues as well as any politician in America today. The important thing was, she managed to look presidential, willing to give the president the benefit of the doubt while appearing tough on terrorism.

Grant smiled. He glanced at the painting of Jane Grey before the executioner's block, then back to the image of Governor Archer on television. She practically filled the screen, her late-forties face with just enough lines to be seasoned, with just enough gray in her walnut-colored hair to give the aura of experience, yet radiating youth and energy and vitality.

The plan was working perfectly.

11

THOROGOOD MATTINGLY FINISHED THE LAST OF THE prime rib, belched once very softly, and tossed his napkin onto the plate. He looked around, savoring the understated elegance of the dining room with its highly polished wood and paintings covering the walls.

The Eklund was a century-old converted hotel on Main

Street in Clayton, New Mexico, and was the finest dining for over one hundred miles in any direction. It had been restored in the early 1990s to a shade of its former Wild West glory, and its famous bar was much the same as it had been in 1899.

Mattingly had only been to the Eklund a handful of times since its restoration. These days he didn't like driving more than a few miles at a time. His arthritic hands and legs didn't like the cramped driving position, and his failing eyesight made it even more difficult. But this was a special occasion: He was going to one-up old Charles Brandon, or whatever his name was now.

Good Mattingly had finally done the right thing. Sending that message to Eric Miles was going to make it right. It would bring his life back into balance, and Mattingly could die with a clear conscience.

As he paid his waitress with a wad of crumpled bills, he stopped for a moment, frowning at his reflection in the window across the way.

But you called Brandon, too, you fool, he thought.

"Well, that was a mistake," he told his reflection.

"Excuse me?" said the waitress.

"Nothing," Mattingly said. "Here, keep the change."

She calculated the tip. "But, sir, that's way too much for just—"

Mattingly flapped a hand at her and slowly walked out of the dining room. His old pickup truck was just across the street. Main Street in Clayton wasn't busy at just after five o'clock on a Monday afternoon, though it was positively congested compared to Kenton. Mattingly smiled a little at the thought of a traffic jam in this part of the country. A traffic jam out here might mean a tractor and a cattle truck going the same direction on the same road.

He drove his old truck east and was out of Clayton in two minutes. There were two giant cattle feedlots just outside of town, and Mattingly smelled them before he saw them, thousands of cattle in pens being fattened for slaughter. He turned the old truck north onto New Mexico 406, heading back for the state line and home thirty-some miles away.

Good Mattingly had decided many years ago that this stretch of state highway between Clayton and the state line was the loneliest, emptiest two-lane road in America. He couldn't count the number of times he'd driven it and not met another vehicle in either direction.

He only thought of the lonely nature of the highway because he'd just spotted the dark blue SUV half a mile or so behind him.

The SUV, something like a Suburban or an Explorer—he couldn't keep up with the models anymore—had been there when he drove himself to dinner earlier. He'd first noticed it behind him halfway to Clayton; then it had disappeared once he got into town, and he'd dismissed it as paranoia.

This stretch of road was nothing but grassland, some of it fenced, some of it pure open range, probably one of the last bits of open rangeland in North America. Past the feedlots, cattle straggled close to the road, but none were actually out on the pavement. A few mesas towered in the distance, but this was mostly high-plains country. Nowhere to go.

Brandon wouldn't send someone after me, he thought. *And Eric Miles wouldn't be following me like that.*

He turned up the truck's radio. Reception was awful out here, and all he could pick up was one religious station, playing something called "contemporary Christian music," whatever that meant. Contemporary Christian music to Good Mattingly meant the hymns of his youth in the Methodist Church of Kenton, "How Great Thou Art" and "Amazing Grace" and "Just as I Am, without a Plea."

Mattingly started to hum, not with the music but in spite of it. It was going to be all right. It was all right, after all.

Since he couldn't find classical music or opera on the radio, Drew drove the rented Explorer in silence. He preferred quiet to the babble of a radio while he was working, anyway. In that respect, this country was perfect for him. The silence, he suspected, could be overpowering to some people, to those who weren't accustomed to it. But he understood silence. He had developed a finely tuned sensitivity to it in the various stages of his life. Nathan Grant understood this about him, and Drew's need for quiet didn't infuriate Grant the way it did others.

He'd only had a couple of days to rest since the job at Fort Defiance, the biggest job he'd ever done. Grant had wanted to show him the effect it was having, the scandal they had created. Drew wasn't interested in the long-term effects. Everything for him was a week, a day, an hour, at a time. Concentrate on the job at hand. Do the job, then move on to the next one. That was all there was. Drew took great peace from the knowledge, whether the job was planting roses in his garden or carrying out assassinations.

He began to accelerate, watching the old pickup truck ahead.

Make this one look accidental, Grant had told him the day before. *This is a low-profile job.*

The old truck was weaving ahead of him. Perhaps this job would be easier than he had thought.

Mattingly squinted into the rearview mirror. The SUV was gaining on him. It had Texas plates, but that didn't mean anything. Out here, Oklahoma, Texas, Kansas, New Mexico, and Colorado all touched each other. It wasn't uncommon to see cars from all five states in a single town.

Mattingly's heart began to pound, and he began to feel a bit of a tingling sensation. He couldn't locate where it was coming from, but he felt it like tiny pinpricks on his skin.

He flipped off the "contemporary Christian" station and started to sing the first verse of "Amazing Grace" in his rough baritone.

"Amazing grace, how sweet the sound . . ."

Another glance at the mirror: The blue SUV was coming closer. A man began to take shape behind the wheel.

Mattingly pressed the accelerator to the floor. The old truck's engine whined and jumped ahead.

"That saved a wretch like me . . ." he sang. The son of a bitch wasn't getting Good Mattingly without a fight.

Mattingly squinted again. Coming up was the only turnoff on this whole stretch of road, a narrow New Mexico state road that ran two miles or so east before bending sharply north and turning into a county road when it crossed into Oklahoma. A sign pointed to Wheeless, which always amused Mattingly. It made it sound as though Wheeless were a town, whereas it was just a scattering of three or four houses and an old church. He didn't even know if the church held services anymore, but he did know all the families who "lived" in the community. He'd delivered at least three of them into this world.

Mattingly's eyes blurred. That had been before . . . before he met Charles Brandon. Before the Mesa Project.

"I'll show you," he muttered, then sang, *"I once was lost, but now I'm found . . ."* He wrenched the steering wheel hard right and bounded onto the narrow New Mexico road, fast approaching Oklahoma again.

"Was blind but now I see," he panted, flooring the old truck. He felt the tingling again, looking back over his shoulder. The big SUV was just crossing the junction, now turning, turning wildly.

Make it look accidental, Grant had told Drew.

That had become more difficult. The old man had obviously spotted him. He'd underestimated Thorogood Mattingly. An eighty-year-old ex-doctor widely regarded as crazy . . . Drew shook his head. That had been a mistake. *Never underestimate.*

The Explorer's big engine roared. The speedometer edged up past seventy. He would overtake the rickety old truck within a few seconds.

There used to be a sign that indicated the sharp turn where the road bent north, but it had long ago been knocked down, a victim of kids from Clayton or Boise City who had used it for target practice on long summer evenings. Mattingly was betting heavily that his pursuer wasn't familiar with the area and hadn't driven this road before. *Hell, people who* are *familiar with the area haven't even driven* this road. . . .

He glanced in the mirror again. The big vehicle was almost on his bumper.

Ahead, the L-turn and the state line loomed.

Mattingly caught a breathless feeling in his chest, something he couldn't quite define. He couldn't tell if it was adrenaline or pain or just sheer craziness, but there it was.

The SUV tapped his bumper.

"Damn you, Brandon!" he roared, then spun the wheel hard to the right. The old truck's tires dipped into a slight depression and sprayed gravel behind him, dust billowing up like a tornado in the high-plains air.

The truck bounded into Oklahoma and Mattingly righted it, bringing it back onto the road. Behind him the SUV kept going straight and thumped into the barbed-wire fence where the eastbound road ended. Mattingly imagined the driver's look of surprise when he realized a crazy old man had gotten the best of him.

Mattingly whooped in the cab of the truck and drove on toward Wheeless.

The impact surprised Drew more than hurt him. He'd been able to brake the Explorer before any real damage was done, though he didn't want to see what the undercarriage looked like. It didn't matter: The vehicle wouldn't be going back to the rental agency anyway.

He didn't get angry. Anger was a silly waste of time and energy, and detracted from the job. This was just a bump in the road—quite literally, this time.

He watched the plume of dust rising toward the north and chastised himself again for having underestimated the old man. The job at Fort Defiance had distracted him, the planning and coordination that had gone into it. Now, days later, it was still with him, and he was having trouble running an eighty-year-old fool off the road in the middle of some of the emptiest country in North America.

He dropped the Explorer into reverse and pulled away from the fence, which was now leaning crazily. The Explorer bounced once through the ditch, then came smoothly back onto the road.

He could still see the dust cloud ahead.

Drew started north.

Mattingly cackled to himself. *Sent your goon after me, didn't you, Brandon? Thought you'd get me here in my own country, did you?*

A couple of structures came into view ahead—the "community" of Wheeless: a couple of frame houses, one trailer, the old white church off to the right. A few miles past that and he could get onto Oklahoma 325 into Boise City. He'd drive straight to the Cimarron County Courthouse. He knew the sheriff, and he'd . . .

Mattingly imagined the conversation: *Well, Good, how come you think this old boy was after you?*

He'd have to tell him what he'd done, what Brandon had done, all those years ago at The Center.

He couldn't do that. Not yet.

Not until he'd talked to Eric Anthony Miles.

The fingers of Mattingly's left hand began to tingle. His wrist started to ache.

"Goddamn arthritis," he muttered.

The roar of another engine overtook him, and from the cloud of dust behind him emerged the SUV, like a shark rising out of black water.

This time the road was arrow-straight and narrow, no clever cutoffs, and Mattingly knew he couldn't outrun the other engine, not in a thirty-year-old truck that hadn't seen a mechanic in at least a decade.

At the edge of his vision the white clapboard of the old Wheeless church slivered into view. It looked nicer than he remembered, painted, the lawn well tended. Maybe they did still have services there.

Mattingly hummed a few more bars of "Amazing Grace," then softly sang, " *'Twas grace that brought me safe thus far, and grace will lead me home.*"

If Brandon's henchman was going to kill him, he might as

well try to attract some attention. He tried to think of the Wheeless families, and who might be home on a late afternoon. There were the Atwoods: The husband and wife were both schoolteachers in Boise City, so maybe they would be home by now. And the Darrens: They ran cattle. Maybe Mike Darren would be driving in from the pasture, coming back home from afternoon feeding.

Yes. Lord help me, this is it. Mattingly hoped Eric Miles would be able to figure it out. Good Mattingly had done all he could.

The pain was creeping up his left arm, stiffening the arm as it went. Mattingly was finding it harder and harder to steer the old truck.

A few more yards . . .

The SUV bumped him, harder this time, and Mattingly's hands flew off the wheel. He screamed wordlessly into the windshield. The pickup began to spin, cutting crazy donut shapes into the lumpy blacktop of the road.

Mattingly grabbed the wheel, struggling with it. Pain gathered into a crescendo at his armpit.

Peering through the dust, he saw the flash of white.

He twisted the wheel with all his strength and steered off the road, onto the nicely mown lawn of the Wheeless Community Church.

He said a silent apology to the families of Wheeless, who would have to rebuild their church, and floored the accelerator.

Just before he crashed into the side of the church, he threw up his hands. He heard metal and glass and wood splintering, and the high-pitched squeal of the SUV's brakes somewhere behind him.

Drew didn't drive across the lawn as the old man had. He turned into the parking lot of the little church, looking around as he did. There were no other vehicles anywhere in sight. The two houses he could see looked dark and quiet. A cow lowed somewhere nearby.

Drew was thorough. He always made sure the job was finished, so he stepped out of the Explorer and walked silently to where the old truck, nose crumpled into junk, radiator steaming, had crashed through the side wall of the church.

The church was all clapboard, no brick, and the truck had driven right through the first three rows of pews. Red hymnals were scattered before the nose of the truck.

He found the old man sprawled across the seat, his face bleeding, a hand clutching his chest. He was still breathing.

"Dr. Mattingly, I presume?" Drew said softly.

The old man raised his head. "Can't . . ." he tried to say.

Drew watched him. The man was essentially dying twice, once from a high-speed car crash, once from the heart attack that was now coursing through him.

Mattingly raised his head. There was blood in his white beard. His bald head gleamed with cuts and abrasions. A look of pain and rage twisted his face.

"Tell Brandon . . ." he rasped.

Then the look changed.

Mattingly's eyes grew wider than Drew would have thought possible, the red lines behind them like lightning bolts. For a moment of terrifying stillness, a look of confusion, then blunt recognition, spread across Thorogood Mattingly's dying face.

"You," he whispered.

Drew stared down at the man. "What?"

Mattingly went stiff, his hand flopping down from his chest. His eyes stayed wide open, staring numbly into Drew's.

Drew began to back away from the wreck, tripping once over a stray piece of lumber. He kept an eye on Mattingly, but the man never moved again.

The job is done, he thought.

But Drew couldn't forget the strange expression and the last word the old man had said before he died.

He climbed into the Explorer. In seconds he was on the road, headed back toward New Mexico. He couldn't afford to get lost in the strange thoughts of dying old men. He had a long way to go, and much still to do.

12

THE DIRECTOR OF DEPARTMENT THIRTY DID NOT LIKE computers. Daniel Winter knew all the arguments in their favor, and he was far from being a technophobe, but the issue was security. For all the triple and quadruple encryption on the government's computer networks, it had been proven time and again that a bright college student could hack into nearly any system on the planet.

So Winter rarely used e-mail. He preferred face-to-face meetings or, at the very least, the telephone. His phones were swept twice each day. No other official in the Justice Department, with the possible exception of the attorney general himself, enjoyed such security. *Or such freedom*, Winter thought. He was essentially left alone to handle his projects.

He slowly swiveled his chair around from the window facing James Madison University and looked at his computer screen again. The subject line of the e-mail read CASE #1 INQUIRY.

DIRECTOR WINTER,

I MUST REPEAT MY REQUEST FOR FURTHER INFORMATION ON BRANDON/GRANT. I DO NOT FEEL THAT I AM EQUIPPED TO DEAL WITH A SITUATION FROM HIS PAST WITHOUT MORE FACTS. MR. GRANT SEEMS TO BELIEVE THERE IS SOME THREAT TO HIS IDENTITY FROM THIS ERIC MILES. I NEED TO KNOW WHY.

PLEASE SEND ALL AVAILABLE INFORMATION ON CHARLES BRANDON'S CRIMES AND ENTRY INTO DEPARTMENT THIRTY ASAP.

FAITH KELLY

So Yorkton's deputy marshal wasn't the type to take no for an answer. Winter smiled. It really would have been illogical to think she was. Winter read the message again. There was no fawning over authority, no wasted words. The young woman was completely no-nonsense, which would be both a blessing and a curse.

He flipped through his Rolodex until he found the number of the Oklahoma City office. He pulled out the card and, with a twinge of sadness, drew a line through the name of Art Dorian, the name he'd written there so long ago. He carefully wrote *Faith Kelly* in its place, then called the number.

When her voice came on the line, he said, "Officer Kelly. Daniel Winter, calling from Virginia. You're still looking for deeper background on Charles Brandon."

"Yes, sir," Faith said.

Not intimidated by superiors, Winter thought. *No hesitation. Good and bad potential.* "Well, it's quite a story."

"Mr. Winter, would you mind telling me why the file is so incomplete?"

Winter smiled. "Politics takes many strange forms, Kelly. Charles Brandon came from a powerful family. His father was a close friend of Henry Kissinger. First of all, you know the personal background, right? Charles Brandon was adopted, not the biological son of the publishing Brandons."

"That's in the file."

"Yes, of course it is. Then you know that the Brandons had tried for years to have a child. They finally gave up and adopted the boy they named Charles. Ten years later, at age forty-three, Clara Brandon conceived a child. After that son was born, the old man, Willis Brandon, washed his hands of young Charles. See, he had a real heir now, a true Brandon. He virtually ignored Charles. Oh, he gave him money and sent him off to college and law school, but he had little personal connection with him. For ten years he'd been a prince. After that, he was an annoyance. Another thing you have to understand is that the old man hated politics and everything to do with it. He was disgusted with the government before it was fashionable. So when Charles, newly graduated from law school, decided to get involved in government, that was the last straw. The old man broke off all relations with him."

"So he didn't use his father's influence to get the job with the House Intelligence Committee?"

Winter leaned back in his chair, crossing his legs at the ankles. "Not directly. Of course Willis never called anyone and asked them to give Charles a job. But everyone on the Hill knew who he was. Charles attached himself to a freshman congressman from Maine, and within a couple of years he was general counsel to the committee. He was liaison between the committee and the CIA, all the military intelligence agencies, the Senate, the White House. He was a master at analyzing information and could memorize complicated data verbatim. His briefings were legendary for their accuracy and insight, and he made the members of the committee look good."

"Always important to congressmen," Faith said.

"Oh, yes. But here's where it all begins to crumble. While he was doing all these brilliant things, he had this strange streak in him. He liked to live well, and with no Brandon money coming in, all he had was his committee salary. It was good, but not *that* good. So he concocted this incredibly wild scheme to make money. But it was deeper than just money. See, he was obsessed with children, with procreation, and with the idea of aristocratic families. When our psychologists interviewed him as he was being processed into Department Thirty, they determined that he was full of resentment toward his family—mainly his adoptive father and brothers: not just for being cut off financially, but for the fact that he was viewed as, well, a bit like damaged goods after a biological Brandon heir was born."

Faith was silent.

"Are you there?"

"I'm here," Faith said.

"Parents have the incredible capacity to inflict so much damage, don't they? And the damage can spread so much further than their own children."

Faith was silent.

Winter remembered her personnel file. *Thinking of your father the detective?* he wondered, smiling again to himself.

"Well, back to the story. Brandon's scheme." He waited a moment, tapping his foot. "We're unclear on how it started. There are several versions, and it's almost the stuff of folklore with Department Thirty now. Somehow Brandon hooked up with a country doctor from Oklahoma, a Dr. Thorogood Mattingly. We think they met when Mattingly came to D.C. on vacation and met with his own congressman, who was a junior member of the Intelligence Committee at the time. That's speculation, though. Somehow this doctor convinced Brandon that he'd stumbled on an incredible new treatment for infertility but that he couldn't get anyone in the medical establishment to listen to him."

"Infertility. You're not serious."

"Oh, I'm very serious, Officer Kelly. It's bizarre, it's convoluted, and it's how Charles Brandon became your friend Nathan Grant. Evidently this Dr. Mattingly had tried to peddle his ideas everywhere. Are you familiar with the drug Pergonal?"

"I've heard the name."

Winter nodded. "It was the first real hormonal drug treatment for infertility. But it didn't come along until the sixties. Here was this Mattingly, a country doctor from the middle of nowhere, claiming to have a treatment ten years before Pergonal. He'd developed the drug, which was supposed to use the hormones FSH and LH to correct abnormalities of ovulation in women who couldn't conceive. He came up with a regimen of injections, along with some kind of herbal supplement and, as he put it, 'the air of the high plains.' It sounded like so much snake oil to me, and indeed it was, with the consequences much more terrible than anyone could have imagined."

"What happened?"

"What happened was that Mattingly and Brandon placed ads in magazines and newspapers touting their miracle cure for families who couldn't have children. They were in tabloids and such, things read by lower-income people, not particularly well-educated people. Blue-collar, small-town people, mostly, desperate to have children. For a fee, an outrageous fee in most cases, Dr. Mattingly and his associate, a 'highly placed U.S. government official,' as the ads put it, would offer their revolutionary new treatment. They wiped out the savings of many of these young couples, squeezed every penny out of them. Over a ten-year period they 'treated' twenty couples.

"Mattingly called it 'The Mesa Project.' They built a facility far out in the desolate high plains country of the Oklahoma Panhandle, near Black Mesa. It's quite a striking landmark, I hear. Do you know it?"

"No. But I haven't lived in Oklahoma that long."

"They would bring the couples in and they would actually live in this 'Center,' as Mattingly called it, for a year, through conception, pregnancy, and delivery. It was an amazing scheme. And Charles Brandon was behind it, all the while protecting our government's intelligence secrets."

"The treatment," Faith said. "What about the treatment? Did it work?"

Winter sighed. "That depends on what you mean."

"I don't understand."

"As you might imagine, I did quite a bit of research on this at the time, as did Arthur Dorian. By the time Department Thirty had come into existence and contacted Brandon in prison, there were real, FDA-approved infertility drugs on the market. Pergonal was one of them. Mattingly's drug acted just like Pergonal, with one large exception. The way I understood it, Pergonal and his drug acted alike in that they bypassed the natural control systems of the woman's body. Therefore, strict monitoring is necessary to reduce the likelihood of complications."

"Complications."

"Such as multiple pregnancies. Such as infection to the fetus." Winter waited a moment. "Mattingly didn't know this. This was his big mistake. Years later, when the real drugs began to develop, there were safeguards in place."

"What happened?" A note of unease had crept into Faith's voice.

"Each of the women Mattingly 'treated' became pregnant

with twins. They all conceived and delivered twins. But then . . ." Winter stopped, the phone to his ear, swiveling back around to look out at the gray stone of the university across the street.

"Sir? Mr. Winter?"

"Yes, Kelly. Every one of those babies died within a few hours of being born. We don't know why. And Dr. Mattingly wasn't set up to deal with critically ill infants."

"Every one of them?" Faith whispered. "Twenty women . . . forty babies? My God, *forty babies?*"

Winter read the disbelief in her voice. "All except one. Thirty-nine babies died, one survived: the last one, born in the summer of 1965. Mattingly had kept tinkering with his system, trying to perfect it, insisting that it would eventually work, while Charles Brandon sat back and collected the money. But one baby survived." He sat back, waiting.

Faith Kelly breathed on the phone line. "Eric Miles," she finally said. "He's the one who survived."

"Very good. His twin died, and his mother suffered complications and died in childbirth. But Eric Miles survived." Winter stopped: It sounded like the young woman was writing.

"Why?" Faith finally said. "Why did he survive when all the others died?"

"Again, we don't know. But that's really irrelevant to us anyway. What happened is this: His father grabbed him and ran. An anonymous call came in to the FBI a couple of days later, detailing this strange scheme taking place out on the plains. Then they disappeared. The father was never heard from again. We think, though we can't prove it, that Brandon had him tracked down and killed before the Bureau closed in. Brandon was arrested and charged with forty counts of manslaughter."

"Forty? But Eric Miles survived. That's thirty-nine."

"Miles's mother, Kelly. If his mother hadn't been placed into the position she was in by Brandon's conspiracy, she would not have died." Winter coughed lightly. "Everyone in this case—and I mean everyone—wanted to make it go away:

Brandon himself, his powerful family, the House Intelligence Committee, even the prosecutors. Brandon pled guilty at his preliminary hearing, he was sentenced, and the records were sealed. The doctor was stripped of his medical license and signed a nondisclosure agreement."

There was a tapping sound on the other end of the line. "And Eric Miles isn't heard from until Brandon—I mean Grant—gets this so-called reliable information that Miles is about to find out who he is."

Winter ran a finger along the edge of his desk. "Not exactly."

"Excuse me?"

"Eric Miles has lived in total ignorance of all this. He's lived under another name for his entire life. The name is Eric Anthony."

Faith was silent a moment. Winter heard her breathing lightly on the line.

"The name's familiar," she finally said.

"The Hawthorne scandal five years ago."

"Oh, shit."

"I guess you remember it," Winter said. "I'll e-mail you his file. Either your local FBI field office or the Marshals Service should have a copy of the videotape. I'm told many offices do. Read the file, watch the video. Truly amazing string of events. You don't know the meaning of the phrase *small world* until you understand how bound up together all of us are. This is part of what makes Eric Miles extremely dangerous, since he's started asking questions. If he finds out who he really is—if he finds out who Nathan Grant really is—God help us, Kelly."

Winter hung up a moment later and turned back around to the window. Tourists were milling on the street below, and as always the D.C. traffic was moving at a nightmarish crawl. He steepled his fingers in front of his face. Hopefully he'd told her enough of the truth to get her to do her job, to find Eric Miles before Miles found Brandon/Grant. In reality, Winter thought, Faith Kelly could be much, much more dangerous than Eric Miles.

13

FAITH HUNG UP THE PHONE AND STARED AT IT FOR A moment, as if she couldn't believe what she'd heard. In fact, digesting what Winter had told her would take a while yet.

Thirty-nine dead babies.

And then there was Eric Miles—Eric Anthony.

She thought back to Nathan Grant's study, the picture of the execution of Jane Grey, Grant's strange fixation on a footnote to sixteenth-century English history.

"Crazy," she said aloud, took a long drink from a bottle of water, and stared out the window at the tourists at the memorial for a few minutes.

When she turned back around, there was an e-mail waiting from Winter, with ERIC ANTHONY/MILES in the subject line.

She opened the attachment and printed the file, all twenty-nine pages of it. She leafed through it, then walked down the hall to the Marshals Service office, file in hand. Most of the other deputies still weren't sure what to think of her, of the strange way she'd suddenly wound up working for Department Thirty. But a couple of her friends, Mayfield and Leneski, spoke to her, and the new chief deputy gave her a friendly handshake. She asked if she could have access to the videotape library. The chief's smile faltered a bit but he agreed.

Sure enough, she found a plain black videotape with a label reading WELDON HAWTHORNE, FROM CBS. She felt an uneasiness in her stomach, like a gnawing hunger that wouldn't go away. She found an empty conference room with a VCR.

Sitting at a desk reminiscent of those in most college classrooms, she settled back, her legal pad in front of her, ready to take notes. A blue screen led in, then was replaced by a grainy picture of a shopping center parking lot, the tape clearly from a surveillance camera.

Five minutes later the pad sat untouched; her pen had dropped on the floor.

"Oh my God," Faith said.

She slowly rewound the tape and watched it again. After the second time the thoughts began to tumble through her like rocks rolling downhill. *Charles Brandon, Nathan Grant, Eric Anthony, Eric Miles, thirty-nine dead babies . . . My God, what have I stepped into here?*

She rewound and started again. An older man sat in his long black Lincoln, alone, nervous, looking all around him. Another car, a blue Honda, pulled nose to nose with the Lincoln in the parking lot. A second man, younger, medium height and medium build with glasses, nothing outstanding about him, stepped out of the Honda and stood beside the open door.

The older man got out of the Lincoln and became instantly recognizable as United States Senator Weldon Hawthorne, senior senator from Ohio and one of the deans of the Senate. His craggy face and trademark rumpled suit eliminated any possibility of mistaken identity.

The younger man said something. Hawthorne pointed at him. The famous face turned angry. Hawthorne stabbed his finger at the man as if it were a sword. The younger man held up both hands and said something else, taking a step back, then putting both hands in his pants pockets.

Hawthorne kept approaching, growing angrier. He reached into his coat pocket and drew out a gun. Faith couldn't tell what kind from the video, but it looked like a small revolver.

The younger man—*Eric Miles*, she thought, trying to begin thinking in that context—put both his hands out in front of him. Even though there was no sound, Faith could see that he was saying, *"Stop! Stop!"*

Hawthorne raised the little revolver and aimed it loosely in Miles's direction. The gun bucked and the Honda's windshield shattered.

Eric Miles ducked out of sight, into the car. Faith saw him fumbling around inside. Hawthorne was shouting now, his face red, gesturing wildly with his gun. Miles's head popped back out, still yelling for Hawthorne to stop.

Hawthorne fired again. Faith couldn't tell where the shot went, but Miles ducked out of sight. When he came back up, he held a gun of his own. It looked like a government-issue nine-millimeter automatic. Miles held it in a firm firing stance with both hands. He was screaming at Hawthorne, and even without sound Faith could tell what he was saying: *"Drop it! Drop it!"*

Hawthorne didn't drop it. The old man maneuvered around the side of the Honda, directly parallel to Miles. He waved with the gun. Miles went on screaming at him. A strange smile appeared on the senator's face. He raised his gun arm.

Faith leaned forward. It was almost as if the video had slowed, lapsing into slow motion. Hawthorne's arm was up, the grin still on his face. He showed no sign of dropping the weapon. Faith watched his hand, his index finger curling around the trigger guard. She saw the motion as his finger slipped back onto the trigger itself. She swore she could see his muscles tighten around the trigger.

Miles shouted something else—she couldn't tell what— then she saw him take aim across the hood of the car. She saw the automatic shake ever so slightly in his hands, and she saw him fire.

Senator Weldon Hawthorne's head dissolved into a spray of red, gray, and white. He stumbled backward, then fell to the side. His fingers clawed against the side of the Honda like a rock climber looking for a handhold, then he was on the ground and absolutely still.

Miles dropped his weapon and vaulted the Honda's hood. When he saw what was left of Hawthorne, his legs went out from under him and he fell to the concrete, bracing his fall with both hands. Then he was on all fours, and his face was turned more or less toward the security camera. For a terrifying second Faith thought he was looking straight at her, as if pleading through the lens of the camera for some help.

Faith shuddered. She saw that the man was crying, then the screen went blank.

"Holy shit, Faith," said a voice behind her, very near.

Faith jumped, banging her knee on the underside of the desk. She turned around. Scott Hendler stood in the open doorway.

"Scott," she breathed. "You—" The words wouldn't come, her throat hard and tight.

Hendler nodded toward the blank video screen. "Are you hooked up with that mess? The Hawthorne case, the—"

Faith found her voice. "Scott, come in and close the door."

Hendler didn't move. "Jesus, Faith, what could Thirty have to do with—"

"Scott, for God's sake and mine, get your ass in here and shut the damn door!"

Hendler closed the door. Faith exhaled slowly, her heart thrumming like a bass line in a rock song. "What are you doing here, Scott?"

Hendler sat down in the desk next to her. "I was in the building dropping off some papers to the U.S. attorney, and I thought I'd come up and see you." He pointed at the dark TV. "What's that all about?"

"You know I can't talk. How much did you see?"

"Just the last minute or so. But I've seen it all before."

Faith nodded. "I was still in college, but I remember the scandal." *Thirty-nine dead babies and one live one,* she thought. *And the man who shot Senator Weldon Hawthorne five years ago is the live one.* "I don't believe in coincidence," she muttered.

"What?" Hendler said, leaning toward her.

"Nothing." She looked at him. "So you just stopped by to say hi, huh?"

Hendler smiled crookedly. "Oh, no. Thirty's not the only department with ulterior motives, you know."

Faith's eyebrows went up.

Hendler laughed. "Oh, relax. Department Thirty's made you jumpy. But I guess that comes with the territory. I just wanted to tell you what I heard about your new boss."

"Winter?"

"Himself. He's from an old family of Boston lawyers.

Every male in his family for five generations has been a lawyer. He went into government young, and was in his current job before he was thirty. From what I can tell, the thing Daniel Winter is most interested in is . . ." He leaned close to Faith.

Faith waited a moment. "What? Come on, I'm in no mood to fool around."

Hendler smiled. "Of all the rotten luck. Winter is mainly interested in Winter, in his own power." The smile faded. "Seriously, Faith, everyone I talked to made a point of saying one thing about Daniel Winter: *Don't trust him.* Don't believe anything he says, because it might be true and it might not, depending on what's in it for him."

Faith sat back, glancing at the blank TV in front of her. In fact, something Winter had said on the phone didn't sound right. Something in the midst of Charles Brandon and Eric Miles and thirty-nine babies . . . but she couldn't quite reach it. When her mind tried to get around it, it slid away like a child on the playground who taunts and then runs away.

"You know, Faith," Hendler said, "you were a good deputy marshal. But maybe you're not cut out for Department Thirty."

Faith smiled, remembering something Yorkton had told her last year. "But maybe that makes me just right for Thirty after all."

Hendler shrugged and stood up. "I guess I'd better get back to the office. I have approximately nine million reports waiting to be written. What are you going to do now?"

Faith waited before answering. "I have another phone call to make, and then . . . then I guess I'm going to try to find Eric Anthony." To herself she added: *Eric Miles.*

"Eric Anthony? The one who shot Hawthorne? You're kidding. Is your—"

"Scott."

Hendler recognized the tone. "No, I don't want to know. See you later, Faith. Maybe we can get together sometime this week?"

"Mmm," Faith said, far away from this little room and Scott Hendler.

"Faith? Maybe Friday night? Carpenter Square Theater's opening that new play. I've got season tickets. Faith?"

Faith finally looked up at him. She was reminded of his Bureau nickname, Sleepy Scott. He managed to look both boyish and wizened at the same time. "Sure, Scott," she finally said.

Hendler smiled. "Pick you up at your place at seven?"

Faith tapped a nail on the desk. "Okay. Thanks for the stuff on Winter."

Hendler left the room, closing the door very quietly behind him. Faith stared after him for a few seconds, still thinking less of Hendler than of Winter, trying to get to what Winter had said that bothered her so much.

She sat quietly, running her mind over all that had happened since she'd become a Department Thirty "officer." There was still one thing she hadn't done. For some reason she couldn't go further until she did it.

She pulled out her cell phone. She'd memorized the number more than fifteen years ago—more than half her lifetime.

"Evanston Police."

"Captain Kelly, please."

She waited, drumming on the desktop, glancing occasionally at the darkened screen, as if she could still see Weldon Hawthorne and Eric Miles in their grotesque ballet.

The voice boomed at her: "Joe Kelly."

"Hi, Dad, it's me."

"Well, Faith Siobhan, how does a decorated deputy U.S. marshal have time to make calls to a lowly suburban cop?"

As always, she didn't know how much of Joe Kelly was dry sarcasm and how much was serious. She shook her head.

"Dad, I—" *What the hell am I doing? I can't tell him anything!*

"What's up, Faith? Come on, kid, spit it out. All hell's broken loose here: I've got a serial rapist in Evanston that's struck three times now."

"Dad, I have a new job."

Silence.

"Dad?"

"What do you mean, a new gig in the Marshals Service? They transferring you out of Cowtown?"

Faith winced. As far as Joe Kelly was concerned, there was no civilization south or west of Chicago. "No. I'm out of the Marshals Service."

More silence, that damned heavy, oppressive silence that had filled the space between Faith and her father for her entire life.

The words started to tumble out of her. "I'm still in DOJ, but it's a pretty highly classified assignment. The pay is great and there's some pretty interesting—"

"Seems like you worked awfully hard to get into the Marshals to dump it after barely two years."

Faith wanted to throw the phone across the room. "I didn't 'dump' it. It's just something that came up."

"This related to that business last year?"

Now Faith was silent.

"Oh, hell. All that grief I took from you for your whole life about how you were gonna be a cop and to hell with what I thought was best for you. And you go give it up after two years to do some secret-agent bullshit."

The back of Faith's neck felt hot. "Dad, I just wanted you to know."

"Well, now I know."

Then Joe Kelly was gone and Faith was listening to a dead phone.

"Well, shit," she slowly said aloud. *What did you expect? Congratulations? A pat on the back? That he would say he's proud of you? Not from Captain Kelly, no way.*

Faith exhaled long and slowly. She had a job to do. Charles Brandon/Nathan Grant, Eric Anthony/Miles, and thirty-nine dead babies. She couldn't afford to think about her father. She stuffed the phone call deep into her subconscious, like garbage into a plastic bag, then gathered up the videotape and her notes. She had to find Miles.

14

ERIC COULDN'T FOCUS ON VOTING RECORDS OF POLITI-
cians, nor on the number of gross ratings points for a certain TV advertising campaign. The research was stagnant,
and the report he was supposed to be writing was only
halfway finished, with a looming deadline. He'd pushed
himself away from his computer in the home office and
walked around the house. With Patrick at school, all was
quiet.

He'd been rereading a paperback edition of Michael
Shaara's *The Killer Angels*, about the battle of Gettysburg, one
of the most remarkable books he'd ever read. Usually he
would mull over whether Buford should have gotten credit
for saving the Union or whether Longstreet should have
pushed Lee harder to move to the right in the battle.

But today it didn't work. He was nowhere near Gettysburg, and Buford and Longstreet and Lee were all dead and
Eric really didn't care. He was in a hidden cemetery on the
border of three states, looking at his own name—a name different from the one he'd grown up using, no less—and birthdate on a grave marker. His own name, and that of one
other: *Edward A. Miles.*

I have a twin, he thought. *Or had one. Or do I? Hell, I don't
know what it means. Why is that marker there in the first place?
Because I'm alive, thank you very much. And since I'm not buried
there—who is?*

His mind arched and twisted, trying to wrap itself around
what he had seen on Saturday. He didn't know what confused him more: the idea that he might have had a twin, or
the fact that there was a grave marker bearing his name and
birthdate. It was too much to process, like a computer with
no memory left.

He blinked several times, trying to orient himself back
into his house, to something real and tangible. He wandered
back into the office and logged onto his e-mail account.

There were a couple of spam messages about home mortgage refinancing and various health aids, which he deleted quickly. Another was from an old college friend, forwarding some political humor.

One e-mail's topic was listed as TWINS AND STONES.

Eric jerked involuntarily, knocking a stapler off his desk.

The sender was T. G. MATTINGLY.

Who the hell is T. G. Mattingly?

Eric's heart thundered. His mind twisted a little more, a rope being slowly knotted.

Then he had it: the old man from Kenton at the tourist shop. "*Good Mattingly. It's really Thorogood, but who would want to call a kid that?*"

The old man had said *twins and stones* didn't mean anything to him.

Eric tapped his forehead, hummed a bar or two of something.

He opened the e-mail.

DEAR ERIC ANTHONY MILES,

I LIED TO YOU. I KNOW ALL ABOUT THE TWINS AND STONES. I CAN HELP YOU. I HAVE RECORDS ON ALL THE MOTHERS. YOU SHOULD KNOW THE TRUTH. PLEASE COME BACK TO KENTON.

THOROGOOD GORDON MATTINGLY, M.D.

P.S. I DELIVERED YOU INTO THIS WORLD, AND I GUESS I AM PARTLY RESPONSIBLE FOR ANYTHING THAT HAS HAPPENED TO YOU. PLEASE COME.

Eric sat there motionless, thinking of the bald, bearded old man with the deep voice, selling postcards and key chains from a tiny building in a tiny, remote town.

I can help you.

Look for the twins and stones, the directions had said. *I hope you will understand.*

Eric looked at the blinking cursor again.

I delivered you into this world.

Thorogood Gordon Mattingly, M.D.

A doctor. The old man was a doctor.

"Oh my God," Eric said. He shot out of his chair as if he'd been pushed off a ledge. He made a fist and banged his filing cabinet as hard as he dared. His mind started racing down pathways. He would fly back to Kenton and talk to Mattingly. He would find out what the hidden graves meant. He would need to find someone to finish writing the report, and arrange for Laura to take care of Patrick. This wasn't the kind of trip that he wanted to take Patrick on.

Eric frowned. Getting Laura to do anything with Patrick was difficult, and usually ended up with he and Laura either staring each other down or shouting at each other. The frown deepened. She could take Patrick for a day, maybe two. It might crimp her billable hours and her time at the country club, but Eric didn't care. Another thought came to him: Laura was a lawyer, and a very good one. He might need some legal advice in this business.

Two minutes later he was in his Honda, backing out of the driveway. In another minute he was headed south toward downtown.

In the flow of traffic two others cars were behind him, then a gold Mazda Miata settled in going the same direction. Eric didn't check his mirror. He didn't see the Miata.

The law firm of Newcomb, Clare, and Boss was the most prestigious in Oklahoma. It had grown from a street-corner practice in the Dust Bowl era to a firm with offices in Houston, New Orleans, Chicago, and Washington. It dealt mainly with corporate litigation, although there was a small criminal division that took the occasional high-profile case. It also managed a lobbying division from the D.C. office, and the firm was well known in the halls of Congress.

Befitting its status, it occupied four floors of the Bank One Tower at Main and Broadway in the heart of downtown. Oklahoma City is not a high-rise city, having preferred sprawling outward across the plains, but it does sport a modest high-rise section, with the Bank One Tower as one of the anchors.

When Eric stepped out onto the eighteenth floor, he emerged into a world of brass, black marble, and tinted glass. Newcomb, Clare, and Boss had evidently decided not to go with the "regional" decorative scheme of many Oklahoma businesses. There were no paintings of Western scenes here, no turquoise art and silver. Everything was ultramodern and vaguely European.

The receptionist sat behind a glassed-in partition with a slender headset and tiny microphone attached to her as she routed calls. She was a formidable-looking blond woman in her forties.

She smiled at Eric and raised a finger as she routed another phone call.

"Hi, Cindy," Eric said. "Laura in her office?"

Cindy checked a computer screen in front of her. "Hello, Eric. When are you going to bring that precious little boy to see me again?"

"Maybe soon."

Cindy cocked her head. "You all right?"

"Nope. Is Laura in?"

Cindy frowned. "Yes, but she's—"

"Thanks, Cindy."

Eric started down the hall, moving slowly through the labyrinth like a rat in a maze. When he saw the door with the brass nameplate reading *Laura Northrup-Anthony*, he stopped for a moment. Should he tell Laura that even her name wasn't what she thought it was? He squeezed his eyes closed, feeling the hallway start to spin around him.

He breathed deeply, then opened his eyes again, and opened Laura's door without knocking. Laura was just picking up the phone.

"Bet you ten bucks that's Cindy telling you I'm coming," Eric said.

Laura rolled her eyes at him and answered the phone. She listened for a moment, then nodded. "Thanks, Cindy." She put the phone down. "No bet. Don't you ever make appointments?"

"Nope." Eric settled into a chair and looked at his ex-wife. She was every inch the corporate litigator, with her "lady-lawyer" shag haircut, navy blue designer suit, and slim gold women's Rolex.

A long way from the girl I met our freshman year at Oklahoma State, Eric thought. They'd met in a political science club meeting and had gone for a beer at Eskimo Joe's afterward. Back then she had "big hair" and wore tight jeans and Western-cut shirts, a small-town girl from Newkirk, Oklahoma, to whom places like Oklahoma City were exotic. She'd been enraptured by the fact that Eric had lived in Los Angeles for most of his life. They shared grand ambitions, and Laura Northrup was the most driven person Eric had ever seen. She'd escaped a horrible home life: Her father had disappeared when she was four, and her mother was a paranoid schizophrenic who once attacked Laura with a knife because she thought Laura had told a neighbor that the family didn't have enough to eat.

By any standard she was a beautiful woman, with that flawless porcelain skin, huge expressive blue eyes, and a figure she worked on with ferocious intensity at one of those exclusive women's fitness centers.

"What's up?" she said. Even her Oklahoma drawl was gone. The years they'd spent in D.C. had softened it, and she'd worked hard to lose the accent altogether. "I have a report due in Clare's office. Can this wait?"

Eric looked at her for another moment. It was hard to believe this was the same woman that laughed at bad puns, wept at Hallmark commercials on television, and liked to make love in sleeping bags while camping beside rivers.

Eric shook his head. "I need you to take Patrick for a day or two."

She'd been shuffling some papers on her desk, and she stopped abruptly. "Why? What's the problem?"

"I have to go out of town."

"Just like that?"

"Just like that."

Laura shook her head. "Can't do it. Not right now. Maybe next month. If you could—"

Eric leaned forward. "No, I'm not going to make an appointment with your secretary so that you can take care of your son."

"That's not what I was going to say. I could just use some notice."

"Well, life doesn't always give you notice."

Laura leaned back in her chair and crossed her legs at the knee. "What's with you? Ever since Colleen died, you've been very out of sorts."

"There's a lot going on."

"Oh, well, that explains everything. There's a lot going on. Welcome to the club. Now why don't you just—"

"Laura, I think I might have a twin," he blurted.

She stopped, her hand suspended in midair over a file folder she'd been about to open. "What?"

Eric dropped his head. "It doesn't make sense. But I think—I think that at some point I might have had a twin."

Laura was silent for a moment. "The black hole."

Eric nodded. When they'd first begun dating back at OSU twenty years ago, they'd had many long, late-night conversations. Eric had tried for the first time to verbalize the strange feelings he sometimes had—a feeling of *incompleteness*, that a part of him was missing. It had helped bring them together. He'd always chalked it up to his unconventional upbringing with Colleen. Laura had lost her only sister to leukemia when she was ten and her sister twelve. At the time Laura had told him he was more empathetic than anyone, and yet, he'd never lost a sibling. He'd called his feeling "the black hole." Later he'd read an article about surviving twin syndrome, based on studies of one twin who had survived when the other had died at birth.

"How did you—" Laura said. All the defensiveness, all the aloof arrogance, faded from her beautiful face and for a moment Eric caught a glimpse of a nineteen-year-old girl from small-town Oklahoma.

Eric shrugged. "I'm not sure what to believe." He told her all of it, Colleen's dying words to him, the name, the trip to Boise City, the grave markers, the e-mail from Mattingly.

She listened without speaking, steepling her index fingers and touching them to her lips. Eric recognized the gesture. He'd once thought it made her look intellectual. When he finished, she sat without moving for a moment.

"Eric—" she said.

He looked up. She rarely called him by his name anymore.

"I know," he said. "It's insane."

"Totally. You're sure . . . I mean absolutely positive . . ."

Eric nodded vigorously. "No doubt." Unable to sit still any longer, he popped up and started to pace the office. "You see why I have to go back out there. This old man, Mattingly. He knows something. He—"

Laura's phone rang. She picked it up, said her name, and listened. She furrowed her brow, looking just like Patrick as she did. "Yes, Mr. Watson. I was just reviewing it." She made a "talk-talk-talk" gesture at Eric with her hand.

Eric tuned her out, pacing, jingling keys and coins in his pants pocket. The faster he paced, the faster he palmed the items in his pocket. He tried to focus on the grave markers while Laura droned on about evidentiary hearings and discovery motions.

Eric flopped back into the chair as Laura made frustrated noises into the phone. He saw a copy of that day's *Daily Oklahoman* on the edge of her desk and began to flip idly through it. Teacher layoffs, drug busts on I-40, budget deficits. Eric turned a few pages. In the state section, a tiny item caught his eye, a two-paragraph filler.

A Kenton man died Monday evening in a one-vehicle accident in rural Cimarron County in the western Oklahoma Panhandle. Sheriff's officers said Thorogood Gordon Mattingly, 80, died when his pickup truck slammed into the Wheeless Community Church shortly after six p.m.

Cimarron County Deputy Sheriff Dale McCabe said officials believe Mattingly, a retired physician, suffered a heart attack, causing him to lose control. This is the first traffic fatality in Cimarron County in more than four years.

Eric gripped the paper hard, crinkling its edges. Laura frowned at him from across the desk.

Mattingly dead. Eric had seen him Saturday at noon. Later on Saturday he'd sent the e-mail message. Monday he was dead.

You should know the truth. I can help you. Please come back to Kenton.

Eric's head began to throb as if someone had kicked the backs of his eyeballs with steel-toed boots. He stood up abruptly, letting the crinkled newspaper slide to the floor. His mind started to crawl over scenarios. What could he do? He wasn't a U.S. government employee anymore, just a researcher with a notorious screwup in his past.

It all came back to the strange hidden cemetery, the pairs of twins, the stone with his name and Edward A. Miles and July 27, 1965, etched on it.

Since I'm not in that grave . . . who is?

Laura hung up the phone with an expulsion of frustrated breath. "Some clients think they own me." She glanced at Eric, who was leaning now against her bookcase, hands in pockets. "What the hell did you do to my newspaper? Get mad about the editorial page again?" She broke off, seeing his face. "What? Eric, what?"

"The old man. Mattingly, the one who e-mailed me."

"What about him?"

"He's dead."

"What?"

Eric swept a hand toward the paper on the floor. "Car accident last night. The cops think he had a heart attack at the wheel and drove his truck through the wall of a church."

Laura stared for a moment. "You're kidding."

"Do I look like I'm kidding?" he snapped. He thumped

his foot, heel to toe, on the floor. "God, what do I do now? There has to be an official channel I can go through." He looked up at her. "What's the process for ordering a grave exhumation? If I find out who's really buried out there—"

"Whoa, stop right there. Getting an exhumation order's not the easiest thing in the world, especially for some pie-in-the-sky—"

"Laura!"

"Look," she said, leaning forward and planting closed fists on the desk, "The DA would have to ask a judge for an exhumation."

"That's okay. You know the DA and you could—"

Laura held up a hand. "Even then, the exhumation can be requested only in certain circumstances."

"Like what?"

"Like a death certificate wasn't issued for one reason or another. Legally you would have to convince the DA, who would then have to present enough facts to a judge, who could then order the grave to be opened. And keep in mind, it wouldn't be the Oklahoma County DA we're talking about. You'd have to go to whoever has the jurisdiction out there. Didn't you say it was right on the state line? It might not even be in Oklahoma jurisdiction. You might have to go through New Mexico or Colorado."

"But—"

"And one more thing: Next of kin must be notified so they can attend the hearing."

"But I *am* the next of kin!" Eric shouted. "The goddamn stone's got my name and date of birth on it!"

Laura waited a moment. "And Colleen told you that your last name was really Miles?"

Eric nodded.

"And she wasn't—"

"No, she didn't seem crazy."

"Getting a grave opened isn't as easy as it looks in the movies. There are a lot of legal proceedings that have to take place."

Eric waved a hand dismissively and started to pace again,

jingling change in his pockets. Something clicked and he stopped in mid-step. Laura was still staring at him in her defensive lady-lawyer posture. "What did you say about the death certificate?"

"If a death certificate wasn't issued at the time of death, that strengthens the case for the exhumation."

"Paperwork," Eric muttered. "The official world runs on paperwork. If someone took the trouble to place these graves way out in such a remote area, and in such a way that no one would know they were there if they weren't looking specifically for them, you'd think they wouldn't want anyone to know what had happened. So they wouldn't go through official channels, would they?"

"What are you saying?"

Eric got his jacket and headed for the door. "I'll let you know when I need to drop Patrick off. I have a feeling I may still need to go back to Kenton."

"Where are you going now?"

Halfway out the door, the rest of his day forgotten, Eric said, "To look for my own death certificate."

15

THE OKLAHOMA BUREAU OF VITAL RECORDS WAS located in the State Health Department building, along Northeast Tenth Street, east of downtown and near the sprawling University of Oklahoma Medical Center complex. Eric left the Honda in the building's parking garage and hurried through a foyer. He was greeted by signs announcing construction, and sheets of heavy plastic hanging from the ceiling. Beyond it he could see plaster and stacks of lumber. A sound of hammering echoed from somewhere.

A security checkpoint sat at the entrance to a hallway: another consequence of September 11, Eric thought. You had to go through checkpoints to enter almost any government building, even those with no security issues whatsoever. He showed the guard his driver's license, signed the visitor's log—once again he hesitated when signing his name, then remembered that he was still Eric Anthony in the eyes of the official world—and asked for directions to Vital Records.

He went down a hall and around a corner. A sliding door opened into a large room with glassed-in cubicles on the right, an institutional waiting area to the left. A large raised wooden table stood just inside the door, covered with forms and a few pencils. A handful of people sat in the waiting area.

Eric went to the table and looked at the first form, the one for requesting birth certificates. He started to put it aside, then looked at it again.

If I died, I would first have to be born, he thought. It sounded like a riddle.

He filled out a request for his birth certificate, then hesitated a moment. Before he knew it, he was thinking of the black hole, the times in his boyhood when he felt something was missing, something he couldn't define, much less understand. Later he'd chalked it up to adolescence. But he'd wondered if the feeling would follow him for his entire life, that tunnel of nothingness deep inside him.

Very carefully, Eric took another form and wrote EDWARD A. MILES in the space for the name. Even writing the name seemed bizarre and unfathomable. He filled out forms for death certificates, then took them to the glassed-in cubicle. A bored man behind the glass asked him for his identification and twenty dollars to cover the fee for the documents. Nothing showed on the man's face until he looked carefully at Eric's driver's license. Then his eyes shot to the forms Eric had just given him.

"What are you trying to pull?" the man said.

"I know it looks strange," Eric said. "It's a long story."

The man looked at him with an I've-seen-it-all expression on his big face.

"Please," Eric said. "Can you check?"

The man was silent a moment. "You don't look crazy. But then, I guess most crazy people don't." He shrugged. "Why not?" He keyed a few strokes into the computer in front of him.

The man frowned.

Eric leaned forward.

The man typed some more, and the frown deepened.

"What?" Eric said.

The man held up a finger in a Wait-a-minute gesture and moved his computer mouse around, clicking several times in rapid succession.

Eric snaked a hand into his pants pocket and palmed his keys, rolling them around in his hand. He tapped his foot against the carpet.

The man behind the glass looked up at Eric. "Well," he said.

Eric leaned in a little closer.

"It looks like you and Edward don't exist."

Eric stared.

"And least not in Oklahoma," the man said.

"There's nothing?" Eric said.

"No, sir. I have no record in the database."

Eric sat back, his heart pounding. He thought of Kenton, of old Good Mattingly—*I can help you*—of the fence line that ran toward the horizon from the three-state marker.

New Mexico. Colorado.

The records had to exist in one of the other states.

Eric stood up. The man gave him back his twenty dollars. "Here," he said. "The money's only if you actually receive documents."

Eric nodded. "Thank you."

"Good luck."

Eric started out the door, but his mind was miles away. He had to find a way to get to the records offices in New Mexico and Colorado. Would they accept a request by phone? By e-mail, perhaps? There had to be paperwork somewhere. Colleen had said she requested a birth certificate for him in California, but there had to be an original one somewhere.

No one could exist in America without leaving a trail of official documents. Eric, of all people, knew that. His career had been built around following such trails, analyzing data, finding information.

He stepped out of the Vital Records office and back into the hall. With all the construction, he was unsure for a moment which way to go. He took a tentative step around a blind corner and nearly collided with an elderly man in a wheelchair being pushed by a college-age girl.

"Careful there," the old man said.

Eric threw both hands up as a defensive measure and spun away from the wheelchair, balancing on one foot. "Sorry," he muttered.

He kept his balance but stumbled into a little alcove across the hall. Sheets of plaster were stacked against the wall. After he righted himself and the wheelchair was out of sight, Eric saw that the alcove was actually a miniature hallway that created a shortcut to the direction from which he had just come. It ended in view of the door to Vital Records, but Eric hadn't seen it when he'd entered and left the bureau. Plaster and paint buckets lined the short passage.

Eric was just about to turn back the direction he'd been going when something caught his eye. He stopped cold.

At the other end of the little hallway was a young woman with red hair, wearing jeans and one of those 1930s-style "newsboy" hats—flat on top, short brim—that young women liked to wear these days. She was reading the *Oklahoma Gazette*.

Eric froze. He blinked.

You're being paranoid, he told himself.

No, it was true. He'd seen her before. Today. Recently.

Then he had it: She'd been in the eighteenth-floor lobby of the Bank One Tower when he came out of Laura's law office.

Eric's heart flipped. She'd been standing by the elevator, leaning against the wall, reading the same paper. The *Gazette* was interesting, but no one could read it for that long. He started to back slowly out of the alcove.

The young redhead's eyes casually lifted from her paper. It

occurred to Eric that he would never have seen her in this building if he hadn't run into the man with the wheelchair.

Who was she?

Eric was almost out of the alcove. The redhead looked up again, and this time her eyes narrowed. She folded her paper and looked around, a little less casually this time. She glanced all directions, finally chancing a look back over her shoulder.

Their eyes met.

Eric turned, nearly tripping over a bucket of paint. He slipped out of the alcove at a fast walk, heading back toward the parking garage.

"Dammit," Faith whispered.

She'd found the perfect surveillance post in the little alcove. She'd been able to watch the door to Vital Records without being seen. And then for some reason Eric Miles had wound up in the alcove himself and they'd seen each other.

She dropped the *Gazette* into a trash can and looped around the corner. She saw his dark green jacket just disappearing around another corner ahead.

Faith started to jog.

All the things she'd learned so far flashed through her mind: Charles Brandon and his strange obsessions; his mysterious contention that Eric Miles was a threat to his identity; the vague nature of Brandon's Department Thirty file; and the call from Winter. Thirty-nine babies, one survivor. Eric Miles and Senator Hawthorne. Tracking "Eric Anthony" down from a directory of metro area advertising firms, following him to the downtown law office, tracking him here.

Her head ached. It was all too convoluted, and she still had a bad feeling about the call from Winter. *Does Department Thirty ever make sense?* she wondered. *Do you ever figure out what's truth and what's fiction?*

Up ahead an elevator dinged. Faith swore under her breath again. What the hell was he doing now?

She rounded the corner just as the elevator doors

slammed shut and the car started up. The corridor was otherwise empty. Faith banged on one of the doors. *Lost him.* Even worse, he knew she was there.

"Goddammit," she said aloud.

A hand fell on her shoulder. Faith jumped and clawed at her shoulder holster. She spun around.

"Were you looking for me?" Eric Miles asked.

Faith winced. She'd been taken in by the old elevator–office building trick. Send an empty car up, hide in a stairway or around a corner, and wait for the pursuer.

"Mr. Miles, I presume?" she said.

"Depends on who you ask. Nice hat, by the way. Who are you?"

A couple of people walked by.

"Let's go somewhere else," Faith said.

"Sorry. Not until we're properly introduced and I know what this is all about and how you know about the name Miles."

"You're just going to have to trust me," Faith said. Just like Art Dorian, she no longer had government-issued credentials. No badge, no ID. Just her own wits.

"Oh shit," Eric said. "Who do you work for?"

"We have something in common. I work for the U.S. government."

The coffee shop was called Java Dave's and sat a few blocks west of the medical complex on Tenth, just off Broadway. They both took dark roast coffee, black.

Eric leaned back, holding his cup with both hands. "Who do you work for?"

"Mr. Miles . . ." Faith said carefully, then stopped. "Or do you prefer Anthony?"

Eric laughed without humor. "Take your pick. I'd prefer the truth, but that seems to be out of the question."

What could she say to him? "You used to work for the Federal Election Commission."

"This isn't about my old job."

Faith nodded. "You know the value of security."

Eric waited.

Faith cleared her throat and took another sip of the dark coffee. "Let's just leave it right there. I can't go into detail about what department I work for."

Eric leaned back in the wooden chair. "Okay, we'll leave it there for now. Why are you following me? Checking up on old government employees? Making sure I'm staying out of trouble, that sort of thing?"

"Something like that," Faith said. She thought for a moment. "What were you doing at the Bureau of Vital Records just now?"

Eric brought the chair back down with a hollow thump. A little coffee sloshed onto the table. "What does anyone do at the Bureau of Vital Records? Come on, now, Kelly. You can do better than that." A thought seemed to come to him. "You know, I bet I could find out what I want directly from you. What Vital Records couldn't tell me, I suspect you can. Since you say you're a federal minion, you probably have all kinds of information."

Faith's anger flared. She pulled off the gray hat and slapped it onto the table. She ran a hand back through her hair. "I'm no one's minion. Let's get that straight. And I know a thing or two." She leaned across the table. "But I think I should tell you that you're on the edge of big trouble. I don't know what you're up to, but you should go back to your home office and leave it alone."

Eric leaned in as well, until their faces were inches apart. "You want to intimidate me, Kelly? Don't go there, because you can't do it. There's not much that can intimidate me anymore. So you'd better find another strategy, because that one's not working."

"I've seen the tape," Faith said.

"So have millions of other people. I understand it's a big seller in the underground. The antigovernment nuts have taken it to heart. Some of them sympathize with me, some with Hawthorne. Big deal, you've seen the tape." Eric sighed. "Did you manage to trail me to Kenton on Saturday? Did you talk to Mattingly after I left?"

The animation drained out of Faith's features. *Kenton. Mattingly.* He'd already been there. He'd talked to Mattingly, the doctor, the one Charles Brandon had recruited. He was further along than she'd thought. A thought came to her: How had Brandon/Grant known Eric Miles was poking around in his history?

"You know what, Kelly? Someone must really think something is up if they've assigned an officer to hang around me five years after the whole Hawthorne mess. And you know what? Something *is* up. I've learned a few things lately about my own background. Not answers, mind you, but questions. Questions I never knew to ask before."

Faith waited. "I wouldn't ask too many if I were you."

"Didn't I tell you I'm not intimidated by that sort of thing? Veiled threats don't impress me."

"It's not a threat, and it's not intimidation. I'm just telling you that there are questions you shouldn't ask because you can't get the answers."

Eric mopped up a few drops of coffee with a napkin. "Well, let's try this one: Do you know about the twins and stones?"

Faith's green eyes widened. Unconsciously she scratched her scar with one nail.

"Where'd the scar come from?" Eric asked, his tone softening.

Faith shrugged. "None of your business."

"No, I guess not. But you didn't get it as a kid. It's fairly recent, so I was curious."

Faith stared at him.

Eric smiled. "I'm an observer. I look for things. Numbers in big computer files, single sentences in reports, little quirks of people. You're in a difficult situation here with me. Neither of us is quite sure what's going on with the other. And what do you do? You touch that scar. It's recent."

The stare faded to a look of quiet respect. "Point taken. It is recent, but I'm not discussing it."

"Fair enough. I tell you what, Faith Kelly of the U.S. government. Sometime in the next few days, I'm going to be heading back out to Kenton. There are still some things I have to find out. A man named Mattingly was going to help me, but now he's dead. I'm going to try to see what he was going to tell me. You come with me. You can write a report to whoever it is you report to that says you stayed right with me all the way. Maybe we'll both learn some things."

Faith sat there a moment, tapping her coffee cup. This was like no surveillance she'd ever studied at the academy. But then, she reminded herself, in Department Thirty all the manuals and rule books were moot. It was all information and instinct. And besides, Eric Miles was no ordinary advertising researcher. It seemed strange that he was connected both to Charles Brandon/Nathan Grant and Senator Weldon Hawthorne, in different ways. *Very strange.*

"Deal," she said.

"Do you like to fly?" Eric asked.

"Not especially."

Eric smiled at her for the first time. "You will soon enough," he said.

16

GRANT RARELY CAME INTO OKLAHOMA CITY THESE days. He preferred to stay in his estate on Lake Texoma, only driving to the city for occasional visits to some of his real estate developments in the area. Drew could usually handle any errands he needed done, and of course he didn't like to be far away from whichever wife he was currently married to. Rachel had been an energetic companion these last eight years. She wasn't particularly bright, but she was devoted and didn't ask many questions.

He'd been thinking a great deal of Eric Miles and of young Officer Kelly, almost to the point of distraction, which he could ill afford. This part of the plan required his full attention, and he had to move very, very carefully. He tried to put Kelly and Miles out of his mind. If need be, he would have Drew send a message to one or both of them. A message they wouldn't be able to ignore.

Grant stopped the Range Rover in front of one of the palatial Victorians that anchored the east end of Heritage Hills, Oklahoma City's oldest neighborhood. He smiled. It had been a while since he'd been here. As he stepped up the sidewalk he thought of John Dudley, the duke of Northumberland, the man who had ruled England through Edward VI and had tried with Jane Grey.

My Lord Duke, I will succeed where you failed, Grant thought. It left him almost breathless.

He didn't have to knock on the door. It opened as he approached it, and he looked into the face of Hank Archer. The old man was seventy-five, a couple of years younger than Grant, and small, only five feet six, now bent with arthritis. His once-piercing blue eyes were shot through with red and perpetually watery, making the old man always look as if he were about to begin weeping. He wore a perfect charcoal-gray suit and pale blue silk tie, the same color his eyes had once been.

"Hank, how are you?" Grant said.

Archer grunted. "Come on in. Be quick about it."

Grant smiled again. Hank Archer was the current patriarch of one of America's most powerful families. Their money had come from oil, but their real wealth was political power. Hank's father, Woodrow Archer, had served Oklahoma as a four-term U.S. senator. Woodrow's brother, Leon, had advised presidents of both parties on foreign policy and trade issues. Woodrow and Leon's father, Mason Archer, had been a secretary of the Treasury.

Hank himself had been deputy secretary of state under Lyndon Johnson, and ambassador to Spain under Ronald Reagan. He often pointed out to anyone who would listen that he was the only living person in the country to serve in appointed positions in two such philosophically opposed presidential administrations. The old man had run for the

Senate once, but he had no personality and was unable to connect with voters.

"Nice to see you, too, Hank," Grant said.

They walked through the entryway, passing the Renoir on the wall, brass fixtures in the hallways, mahogany paneling. At the rear of the house the two men paused at the door of an office-study.

"You sure she's ready for this?" Archer said, grabbing Grant's sleeve.

Grant pulled away from him. "Hank, her whole life has been leading to this point. How could she not be ready?"

The old man tapped his foot and sucked at his teeth.

Grant grimaced. Even aristocrats had disgusting habits. "This is what you've wanted, Hank. I'm helping you to get what you want. Isn't that what I've always done?"

Archer flinched as if he'd touched something very hot.

Grant smiled his cold smile again and they went into the study.

The governor of Oklahoma was standing there behind her father's old desk, the phone to her ear. She nodded neutrally toward her father, then caught sight of Grant and smiled warmly. She held up a finger in a Wait-a-minute gesture, then went back to her conversation.

Grant knew Angela Archer was forty-nine but could seem either older or younger, depending on the situation. Like her father, she was small, only five three, but her supporters couldn't be convinced of that. She was a giant in the political landscape of the state. She had managed to connect with people where her father had not. She could convince the blue-collar people in rural places like the panhandle or Little Dixie that she was just like them even though she'd never had to worry about money, nor really even work for a living, in her life. She could also sit in corporate boardrooms and talk the talk of multiple billions of dollars.

She had always been a maverick of one kind or another. Living in a conservative Bible Belt state, she had never taken her husband's last name. Of course, after his sudden death from a brain embolism at age thirty-two, there had been no need then to "revert" to the name Archer. After business degrees from Wellesley and Stanford, she'd puttered around with the family oil business for a few years, then jumped directly to a seat in Congress. No city council or state legislature for Angela Archer. She served three terms in the U.S. House, then came home to run for governor. She was elected Oklahoma's first woman governor with sixty-nine percent of the vote, trading heavily on her family name and the Archers' generations of service to Oklahoma and the nation.

Her political positions were all over the spectrum. She strongly supported the death penalty but at the same time worked for civil rights protection for gays and lesbians. She was hawkish on defense and security issues, unusual for a female politician, but also lobbied for a Canadian-style single-payer health care system. She infuriated both her own party's leadership and that of the opposition, who could never pigeonhole her.

Grant smiled at the thought. It was what made her such an excellent candidate. It was part of what would put her in the White House. That, plus her personal charisma, a ton of money, and the information in the manila envelope Grant was about to give her.

"Calvin, you're the speaker of the House," Governor Archer said into the phone. "You have more power than I do. You know that." She winked toward her father and Grant. "You go back and tell Harry that he's not getting another dime for corrections unless he stops holding up the teacher salary bill. Have him do the math."

She hung up and looked across the room, the legendary green-gray eyes radiating confidence and energy. Grant felt powerful just looking at Angela Archer.

"Well, my two favorite old men, in one place," she said. She came around the desk, squeezed her father's shoulder, and enveloped Grant in a tight embrace. After holding him for a moment, she took both his hands and stepped back. "Nathan, Dad didn't tell me you were coming to town today.

He just said to clear my calendar for a while this afternoon."

"I wanted to surprise you," Grant said.

The governor dropped one of his hands and waggled a finger in mock reproach. "Politicians don't like surprises. It's so good to see you. You don't get to the city very often these days."

Grant shrugged. "Rachel keeps me pretty busy with projects close to home."

"And how is she?"

"She's well. Very well."

The governor waved both men to chairs. Grant sat in a deep leather armchair, but her father scowled and stayed where he was.

"You know, Nathan," Angela Archer said, "I thought of you just the other day. One of our esteemed legislators, one of the ones who isn't near as smart as he thinks he is, was babbling on about the image of our state and how we needed better public relations, blah, blah, blah. Out of the clear blue sky he says we should follow the example Henry VIII set in England in his day.' He made the rest of Europe pay attention to England for the first time. People *noticed* the country during his reign.' You would have been proud of me, Nathan. I told him Henry VIII's reign was a classic example of style over substance. When he died the country was nearly bankrupt, and the social problems his Reformation created left more people in deeper poverty than ever before."

Grant smiled. "See, you were listening when *I* was blathering on about the Tudors all those times when you were a girl."

Angela Archer laughed. "I told my legislative friend that if we'd pay more attention to tiny little things like education and health care and reforming the state tax code, that would improve our 'image problem' a lot more than a slick PR campaign." She sat back down on the edge of her desk. "Well, then, I know you didn't come all the way to the city to listen to me tell you how much I learned about Henry VIII."

"How was New Hampshire?"

"Green. Very green. Lovely state, though the people can be

a little dour. That old Yankee reticence, I suppose. Plus, they've seen so many politicians . . ."

"I saw you on CNN," Grant said. "Good appearance. How's the campaign organization coming along?"

"Beautifully. Everything is just about in place. I want to announce on Memorial Day."

"Good patriotic tie-in," Hank Archer said. "My idea."

"Credit where credit is due, Dad," Angela Archer said. "It was a good idea. Patriotism is everything these days, at least the appearance of it. I'll have Dad there with me, and Uncle Jack. You remember him, don't you, Nathan? He was in the state legislature for more than twenty years, and was one of Clinton's unofficial economic advisors later."

A long silence followed, and Angela Archer looked at both men carefully. Finally she moved back behind the desk and sat down. "You two old codgers. Most people say more than they know. But you two always know more than you say. It can be a wonderful quality at times, and infuriating at others."

"Nothing escapes you, my dear," Grant said. "Have you seen the President's poll numbers?"

"Down twelve points since the bombing in Illinois and that press conference where someone tried to connect him to the terrorists," the governor said immediately. She shook her head. "Terrible thing. Not just a mess for the President, but for the country as a whole. And the FBI can't find any of these Sons of Madison United people to question them. It's like they don't exist, except we know that they do."

"And now they've struck again," Grant said.

Angela Archer leaned forward, planting flat hands on the desk. "What?"

"You haven't heard?"

"No, I've been tied up on the phone all day with these budget negotiations."

Grant lowered his voice. "A rural sheriff's office in Saint Marys County, Maryland. I heard it on the radio driving up here."

"What happened?" Hank Archer said.

Grant glanced at him, then back to his daughter. Everything hinged on how he played the next few minutes. He wondered where Drew was, if he was already en route back from Maryland now. He still had other jobs to accomplish as well.

"More explosives?" Angela Archer said.

"No," Grant said. "Sniper fire."

The governor of Oklahoma sucked in her breath. "Mother of God," she whispered.

"The sheriff's department had just concluded their morning meeting. The deputies were heading out to their patrol cars. The working theory right now is that the sniper was on top of a warehouse building across the street. It would've been a distance of around two hundred yards."

"How many—" Angela Archer said.

"He killed five deputies. Three others were wounded. That department is in a shambles now." Grant shook his head in apparent sorrow.

"I have to call the governor of Maryland," Angela Archer said.

"How do you know it's these Madison people?" Hank Archer asked, sucking his teeth.

Grant winced. "Evidently they did the same thing as before. About two hours after it happened, a call came in to CNN, NPR, and *The Washington Post*. Same voice as the first one. I heard the tape on the radio."

"But aren't these people big into symbolism?" Hank Archer growled. "Fort Defiance and all that. They made such a big deal of it. What's the significance of some little sheriff's office in Maryland? I mean, five deputies is bad, but nothing on the scale of what happened in Illinois."

"I wondered that myself, Hank. It seems Saint Marys County, Maryland, is the oldest sheriff's department in the country. It's been in existence since the 1640s, colonial days."

There was a moment of silence. "The symbolism of striking at the nation's first law enforcement office," the governor said. "Who *are* these people?"

More silence, then Hank Archer said, "This whole situation is also changing the political landscape."

"Yes, Dad, but I can't say that publicly. I won't be seen trying to take advantage of it."

Grant nodded admiringly. "You've done a good job of using it while staying above it so far."

Angela Archer tugged at one of her earlobes. She'd been doing it ever since she was a teenager, and it had become a trademark gesture, one that political cartoonists loved to exploit. "It's a nasty, ugly situation. An obscure governor from a small middle-American state is going to have to be very, very careful what she says about something like this."

"Ah," Grant said. The timing was right. He passed the envelope across the desk to the governor.

"What's this?"

"It's going to get you elected president."

The famous eyes sharpened, and Grant saw the astute politician in Angela Archer emerging. "Summarize, please."

Grant relaxed. He'd already been over the material many times. "Go back nine years. The President still hadn't even run for governor at that point. He was just a fairly obscure businessman with ambition and some outrageous views."

Angela Archer didn't move, watching him with the eyes of an alert student listening to a beloved teacher. Hank Archer shuffled his feet and sucked at his teeth.

"There are three small things in that envelope," Grant said. He ticked them off on his fingers. "One, a photocopy of a check drawn on his personal checking account, made out to Wayne Devine, the founder of Sons of Madison United. The check is for five thousand dollars. In the memo line it says 'special projects.' There's a handwritten note with it. Among other things, it says, 'I can't say it publicly, Wayne, but you know I'm with you all the way.'"

"My God," Hank Archer said. "So he *was* connected to these bastards. He's been trying to convince everyone he's just a middle-of-the-road moderate, and has never said or done anything extreme—"

"Dad," Angela Archer said, then looked back to Grant. "Nathan?"

"Item number two: a sheriff's raid on Wayne Devine's home in the Arkansas Ozarks, three years later. It uncovered all kinds of illegal and unregistered weapons, including potential bomb-making supplies. You have the copy there of the arresting officer's original notes."

"Back up," the governor said. "All we've been hearing is that the Sons of Madison United have never actually committed any crimes before."

Grant smiled.

"Bastards," Hank Archer said. "Killing peace officers. *Bastards!*"

"Wayne Devine was never arraigned. He never spent a single night in jail. His release was quietly arranged by the state attorney general of Arkansas. The raid, he said, was a 'mistake.' Item number three: a copy of a letter written by the man who is now President of the United States, by that time a first-term governor, to that state attorney general. Bear in mind, the two men lived in different states. The letter said in part: 'Thank you for taking care of that business with Devine. He and SOMU really don't need to be in the news that way. I won't forget what you did.' That state attorney general went all the way to Washington with him: He's now the AG of the United States."

"Why, that sorry son of a bitch," Hank Archer said. "It proves he not only lied about never having any connection to the group, but he can't weasel out of it by saying he didn't know they were a violent group. He bloody well knew what they were all about, and got the founder off the hook. I never thought I'd live to see this: the President of the United States of America, in bed with some of those goddamn antigovernment terrorists. Cop-killers, no less. I knew he was a nut, but not that much. There goes his Mr. Moderate image."

Archer had summarized it perfectly. All Grant's plans had come to this point. Like the duke of Northumberland with Lady Jane Grey, he had worked carefully, behind the scenes, for a very long time to consolidate his power. Now he was on the cusp of the ultimate power. He had opened the door, and Angela Archer simply had to walk through it.

Governor Archer sat back down in her father's chair. "Nathan . . ." She stopped.

Grant nodded. Angela never simply blurted out words. She always considered very carefully what she was going to say. She would be thinking now, turning the implications over in her mind.

"Nathan," she said again. "You can prove all this? You can back it up?"

"Would I have brought it to you if I couldn't?" Grant said.

"Nathan," she said a third time. "You have the keenest political mind of anyone I've ever known. To have never served in politics or government, you have the most incredible instincts. I trust you above all my political advisors. You know that."

Grant frowned. He didn't like the way this was sounding.

"But I don't know about this one," the governor said. "It's past history, there's no bearing on the President's policies or job performance. . . ."

"Angela, goddammit!" Hank Archer exploded. "It's obstruction of justice! The man now in the goddamned White House got one of his cronies off, one whose group is now going around blowing away police officers!"

Angela Archer folded her hands together as if praying but kept her chin up, meeting her father's iron gaze. "I agree it's a character issue, Dad, but—"

"Do you want to be president or not?" her father thundered.

The governor flinched slightly. "That was uncalled-for, Dad." She turned back to Grant. "Nathan, you're certain of your information? Your sources are solid?"

"Absolutely," Grant said.

Angela Archer sighed. "If we were to use this—*if*, I said, Dad—it couldn't come from me."

"Of course not," Grant said. "We'd engineer an anonymous leak to the media and let the story take on a life of its own." His tone changed, became almost paternal. "Angela, my dear. You've known me all your life. This information can get you where you want to be. The first woman, the first Oklahoman to be president of the United States. And I'll be with you all the way."

"I need to think about this," Angela Archer said.

"Don't think too long," her father growled. "You know, strike while the iron's hot and all that."

"I need to think about this," Angela Archer repeated.

Grant stood up. "I have some other business in the city. I'll take care of it and you can let me know. You have my cell phone number?"

"First one in my Rolodex." The governor came around the desk and embraced him. "You've always looked out for me, Nathan," she whispered.

He patted her hand. "Of course, Governor." He smiled and left the room, Hank Archer trailing him.

At the door of the house Grant turned to the old man, no longer smiling. "Hank, she can't be obstinate about this. We need to move on it. The media will rip the President to shreds, and by the time the primaries come around, he'll be so bloody he'll draw opponents from inside his own party. The party will split, and even when he's renominated, he won't have a prayer." He leaned down until his face was only inches from Archer's. "She *will* use this."

The old man backed up a step, fear flickering through his eyes like a dying flame. "She's stubborn. And, by God, she's nearly fifty years old. She doesn't always listen to me anymore."

Grant's voice dropped to a menacing whisper. "She will, Hank. You will convince her, won't you? *Won't you?*"

Archer recoiled from him.

"Remember, Hank. You will convince her. You have no choice."

Grant turned his back on the man and started down the sidewalk toward his car.

PART TWO

17

FAITH SNAPPED AWAKE ON SATURDAY MORNING AND FOR a moment wasn't sure where she was. There was a digital clock somewhere near her, floating seemingly disembodied in the dark. The red numbers said 5:16.

She blinked, not moving, letting her eyes adjust to the darkness. It took several moments to realize she was in her own bed, in her own house. On the wall opposite her was a framed poster of thousands of runners beginning the Boston Marathon. Next to it was a photograph of white-capped waves crashing against some unknown shore.

Faith sat up. She blinked again, trying to remember last night. She'd gone to the play with Scott Hendler; they'd stopped for ice cream, like a couple of kids. A few minutes after that he'd kissed her, and Faith had felt herself surrendering, all her carefully constructed defenses giving way.

She hadn't been with a man in nearly two years. The last man she'd dated, a perpetual philosophy graduate student, had looked on her more as a curiosity than a companion or friend or lover. Of course, she'd also used him, flaunting his earring and his trust fund and the fact that he was neither Irish nor Catholic at her father. In the end she'd wound up throwing an omelet at the man.

Then there was Scott Hendler, a decent, intelligent, somewhat understated, prematurely balding FBI agent. Joe Kelly would like that: Scott was a cop. A *federal* cop, but a cop nonetheless. He had his quirks, like using the phrase "Holy shit!" as an all-purpose exclamation. Faith didn't mind the profanity—she'd grown up with it, after all—but she wished he'd find a different phrase to use on occasion.

She'd returned his kiss, thinking how good it felt; then,

like a knob being twisted somewhere, she asked herself, *What the hell are you doing?*

She gently pulled back from him, put her hands on his shoulders, and said, "Not yet, Scott. My life is complicated enough these days."

They didn't talk much as he drove her home, then he assured her that it was okay. She believed him. He didn't try to kiss her again, just squeezed her hand as she got out of the car.

She got up and made coffee, then poured the first cup. It was bitter but she needed it. She sat back down at the table, sipping, wondering about opportunities granted and chances missed.

No time for that.

She tapped nails on the table top. Too much on her mind. Department Thirty and her father and Eric Miles and Nathan Grant. She was flying with Miles today to wherever it was the old man had lived, the old man who'd said he could help Miles and had then died in the car accident. Plus, she still had the conversation with Daniel Winter in her mind, the conversation that wasn't quite right.

She tapped some more. Scott. *Scott!*

After a moment she had it. Hendler was the one who'd come to her aid last year, when she lay on her dining room floor with shards of glass embedded in her face. He had sat beside her and held her hand, rode with her in the ambulance, and stayed with her until they took her to surgery. He hadn't said much, but he'd been there the whole time.

And now he'd figuratively come to her "rescue" again.

Except she hadn't let him this time.

"Dammit," she said aloud. She made a mental promise to talk to him later. Sometime when her life wasn't in an uproar.

If that time ever comes, she thought.

She went for her run, showered, and dressed in a long button-down shirt over her Federal Law Enforcement Academy T-shirt and khaki slacks. At just past ten A.M., Faith drove the Miata slowly down Northwest Twenty-first Street through the Gatewood neighborhood. She checked house numbers for the address Eric Miles had given her, but after she saw the house, she knew it was unnecessary. Miles was right: It was the worst-looking house on the block, with a half-done paint job and ripped storm windows.

She parked on the street, under a towering elm tree. She recognized Miles's Honda in the driveway, behind an old burgundy Cadillac the size of a small yacht. As she started to climb out of the Miata, her cell phone rang. She heard her father's voice when she answered it.

"Faith?" Joe Kelly said. "Where have you been? I called your house last night."

Not now, she thought. "I was out for a while, Dad. What's up?"

"Out?"

"Out. The opposite of in. Why didn't you leave a message?"

"I hate those damn answering machines. Out where?"

Faith leaned against the car. "Dad, I'm working. What were you calling about?"

Joe Kelly paused a beat. "Still won't tell me about the job, then."

Faith walked a few steps up the sidewalk. "Dad, if you've got to tell the boys on the force something, tell them I'm working in 'special projects' for the Justice Department. That's the truth. I can't go into it. Why *did* you call anyway?"

"Have you heard from your brother lately?"

Faith tried to think. "He e-mailed me a week, maybe two weeks ago. Typical Sean. Just 'Hi, I'm checking in, how are you, good-bye' and that was it."

"Ah, well." Joe Kelly exhaled noisily into the phone. "Since they moved Customs under Homeland Security, he's gone a lot more of the time. You'd think kids would give a little more thought to letting their folks know they're not dead."

Faith heard her mother's influence in that statement. Joe Kelly, on his own, would never have said such a thing. She decided to try a different tack. It was always safer to talk to him about his own work. "How's the serial rapist case? Any good leads?"

Joe Kelly's whole tone changed, as if he'd skated from thin ice onto something much more secure. "Not yet. But I've got Norm Delton running the case and he's good. He was asking about you yesterday."

So that's it, Faith thought disgustedly. Norm Delton was a couple of years older than she, and she'd dated him for a short while back in high school. It had been her father's fantasy: that she'd teach English, marry another local cop, and pop out fat-cheeked babies every year or so. "That's good, Dad. Well, tell him I said hello."

"Yeah, I guess. I know he'd like to see you the next time you're home."

"Dad—"

"I'll give him your phone number, if that's okay."

"No, it's not okay, and I'm not interested in Norm Delton."

"Yeah, well, that figures, huh? You were never interested in anyone your parents actually respected. Better go. I've got to head up to the office and do some paperwork on this vehicular manslaughter deal. Guy was drunk in the middle of the day, plowed through a store window, and killed an old woman and a little kid. I wish the DA would bump it to second-degree murder, but he won't." Joe Kelly cleared his throat. "Of course, a silly little local manslaughter case wouldn't interest a secret agent like my girl Faith."

"You know, Dad, you don't have to . . ." The sentence died in Faith's throat.

Joe Kelly caught the tone. "Faith?"

Manslaughter. A silly little local manslaughter case.

"Well, I'll be damned," Faith murmured. "Dad, manslaughter's a state charge, isn't it?"

"Of course it is."

She started back down the sidewalk toward the address Eric Miles had given her. "That's it. That's *it*. Dad, I have to go."

Faith clicked the phone off. Now she knew what Daniel Winter had said that bothered her so much. Winter told her that Charles Brandon had been charged with forty counts of manslaughter and sentenced to Englewood Federal Correctional Facility in Colorado, where he'd served five years before he was brought into Department Thirty.

But Englewood was a *federal* prison, and manslaughter— even forty counts of it—would have been state crimes: He should have been sent to a state prison.

She remembered what Hendler had told her about Winter: *Don't trust anything he says.*

"Lied to me," she said.

Her irritation began to grow into full-blown anger. With incomplete files and cases that didn't make sense and superiors who lied to her about those cases, how the hell was she supposed to do her job? What was the extent of the lie? The crimes, the punishment . . . how far did it go? Was anything Winter told her about Charles Brandon and Eric Miles the truth?

Her phone rang again. She checked the caller ID. Her father, calling back to yell at her for hanging up on him.

"Sorry, Dad," she said, and turned off the phone.

She didn't care how slick and secretive and important Department Thirty was. If she didn't have all the facts, she couldn't do the job they'd hired her to do. Hard on the heels of that thought: *So why did he lie?*

She looked up at the house. It occurred to her that she and Eric Miles were looking for the same thing. From different directions, and for different reasons, but nonetheless they could help each other. She would have to tread very, very carefully, to see that she didn't compromise Brandon/Grant's security—that *was* her job, after all—but Miles could help tie together all the threads that hung off this case like tails trailing after kites in the wind. Suddenly the idea of spending a day poking around in Miles's past was a lot more appealing than it had been before.

18

THE STONE PORCH HAD BEEN PAINTED ONCE LONG AGO, but now even it was peeling, shades of gray under a dull green. A sagging glider swing sat near the door. *The house of someone with other things on their mind,* Faith thought.

The wooden door was open, and Faith rapped her knuckles on the glass storm door. It was dirty and she couldn't see much through it. A vague shape inside moved around and waved a hand.

She walked in and, just as her law enforcement training had drilled into her, immediately checked the corners of the room. It was messy, no surprise there, but with several crates and boxes stacked on top of furniture. The only intact piece of furniture was a blue beanbag chair occupied by a young boy playing a handheld electronic game. The boy didn't look up.

Eric Miles was standing on a chair in front of the stone fireplace, both his hands around a large framed poster of some sort.

"Moving in or out?" Faith said.

"Neither," Eric said.

"Oh?"

"This isn't my house. It belonged to the woman who raised me."

Faith thought back to what she'd read in Miles's file. "And who was that again?"

"Second cousin of my mother's. She died not long ago. I'm trying to get it cleaned out as much as I can. It's been slow going. My mind's been otherwise occupied. Fancy that."

The little boy, with his fair skin and huge blue eyes, had looked up from his game. Faith caught motion out of the corner of her eye. The boy's hands gestured in his father's direction. Eric gave him a quick smile, then signed back. Patrick looked up into Faith's eyes, made his hands-over-the-ears and head-shaking sign, then introduced himself.

Faith froze for a moment. Then she remembered: Grant had mentioned that Eric Miles's son was deaf.

"He's saying—" Eric started, then cut himself off.

Faith looked down at the boy and signed, *Hello, my name is Faith.*

Patrick's eyes widened with delight. *I have a Game Boy*, he signed, and showed Faith the game.

Faith studied the tiny digitally animated *Star Wars* characters moving across the little screen, then signed, *Cool game. Are you pretty good at it?*

Level seven, Patrick signed with a smile.

"Well, you're a surprise, Kelly," Eric said. "Patrick isn't used to very many other adults knowing sign."

"My best friend in middle school was deaf," Faith said. "I learned to sign and it was like having our own secret language that no one else knew. At least none of the other kids. Then she transferred to the Illinois School for the Deaf. I'm a little rusty."

"What was your sign name? I don't think that's the sign for *faith*."

Faith smiled. "It's not. I didn't like the regular sign for the word *faith*, so my friend created this name for me." She made an *F*, thumb and forefinger tips touching, with the other three fingers straight up, then put her hand at her temple and lowered it into the palm of her other hand. "My friend said I'd someday use my head and hands to do things, so that was my name." She shrugged.

"Definitely a surprise," Eric said. "Patrick's going to be joining us today."

"Oh?"

"His mother had . . . another commitment."

Faith noticed he couldn't hide the frustration in his eyes.

"Don't worry, he's an old hand at flying," Eric said.

"Wish I could say I was," Faith said.

Eric smiled. "Could you help me with this?"

Faith walked to the fireplace and looked up at him, still standing on the chair. Did she know anything about the man, other than what she'd seen on the Hawthorne videotape? Had anything Winter told her been true? The anger tried to surface again. *SOB lied to me*, she thought.

"What is that?" she said, pointing at the poster.

"Movie poster."

"What are you going to do with it?"

"Burn it, I think."

Faith stepped back in surprise.

"Sorry," Eric said. "It should never have been here. But I had to look at it every day after we moved to this house, and I was reminded of things that I shouldn't have had to think about."

Faith peered around him. *"Angels Cry,"* she said. "Good film. I just saw it on late-night cable a couple of months ago. What's the problem with it?"

Eric lifted the whole poster off the nail where it had been hanging and carefully handed it down to her. She took it and held it at arm's length, looking at the shadowy images of the man and woman and the ghostly shattered-glass effect that covered the whole picture.

Eric looked at her as if sizing her up, questioning her worth. He stared at her so long Faith began to get annoyed. "You want to say something, Mr. Miles?"

Eric shook his head after a moment. "No."

"What's wrong with this movie?"

"Is this an official U.S. government interrogation?"

"No, but I'm curious why you'd want to burn an old movie poster."

With sudden vehemence Eric pointed to Colleen's intense photo on the poster. "See that woman?" Faith nodded. "The actress Colleen Fox. Real name Colleen Cunningham. Owner of this house. My mother's cousin. She died a week and a half ago. You remember the scene at the end of the movie where her character shoots and kills her husband, after she figured out that he was the serial killer and had been torturing coeds in their basement?"

Faith nodded silently, intently.

"I watched that scene when I was seven years old. I saw it at the Hollywood screening and then I saw it over and over again. I saw the woman who was the only family I knew shooting and killing a man, larger than life. Even years after the nightmares stopped, I had to come in here and see this damn poster hanging here."

Patrick had looked up from his game again and was watching them.

Sorry, Eric signed, then turned back to Faith. "He picks up on my moods. My posture, body language, all that nonverbal stuff. Once he even told me I had a certain smell. Not sure what he meant by that". He cleared his throat. "Didn't mean to rant. Colleen was really a good woman and she did the best job she could with me, considering the circumstances."

Faith looked at him silently. He was a complicated man. The fact that the man who'd helped to ruin and then killed Senator Weldon Hawthorne was traumatized by a movie poster, and was obviously a caring single father, didn't jibe with the image she'd had of him. In talking to Grant, and then Winter, he was a factor in a case, a variable to consider and then handle. In this dusty house the little boy playing his game with its electronic sounds and boxes of who-knows-what on top of all the furniture, he was a man having trouble figuring out what was going on around him.

It's about the people, Art Dorian had told her last year, not long before he was murdered. *If we don't serve the people, the rest doesn't matter a whit.*

She thought of her father and Daniel Winter and Scott Hendler and Brandon/Grant. It was difficult to bear in mind that she was supposed to be working on behalf of Nathan Grant, after Winter had lied to her about at least part of his history. It was also difficult to think of Eric Miles as being a threat to Grant's security.

Eric turned the *Angels Cry* poster facing away and leaned it against the fireplace. "I don't particularly trust you, Kelly, but I'm thinking that maybe the two of us can help each other. How long have you had this covert government gig?"

Faith folded her arms across her chest.

"I'd say not very long," Eric said, "but that's just a guess. Do you have sunglasses?"

"No, I never wear them," she said after a moment.

"We'll be up where the glare can be pretty strong. How about a hat, something with a bill? Sorry, your cute little gray hat isn't quite what I had in mind."

"I might have something in the car."

"Get it," Eric said. "Let's fly. We both have things we need to find out."

A little less than an hour later they were at Wiley Post Airport in far west Oklahoma City, where Eric had pushed the Cherokee Arrow out of its hangar and was preparing for take-off. After he completed the outside part of his preflight checklist, he motioned for Patrick to get in.

The boy, with his Game Boy in one hand and a battered U.S. road atlas in the other, climbed into the backseat.

"A road atlas?" Faith asked, looking at Eric.

Eric shrugged. "He's crazy about maps. He's better with geography than most adults I know." He stepped up onto the wing, ducked his head, and crawled across to the pilot's seat. "Come on up."

Faith ducked down but not quite far enough, bumping her head lightly on the door frame. "Ouch! Dammit!" she muttered.

Eric looked at her thoughtfully. "Forgive my saying so, but when did secret government agencies start hiring six-foot-tall redheads as field officers? Doesn't quite fit, does it? No offense."

Faith ducked farther and slid into the seat. "None taken, and I'm only five ten. I sort of backed into this job, and no, I'm not going to tell you more than that."

"Fair enough. After all, you're investigating me." He looked pensive for a moment, lost somewhere in his own thoughts. "We'll see, I guess."

Eric turned back toward Patrick and signed for him to fasten his seat belt. The boy did, then Eric checked the clasp. Father and son gave each other thumbs-up signs.

"All right, Agent Kelly—"

"Don't call me 'agent,'" Faith said, trying to stretch out

her legs in the cramped space. "Not much legroom in here."

"I have a friend who's six eight and weighs over three hundred pounds. If he fit in here, you can fit in here. What do you want me to call you?"

"Kelly or even Faith will do. Be honest. Don't you think the whole 'agent' thing is kind of silly?"

Eric smiled. "As a matter of fact, I do. Pull the door closed, please." Faith did, and Eric consulted a laminated sheet of paper. "Now, Kelly, or even Faith. I see you've already found your seat belt. Very good. See that door? There are two latches on it, and since this is a one-door right-side airplane and you're sitting beside it, you need to know where they are."

A nervous look crept onto Faith's face. She imagined that her scar began to itch.

Eric smiled. "It's safer than driving that little car of yours. Trust me. There's one latch connected to the door handle and one overhead that seals the top of the door. See them both?"

Faith looked, located both latches, and nodded.

"Excellent. We'll make a flier out of you yet. You also need to know that the fire extinguisher is located below and behind my seat. See it?" Faith nodded again. "Now, if we get into trouble, you get out and go to the rear, to keep away from the propeller and any possible engine fire. Don't wait on me. I'll have plenty to do securing the airplane. A pilot is a bit like a ship captain in that we're expected to be the last one off, make sure the passengers are safe, and go down with the ship if necessary."

"You're kidding."

"Nope. I kid about a lot of things, but not about airplane safety."

Faith looked over her shoulder. "Will he be all right?"

Eric smiled with pride. "Patrick's fine. He's a good flier, and he knows all the procedures." He reached back and squeezed his son's leg, which turned quickly into a tickle.

Patrick signed *Stop, Dad!* several times, though he was smiling as he did it. Faith couldn't help smiling at the little display herself, then the smile faded as she remembered that this man had lived nearly forty years before finding out what his real name was and that he had no idea of the strange circumstances surrounding his birth.

"Let's go, then," Eric said. "Ready?"

Faith shrugged.

"I'll take that as a tentative yes." Eric pointed to a pair of headphones hanging on a hook in front of her. "Put those on. It's the only way we'll be able to talk to each other during the flight."

Faith put on the headphones over the Chicago Cubs baseball cap she'd found in the backseat of the Miata. She adjusted them and pulled the boom microphone close to her mouth. She'd worn similar gear in Marshals Service ops. *Was I ever in the Marshals Service?* she wondered. *Seems like a long time ago, or even a hallucination.*

"Test, test, test," she said.

"Very good," Eric said. He'd slipped on his own headset and adjusted the mic. "Now let's see if this thing works."

He turned on the engine, and Faith watched the propeller roar to life. Patrick looked up when he felt the vibration, then went back to his atlas.

"What do you know," Eric murmured, "it still works. I hope you attended to nature, Kelly. We're looking at about a two-and-a-half-hour flight into Boise City World Intercontinental Airport."

Faith stared at him.

"It's actually a very, very sleepy little airport in the middle of nowhere," Eric said. "I'm just being a smart-mouth."

Fifteen minutes later they were in the air and Eric had punched in Boise City's code on his GPS unit. Faith sat stiffly, watching the land recede. She'd listened as Eric engaged in a series of radio calls with the Wiley Post tower, and listened in the headset to a bunch of unintelligible numbers—which seemed to make sense to Eric—flit by her.

"Ever flown GA before?" Eric asked, making an adjustment on the panel to his right.

"GA?"

"General Aviation. Noncommercial flight."

"No. I'm fond of terra firma, thank you."

Eric shrugged. "Up here you get a feel for the country. See, there's Lake Hefner over there. Looks like the sailboats are out." He scanned the sky. "Great day for flying, I'll tell you that. I don't see a cloud anywhere. One thing about Oklahoma, compared to where I used to live in L.A.: When they say clear skies here, they mean truly clear skies."

Faith took a glance at him, noticing the few soft lines around the man's eyes. She didn't think they'd been there in the Hawthorne video, even though she hadn't seen any close-ups. Maybe she was imagining things.

"Tell me about where we're going," she finally said.

Eric waited so long she thought he wasn't going to answer her. He was scanning the western horizon ahead and periodically glancing down to the instrument panel in front of him.

"My wife used to tell me that I was more comfortable talking to perfect strangers than to the closest people in my life," he said. "Now I can look back on that and see she was right. She and I were better together when we were first getting to know each other, back in college. Later . . ." He shrugged.

"I understand," Faith said.

"Do you?" Eric glanced at her. "Maybe you do. After all, I don't know you." He smiled toward the windshield. "The woman in the movie poster—Colleen. She raised me. We left L.A. in 1978 and moved back to Oklahoma City, to that house where I was this morning. She wasn't getting any more good roles and was tired of playing all the Hollywood games. Stop me if you already know all this."

Faith shook her head vaguely.

"A little while ago Colleen died of cancer." Eric tapped the control yoke of the plane, then began to tell Faith what Colleen had said to him the day she died.

By the time he'd told her about Good Mattingly's e-mail, they were over the flattening plains of western Oklahoma.

"Look there," Eric said, pointing out the window. "That's the Gage VOR. Not many landmarks out here."

Faith peered where he pointed. Against the flat landscape was a small white rectangular building topped by a white structure shaped like an old-fashioned milk bottle.

"VOR?" she said.

"VHF omnidirectional range station."

"Oh, that clears it all up."

Eric smiled again. "AM radio stations just below the frequencies used for voice in aviation. It's a navigational tool."

They both fell silent. Faith was suddenly aware of the pressure of the headset against her ears. She thought about what Eric had just spent half an hour telling her. It filled in a couple of holes for her, but then, how did she know what was true and what wasn't?

There had to be more. There had to be something in the here and now, some connection between Daniel Winter and Eric Miles and Brandon/Grant that caused Grant to be afraid of Miles, and Winter to lie to one of his own people about it.

She watched a few more miles roll away beneath them, trying to ignore the familiar queasy feeling in her stomach. She glanced back at Patrick Miles. He'd put aside his map and was playing with his Game Boy again. He somehow sensed she was looking at him and raised his head. He smiled his beautiful, open, wide-eyed smile and bent back to the game.

In another few minutes it came to her, like someone grabbing her by the shoulders and shaking her.

Hawthorne.

The man sitting beside her had been part of the investigation that led to the ruin of one of the most powerful members of the United States Senate. Then, after the man had resigned in disgrace, he and Eric Miles had met in that suburban parking lot and Hawthorne had started shooting. In self-defense Miles had shot back and Hawthorne was left dead on the pavement.

Eric Miles, under the name Eric Anthony, had been involved in the Hawthorne case. Daniel Winter had lied to Faith about Charles Brandon's crimes. Faith had stopped believing in coincidence a little over a year ago. She was reminded of those hideous story problems in high school algebra class, with solutions that went: *If A equals B, and B equals C, then A must also equal C.*

"Hawthorne," she said aloud.

"Excuse me?" Eric looked at her, frowning, then looked quickly away.

"Tell me what really happened," Faith said.

He waited a long time. "That's a totally different story."

"Maybe it is and maybe it's not," Faith said.

19

ERIC SLOWLY TURNED TO LOOK AT FAITH. HE MET HER green eyes, then turned away again. He did an instrument check, then looked over his shoulder. *How you doing?* he signed to Patrick.

The boy gave him a thumbs-up, then signed, *How far? Another hour.*

Patrick gave an exaggerated sigh. Eric smiled a little, but it faded quickly as he turned back to the front of the airplane.

"Hawthorne," Faith said.

"Why? I'm sure you know all the gory details already."

Faith nodded. "But I want to hear it from you."

Eric was silent for a while. "My life . . ." He stopped. He felt like putting his hands in his pockets, but he didn't do that while flying the airplane: his own personal rule, even with the autopilot engaged. "My life has been mainly a weird black hole, with these strange feelings." He searched for the word. "Hollow. No, that's not it, either. Just like something's missing, incomplete. I've always just dealt with it and gone on. So it's been this sense of something missing, punctuated by short periods of explosion. The early days of my marriage to Laura, the Hawthorne case, Patrick's birth—intensity in the middle of all that emptiness. From being hollowed out to overflowing. You understand that?"

"Yes."

Eric looked surprised, then his eyes almost unconsciously honed in on Faith's scar. "Maybe you do. After I graduated from college, I worked for a couple of political consultants in Oklahoma City, doing basically what I'm doing now: researching issues, opposition voting records, planning advertising strategies. I did that for nearly ten years. Laura's law career was going great guns and her firm had just opened an office in D.C. She always craved being close to power, so she jumped at it. I got a job with the Federal Election Commission. Same sort of work, analyzing reams of data, except now I was looking for abuses of the campaign finance laws."

"Important work."

Eric nodded. "I thought so at the time. I had this burning desire to help make politics work again, make it *clean* again. I was all fired up with righteousness. I was going to help make Washington a better place."

Faith caught the sarcasm, tinged with bitterness, in his voice. "Not a bad ambition."

Eric shrugged. "Naive and silly. Our government may be the best in the world, but it still has its warts." He shrugged again. Short of putting his hands in his pockets, it was all he could do. "Mostly we found abuses in various political action committees, PACs, contributing above the legal limit, that sort of thing. In most cases the elected officials themselves had no idea they were getting illegal contributions. It was just the campaign fund-raising machine. The campaign committees refunded the money and went on. I spent a lot of time reading reports and reviewing bank accounts and going through documents and databases."

"That's what most investigations are nowadays: paper trails and computer files."

"Yep." Eric made a slight adjustment on the instrument panel in front of him. "I started to see some strange numbers popping up in some quarterly reports, things that didn't add up. The amounts that people said they were giving didn't match up with what one senator's campaign said he was receiving."

"Hawthorne," Faith breathed.

"The honorable senior senator from the state of Ohio, Weldon Paul Hawthorne, chairman of the Senate Judiciary Committee, member of the Appropriations and Foreign Relations committees. Powerful man with a lot of clout on the Hill. I got a court order and started tracking his money. He was getting huge amounts, in the millions of dollars, from two industrial concerns in his state. Only a fraction was going into his campaign accounts."

Faith was riveted to him now. She was totally oblivious to the airplane and the land more than a mile below. "And the rest?"

"Offshore accounts. Jamaica, Grand Cayman. At this point it became a formal investigation, so I turned it over to my partner, who was a real field officer. In the Investigative Division of the FEC, we all worked in pairs: one field investigator, one analyst. I, of course, was the analyst, so I kept researching while my partner, a guy named Ted Carpenter, interviewed Hawthorne. We confronted him with all the records, and Hawthorne stood there and denied all of it. With the paperwork right in front of him in black and white, he insisted he didn't have any offshore accounts and wasn't taking any illegal contributions. The boss wanted to turn up the heat on Hawthorne, so we leaked to *The Washington Post*. The *Post* ate it up: The reporter was some young kid who thought he was the next Woodward and Bernstein rolled into one. Hawthorne went ballistic, of course."

"I remember," Faith said. "I was in grad school at the time. He made all these speeches on the floor of the Senate about witch hunts and lynchings and all sorts of things."

"Like to watch C-Span, do you?"

Faith shrugged. "Occasionally. It's an education. Mind-numbing boredom, mostly, with little spurts of both greatness and corruption thrown in now and then."

"See? Just like my life."

Faith's face darkened. "I didn't mean—"

"I know you didn't mean. Yeah, Hawthorne went through the roof. He called our office five times a day, and his attorney called another five times a day. Then, about that time I started to find credit card receipts from hotels on Grand Cayman, extravagant parties thrown by the senator with vast amounts of liquor. There was even a receipt from an 'escort service,' a discreet one that deals in both young women and men. *Very* young, if you know what I mean."

Faith whistled.

"Uh-huh," Eric said. "I couldn't figure out if Hawthorne was stupid or just arrogant to use a campaign credit card to pay for these things. I finally decided he was a little bit of both. I guess that doesn't say much for the good voters of Ohio. Of course, Hawthorne bit back and this time he singled out the FEC in particular. He pointed to us as evidence of a government agency run amok, as an evil entity set out to destroy good public servants. Et cetera, ad nauseam. Here's Carpenter, a terrific guy with three young kids, and he starts getting hate calls at home. Me? No one knew me. I was the guy in the basement staring at the computer, the guy who wasn't there. I'd set all this in motion, and yet Carpenter was the one getting dragged through the muck."

Faith noticed that Eric was staring straight ahead, his jaw set, hands tightly grasping the control yoke even though the airplane was still on autopilot. "Look there," he said, pointing down. Faith looked: There was a small, dark body of water below them. "Lagoon from one of the big hog farms. That's the big industry out here in the panhandle now. Guymon's not too far off. We'll be into Boise City pretty soon." He gripped the yoke again. He lowered his voice instinctively. "Laura was pregnant with Patrick right then. She hadn't wanted to get pregnant, kept putting me off about it. She was all fired up about being in D.C., and a baby was the last thing she wanted. But somewhere along the way she must have forgotten to take a few pills. So anyway, she was pregnant when all this was going on. Her blood pressure started spiking, and the doc put her on solid bed rest for the last two months of the pregnancy. She hated that." He smiled hollowly.

Faith said nothing.

"You're a good listener, Kelly," Eric said suddenly. "Thanks."

Faith shrugged.

"So all this hit the fan. Carpenter was about ready to turn it over to the U.S. attorney, and we were sure we could get an indictment. Then Hawthorne resigned. Just quit. Remember how he stood there and cried on the floor of the Senate? And all the senators, even the ones who hated him, stood up one by one and applauded? Stirring moment. That made it past C-Span all the way to the evening network newscasts.

"We weren't sure what to do right then. We were pretty sure we could indict Hawthorne on fraud and conspiracy, even if he wasn't in the Senate any longer. So we sat on our hands for a while. Carpenter was a mess, stalking around the office. He made it sound like he not only wanted Hawthorne out of office, but wanted him totally ruined." Eric bowed his head. "Which he pretty much was, by that point."

Eric stopped talking and glanced back at Patrick. The boy had abandoned both his game and his map and was looking out the window at the treeless landscape below.

Faith waited awhile, then said, "What about the parking lot?"

Eric cleared his throat. Faith winced at the sound in the headset.

"Sorry," Eric said. "Tell me something."

"What?"

"The scar."

Faith shook her head. "No."

"Why not?"

"None of your business."

"And all this about Hawthorne is your business?"

"It might be," Faith said.

"Could you be a little more vague?"

"Probably not."

"Do you seriously think, *Agent* Faith Kelly, that Hawthorne has something to do with your case, or my case, or however you want to look at it?"

Faith waited a moment. "I think it might."

Eric nodded. "Vague. Tell me about the scar."

Faith sighed.

"Look at it like this," Eric said. "Remember in *The Silence of the Lambs* where Anthony Hopkins tells Jodie Foster he'll help her catch the killer if she'll let him get inside her head?"

"I think you watch too many movies."

"I grew up with an actress. What can I say?"

Faith sobered quickly. "Look, the scar came because someone I thought I trusted was corrupt. He betrayed both me and the whole system. His betrayal led to someone I was very close to being killed. It led to two innocent bystanders being killed. Then this man, the corrupt one, tried to kill *me*. The scar's a souvenir of that."

Eric was quiet for a few moments, listening to the airplane, watching the sky. "Maybe you do understand more than I give you credit for. Six weeks after he resigned from the Senate, Hawthorne called Carpenter on the phone. He's humble and contrite and says he wants to talk face-to-face, one-on-one. Carpenter asked me if I wanted to go along. I thought about it long and hard and decided to go. The morning of the meeting, Carpenter got a call. His father, out in Oregon, had just had a stroke. He had to fly out immediately. He took me aside, told me I'd have to go alone. We couldn't break the appointment."

Faith's gaze was steady on him. "What about the gun?"

"Everyone in the investigative division was issued three things after they came on board: credentials, a laptop, and a sidearm. It's like FBI agents who work in the lab: They still have Bureau-issued weapons because they're still FBI agents. Same principle. My gun mostly stayed in a drawer. I went through the basic firearms course, but that was about it. I was a terrible shot." Eric tapped fingers on the yoke. "Since you've seen the tape, you know what happened. Hawthorne started shooting that little pistol and wouldn't stop after several warnings. I grabbed my gun and fired back. I meant to hit him in the leg or the arm, just to disable him, make him stop shooting, for God's sake! But you know what, Kelly?"

"What?"

"Just like I said, I was a terrible shot. So my arm or leg

shot turned into a head shot and Hawthorne was dead, right there on the security tape for the world to see. Less than a month later Patrick was born prematurely. A month after that, with Patrick still in the neonatal intensive care unit, I quit the FEC. I turned tail and ran back to Oklahoma. Laura came with me but filed for divorce ten months after that. We were going through Patrick's hearing screenings at that point, and it was becoming obvious something was wrong. She couldn't handle it. She didn't even try for custody. I got the job with Solomon and Associates. The senior partner is an old college friend. I could work at home. Hawthorne was dead, and everything I was before that died with him. It was like the phoenix, you know, except I didn't quite get all the way up out of the ashes."

They were both silent for a while.

"And you know what happened next," he said. "It came to light that all the records, every document in the Hawthorne case, had been falsified. It wasn't true, none of it. The bank accounts, the hookers, none of it. It had been very carefully put together to destroy Hawthorne, done so well that it could fool the best investigator." The bitterness had crept into his voice again. "It fooled everyone, and there was never a single concrete lead into who or why."

There was a long silence. "Thanks for telling me," Faith finally said.

Eric shrugged again. He hadn't told the story in a long time. The last time had been before a board of inquiry five years earlier. The killing was clearly self-defense, but he'd been issued a formal rebuke for not having more closely verified the documentation of the case. Eric turned down every media request for interviews, though he could have made a lot of money if he'd granted one. He'd turned down a six-figure book deal from a major publisher. It would never go away, but he'd at least walked away from it, walking figuratively as far as he could go, to his little home office in Oklahoma City.

He looked at Faith Kelly. She was staring out the windshield, the bill of the Cubs cap pulled low over her eyes against the glare, her red hair pulled through the opening at the back of the cap. What was her part in all this?

This was all about people not being who they once were. It was all about information exchange.

Eric A. Miles.

Edward A. Miles.

July 27, 1965.

Gone home.

Eric shivered, then did put his hand in his pocket, wrapping his palm around keys and coins.

He remembered Good Mattingly's message: *I delivered you into this world, and I guess I am partly responsible for anything that has happened to you. Please come.*

But the old man was dead, his truck crashed into a church on a country road.

Please come.

"Here I am," Eric said, and began his landing approach to Boise City.

20

AN HOUR LATER THE AIRPORT'S COURTESY CAR, THE ancient Suburban, rolled down the little hill into Kenton. Patrick Miles had spent most of the trip from Boise City in a state of nervous excitement, remembering the adventure of last weekend. Eric was mostly silent. Faith watched the country roll by, thinking—as Eric had done a week ago—that this didn't look much like the Oklahoma she knew.

Eric pulled the Suburban into the single parking place in front of the little white building, where he had signed Good Mattingly's guest book. The building was locked. Faith leaned against the window and looked inside, taking in the rack of postcards spilled on the floor.

"It's closed," said a voice, "and it ain't opening back up again unless you want to run it."

They turned. A burly man in his fifties, with thick, muscular arms and neck, was standing by the side of the road. He was almost totally bald on top, with a firm, distinct jawline and hooded eyes. He wore a white T-shirt, jeans, and cowboy boots, and was smoking a cigarette.

"The old man's dead," the man said. "You want to buy the place?"

"Did you know Mr. Mattingly?" Eric said.

"Old fart was my uncle." The man extended a hand. "Jimmy Herrin. How did you know him?"

Eric shook his hand. "Just met him coming through here," he said vaguely. "I'm sorry about what happened."

Herrin shrugged and spat in the road. "He was a crazy old SOB. I always thought he was too crazy to die. Guess I was wrong, and now there's a big hole over in the Wheeless church."

"You didn't think much of him?" Faith said.

"Oh, he was my uncle, Mom's last surviving brother, but he was crazy as a bedbug. He was a doctor, you know. Delivered half the babies in the western panhandle for years. Delivered me, come to think of it. He even did some real serious research on helping people have kids. You know, people who weren't able to."

"Infertility," Eric said.

"That's the word. Then he went off on a trip, early seventies, I think it was. Just disappeared for a month. When he came back, he said he wasn't practicing medicine anymore, just gave it up. He just rattled around his old house out there by the mesa. He used to have his office in there, and I'd come in to check on him and catch him just sitting on the examining table, staring out the window, out toward Colorado."

"He had an office in his home?" Eric said, speaking to Herrin but looking at Faith.

"Oh, yeah," Herrin said. "There he was, last house out on the road past the mesa, with a doctor's office out there. You know, his house is the furthest west of any house in the state of Oklahoma. He was proud of that. Crazy old fart," he added, scraping his boot along the pavement. All the time they had stood and talked, no other cars came or went along the road. "Guess I'm going up to the Merc for a dinousaur burger. Then I'm headed back over to Boise City."

"Dinosaur burger?" Faith said.

"Try one for lunch." Herrin winked.

Eric drove all the way to the fork in the road that led to the three-state marker, then turned the Suburban around. He turned into the long gravel driveway that led to the last house on the road. He drove past a crudely lettered mailbox with *T. G. Mattingly, M.D.* scrawled on it in red marker.

There was no vehicle in the driveway, but deep ruts showed that one had been parked here often. Eric pulled the Suburban parallel to the house, which was painted a light gray, with an old-fashioned wraparound porch running the length of it. They got out and surveyed the porch, then Faith and Eric walked toward the back, Patrick trailing a few steps behind.

Faith cocked her head as if listening. "Awfully quiet out here," she finally said.

Eric nodded. "Tell me about it."

A set of six wooden steps, the painting flaking slightly, led up to a back door. Large windows flanked the steps on either side. Faith looked the house up and down.

"So what's U.S. government policy in this situation?" Eric asked.

Faith looked at him, then back to the house. She started up the steps and rattled the back doorknob. Locked.

"Uh-huh," she muttered.

She looked through the windows. The one to her right was heavily curtained and she couldn't see through it. The one to the left looked into a laundry alcove. She saw an ancient washer-dryer set, bottles of detergent lined up neatly on a wooden shelf. Faith reached out and ran a hand along the storm window. The bottom of it rattled.

"Hello?" she said, running her hand all the way to the bottom. The lower-right screw was missing.

"You have any tools?" she called down to Eric.

"Sorry, I don't. I carry a few in the airplane, but that's forty miles away."

"What about the airport car?"

Eric shrugged. "I'll check."

He and Patrick walked away while Faith tugged on the screen. Two minutes later Eric came up the steps with a small, rusting toolbox. "It was under the backseat," he said. He found a screwdriver and started to work one of the other screws.

Then he stopped suddenly.

"What?" Faith said.

"Patrick. He doesn't need to see us breaking into this house."

Faith smiled. "Of course. You're right. Take him around front and I'll do this." She looked at him with a mixture of apprehension and admiration. *This* man was a threat to Department Thirty security?

Eric signed to Patrick and they walked back around the side of the house. Faith worked quickly with the screwdriver, loosening and removing all the screws from the storm window. She could barely reach the top ones, extending her arms all the way to reach them.

There are advantages to being nearly six feet tall after all, she thought vaguely.

When she had the screen off, she looked around for a moment, then descended the steps to the detached garage. It contained the usual assortment of junk and yard implements as well as a box of rags. Faith found an old towel that looked big enough for her purposes, then went back to the house.

She wrapped her right arm in the towel, looping it over twice, and thought: *Long way from being a federal marshal, Faith Siobhan.*

In one harsh motion she rammed her towel-encased elbow into the glass of the window. The glass erupted into a sunburst but didn't shatter. She cocked her arm again. This time it came apart, raining shards onto the ground below.

She then used the towel to clear out the remaining jagged edges from the window frame.

When all the glass was out of the way, she dropped the towel and grabbed the ledge of the window, swinging her body away from the steps. With her arms she pulled herself through the window and onto the top of Good Mattingly's washing machine.

Thirty seconds later she'd opened the door from the inside and retrieved Eric and Patrick from the front.

The house itself was neat and orderly, with the exception of a single bowl and cup in the kitchen sink and an empty Campbell's Chunky Soup can beside it. Good Mattingly had no family pictures downstairs, just a couple of generic Western landscape-type paintings and a few old brass pieces that looked like they hadn't been polished in years. The furniture was straight out of the 1950s.

"Definitely an old man's house," Eric said mildly. He looked at Patrick and signed, *You want to watch TV?*

Patrick shrugged and signed, *Okay.*

Eric turned on the television and fiddled with the satellite receiver. There was no cable service out this far. When he got it working, he flipped channels until he found Nickelodeon, and Patrick settled in on a frayed old quilt that covered Mattingly's sofa.

Faith and Eric checked the downstairs rooms, the living room, kitchen, bathroom, and a bedroom that was empty except for an unvarnished wooden table.

They climbed the stairs, noticing the chair sitting at the top. "Strange place for a chair," Faith said.

"Arthritis," Eric said after a moment.

"What?"

"I bet he had severe arthritis. When I met him last Saturday, he seemed to move very stiffly, very carefully. I had a professor at OSU who had arthritic knees. She lived in a two-story house but refused to get a chairlift. So she kept a chair at the top of the stairs to rest in after she climbed the stairs."

Faith looked at him, impressed. "Very good, Mr. Miles."

"Thank you, Kelly."

Faith looked at him strangely but kept quiet. The man was an enigma to her. Of course, if he was truly the fortieth baby, his entire life had been conceived in strangeness. He thought of what he'd told her about his parents and Colleen Cunningham, whom Faith had known from movies as Colleen Fox. Maybe the answer was here in this neat, out-dated old bachelor's house.

They stepped into the office, the first door at the top of the stairs. The blinds were up on the window. Eric walked to it and looked out at the mesas of Colorado off to the north. A little way out, perhaps the distance of a football field, was a barn. No, not a barn, more of an outbuilding. It looked in serious disrepair.

"Hmm," he said.

Faith sat down at Mattingly's desk, the old-fashioned wooden chair squeaking under her. She pulled off her cap and ran both hands through her hair. "I wonder what we're looking for."

"His e-mail said he knew 'all the mothers.' That's how he put it. What does that mean? It also said he delivered me into this world." He stopped, standing in the middle of the room. "I don't even know which way's up anymore. My whole life I've been oblivious to what was going on around me. No matter how crazy things were, I was calm and could still do what needed to be done. That's who I am; that's what I do."

Faith swiveled in the old chair and watched him.

"It got me through life with Colleen, through college, through the FEC and Hawthorne, Patrick's birth, his deafness, the divorce, flight school, everything. Now I don't have a clue. Now I find out my last name isn't Anthony. Now there's someone buried in a grave with what's supposedly my real name and my birthdate on it. Now there's a twin that might or might not exist. Is he alive? Is he dead? Or is it just some stupid fantasy of a crazy old ex-doctor?" Eric swept his hand around the room, then fixed his gaze on Faith's sharp green eyes. "And you. You know more than you'll tell me. I'm under investigation. For what, I don't know. But you, with your scar from someone you once trusted, you're mixed up in the middle of this."

Eric leaned back against the examining table and jammed his hands in his pockets.

"Let's get busy," Faith finally said. "You want answers; maybe they're here. How are you with computers?"

Eric didn't move from the table. "I spend my life in front of one."

Faith got up from the chair and squatted in front of the old gray three-drawer filing cabinet—very similar, she realized, to the one in her office, Art Dorian's old office. It occurred to her that from what she knew of Thorogood Mattingly that he and Art Dorian were somewhat alike. Neat, seemingly organized, literate about computers but distrustful of them. Perhaps, she thought, just like Art, Mattingly would have kept his records on paper and not in a computer database. That was why she wanted Eric to work the computer while she sifted through the filing cabinet.

She pointed to the chair and the desk. "That's all yours, then. I'll start here."

They worked silently, side by side, Eric tapping computer keys while Faith pulled out file folders.

"Nothing here," Eric said half an hour later. "His computer wasn't even password protected. It came right up. No word processing documents. The only e-mails in the inbox were spam, and the only one in his sent box was the one to me. I'd say our Dr. Mattingly didn't use the computer too much."

"There aren't any—" Faith said, shifting against the stack of manila folders. She'd just opened a folder toward the back of the cabinet and pulled out a single sheet of paper with the word *Brandon* and a phone number on it.

"What?" Eric said.

"Nothing," Faith said quickly. "I thought it was something but it wasn't. These files don't have anything related to his practice. It's just old electric bills, old phone bills, credit card slips. That sort of thing."

"That would be too easy," Eric said, "to have medical records stored in what used to be a medical office."

Faith smiled cautiously. "Of course."

Eric stood up, rolling the kinks out of his back. His face still held the lined, haunted look Faith had noticed back in the airplane. "I'm going to go check on Patrick." He left the room, wooden floorboards creaking.

When his steps had faded, Faith carefully took the paper with the phone number on it and folded it into the pocket of her pants. She had no way of knowing how old the paper was, though it seemed somewhat faded. She let her mind trail over the possibilities. If it was a current and working number, that would explain how Grant had it "on good authority" that an issue "from his former life" was about to crop up.

Somewhere, someone was lying. With a start, she realized she was one of the liars. She could come right out and tell Eric Miles who Charles Brandon had been and what he had done—at least what she knew of it. But no, she was to protect Brandon/Grant. She had become one of the liars.

If you'll tell a lie, there's nothing you won't do, her father had preached at her for years. *And the more you lie, the more you have to lie.*

Faith took a deep breath, stood up, walked out of the office and down the stairs. Eric and Patrick were standing in Good Mattingly's kitchen, the door of the freezer open before them. One of the old wooden dining room chairs had been pulled over in front of the refrigerator-freezer combo.

"Looking for clues in the ice cubes?" Faith said.

Eric turned toward her. In his hand was a white plastic grocery sack that looked like it was wrapped around something.

"What is it?" Faith said.

"Patrick got hungry," Eric said. "He didn't find anything in the refrigerator, so he pulled over a chair and opened the freezer. This was in there."

He placed the bundle on the table and slowly unwrapped

the sack. When the end was open, he pulled out a small stack of manila files rubber-banded together.

Eric looked up. Patrick was bouncing excitedly around the table, proud of what he'd found that was so obviously important to the adults.

Good job, Faith signed to him.

Thank you, he signed back. *What is it?*

We'll see, Eric signed. *Go back and watch TV. We'll go get some lunch in a little while.*

Patrick rolled his eyes. His father made a shooing motion with both hands and the boy went back to the living room.

"So he thought someone would come looking for these," Eric said. "But who? Why hide them?"

Faith thought of the slip of paper in her pocket. *Brandon. Grant.*

"You know, don't you?" Eric said. "You know who he was hiding them from. You're protecting someone."

"Let's take a look," Faith said.

"You didn't answer me."

"No, I didn't."

She met his cold stare.

"Do you want to see these or not?" she said. "There are things I know, but a lot I don't. Now, let's take a look."

They sat at the table, Eric taking the top half of the stack and giving the others to Faith. He opened the top file, feeling the cold stiffness of the paper under his fingers. The top sheet had the name *Thorogood G. Mattingly, M.D.* printed in ornate script across the top, followed by the address—a Kenton rural route—and phone number. The words *General Medical Practice* followed.

Eric began to scan down the sheet. It was a medical history of a young pregnant woman named Mary Jane O'Dell, whose address was listed as Wheeling, West Virginia. Her date of birth was 1935. Under "spouse" the entry was Arlen Henry O'Dell, date of birth 1933. Mary Jane O'Dell's date of "admission" to Mattingly's care was February 1, 1954.

O'Dell. O'Dell.

Why is that name familiar? Eric thought. Then he had it:

He pulled out his little spiral notebook and flipped to the notes he'd made at the three-state marker, at the makeshift cemetery. The first stone he'd found, the one with the gold border around it, was for Brenda and Linda O'Dell, born and died March 31, 1955.

"Look at this," Eric finally said.

He explained to Faith what he'd found, then showed her his notebook where he'd written the names of the two babies.

Faith's eyes narrowed. "But I don't see—"

Eric paged through the file. He found several notes on "treatments" being administered throughout February, March, and April of 1954 to Mary Jane O'Dell. Many of the notes were signed by Mattingly, but a number were signed by "Helen Harker, R.N." Eric wrote the name in his notebook.

A note dated in June confirmed that Mary Jane was pregnant, and the rest of the notes tracked her prenatal care. At the back of the file were several pages detailing her labor, and her delivery, at 4:14 A.M. and 4:22 A.M. on March 31, 1955, of identical twin girls, whom the mother named Brenda and Linda. The twins were born thirty-three weeks into the pregnancy but were otherwise healthy.

There were two more pages detailing the babies' respiration and progress of their first few days. Most of the pages on the babies, after their birth, were signed by Helen Harker. Stapled to the back of the file was a final note. Scrawled in what Eric had come to recognize as Good Mattingly's handwriting was: *Released to C.B. April 4, 1955.*

The rest of the page was blank.

Eric sat back, his heart hammering against his rib cage. He remembered the stone: BRENDA AND LINDA O'DELL. GOD'S ANGELS.

He shook his head.

The babies lived.

Sitting beside him, looking at the file, Faith said, "Holy shit," very softly.

Eric began to look through the other files. All were the same, and all ended the same way, with a set of twins born, and then "released" to "C.B." within a few days or weeks of their birth.

The final file was at the bottom of Faith's stack. The mother's name was Margaret Eleanor Miles, the address in Kerry's Landing, Oklahoma. Spouse: Terry Lynn Miles.

Most of the file was the same as the others, except it seemed to have taken Maggie Miles longer than any of the other mothers to conceive.

But the records ended with Maggie's thirty-seven week checkup.

There was no sheet stapled to the back of the file detailing the birth of twins.

No mention of boys named Eric A. Miles and Edward A. Miles.

Nothing. At thirty-seven weeks pregnant, it was as if everything about Maggie Miles had fallen away into a black hole.

Eric wanted to scream.

Faith said, "There's no—"

Eric stood up and walked away from the table, to where Patrick sat on the couch watching *Rugrats*. Of course Patrick couldn't hear it, and of course Good Mattingly didn't have closed captioning on his television, but Patrick smiled at the absurd antics of Tommy and Chuckie anyway.

Eric put his arm about the boy's shoulders, then it turned into an embrace. Patrick first smiled, then squirmed, then frowned, furrows slashing into his forehead.

Eric's eyes had filled, and while no tears fell, he had to blink hard to keep them away.

Daddy, what? Patrick signed, then his little white hands moved up his father's cheek.

Eric just shook his head.

Don't cry, the boy signed.

Eric shook his head, blinking again.

Daddy, don't cry. More urgent, choppy hand motions this time.

Eric pulled Patrick closer and held him.

Faith stood unsteadily from the table, clutching Maggie

Miles's medical records as if they had magical powers. She took a couple of steps toward the living room.

Eric looked up at her. " 'Released to C.B.' Who's C.B.?"

Faith stopped walking.

"Where did these babies go? Why do they have grave markers down this road?"

"I don't know," Faith said, her voice barely a whisper.

"And what about C.B.?"

Faith was silent.

"Kelly?" Eric said.

"I think we'd better get back to Oklahoma City," Faith said.

21

NEITHER ERIC NOR FAITH WAS HUNGRY, BUT PATRICK was, so they bought the boy a "dinosaur burger," which turned out to be a very large, remarkably good hamburger, from the grill at Kenton Mercantile. The store was equal parts grocery, video rental shop, tourist gift shop, lunch counter, and general gathering place.

Ten minutes later they were back in the rickety Suburban. In less than an hour it was parked on the grass at the Boise City airport again. While they were in Kenton, another small plane had come in and was tied down on the ramp. Otherwise the airport was as still as ever, no signs of life anywhere.

After Patrick had climbed into the Arrow and fastened his belt, Eric took Faith's arm before she put her foot on the step up to the wing.

"Tell me one thing," he said.

Faith stared at him warily.

"Tell me the truth." He tapped the sack of folders she held. "Did you know about this? Did you know all these babies were alive?"

"No," she finally said after a long moment.

Eric didn't let go of her arm. "But you know who C.B. is."

Faith didn't answer.

"You do," Eric said. "I saw it on your face back there in the kitchen."

"Is that a question or a statement?"

"You tell me."

Faith shook her head and broke eye contact. "Let's go. I need to get back to the city, and I need to make some phone calls."

Eric squeezed her arm harder. "You know who it is."

Faith set the bundle of files down on the airplane wing and, one by one pried Eric's fingers off her arm. He didn't resist. "Yes, I do," she said.

"Then tell me—"

"This is so complicated that I don't even know how complicated it is."

Eric stared at her for a long moment, then climbed past her and settled into the pilot's seat. Faith gathered up the files, ducked her head, and crawled in, pulling the door closed and latching it after her.

"Good job," Eric said. "Now let's get out of here." He looked sideways at her. "You understand that up until a couple of weeks ago, I had certain assumptions about my life that I figured were true. Then Colleen told me that story, and—"

"Let's go," Faith said.

Eric nodded.

They were in the air shortly, Patrick scrutinizing his road atlas, carefully studying a map of Massachusetts. Faith began to leaf through the files again, looking at dates, at names, and at nineteen sets of twins.

Released to C.B.

Charles Brandon.

Nathan Grant.

She glanced at Eric. Why hadn't he and his twin been "released" to Brandon like the others? They were the last ones—at least it seemed Winter had told her the truth about that. But what difference did that make, Eric and Edward

Miles being the last twins born under Brandon's "scheme"?

Too many questions. Her life was nothing but questions. A minute later the airplane's engine sputtered and died.

"Hello?" Eric said.

"What happened?" Faith said, sitting bolt upright. She instinctively looked back at Patrick.

The boy was staring ahead. He caught Faith's eye and signed, *What?*

I don't know, she signed back.

"Our engine just failed," Eric said.

"Oh, shit," Faith muttered. A strange feeling crept down into her stomach. It was as if she had swallowed something whole and it had been lodged in her throat but had just been shoved forcefully down into her gut.

The vibration she'd come to expect from the little airplane had stopped. She pulled one headphone away from her ear and heard only rushing air, no engine noise.

Eric scanned the instrument panel. The Arrow was beginning to descend.

"Are we going to crash?" Faith breathed. Her heart was hammering so hard she thought that she could hear it over the wind.

Eric glanced at her but said nothing. He reached below and to the left of the control yoke and pulled the fuel tank selector switch toward himself.

The engine caught and roared to life. Eric pulled the nose of the plane up again.

Faith exhaled, gripping the sides of her seat.

"What happened?" she said after a moment.

"I told you, the engine failed," Eric said. He looked back over his shoulder. *You okay?* he signed to Patrick.

The boy gave a shaky thumbs-up.

"Well, why?" Faith said. "Why in the hell did your engine fail?"

Faith heard Eric's rush of breath in her headset. "Bad fuel in the left tank, most likely. Maybe water in the tank."

"What did you do?"

"Switched over to the right tank. We should be able to

make it home on the right one." He glanced over at her; they were now flying as if nothing had happened. "Why was it you said you didn't like flying?"

Faith didn't answer. The lurch in her stomach had finally subsided and her heartbeat had slowed down.

"Are you all right?" Eric asked her.

"Yes," she said, closing her eyes.

"That was quite an adventure."

Faith opened her eyes and stared at him, but he wasn't looking at her.

Faith sat stiffly, hands still clutching the sides of her seat, for a good ten minutes before she began to relax. She looked over at Patrick. He was back to studying Massachusetts in the atlas.

Maybe I hallucinated the whole thing, Faith thought. *In fact, maybe I hallucinated the whole day and I'm still having ice cream with Scott Hendler.*

Don't be stupid, she thought after another moment, taking care not to say it out loud.

A few more minutes went by. The records from Mattingly's freezer had slipped off her lap when the engine had died. Faith leaned over and began to pick them off the floor, taking care to rearrange them in chronological order.

She'd recovered all but the last two when the engine died again.

Faith straightened up. "What—"

"I believe we're in a moderate amount of trouble this time," Eric said.

Faith looked at him. His voice was calm, but his forehead was fringed with perspiration.

"Now, where are we?" Eric muttered, pulling out a chart from a pouch beside his seat.

"What are you doing?" Faith said, her voice rising slightly.

"Trying to find a place for us to land. We're just southwest of Gray, Oklahoma, and a little northwest of the airport at Perryton, Texas. I don't think we can quite make it there."

"Then what do we do? Are we going to crash?"

Eric glared at her. "Would you tend to Patrick, please? I'm about to be very busy."

Faith stared at him in disbelief for a moment, then turned. Patrick was staring ahead, wide-eyed.

Your dad's going to take care of us, she signed to the boy, then held out her hand.

Patrick, already a fair-skinned child, had gone even more pale. He reached out his small white hand and slipped it into hers. She squeezed and held on.

The stone descended into Faith's gut again. The vibration had ceased, even though the propeller was still turning. Eric was using his right hand to roll a small wheel located between their two seats.

"What are you doing?" Faith said again. The plane dipped farther.

"I'm adjusting the trim for the best glide airspeed."

"What?"

"Quiet, now." He thumbed the radio switch on the yoke. "Kansas City Center, Cherokee two-eight-one-one Bravo, with engine failure, declaring an emergency."

Several seconds passed. Faith felt her scar begin to itch. She swallowed hard, still holding Patrick's hand. The boy had gone the color of paste, and his huge blue eyes were locked onto hers.

A deep male voice in the headset said, "Cherokee two-eight-one-one Bravo, say souls and fuel on board."

"Center, one-one Bravo," Eric said. "Three on board. Two hours and forty minutes fuel remaining."

Faith tuned out the voices in her headset. The rock had settled permanently in her stomach as the airplane began to descend sharply. She closed her eyes, tuning out everything but Patrick Miles's hand in hers.

She had no idea how much time had passed when Eric said, "I'm set up to land in this nice wheat field over here."

Faith looked out the window. "What do I need to do?" she said after a moment.

"Glad you asked, Agent Kelly. As we're coming in I'll need

you to open the door and hold it open while I land the airplane."

"Open the door? You want me to open the door while we're still moving?"

"If there's damage to the airframe while we're coming down, we don't want the door getting jammed. You don't want to be trapped in here, do you?"

"Ah, no."

"I didn't think so."

The ground, thick and green with wheat stalks, was coming fast. "What else? Anything else you need me to do?"

"Pray?" Eric said.

"What?"

"You have red hair and your name's Kelly. You're a good Irish Catholic, aren't you?"

"Sort of, I guess. You?"

Eric's eyes were still straight ahead. "Liberal Protestant. There are such things in Oklahoma, believe it or not."

Faith closed her eyes and tried to think of praying the rosary, but nothing would come, only a windy silence inside. She felt betrayed by her own name. *Faith, faith. What faith?*

"We're going to land gear up," Eric announced. The fringe of sweat had circled all the way around his head now. His hair was damp and matted.

"Isn't that dangerous?" Faith's scar was almost burning, or at least she imagined it was.

"Landing in a field like this, it minimizes the chance of one of the wheels getting stuck in a rut or a gopher hole or something and flipping the airplane over. Here we go now. Turning off the ignition and master switch. If you'll just unlatch that door now and hold onto it . . ."

Faith squeezed Patrick's little hand one last time and signed, *Hang on, it's okay.* She undid the latch on the top of the door, then the one on the handle.

"Open it!" Eric shouted.

Faith pushed the door open, feeling the air rush like water over a falls. She opened her mouth as if to scream, but nothing came out. She caught motion behind her. Patrick had thrown his hands up over his face.

The ground thundered toward them. The stalks of wheat were distinct now, lush and green, not quite knee-high. Faith had the ludicrous thought that she could reach out through the open door and just grab onto one.

The tail of the Arrow impacted the ground, then the nose pitched forward and began to dig into the dirt. Faith lurched in her seat. Mattingly's files scattered onto the floor again. Metal scraped on the earth.

"Come on," Eric whispered as the airplane began to ski along the surface of the field, churning up the wheat. "Please."

Faith held her breath, the metal of the door cutting into her hands.

The Arrow's speed began to lessen. Faith listened to the sick crunching beneath her and was quietly thankful she hadn't eaten anything back at the Kenton Mercantile.

Then it was over and the plane stopped moving. It was as if a switch had been flipped on a giant panel somewhere, and now everything was in the Off position. It was quiet, dangerously so.

Faith looked around. The propeller of the airplane was bent. She looked out the door she still held. Behind them a new rut was churned up in the wheat field. She started to move in her seat and found she couldn't work the latch on her seat belt. She hadn't realized she was dizzy before, but the world was spinning, a giant roulette wheel in this rural field.

Movement: Eric was getting out of his own belt, reaching behind him. He grabbed Patrick and held him as tightly as he could. Tears were streaming down the boy's face, and he was shaking uncontrollably. Eric didn't talk, didn't sign, but just held Patrick and let him cry.

Faith was finally able to get out of her belt, and she pushed the door all the way open. She crawled awkwardly out on the wing, dragging her long legs behind her. Her legs felt as if they had hundred-pound weights strapped to them: They didn't want to cooperate. When she had her entire body extracted, she slid down off the wing and toppled over in the wheat.

She sat that way, breathing hard, for several minutes, before she trusted herself to get up. She steadied herself against the wing and looked around. Nothing but wheat, as far as she could see.

There was noise above her, then Patrick and Eric came out the door, just as awkwardly as she had.

"Are you hurt?" Eric asked.

"I don't think so," Faith said. Her voice sounded strange, far off, disconnected from this field. "What about you two?" She signed the last as she spoke it, amazed that her hands could find the words.

"We're okay," Eric said.

Okay, Patrick signed. He was still paper-white.

They all took a few steps away from the airplane.

"Dammit to hell," Eric said, and didn't bother to apologize. He walked all the way around the airplane. "Dammit, dammit, *dammit!*"

Faith stayed with Patrick, holding the boy's hand, just as she had done when they were in the air. *Is Daddy okay?* he signed.

Faith nodded. *He's okay. Just mad now.*

Patrick frowned.

Not at you, Faith signed quickly.

Patrick pointed at her questioningly.

Faith smiled a little, then shrugged. *Not so sure about that one.*

Eric had crawled back into the cockpit and came out a couple of minutes later with his cell phone and a small toolbox. "I called the flight service station out of Fort Worth and let them know what happened," he said. His voice sounded as disconnected as Faith's had. "We're in Ochiltree County, Texas. They're notifying the local authorities."

Without waiting for a reply of any kind, he walked around the other side of the ruined Arrow. Five minutes later he came back around to the side where Faith and Patrick stood. His face was clouded with anger.

"What?" Faith said.

Eric didn't answer. She saw him take a screwdriver out and begin to pry something on the airplane. She heard him mutter several unintelligible words, and within a few minutes he walked to her and thrust two small objects into her hand.

She held them up. They were two halves of a broken pencil, a plain yellow number-two pencil. They were soaked and smelled of fuel.

"What does this mean?" she said.

"At first I thought it was a fuel problem," Eric said, his voice tight. "But I checked the tanks before we left Boise City, and the gauges showed there was fuel in the tanks."

"So?"

"So . . . the fuel tank vents were plugged."

" 'Plugged'? What do you mean, 'plugged'?"

Eric scuffed his feet along the ground. His entire body had taken on the appearance of a spring too tightly wound. "Fuel in the tanks is replaced by air as it's pumped into the engine. If the vent is plugged somehow, it causes a vacuum in the tank. Eventually that prevents fuel flow and starves the motor." He pointed to the pencil halves. "Someone put that in the vents and plugged them up on both sides."

Faith looked at the pencils, then at Eric. Up until that moment she hadn't considered that it was anything but an accident. Her mind tumbled like clothes in a dryer. *Grant? Winter?* she thought. *But that makes no sense.*

"Someone was trying to kill us," she finally said. She quickly turned away from Patrick.

"He doesn't lip-read," Eric said. He put a hand in his pocket, but kept it still. "No, they didn't want to kill us."

"Oh?"

"More like . . . get our attention." The anger came back to Eric's face. "I'd say they did. Your pal C.B., maybe?"

"That doesn't make any sense," Faith said.

"Well, tell me something that does," Eric snapped. "If they wanted to kill us, they could have done something else. Someone who knew to jam an airplane's fuel tank vents would also know that a reasonably conscientious pilot could find a way to get the plane down without getting killed. No, I'd say someone just fired a shot across my bow. I want to know who. I want to know what's going on here."

He took a step toward her.

Faith's body tensed. Her Glock was in her purse, back on the floor of the plane.

"This has gone far enough," Eric said.

"I agree," Faith said.

"Tell me."

Faith shook her head. "I—"

"You tell me, goddammit!" Eric shouted, his voice rising with the wind into the empty country.

Patrick stepped between them.

They looked at each other, then at the boy.

She held my hand, Patrick signed to his father.

Some of the rage seemed to melt away from Eric.

"Listen," Faith said quietly. "They've lied to me too. I'm supposed to have all the information, but I don't. I don't know what's real and what's not."

"Can you find out?" Eric said.

Faith thought about it. "I don't know about you, but I hate being lied to by people I'm supposed to be able to trust."

Eric nodded.

"I'll find out," Faith said.

"I'll come with you."

Faith waited. "There will be things I can't tell you along the way. You understand that."

Somewhere not far away, they heard an engine. "That'll be the sheriff," Eric said. "Hopefully I'll be able to arrange for transportation back to Oklahoma City, and for a truck to come get my airplane. I hope the farmer who owns this field doesn't sue me." He smiled wanly. "But then, that's the least of my worries."

Faith wasn't listening. Her mind was racing through the conversations she'd had since she began working for Department Thirty. Yorkton, Winter, Brandon/Grant, even Scott Hendler.

She thought she heard her father's voice again: *If you'll tell a lie, there's nothing you won't do. And the more you lie, the more you have to lie.*

"Dad, you were right," Faith said, and started walking toward the sheriff's deputy who was coming across the field toward them.

22

IT WAS DUSK, THE SUN SETTING SLOWLY BEHIND THEM, by the time Eric, Faith, and Patrick were back in Oklahoma City. The Ochiltree County sheriff's deputy, after consulting his dispatcher, insisted on driving them back himself. He was a slim middle-aged man named Ferguson, and shattered every possible stereotype of rural Texas law enforcement. He did not wear a cowboy hat or boots, did not chew tobacco, was articulate and soft-spoken. He played tapes of Debussy and Vaughan Williams in the patrol car during the four-hour drive back to Oklahoma City.

Patrick slept for much of the trip. Faith and Eric dozed at various times themselves, neither saying much. Eric had Ferguson drop them back at the airport, and he drove back to Colleen's house, since Faith had left her car there.

Eric stood in the driveway in the cool spring evening with Patrick on his shoulder and said, "Now what?"

Faith tapped the medical records. "I'm going to follow up on these. I have to know at what point, and for what reason, people stopped giving the facts of this case, even within my department."

Eric stared off into the distance, toward the sunset, the way they had just come. "I think I should see if Laura can keep Patrick for a few days, and her 'other priorities' be damned."

Faith waited a moment, then nodded. "I think that might be a good idea."

"Good night . . ." Eric seemed to think for a moment over what to call her. ". . . Faith."

"Good night, Eric."

Eric watched her climb into the little gold Miata and drive west, as if drawn back toward the place they'd already been that day. He watched until her taillights turned north on Penn.

"Come on, big boy," he said, shifting Patrick from one shoulder to the other. "Let's go home."

Eric and Patrick lived in a modest house a couple of miles northwest of Colleen's Gatewood home. The interior was entirely unassuming, in blues and browns, neither neat nor sloppy. A few toys were on the floor, and there were several pictures of Patrick. There were a few more of Patrick and Eric together: at the beach, at Frontier City, at the annual school carnival. There was one of the two of them, standing beside Colleen, who beamed out her movie-star smile.

Eric put Patrick to bed, and the boy barely stirred.

Quite a day for a five-year-old, Eric thought. *He was in a plane crash and can tell his friends about it at school on Monday.*

Bone-weary, his mind overloaded to the point of numbness, Eric walked back into the living room. He stood for a moment, as if uncertain what to do, then began to feel the anger again, the same feeling he'd had as he stood beside his ruined airplane.

Patrick could have been killed. He could have been killed himself, regardless of what he'd told Kelly.

Kelly.

She could have been killed too. Whatever she was, who-ever was after him didn't mind killing her in the process. He wasn't sure yet what that meant.

He wandered around the living room for a few seconds, then his eyes fell on the security panel beside the front door.

He almost never activated it. It had come with the house, and he only turned it on when leaving town for more than a day at a time. He reached out, punched in the four-digit code, and listened as the mechanized voice said, "Security system activated."

He made sure the back door was locked, then checked every window in the place, remembering how they'd broken into Good Mattingly's house. There were no loose screws.

His mind still churning but not knowing what else he could do, he went to the refrigerator and pulled out a beer. He drank rarely, and he liked to joke that a six-pack would last him half a year—one beer per month.

He rolled the beer can against his forehead and turned on the TV. The news anchor had just returned to the screen after a field report from a White House correspondent. "Certainly, Jeff," she said, "this is the biggest political crisis the President has faced."

Eric sat down. The anchorwoman shuffled some papers in front of her. "Recapping this breaking news story, it now appears that the President may have had prior connection to the Sons of Madison United, both before and after entering politics. He is reported to have contributed money to the group and used his influence when he was governor to help SOMU founder Wayne Devine escape a series of weapons-related charges several years ago. Documents obtained by CNN show that the President used his power when he was governor to help Devine avoid prosecution and even had his record expunged.

"The White House has thus far had no comment on the allegations. Senator Max Candell of Louisiana, chairman of the Judiciary Committee and one of the President's most vocal critics, is already calling for an independent counsel to be appointed to look into the case and how it relates to the recent terrorist activites claimed by SOMU. Either way, the President has become increasingly embattled and is drawing fire from across the political spectrum.

"On a related note, several organizations of law enforcement officers have cancelled scheduled conventions, and cases of 'blue flu' have been cropping up from California to Virginia, with many officers being afraid to report for duty."

Eric changed the channel. The two leading contenders for

the opposing party's nomination were being interviewed on another network. Senator Blanchard of Michigan not only appeared old and tired but spoke in an uninspiring mumble. By contrast, Oklahoma Governor Archer radiated calm and confidence and vision, never criticizing the President directly but managing to convey the impression that she was mightily disappointed in him.

Eric turned off the TV. No more politics. He caught sight of his telephone answering machine, its blinking light like an accusing eye. Everyone he knew had digital voice mail, but Eric had clung to the microcassette answering machine he'd had for more than ten years. He jabbed at the button. First message was from the director of research at work, reminding him of Monday morning's staff meeting.

"Yeah, yeah, yeah," Eric muttered, sipping the beer.

The next message was a telemarketer offering him a superb "home improvement package." The next one was silent for several seconds, but Eric could hear breathing on the tape.

"Mr. Miles," said a man's voice.

Eric sat up straight when he heard the name spoken.

"How was your flight today? Safe, I trust. Those small airplanes are so dangerous, I've heard. Anything could happen. *Anything.*"

Eric stood up, spilling beer all over the carpet.

"Perhaps it would be best if you didn't travel out that way anymore. Perhaps it would be best if you simply forgot about any questions you might feel like asking. After all, as I said, anything could happen."

There was a click, and the tape stopped.

Eric stabbed the button again, replaying the message.

Listening to the calm, almost serene, inflection of the man's voice, Eric felt the beginnings of the rage again. They had almost killed Patrick and him today. His airplane was ruined. His life had been shaken, the same way Patrick liked to shake those little Christmas snow globes.

"Son of a bitch!" Eric shouted at the walls.

He grabbed his wallet and pulled out the card Faith Kelly

had given him. He got no answer at her office or home numbers, so he tried her cell.

When she answered, he said, "It's Eric. Where are you?"

"On my way home. What's wrong?"

"Listen to this." He held the receiver down by the little speaker and played her the message.

"Well . . ." she said.

"Yeah, 'well' is right. Who is he? Dammit, Kelly, *who is he?*"

There was a pause. Eric heard muted music in the background, as if from a car stereo. Something melodic and flowing, like jazz. "Take the tape out of the machine," she said.

"What?"

"It's evidence now. Take it out, put it aside. I'll need it."

"But you—"

"I'll come and get it. Just be still."

She clicked off, and Eric was left standing alone in the room, beer soaking into his carpet. He barely noticed.

Faith was on May Avenue, a few blocks from the turnoff to her house. She didn't really like talking on the phone in the car, and especially not for involved conversations. Considering what she'd just heard, she was surprised she could hold the Miata on the road.

She pulled into a little strip mall and sat there for a moment. Her own rage was building.

"Screw Department Thirty," she said aloud, then she thought: *No, dammit. I have a job to do, and I'll do it. But on my terms from here on out.*

She was almost shaking with anger. She thought of Patrick Miles's little hand in hers, of his huge blue eyes, crowded with fear as his father's airplane went down.

She flipped open her address book so hard that it fell on the floor, and she had to lean over to pick it up. After she punched in the number, she got out of the car and slammed the Miata's door, pacing up and down the parking lot.

When Grant came on the line, she said, "What the hell do you think you're doing?"

"Excuse me?" said the voice she'd just heard on Eric's tape.

"It's Kelly. What is the matter with you? Have you lost your mind?"

Grant paused. "Take care in your tone with me, young lady. I won't be spoken to that way."

"I don't want to hear it. I don't know what you think you're doing, but it stops now. Leave Eric Miles alone. Do you hear me? I will handle it."

"I'm afraid I don't—"

"*Stop it!* Just stop it! Miles and his little boy were almost killed today. So was I! You leave it alone. I am handling this investigation, and you stay out of it! Are we clear?"

Silence.

"I'm talking to you, Grant! Do you understand me?"

"I don't care for you, Officer Kelly. Professor Dorian never talked to me this way."

"And he never knew the truth about what really happened to those babies, either, did he?"

Grant waited a long moment. When he spoke again, his voice was low, dangerous. All the malevolence Faith had sensed from the man in person was right there in his voice. "I haven't been satisfied with your handling of this Miles situation. One does what one has to do. I am involved in many important projects, *Officer* Kelly." He bit off the title, showing sarcasm for the first time. "It's your job to see that Eric Miles doesn't disrupt them. And I'll say this one more time: I won't be talked to this way. You'll show me more respect."

"Those babies lived. I have the proof. I have Mattingly's medical records. I don't know what the game is with all the gravestones, but I know the babies didn't die at birth. *What did you do with them?*"

There was another long silence. Faith heard Grant breathing on the line. Then the phone abruptly clicked in her ear. "You arrogant old bastard," she said to it.

She stalked up and down the parking lot, oblivious to the Saturday evening traffic passing on May. A Hispanic woman came out of one of the stores in the strip mall and looked at her strangely.

Faith got back in the car and gripped the wheel of the Miata. There were many things that bothered her about Nathan Grant, but something in particular about this conversation dug at her. Grant never denied having anything to do with the airplane sabotage. He didn't even bother to dispute it.

But that wasn't it. What was it he'd said?

I'm involved in many important projects.

If Grant was living his life under Department Thirty as he was supposed to—as he was *required* to—then he was an ordinary small-town real estate man. A successful one, to be sure, but just a real estate developer nonetheless.

What important projects could he be involved in that Eric Miles would disrupt?

Even on the off chance that Eric discovered that Nathan Grant was once Charles Brandon, what difference would it make? He'd been Grant for more than thirty years. What could they find that would damage Grant in the here and now?

She started the Miata, then called Eric. "Save that tape," she said. "I have to go to the office first."

She slipped the Miata into gear and headed south toward downtown.

In her darkened office she stared at the catfish on the wall and thought about taking it down. *No. It belongs here, even if I don't.*

She turned on only the little desk lamp, giving a tiny, ghostly circle of light to the room. She booted up the computer, then inserted the disk Yorkton had given her, the one with all the Department Thirty procedures and protocols as well as information on her individual cases.

She opened several files, not finding what she wanted. She knew there was a way in there to catch Grant, and a way to deal with him once she caught him.

She read six more files of mind-numbing bureaucratic blather before she found it.

"Yes, sir," she whispered to the computer screen, then reached for the phone.

When Dean Yorkton's voice came on, he said, "Well, Officer Kelly. To what do I owe the pleasure? I didn't think I'd be hearing from you so soon."

Faith didn't smile. "I have a serious procedural question to ask you."

All the levity whisked out of Yorkton's voice. "I'm listening."

"Section six, paragraph two of the Department Thirty Protection Agreement. The agreement all our cases sign when they agree to accept a new identity."

"Yes, I'm familiar with it. What about it?"

"There are two requirements. They agree to provide—"

" 'Information pertinent to, and/or relative to, the cases and issues mentioned in the above paragraph,' " Yorkton quoted.

"But it's the next part I'm interested in. They stipulate that as part of their agreement, they will never engage in any further unlawful or criminal activity while under the protection of Department Thirty. Failure to comply will result in the agreement being null and void, protection rescinded, the new identity terminated."

"Yes, yes. It's a standard clause. We don't want them out committing more crimes while they're under our protection, now, do we?"

Exactly, Faith thought. "So if I can prove that one of my cases has committed, or is in the process of committing, 'unlawful or criminal activity,' then they're out."

Yorkton didn't reply at once.

"Yorkton?" Faith said.

"Are you telling me you have evidence of such activities?"

"Not yet." *Unless you count attempted murder,* she thought. "But I have a strong suspicion—"

"Tread carefully, Officer Kelly. You're new at this, and it's a very serious business. Have you talked to the director?"

Faith swallowed, biting back an angry reply to the patronizing tone. "Yes, it certainly is a very serious business, and no, I haven't talked to the director. But I do believe something's going on here, and I think the department has to address it."

Yorkton waited again. "Your evidence must be solid. There can't be any mistake."

"I understand that."

"I won't ask you which case. I don't need to know. The field procedures are there in the information I gave you."

"I have it right here."

"Kelly?"

"Yes?"

"Be careful. I don't mean to give offense, but I wonder if you know just what you're doing down there."

"Maybe I don't," Faith said. "But then, as you've said yourself, maybe that's better, in a way."

"Maybe it is," Yorkton said.

Faith hung up and sat back, feeling a rush as intense as if she'd just run a marathon.

I'm involved in many important projects, Grant had said.

"I just bet you are," Faith said, then switched off the lamp, plunging the office back into full darkness.

23

ERIC FUMBLED AROUND THE HOUSE ALL DAY SUNDAY. He didn't go to church, he didn't work in the yard, didn't watch television. He made Patrick's meals, read with the boy for a little while, then sent him into the backyard to play.

At six o'clock Monday morning, showered and fully dressed, Eric called Laura's home number. He knew she put in obscene hours at the firm, and he'd have to catch her early before she left for downtown.

"Laura Northrup-Anthony," she answered, rushed.

She can never just say hello, Eric mused. "It's me."

"What do you want? I'm heading out the door."

"You need to take Patrick for a few days."

Big sigh into the phone. "I told you when you were in my office ranting the other day—"

"Someone tried to kill me on Saturday, Laura."

Silence.

He explained what had happened, carefully avoiding any details about what they'd found in Good Mattingly's house.

"What are you doing?" Laura finally said, almost in a whisper.

"Don't know. But I think he should stay with you until this mess is cleared up."

Laura was silent for a long time. "I guess so. Have you talked to the police?"

"Sort of."

"What do you mean, 'sort of'?"

"It's complicated."

"I guess it is." She waited.

"I can't get into it."

"I'm sure you can't." A touch of disdain crept into her voice. "This is hard for me, you know."

What, thinking your son was almost killed, or the inconvenience of having to look after him for a few days? Eric tried to drive the thoughts out of his head. If he dwelled on bitterness, it would start to control him. He couldn't allow that, for Patrick's sake. "I know," he finally said. "I'll take him to school this morning, so you have the whole day to juggle your schedule."

"Thanks." She sounded relieved.

Eric hung up and made Patrick's breakfast, then helped him get ready for school. After he'd seen Patrick safely to his classroom, he sat for a moment in the Honda, idling in the school parking lot. He took out his ever-present spiral notebook and flipped it open. While Patrick had eaten lunch at the Kenton Mercantile on Saturday, Eric had copied down the names of all the mothers and fathers and their addresses from Mattingly's files.

He'd drawn a circle around *Margaret Eleanor Miles* and *Terry Lynn Miles* and their address: 207 North 7th Street, Kerry's Landing, Oklahoma.

He found Kerry's Landing in Patrick's road atlas. It was in southern Marshall County, south and east of Madill, right on

Lake Texoma. He remembered he'd heard that the town was a resort community on the lake and was also home to a small liberal-arts college.

And it was where his parents had lived.

Eric pulled out his cell phone and called Solomon and Associates. When his boss came on the line, he growled, "Where the hell are you? Staff meeting, remember?"

"I won't be in today. Something's come up."

"What?"

"Personal business."

"Eric, are you crazy? These reports—"

"I know that. Get Dodds to finish them. She's good."

"For God's sake, Eric! What's the matter with you?"

Eric shrugged. "I can't explain. I'll call when I can."

"Eric—"

Eric pushed the End button. Fifteen minutes later he was on Interstate 35, heading south.

It was just past eleven o'clock, iron-gray clouds rolling across the sky, when he slowed the Honda to drive through Madill, seat of Marshall County. He took a wrong turn and wound up having to loop the courthouse square three times before figuring out where to go. The square made him think vaguely of Boise City. Both towns had large gray courthouses and a ring of small businesses around them. But there the similarities ended. Madill was pleasant and appeared to be thriving, whereas Boise City seemed to Eric to be barely breathing.

Back on the right road, Eric headed south out of town. Four miles later a huge sign pointed to the turnoff for Kerry's Landing: *Pop. 4018, Lake Country's Playground and the Home of South Central College.*

He reached the city limits in another five miles, passing an identical though smaller sign. Its logo included a graphic of Lake Texoma itself, the shape that of a Chinese dragon, twisting and writhing to every compass point.

He didn't see anything like a historical society, so he finally stopped at the Kerry's Landing Chamber of Commerce, which sat a block east of the town's single traffic signal on the main drag, which was called Chickasaw Boulevard. He went into the little brick storefront building and found a middle-aged Native American woman behind the reception desk.

She looked up and said, "Morning."

Eric bobbed his head. "Hello. I wonder if you can help me. I'm doing some family research, and my parents were originally from here."

The woman smiled a little. "Where do you live now?"

"Oklahoma City."

She nodded, as if that explained everything. "Who were your folks?"

"Miles. Terry and Maggie Miles."

"Don't know them. But I just moved here in '86."

"Oh. They left around 1964."

"Go down to the newspaper office. They know everything. Ask for Curtis."

"Thanks. Where is it?"

The woman laughed. "Two doors east, honey."

Eric thanked her again and walked back outside. The air was beginning to feel heavy and thick, a spring thunderstorm coming. Spring in Oklahoma was volatile, green and gorgeous one moment, dark with the threat of incredibly violent storms the next. He turned east.

The front room of the newspaper office was small and cramped, with one sad armchair by the window. Several bundles of the *Kerry's Landing Register* were stacked on the floor. The place smelled vaguely musty, as if it hadn't been aired out in a while. It was paneled in dark wood that had begun to peel away from the bottom of the wall in places. From somewhere behind this room he heard activity—lots of it.

A small bell had tinkled when he walked in, and it took a couple of minutes for someone to come to the front room. A head popped around a corner, young, college age, female, blond. "Hi. What can I do for you?"

"I was told to ask for Curtis."

"Oh, boy. He's on deadline, but hold on."

The head disappeared. A few minutes later a man came

around the corner. He looked to be around sixty, of medium height and build but with a remarkable face, seamed and wizened. It was a face that said it had seen just about everything, and was skeptical of most of it.

"Mr. Curtis?" Eric said.

"Not Mister. Just plain old Curtis." When he spoke, it was in a resonant baritone that reminded Eric of country preachers. He came around the counter, hand extended. The seams on his face knitted. "Have we met before?"

A knot started to twist in Eric's stomach. "I don't think so. I'm Eric Anth . . . Eric Miles."

They shook hands. "Eric Miles. Where are you from?"

"I grew up in Los Angeles and later Oklahoma City. I live in the City now. But my parents came from here. That's why I'm here, doing some family research."

"Oh, thunder," Curtis said. "Miles, you said. Terry and Maggie Miles."

Eric nodded, his heart thumping. "Did you know them?"

Curtis held up a finger in a Just-a-minute gesture, then leaned back over the counter. "Jenny! I'm going out. Back in a little bit."

"What about this city council story?" the young woman's voice drifted back.

"Read my notes and write it," Curtis called. He turned back to Eric. "You want some lunch?"

"Lunch?" Eric hadn't eaten much since Saturday, and he realized he was starving.

Curtis smiled. "I guess so. Come on, let's go over to Eva's." They walked back outside. A few fat drops of rain plinked onto the sidewalk. "Ah, spring. You don't like the weather in Oklahoma, wait five minutes."

They walked past the chamber of commerce and turned at the traffic light. A block later they walked into another storefront building, this one with *Eva's Grill* stenciled in rainbow colors across the front glass. People called and nodded to Curtis, and regarded Eric curiously. They took a booth with red leatherette seats. A young waitress who also looked like a college student gave them menus and tall glasses of water.

Curtis didn't look at his menu. "Number four, no onions, and iced tea."

The girl looked at Eric.

"Oh. What's good?"

"All of it," the waitress said. "This is Eva's, after all."

Eric looked at Curtis.

"Eva's has a bit of a reputation in the area," Curtis said. "Try the hot roast beef sandwich. We might have to roll you back to the city, though."

"Sounds good."

The girl disappeared, and Eric said, "You knew my parents."

Curtis sighed and scratched his cheek. "I grew up with Terry. He was a couple of years younger, but . . ." He shrugged. "It's a small town. I knew him. He was a track star, even set a few school records. But what he really liked was cars. He could take an engine apart and put it back ten times better than when he started. But you already knew that."

Eric shook his head. "I was raised by a distant cousin, Colleen Cunningham. Did you know her? I don't think she lived around here, but she was my mother's second cousin."

"Don't know any Cunninghams from The Landing. Maggie's people weren't from here originally. They moved here when Maggie was in high school. Her name was . . . what was it? Must be getting old. Hendrickson, that was it. Maggie Hendrickson. They came from somewhere up around the city, I think. So what happened to your folks?"

Eric drew back from the abruptness of the question. "How do you mean?"

Curtis looked at him strangely. "They left here and just never came back. Terry was working as a mechanic at the Ford place over at Madill, and Maggie was waiting tables right here at Eva's. But they just disappeared. Cleaned their stuff out of their little place, and no one ever heard a word from them again."

The food came. Eric's consisted of two pieces of white bread topped with a mound of mashed potatoes, roast beef, and brown gravy. Curtis bit into a huge cheeseburger.

"I shouldn't eat this," Curtis said, "but you're only young once."

Eric ate a little.

"They just left," he said after a while.

Curtis nodded. "Not a word to anyone. Terry's dad was dead by then. He died when Terry was little. But his mother, and both of Maggie's folks, as well as Maggie's brothers, were here. No one knew where they went. It was quite the story at the time." Curtis ate some fries, and took a long pull at his iced tea. "And you mean to say you never knew them?"

"No, I—" He swallowed. The last thing he needed to do was tell this small-town newspaperman about the confusion of his name and Good Mattingly and the twins and stones. "Like I said, I grew up with a distant cousin. What can you tell me about them?"

Curtis shrugged. "They were pretty good kids. They got married right out of high school. Everyone thought Maggie was pregnant, but it turns out she wasn't. Two years went by, no baby, and then they just left. Maggie . . . Maggie had style. She was really pretty, blond as they come, and her eyes were sort of greenish-blue. Depending on what she wore, they'd look more blue some days, more green on others. She used to say that it depended on her mood, but I never put much stock in that. She was into everything in school: cheerleader, drama club, student council. And she was big into her church. You'd catch her on breaks here at Eva's reading her Bible."

Eric waited, not sure what to do or say. His parents had never been real to him. They were abstractions, about as relevant to his daily life as the president of the United States was.

Curtis bit off more of his burger, chewing slowly, clearly savoring the taste. Around them, more people had drifted in for lunch. Several spoke to Curtis as they passed.

Curtis finally swallowed. "Terry was a good guy. He had sort of a surly streak, but nothing serious. He started going to church with Maggie, but I don't know that he was ever into it as much as she was. Of course, that's the way it is with most married couples around here. He worked hard, I know that.

He worked at the Ford place but also would fix other's people's cars around The Landing, just to make a few extra dollars."

Eric nodded. "So no one had any inkling of anything wrong before they left?"

"Nope. That's part of what made it such a big deal. In fact, I'd just seen Maggie the day before they disappeared. I was in here for a cup of coffee and a piece of pie, and she served me, and we were talking about the high school basketball game from the night before."

"You mentioned their parents and Maggie's brothers. Are they still around?"

Curtis put down the French fry he'd been about to eat. "I'm sorry, son. All your grandparents are dead. Terry's mother had cancer, something to do with her colon, I think. That was in about 1984 or so. She was only in her fifties. Maggie's two brothers both moved away. They were older, and neither one liked The Landing very much anyway. One was in Atlanta, I think, and the other in Houston. The folks both died. Maggie's mom ran her car off the Roosevelt Bridge and into the lake one night. Her dad had a heart attack a year after that. I guess you don't have any roots here anymore."

The two men looked at each other.

"You know," Curtis said, leaning back against his seat, "I still can't help but think I know you."

"Do I look like either of them?"

"No, that's just it. You really don't. Well, I take that back. I guess your face is shaped kind of like Maggie's. Of course, you have to remember it's been a long, long time since I saw her face, but I think there's a little resemblance there. No, you just seem familiar in some other way." He drank some more tea. "But then, it could be a senior moment. After a while maybe everyone starts to look alike."

Eric ate a little more. The roast beef was tender but he barely tasted it. Terry and Maggie Miles had simply disappeared from their hometown. They cleaned out their house and were gone, never to be heard from again. How, and why, did they get from being a mechanic and a waitress in Kerry's

Landing to Good Mattingly's little examining room at the tip of the panhandle? And what had happened then?

"Is there anyone else around town I could talk to?" Eric finally asked.

Curtis shrugged. "Oh, sure, there's any number of people who'd still remember them, but I'll wager I know more than anyone else. You want to know what's going on in a small town, son, you visit the weekly newspaper. We know more than we print sometimes, but we know an awful lot. Look, if you find out what happened to your folks, drop me a line and let me know."

Eric nodded, his frustration mounting. Instead of finding answers in his parents' hometown, he'd found only more questions.

He picked a little more at his food, then shook hands with Curtis, put some money on the table, and left Eva's Grill. He looked back once and saw the newspaperman watching him.

He found his car and sat in it for a moment. It had rained just enough to wet the streets. Eric scanned the sky. The clouds were still thick and gray to the north, but a few lines of sunlight were beginning to filter through to the south. Strange conditions, as if the weather were waiting for something, for some decision to be made, before committing itself to rain or shine.

Eric drove around Kerry's Landing for a few minutes, feeling lost. The damned black hole he'd felt for all his life continued to dig at him, like a miner with a pick. He passed the neatly manicured grounds of South Central College, and at the edge of town, in view of the lake, he passed several homes that easily qualified as mansions. Looping around the far end of the row of vacation homes, he headed back into Kerry's Landing proper, then he realized what was nagging at him.

Terry and Maggie Miles weren't the only ones who had files in Good Mattingly's freezer. There were nineteen other couples. Nineteen other sets of twins with stone markers, buried in the hard ground where Oklahoma, New Mexico, and Colorado came together.

Eric pulled over at the entrance to Memorial Park and got out of the car. He walked into the park, circling a pond and a swing set. Redbud trees, the Oklahoma state tree, were in full bloom everywhere, the blossoms not red but blazing purple. He found a bench, sat down, and pulled out his phone and his notebook.

He waited a moment. What had Curtis said? *You want to know what's going on in a small town, son, you visit the weekly newspaper.*

Almost all of the couples in Mattingly's records had come from small towns, places Eric didn't recognize. Towns with names like Magee, Mississippi; Hebron, Nebraska; Cranfills Gap, Texas. The O'Dells, from Wheeling, West Virginia, came from the largest city, the only one with which Eric was familiar. He started calling directory assistance and began making notes.

An hour later he had talked to a number of weekly newspaper editors, a few county clerks, and a handful of rural law enforcement personnel. He looked at the notes he'd made.

It's bigger than I imagined.

Then he thought: *Kelly.*

He dug out her card and called the office number. She answered on the first ring.

"Kelly, it's Miles."

"Where the hell are you?" Faith said angrily.

"Hello to you too."

"I've been trying to reach you today. I need that answering-machine tape."

"It's at home. I'm not."

"Obviously. Where are you?"

"Kerry's Landing, Oklahoma."

There was nothing for a moment. "I could have you arrested," Faith finally said. "I could call the local authorities and have them pick you up for interfering with a federal investigation."

"But you won't," Eric said.

Faith's voice rose. "I'm warning you, don't push me. What do you think you're doing?"

"What do *you* think I'm doing? Trying to find out about my parents. What would you do in my place?"

"That's beside the point. I will handle this. Do you get that? Let me say it slowly: I . . . will . . . handle . . . it. Don't you have a job to get to?"

"Well, I did before I left."

"Don't fool around with this. I'm telling you, I'm taking care of it. You're part of the subject of this investigation, not one of the investigators. Remember?" Eric heard Faith sigh, then she said in a mumbling tone, "If only you people would leave it alone."

"What people?"

"Let's just say you're not the only one who's being difficult."

Eric smiled. Despite the situation, he was beginning to like Faith Kelly. He remembered the way she'd taken Patrick's hand back in the airplane, without questioning, without hesitation. "Do you want to know what I found out?"

"Of course. Tell me."

He nodded. She was also smart enough to understand that information was information, regardless of who acquired it.

"Terry and Maggie Miles just disappeared from their hometown. There was nothing leading up to it, didn't seem to be any personal problems, nothing. They just packed up and left and were never heard from again. It got me to thinking about the other couples. I did some calling. All of them were blue-collar, in fairly low-income jobs. None had gone to college. All the women were under twenty-five. Most were from small towns, populations under ten thousand or so."

Eric waited. It sounded like Faith was making notes. "So someone, whether Mattingly or . . . someone else . . . made a profile, and they all fit the profile."

"Sounds like it to me. Your friend C.B.?"

Faith was silent for a long moment.

"Okay, that was uncalled-for," Eric said.

"No, I understand," Faith said. "I know you're frustrated.

You don't trust me, and there's no reason you should. But . . . there's so much I *don't* know. It's like having the beginning and ending of a book torn out and only reading the middle. I think I know the middle, but beyond that, I'm in the dark as much as you are."

"Mea culpa," Eric said. "But I haven't told you the most interesting thing about all these couples."

"And that is?"

"Every single one of them disappeared from their hometown about a year before the date Mattingly listed their babies as being born. They all just packed up and left without telling anyone what they were doing. And none of them, Kelly—not a *single one*—of these young men and women were ever heard from again."

24

FAITH'S LEGS WERE LONGER THAN SCOTT HENDLER'S, so she had to watch her stride, taking care not to outpace him. Still, he was in good shape—but he'd told her he was more into organized activities like softball, adult soccer, racquetball.

As dawn broke behind them, they rounded the last curve back toward Faith's house. Faith had invited him on the run more out of curiosity than anything else. She wanted to see how he'd react, and if he'd grumble about the hour, and how he felt about her not going further with him the other night. He didn't complain and had been on her porch at 5:30 A.M. sharp. He was a good running companion. He didn't talk much, focusing on the road and his breathing. Faith found she liked that. She hadn't run with other people often, but when she did, most seemed to want to have conversations during the run. She preferred the mind-cleansing experience of concentrating solely on the run.

When they reached her house, they both stood and did

some cool-down stretches on the porch. Faith pulled off her green bandanna and wiped the sweat from her face.

"Good run," she said. "Thanks." She smiled at him.

"Thanks for the invitation."

"Wasn't sure you'd come."

Hendler shrugged.

Faith cleared her throat. "Right now—" She wiped her neck. "Let me try this again. Right now, Scott, I need a friend. That's—that's it."

"I know."

She looked at him. He shrugged again.

"You working on anything interesting at the office?" she asked him.

Hendler touched his toes, straightened, and ran a hand across his head, touching his bald spot. "I'm on this bank robbery case. Fat white guy's hit four banks in the metro area."

"I heard about that one. Lots of pressure from the locals."

"Yep. What about you? What are you working on?"

"Oh, you know."

"No, I don't know. Thought I'd ask, though."

Faith stared down at him. She remembered having almost the exact same conversation with Art Dorian just before he died. Strange that she should now be on the other side of it.

"Big stuff," Faith finally said. "Today I'm interviewing a ninety-two-year-old retired nurse. Don't ask me more than that."

"Fascinating." Hendler put mock sarcasm into his voice.

Faith laughed pleasantly. She didn't laugh nearly enough, and it was a pleasure to do so. "Why, Sleepy Scott, you're teasing me."

"Oh, no, I'd never tease a Department Thirty officer. You might make me disappear."

Faith's smile faded and her face fell.

"Oops," Hendler said. "I'm sorry. I didn't mean—"

Faith put a hand on his arm, sighing. "I know. I'm still getting used to all of it, and this case I'm dealing with right now is so . . . so convoluted."

Hendler held up a hand. "Say no more. I'd better go anyway. Call you later?"

Faith was tempted to say yes but at the last second she pulled back, like a horse being reined from a gallop into a slow lope. "Make it later in the week."

Hendler studied her. "Okay, fair enough." Hendler trotted down the driveway to his car. Faith watched him drive away.

Inside, she showered, then dressed. She chose a slightly more upscale outfit than what she'd been wearing most of the time lately. In fact, she wore a below-the-knees skirt, light pastel blue, with a cream-colored blouse. She reasoned that Helen Harker was an old woman and would be more likely to open up to someone who dressed conservatively.

"Dressed more like a girl, you mean," she said to the mirror, then applied a little makeup.

By eight o'clock she was in front of Eric Miles's house. She only had to honk once, and he came down the sidewalk. As always he looked slightly frumpy, as if his clothes didn't quite fit. His hand was in his pocket, palming whatever he had in there.

"Another new look for the ever-changing Agent Kelly," he said, looking at her clothes as he climbed into the Miata.

"Stop calling me Agent. I'm not an agent. Do you have the tape?"

"And all business too. That's good." Eric dropped the little microcassette in her hand. "Tell me about the nurse."

Faith pulled away from the curb. "I did a check of Social Security records. Helen Harker is ninety-two years old. She lives in a retirement apartment on the south side of town."

Eric looked surprised. "She's here? In Oklahoma City?"

"Uh-huh. Moved here from Boise City in 1981, according to her granddaughter."

"Nice. How's her memory?"

"We'll find out."

"There's got to be some mistake," Eric said half an hour later.

Faith checked her notes. "No, this is the address the granddaughter gave me."

Eric looked at the brightly colored building with the high fence and playground equipment. "A day care center."

"Her granddaughter said she was at work, and this is where she works. Speaking of which—"

"He's with Laura," Eric said. "Cramped her style a bit, but I think I made her understand the seriousness of the situation. Let's go."

Faith noticed how his entire demeanor changed when talking about his ex-wife. His shoulders seemed to sag and his face grew longer. She sat for a moment with her hand on the door handle. "Still in love with her, huh?"

Eric turned slowly. "Is this part of the investigation?"

"No."

Eric waited for her to say something else but she didn't. "Most people think I hate her," he finally said.

Faith said nothing.

"There you go again, doing that listening thing," Eric said. "I don't know if I love her, but I don't hate her. I think I love who she was when we met, when we could share our own empty spaces: She had one from the death of her sister. And me? I never knew. Maybe the twin." He looked away, staring into the traffic. "Maybe the twin," he said again, more softly.

"Well," Faith said.

"Well. It doesn't matter."

"Maybe it does," Faith said, then got out of the car.

When they opened the front door of Heart of the Arts Child Development Center, they could hear the sound of kids—lots of them—before they could see them. A small desk sat in the front room, surrounded by a wall of colorful drawings done by the children. Faith noticed a pattern of similarity to them.

A woman in her thirties, short-cropped brown hair with gray streaks, was sitting behind the desk. A nametag identified her as Amy Lane, Director. Her eyes followed Faith's gaze. "It's 'The Snail.' Henri Mattisse. We had the kids do their own impressions of it."

Faith remembered it from her only art history class in college, abstract chains of shapes and colors. She hadn't liked it much then, but was impressed that this little southside day care center had introduced Oklahoma children to French art. "Very nice work. I understand Helen Harker works here."

Lane smiled. "Granny Helen? We'd be lost without her. Could I ask what this is regarding?"

"Certainly," Eric said. "I'm doing some family research, and her name has cropped up in some birth records."

Lane's smile grew. "I hear she helped deliver a lot of babies when she lived out in the panhandle." She stood up. "She's in the four-year-olds' room. I'll cover if you need to talk to her. It won't take too long, will it? The children miss her if she's gone very long."

"I hope not," Faith said.

Lane motioned them through a door that was divided into two halves. Faith and Eric watched as they passed through a room where toddlers were listening to a Haydn string quartet, and a group of three-year-olds were acting out a play.

They went through another door and found a middle-aged Hispanic woman directing children, who were mostly black and Hispanic, to various learning "centers." At one such center a group of five children sat coloring in circular patterns. At the edge of the table, coloring with them, sat an old woman.

"Granny Helen," Lane said softly.

Helen Harker looked up, and at first Faith thought there had been some mistake. She knew from the Social Security records that Helen Harker was ninety-two years old, but the woman at the table could easily pass for twenty years younger. Though her face was quite wrinkled, laugh lines around the eyes and mouth softened her appearance. Her hair was short and snowy white. Her blue eyes were lively and observant behind large glasses in plastic frames.

Faith saw she needn't have worried about her wardrobe. Helen Harker had the distinction of being the oldest person Faith had ever seen wearing jeans. She wore an old-fashioned shift top, and a small silver cross dangled around her neck.

"Yes, honey?" Harker said. Her voice was soft, and while it

sounded aged, it didn't carry the craggy, uneven quality of a woman in her nineties.

"You have some company," Lane said. "I wonder if I could color a mandala with the kids while you visit with these folks."

Harker looked from Lane to Faith and Eric, then back to Lane. "Well, I suppose." She looked at the children. "Will y'all miss me?"

"Yes!" the kids chorused.

Harker patted the hand of the one nearest her and, in flawless Spanish, said, "I will be right back."

She stood slowly and Lane took her place at the table. "Let's walk outside," Harker said. "It's a fine spring morning and we can enjoy the sun."

They went out onto the playground. Harker motioned them to seats at a wooden picnic-style table. "Don't tell me," Harker said. "You saw the article *The Oklahoman* did on me, and want to see if your little one could come here."

Faith and Eric both smiled. "Not quite. I'm Faith Kelly. I'm with the U.S. government." She nodded toward Eric. "And this is Eric Miles. Your name's come up in a—"

"Well, it's about time," the old woman said. "I was beginning to wonder if anyone was ever going to come. I won't be around forever, you know."

"Excuse me?" Eric said, leaning forward.

"You're here because of Good and The Center," she said.

Faith tapped nails on the table. "So you are Helen Harker who worked as Dr. Mattingly's nurse?"

Harker smiled. "Helen Harker Troutman Nordgren Echeverria, actually. Buried three husbands: a German, a Swede, and a Mexican. Also buried two of my six children, and one grandbaby. Married my last husband at the age of seventy-eight. He taught me to speak Spanish, then up and died on me a year later. But I never took any of their names. I figured I'd outlive 'em all. My mother lived to be 104, and her mother lived to 105."

Faith smiled, looking around at the day care center. "So you work with four-year-olds all day long."

"Just half days, really. They're sweet kids and most of them don't have any grandparents of their own. Or if they do, they don't get to spend time with them. So I'm everybody's Granny Helen."

"How long have you been working here?"

"Oh, five years or so. I quit nursing after I moved down here from the panhandle. Moved to the city to be near Katie—that's my youngest granddaughter. She's crazy about me and I'm pretty crazy about her. Now her little boy's about to graduate college. I sat around her house and did granny things for a while, even used to go to the senior citizens' center. But I didn't like all those old people, so I got a job. Ran the cash register at the barbecue place over there on Fifty-ninth Street for a year or two. Filed insurance forms for a couple of doctors. Then Katie told me about this place. She knew Amy, who runs it. I walked in and wouldn't leave until they hired me."

Eric smiled. "Quite a life."

Harker waved a hand dismissively. "That's just the last twenty years. I've forgotten all the really fun stuff." Her tone turned serious. "I saw in the paper that Good died, crashed his car a while back. I even cried a little bit for him, though I hadn't seen him or talked to him in all these years. He and I were close once. Not quite what you're thinking—I know that look—but we were good friends. Most of the men out in the panhandle thought Good was a sissy because he never got married, and the women just thought he was an oddball. I was one of the only friends he had. Worked for him twenty years."

"You don't seem surprised that we're here," Eric said.

"No, sugar, I'm not a bit surprised. Don't look at me like that: When you're my age, you can call people anything you want. No one ever asked me about that business that Good was knee-deep into back in the sixties. I was just the nurse, after all." A note of scorn crept into her voice. "I took care of all those girls. I saw them every day, while Good might see them once a week, and that was just late in the pregnancy. They were *my* girls."

Faith had taken out her small legal pad. "You mentioned 'The Center.' What do you mean by that?"

"Why, that's what they called it," Harker said. "Good and the other fella, the one who was behind the whole thing."

Eric leaned forward.

"But in all that time, in ten years, I only saw the man once, and that was on the last night." She looked away from them.

Brandon, Faith thought. *C.B.*

When Harker turned back to them, her eyes were wide. "I know Good lied to me. He told me later, after he'd quit practicing, just before I moved down here. He said he'd done it to protect me. He'd told me he'd come up with this treatment that would cure infertility. Of course, in those days we didn't know much about infertility. They were just starting to study it. He said he was bringing in young couples to do a research study, and that this big shot was behind it. That's what he told me."

"But you didn't believe him," Eric said quietly.

"I did at first. He was Good, after all. But you see . . ." Harker gazed off into the distance, shielding her eyes from the sun. "It'll be a fine day to bring the kids outside. They always say, 'Granny Helen, will you slide with us?' I can do a lot of things, but these brittle old bones don't want to go down that slide." Her voice trailed off as she continued to look away from Faith and Eric.

The silence drew out, then Eric said, "Granny Helen?"

The old woman turned, a momentary look of confusion on her face. Then she smiled at the nickname. She patted Eric's hand on the table. "You catch on quick." She folded her own hands together. "The Center was a building out past Good's property line. I could never keep the state lines straight out there. For one thing, they kept moving them. Every few years surveyors would come out and make some calculations and move the border a few hundred yards this way or that. I think the building actually sat on the Colorado side of the line. It was like a big barn, except it had electricity and we divided it up into three rooms. Well, they'd be called 'birthing suites' nowadays. You see, back then if you were in a normal hospital, you went through your labor in one room, the delivery in another, and recovery in another. Silliest thing you ever heard of." The old woman gave a small smile. "Good was ahead of his time in that way. He figured it out to let the girls go through the whole thing in one room. Plus, you see, they lived in those rooms."

Faith stopped writing in the middle of taking notes. "Excuse me? They lived in them?"

"That's right, sweetie. Those young couples came to us and they pretty much lived with us for a year. It usually took about two to three months for them to catch pregnant, then they'd be with us all through the pregnancy, until just after delivery. Sometimes we'd have all three rooms filled, sometimes two, sometimes only one. Once we went for nearly a whole year with no patients at all out there." Harker's face darkened and she looked away again, toward the sound of traffic out on the street. She took off her glasses, folded them carefully into her lap, and sat perfectly still.

After a long silent moment she said, "Thank you for being patient. I was ready to tell all this a long time ago, but no one ever came. And now here you are, with Good just now dead. It's funny how things come out." She put her glasses on again.

"What about the babies?" Eric asked. It came out almost as a whisper.

Harker looked at him.

"We found your records," Eric said, "the notes about releasing them to someone called C.B. What happened to them?"

Faith placed her hand on Eric's forearm and squeezed. *Take it easy. One step at a time.*

Harker watched them. "Sure you two aren't married? Well, never mind that. I'm just a silly old lady." She fingered the cross around her neck. "Lord help me," she whispered. "I don't know. After delivery, I took them to our nursery. We had a good newborn nursery set up. It wasn't big, but Good had everything we needed in there. I would clean them up, weigh them, suction out their noses . . . you know, all the usual stuff. Since they were all twins, most of them were a few weeks premature, so we had to watch their breathing, make sure they were all okay. But you know, they were all really healthy. I remember that: None of them had to have oxygen. No infections or anything. I guess Good's herbs helped with that. He never would tell me. So I'd take care of them for a day or two or a week or two, whatever they needed. I slept right there in the nursery, so I could monitor their vitals every few hours. It would always happen that I would go to eat, or to the restroom, or to run an errand or something, and I would come back and the babies would just be gone."

"Just like that," Faith said.

"Yes'm, just like that. I got all hysterical the first time, and Good came along later and calmed me down. Told me the babies were all right, that this was how it had to be. After that I'd go back to the patient room to see if they were with the parents, but the parents would be gone too. It was totally different from the way we delivered other babies, the ones from outside The Center. I always suspected something was going on over on the other side of the building, but it was locked and I never had a key."

"The other side?" Faith said.

Harker nodded. "That building was divided down the middle, and I never once saw what was on the other side." She lowered her voice. "There were people over there, though. I know there were. I could hear them moving around. But Good wouldn't tell me, and I couldn't get in."

Faith and Eric exchanged looks.

"Yes, yes, it was pretty mysterious," Harker said. "I didn't know what to make of it, and after a while I quit thinking about it and just tried to concentrate on taking care of my girls."

"Maggie Miles," Eric said suddenly.

Faith grimaced.

"The last one," Eric said. "Maggie and Terry Miles. There was nothing in Maggie's records about her delivery. All the others—"

"Oh Lord," Harker said. Her face had gone slack. "Oh my Lord in heaven. You're one of the twins. Miles. You're one of Maggie Miles's little boys."

Eric nodded.

Harker let out a little cry, then pushed herself away from the picnic table. She stood and circled away from Faith and Eric, passing behind a grouping of metal playground equipment.

"Mrs. Harker?" Faith said.

"What happened?" Eric said. He directed his voice toward Harker. "What happened to me? To my twin? My parents? What about the grave markers?"

"Slow down," Faith said. She lowered her voice. "She's an old woman. Just settle down."

"I heard that," Harker said, now on the other side of the playground.

The door to the day care center opened. Amy Lane's head appeared. "Granny Helen, is everything all right?" She cast a suspicious look toward Faith and Eric.

"Fine, honey, go back in," Harker said. The door closed. Harker looked at Eric. "What are you talking about, 'grave markers'?"

"Down the road from Mattingly's house," Eric said. He stood up and jammed hands in his pockets. "Just beyond the three-state marker. There are gravestones for all the twins. The dates, the names, all twenty pairs."

Harker's face crinkled. "No," she said. "I don't understand."

"I saw them." He took a few steps around a rough-wood fort. "I touched the stone with my own name on it. Eric A. Miles. And Edward A. Miles. I never knew I had a twin. I never knew my parents." His voice was rising. "Please. *Please!* What happened?"

"Eric, that's enough," Faith said. "I didn't have to bring you here, remember."

"Here, now," Harker said. Her voice wavered a little, then she cleared her throat and it was stronger. "Come here. Eric? Is it Eric? Come here to Granny Helen."

Eric walked unsteadily to the old woman, on the far side of the swings. He stopped within a couple of feet of her, until he could catch the scent of her perfume, something floral and old-womanish. He blinked fiercely.

"Come here," Harker whispered. She took Eric's hand and drew him to her. She opened her arms and pulled him into her embrace. The old woman wrapped her arms around him and held him tightly, patting his back. He put his face against her shoulder and closed his eyes.

"Mrs. Harker—" Faith said.

"No, it's all right," Harker said. "Everyone needs a granny sometimes."

She and Eric held on to each other for several minutes without speaking. When he finally pulled back, he just looked down at her for a moment. "I'm sorry," he finally said.

"What on earth for? Somebody needs to knock some sense into you boys and let you know it's okay to need someone." She looked down at Eric's hands. "No ring. You're not married?"

"Not anymore."

"Buried or divorced?"

"Divorced."

"Kids?"

"I have a little boy. He's five."

Harker nodded. "Do you see him much?"

"He lives with me."

Harker couldn't conceal her surprise. "Well, all right, then. Things do come around, don't they?" She walked slowly back to the picnic table and sat down. "I need to save my standing-up time for chasing the kids later." She beckoned for Faith and Eric, and they joined her. "I held one of you," she said, looking at Eric after he'd sat down.

"What?"

"I don't know if it was you or your twin. I don't know which one of you was born first, and I guess you don't know, either. It was hot that night. I remember there was no wind. That's a silly thing to remember, but you know the wind usually blows like the devil out there in the panhandle, and it was so calm, so still that night. Just hot. We had the windows open in The Center. Your mama's labor was normal and everything was fine. First twin was born, and I took him to be cleaned up. I'd done that and was ready to come back for the second one. I had the baby—you or your brother—all swaddled and in my arms and was coming back down the hall to Maggie's room."

She paused, and this time no one spoke.

"Just before I turned the corner," Harker said, "I heard a voice. I'd never heard it before." She stopped, looking beyond them, somewhere out of time. "I figure on living to 103, you know. Women in my family have been losing a year a generation, so I guess I'll go eleven more years. And if I do, I will never, ever forget that voice or what he said. He said, 'Where's that nurse? They're waiting.'"

They sat for a while, listening to the breeze and the traffic and the sounds of the children inside the building.

"'They're waiting,'" Eric repeated.

Harker nodded. "That's what he said. So I stopped. I wondered who 'they' were, and I figured it had something to do with whatever was going on in the other half of The Center. Then there was a big commotion, people running, other voices, Maggie's husband, Terry. Fine young fella; I liked him a lot. I could hear Good and I could hear Maggie. She was sort of half-yelling, half-sobbing. And of course, this other man. Then there was—"

"What?" Eric said.

"It sounded like they were fighting. Struggling with each other, but I didn't know who it was. Someone fell: I heard them hit the floor. I started to back up. I was scared, didn't know what in the world was happening. Then I heard the sound. It was a gun. Someone shot off a gun in there, and I heard something break, like glass. And people were running. I saw this other man I'd never seen before go running past. He was wearing a suit and expensive shoes. He saw me and stopped, then came after me."

Faith's eyes widened. She'd stopped writing long ago.

"I just wanted to protect the baby. I ran, but he caught me. I'm a little old thing, not all long-legged like you." She nodded toward Faith. "He grabbed me and he tore the baby out of my hands. I thought he was going to drop him, but he tucked him under his arm and ran. Then Good came around the corner. He told me to go somewhere out of sight and not come out until he told me. I was so scared, I just did it. I hid in a closet. There was all kinds of commotion, and it seemed like all night had gone by when Good came back and opened the closet. And he said, 'Helen, it's all over. Go back home, and don't say anything to anyone.' "

Harker waited, bowing her head, fingering her cross necklace. "I went home to Boise City. I never knew where the babies went, or Terry and Maggie."

She stopped, as if she didn't know what else to say. For the first time Faith thought Helen Harker looked truly old, her face more drawn and weathered.

"Why didn't you call the police?" Faith finally asked, in as gentle a tone as she could.

Harker raised her head. "Why, I did, honey."

Faith stared at her.

"For two days I sat in my house and did nothing. Ignored the kids, just sat there. Then I had my son drive me all the way down to Amarillo, and I used a pay phone there by the highway, and I called the FBI. I'd watched all the TV shows, so I knew they could trace those calls. I gave them what you might call your basic 'anonymous tip.' A couple of weeks later Good disappeared. When he showed up again in another month, he said he'd quit medicine forever." Harker looked sad. "I helped ruin a fine man. But something had to be done. I don't know what happened, but I had to do something." She looked up at Eric, her eyes clear. "For the sake of the babies."

Eric nodded, unable to speak.

"I wonder if that was you that got ripped out of my arms that night," Harker said. "I never saw the other twin. I don't know anything about him."

They finally walked back inside, through the day care center, and out to the parking lot. Amy Lane watched them closely as they went by, but Harker waved her off.

At the Miata, Harker said, "How do you drive something so little?"

Faith shrugged. "Thanks for talking to us."

Eric took both Harker's hands. "Thanks . . . for everything."

"Don't thank me for everything," Harker said.

Eric looked at her.

"I haven't told you everything." A car zoomed by going at least twenty miles over the speed limit. "Slow down!" Harker shouted. "There's kids around!" She looked back to Eric. "They never learn. Just before I left the panhandle, Good came to see me one night. He was in his cups, which was strange, because I'd never seen him drink more than a little wine every now and then. Poor man, I felt so bad for him. He slobbered all over me and I held him and rocked him. He finally told me that all the stuff about The Center wasn't gone after all. He had the girls' medical records."

"We found them," Faith said, remembering Patrick standing in front of the freezer.

"And," Harker said, "he said there were other things. He kept saying he had the list and that the list was safe. As long as the list was safe, the babies were safe."

"List?" Faith said. She and Eric looked at each other.

"And then there were personal things from some of the girls, stuff the other man, the big shot, took away from them before they left The Center."

"What kind of personal things?" Eric asked.

Harker looked at him. "Your mama kept a diary."

"My God," Eric said.

"At first I just thought Good was drunk and crazy. And I had a life to live. I was leaving the place I'd lived for seventy years and moving to the big city. So I didn't think about it after that. But, see, he told me where it was. He said you stand at the high-point marker, and you face north, and there's a cedar tree about twenty yards away from it, almost on a straight line. He said it's buried right under the cedar tree, in a strongbox."

"Back up," Eric said. "I don't understand. 'High-point marker'? What do you mean?"

Harker pointed a finger generally northwest. "Up there."

"Up where?" Faith said.

"The highest point in Oklahoma," Harker said. "On top of Black Mesa."

25

DREW PRESSED THE HEADPHONES CLOSER TO HIS EARS, deeply into the music. It was the Bonynge/Sutherland/Pavarotti/Milnes recording of Verdi's *Rigoletto*, a masterpiece that was unparalleled, as far as he was concerned.

There was no outside world when he listened to the opera. Nathan and Rachel Grant and their estate, on which he lived, slipped into suspended animation. Even his own life, such as it was, fell away like rocks in a landslide. He had no recollection of what he had done in Illinois, or the shots he'd fired in Maryland, or even Good Mattingly. There was no memory of having broken apart the pencils and plugging Eric Miles's fuel tank vents with them. There was only the music and the drama, and nothing existed outside it.

He sat on the floor, legs crossed, the headphones his lifeline to the music. His eyes were closed, his head back, his hands raised in front of him like an evangelical worshipper offering praise. The jester Rigoletto was on his way home, brooding on the curse pronounced by Monterone, when he encountered the assassin Sparafucile, sung by Nicolai Ghiaurov. The assassin offered to help the jester to take care of his "problem," but Rigoletto rejected him, saying the word can be as deadly as the dagger.

Although he did not speak Italian, Drew had read the libretto and studied the story so many times over the years that he almost believed he could understand the language of the singers. Language aside, he could *feel* what they said. He could hear Rigoletto's anguish and confusion, the wheels turning in his mind. He felt almost like crying out to Rigoletto, to warn him that it would lead not to the death of the hated duke but that Sparafucile would eventually kill Rigoletto's own daughter, his beloved Gilda.

Gradually, very gradually, Drew became aware of something from the outside world. A slow, steady sound. He tried to force it away. It became more insistent.

"Damn," he muttered, reluctantly removing the headphones. He turned off the CD and walked toward the sound of the knocks on the door.

Grant stood there, looking impatient. "Have you gone deaf?" the man said.

"No," Drew said, then stood aside and let Grant into the bungalow. He had no intention of explaining to Grant what he had been doing. The man would not understand. Outside, up a small curving path, he could see the main house. Behind them was the lake, choppy today as the wind rose and fell.

Drew closed the door and faced Grant. "What is it?"

"Kelly and Miles."

"And?"

"Your message with the airplane was received but ignored."

Drew shrugged.

"The woman is rude and disrespectful," Grant said. "Even worse, for my purposes, she refuses to leave my affairs alone. The timing is bad." Grant began to pace.

"What do you want me to do?" Drew asked.

Grant acted as if he hadn't heard him. "I don't know how Eric Miles first stumbled into Kenton. I don't know what made him start asking questions. But the timing couldn't be worse. And if Professor Dorian hadn't died, I wouldn't have inherited this Kelly, who seems to fancy herself a crusader."

"What do you want me to do?" Drew repeated.

Grant walked up and down, seeming to turn something over in his mind. Drew had watched the man's moods for many years now, and Grant was a decisive man. He was care-

ful, methodical, and patient, and it was unlike him to ago-
nize. Drew was interested in the change. Whatever Grant was
doing, with the terrorist attacks laid at the door of the Sons
of Madison United and all the strangeness related to this Eric
Miles, it had brought out a side of Grant that Drew had
never seen.

"We're too close," Grant muttered, then straightened up
and looked Drew in the eye. He gave a hollow smile. "You
should be thankful that you don't know the bigger picture,
my friend. I envy you, in a way. You're able to do a job and
not concern yourself with the 'why' of it. It's better that
way."

Drew waited.

"Well," Grant said after a moment, "this business with
Kelly has to end. She hasn't stopped Miles's curiosity, and
now she's a bit too curious herself." Grant wiped a hand
across his upper lip. "I want her gone."

Drew nodded passively. "And Miles?"

Grant closed his eyes, then nodded silently. "Both of
them. I just can't take the risk."

"Any special instructions?"

"No, not this time. Just follow Kelly and get it done."
Grant started for the door.

When he had his hand on the knob, Drew said, "You
didn't tell me there would be a little boy on the airplane."

Grant jerked his hand off the knob and wheeled around.
"Don't question me, Drew. Remember that you are nothing
without me. You owe me everything. Is that clear?"

"Perfectly," Drew said, and watched Grant slam the door
and start up the path to the main house.

Grant slid open the back door, the one that opened into his
study, then closed it, locked it, and drew the blinds over it.
He reached for the TV remote and clicked on the big screen.
It settled onto CNN.

Then his eyes flickered from the television screen onto his
computer. He logged into e-mail, to his anonymous untraceable account, and sent another message. This time, a threat—

a specific threat of more violence from SOMU against law enforcement.

This time, the SOMU attacks would climb the ladder to the federal level. Grant wrote to CNN, NPR, and the *Post* that SOMU was going to begin assassinating members of the U.S. Marshals Service, the nation's oldest federal law enforcement agency. They would be random and in various places.

Now the "blue flu" would become an epidemic. And now the president would have to deal with a ticking clock, the threat of more violence against the government he himself oversaw. The questions would grow more pointed. The calls for investigation, which had already begun—just as Grant knew they would—would intensify.

He flinched as the door opened and Rachel came in. "Good, you're back," his wife said.

Grant said nothing, his eyes moving back to the TV screen. CNN was interviewing a member of the new Afghan parliament. *Move on, move on,* Grant silently urged the network.

"Nathan? Hello?" Rachel said.

He finally turned to look at her. She was wearing a soft gray silk blouse with her trademark tight jeans and designer boots. "What?" Grant said.

Rachel caught his tone. "What's wrong?"

"Nothing. What do you want?"

"Don't talk to me that way. I haven't done anything." She planted hands on hips. "I wanted to remind you about the Business and Professional Women's Club banquet. It's tomorrow night, and—"

"Forget it."

"What?"

"Forget it, I said. I don't have time to attend a bunch of idiotic small-town civic affairs."

"Nathan, what the hell has gotten into you? You committed to go to the banquet two months ago. You're going to—"

"Leave me alone, Rachel!" Grant roared. "I don't have time to deal with you right now! I have important things to do!"

Rachel's eyes flared. "I don't think so, mister. Now you can play power broker with the governor all you want to, but

I'm not one of your real estate clients, and I'm not a politician, either. You pay attention to me!"

Grant picked up the first thing he saw from his desk, a glass paperweight he'd bought in Australia. He heaved it toward her.

Rachel dived out of the way, skidding onto the carpet. The paperweight crashed into the huge wooden door and shattered.

"You bastard!" she screamed.

"Get out of here, Rachel!"

"You bastard, how dare you!"

"Get out! Do you hear me, woman? Get out of this room right now!"

Rachel glared, high color in her cheeks. Then she picked herself up and slowly walked out of the study, watching him the whole time. In a few minutes Grant heard the front door slam. Another minute after that and he heard her BMW roaring out of the driveway. Headed to her parents' house, no doubt. Thirty-one years old, and she ran home to Mama every chance she got.

Grant sat down at the desk, slowly calming himself. It wasn't good to lose control. He'd built his life—both as Brandon and as Grant, he thought fleetingly—on control. First Drew, now Rachel. They did not understand. They did not comprehend the pressures he faced, now that the time was drawing near.

CNN had moved on to the federal budget, and Grant muted the sound. His hands were shaking a little. He looked at *The Execution of Lady Jane Grey* and thought of how calmly, how bravely, how tragically, Jane had faced her death. But her manipulator, the "queenmaker" John Dudley, had groveled at the end, had begged Queen Mary to be spared—even converted to Catholicism to try to win her favor. All to no avail. He had lost his head anyway.

Grant placed both hands flat on the desk in front of him and willed himself into being more calm. *Everything is fine. Everything is working. Drew will take care of any problems, and it will all be as it should be. Nothing can stop it now.*

He picked up the phone and pulled another number out of his memory. When it was answered, he said, "Are you coming to the family reunion?"

The man on the other end said, "I'll have to check my calendar," and hung up.

It was a silly code, Grant thought, but the other man had believed it necessary. And, Grant admitted, one could not be too careful. Not now.

Five minutes later Grant's private line rang. "Yes?" he said.

The other man's voice was neither loud nor soft. "What is it?"

"Faith Kelly. She won't go away."

"What a pity," the other man said after a moment.

"And Eric Miles. He's going to have to go, I'm afraid."

Another long pause. "You didn't have to call me to tell me that."

"I could never have done this without you."

"Yes."

"I mean, without all your good intelligence on the President and SOMU, it would never have come together."

"Nothing from the real SOMU group?" the other man asked.

"No. I knew they wouldn't protest. After all, we've done what they've wanted to do for fifteen years, but they were never organized enough or had the money to carry it out. We've achieved their own objectives and given them the credit for it." Grant turned thoughtful. "In the days of the Tudors, if someone had to be gotten out of the way, the king would have his people create crimes for them to have committed. That's how he disposed of Anne Boleyn when he wanted to marry Jane Seymour. Anne didn't commit treasonous adultery or incest. She may have been rebellious, but she wasn't stupid. So Henry had Master Secretary Cromwell create the crimes and mold the evidence to fit it."

"The point?"

"We didn't have to do that with the President. He saved us the trouble of finding a scandal to discredit him."

"Are you forgetting Hawthorne?"

"Well," Grant said. "A minor matter."

"Is there anything else?" A bit of impatience crept into the voice.

"No, I suppose not."

The phone clicked in Grant's ear. He put it down slowly, sat down in his chair, and turned to look thoughtfully once again at the painting of Jane Grey before the block.

In the Department Thirty national office, Daniel Winter kept his hand on top of the phone for a moment after he placed the receiver back in its cradle.

Eric Miles would have to die. And Faith Kelly as well.

Kelly had been a mistake, but then, he'd been caught up in Yorkton's rapture over the young woman, plus the fact that she'd seen Dorian's case files. If only Dorian had lived. His old friend had trusted him, and had never pushed on the Brandon/Grant case. That had been enough: the trust of two men who had once been boys together. Faith Kelly had no such trust.

Winter felt a vague sense of shame, not for what he was doing with Grant, but that he'd had to lie to Arthur Dorian to do it. Arthur had simply never understood power, no matter how much Winter had tried to show him.

And now Eric Miles would die.

Miles, who was an innocent in so many ways. Kelly, who was trying to fill Arthur Dorian's shoes, who had been Arthur's protégé.

Two more lives. In the grand scheme of the game of power, what were two more lives? Winter thought he knew what Arthur Dorian would say. But then, Arthur was gone.

Winter turned off the lamp on his desk and leaned back in his chair, sitting alone in the gathering darkness.

26

ERIC'S THIRD TRIP TO THE PANHANDLE WAS BOTH BETTER and worse than the first two. Worse because he couldn't fly, and this countryside only reminded him of what had happened with his airplane. Better because the six-hour trip from Oklahoma City to Kenton gave him time to think.

He thought about what the old nurse had told them: that all the babies were born healthy and then simply disappeared from the nursery when she wasn't looking. There was Mattingly and another man, who had to be the "C.B." of the doctor's records. A well-dressed man who seemed impatient, who said, *"They're waiting,"* as he and his brother were being born.

His twin brother.

For the first time, he knew Edward A. Miles existed. That was all he knew, but he had the proof that it was no fantasy. Whether Edward was dead or alive now, he might never know. At least Eric understood a little more about himself, about his "black hole." There was another part of him, a part he'd never known existed.

He put his hands to his head and watched the flat country slide by outside the window of Faith Kelly's little Miata. He glanced at her behind the wheel. She was back to the college student/vogue look, jeans and long denim shirt and the little "newsboy" hat. Only this time she wore black hiking boots. She'd insisted that he buy a pair as well.

"Four miles one way," he finally said. They'd already passed through Boise City and were on the last leg toward Black Mesa.

"You've said that five times now since we left this morning," Faith said. "I read about it on the Internet. Yes, it's four miles from the trailhead to the high-point marker on top of the mesa."

"Did I mention that I don't hike and that I don't really like being way out in the country?"

"A couple of times." Faith looked at him again, then glanced back to the road. He was carrying extra weight around the middle but still looked as if he could hold his own. "I'm a runner," she said. "Used to do marathons when I was in college. I'm down to only five miles a day now."

"Oh, is that all?"

She smiled, looking back to the road.

They saw Kenton spread out below, and Faith turned north at the sign pointing toward Colorado. In a few minutes they were in the gravel parking lot of the Black Mesa trailhead.

The trail was fenced off, accessible only by a strange little set of iron steps, three up to a platform, then three down to the other side of the fence. On the outside was a large sign that lectured on the flora and fauna of the area, warned about rattlesnakes, and said that five hours should be allowed for a round trip to the high-point marker.

Eric stared off into the distance, watching the little trail wind away toward the mesa. "Think we'll see anyone else on the trail?"

Faith had just strapped on a backpack and was adjusting her hat. "No other cars in the lot. It's a Wednesday in May. Not quite tourist season and in the middle of the week. I'm guessing we'll have it all to ourselves."

"That's best, considering what we have to do."

Faith nodded. She pulled two plastic collapsible shovels out of the car and handed one to Eric. She put the other in her backpack. He hefted his own pack—not a heavy hikers' pack but a standard one, the kind universally used by college students. It contained sandwiches and trail mix, several bottles of water, and his notepad and pens. Faith was similarly outfitted.

Faith did some stretching exercises against the side of the car. "Let's go. It's already noon. We can eat on the trail. The stuff I read online said there's not a lot of vertical climbing, only eight hundred feet or so, and that's right at the end. For two and a half miles it's just plain old flatland."

"Great," Eric said without emotion.

Your mama kept a diary, Helen Harker had said.

As long as the list was safe, the babies were safe.

But he was one of the babies. If he unearthed the "list," whatever it was, did he jeopardize his own safety?

He remembered the way the old woman had hugged him, the way he buried his head in her shoulder. He'd never felt that before, had never known the touch of a gentle grandmother. Even Laura, when he'd loved her most and fiercest, had never touched that spot in him. Only Patrick came close, he realized.

Up there, Harker had said.

I have to know, Eric thought. *I have to know who I am.*

He went to the iron steps and climbed them, slipping down onto the other side, onto the trail that would take him to the top of Black Mesa. He looked back at Faith; she'd just slipped her Glock into her backpack and zipped it closed.

She saw him looking. "You never know," she said.

"No, you don't," Eric said, and started walking.

The trail was wide at first, two lines of gravel in the grass. It was clear that vehicles had come down this trail at some point. Faith and Eric spotted a few brown cattle grazing close to the trail, but otherwise it was perfectly still. The only sound was their footsteps crunching the gravel.

The trail bent this way and that, and Faith's information was correct: It was mostly flat. After an hour and a half they began to climb slightly. The terrain became rocky. It wasn't a subtle change but sudden, the way a stroke attacks its victim. In the space of a few feet the trail was strewn with rocks.

They dodged them, stepping gingerly. "Thanks for making me buy the boots," Eric said, growing a little short of breath. "I don't think I could navigate this in my Hush Puppies."

Faith, striding across the rocks with her long legs, didn't appear visibly winded. "Probably not."

They stopped for a moment to sip water and let Eric catch his breath. Just ahead and above them, the trail bent at a sharp angle where it began to climb the side of the mesa itself. They could see the trail above.

They went on as the terrain grew steeper and rockier. Faith was in the lead, and would occasionally glance back and say, "You all right?"

"No more burritos for lunch," Eric groaned. "And maybe I'll start running marathons."

Faith worked her way around a boulder. "Just keeping up with that little boy ought to keep you in shape."

"Trouble is," he panted, "I *can't* keep up with him."

They stopped more frequently, hugging the craggy rock of the mesa side. They were high enough now to look back down and have the land below take on the quality of a valley. From this vantage point Eric thought he saw more trees. *Where were they when we were down there?* he wondered.

Then, almost as an anticlimax, they were on top. A single strand of barbed wire, connected to a wooden post on one side and the top of a small tree on the other, stretched above the trail, and Eric and Faith stepped onto the top of Black Mesa.

Eric doubled over, breathing deeply.

"Quite a hike," Faith said.

Eric nodded, still working on his breathing.

"Sure you're all right?"

"Stop asking me that," Eric said. "I'll be all right when I find some answers."

Faith looked at him silently. It was the first either of them had spoken of why they were here.

Eric straightened and drank some water. Ahead and a few feet to the left was a small yellow metal sign: HIGH POINT, it read, with an arrow. The trail continued, winding away from them. Eric squinted into the sun.

"I don't see any marker," he said.

"Neither do I. Let's follow the trail."

"What a rip-off," Eric said, starting to walk again. "You get to the top and you have to walk some more?"

Eric started to notice features of the mesa. He saw where it got its name: an abundance of black, volcanic-type rock visible from the trail. He also found it interesting and paradoxical that both cactus and evergreen trees seemed to thrive side by side up here. There was still no sign of wildlife except insects. Grasshoppers with large red patches under their wings fluttered into and out of their path.

"How close am I?" he said.

"To what?" Faith said.

"To whoever you're protecting."

Faith didn't answer for a long moment. She looked at him, then cut her eyes back to the trail. "Let's find the marker," she finally said.

The hike was challenging but far from the most difficult Drew had ever attempted. In fact, he didn't much care for cross-country hiking, but had done his fair share of it in the line of various projects for Grant.

One of the red-winged grasshoppers flitted by close to his face, and he waved it away. He let himself wonder about the "why" for a moment, breaking his own rule. Since last night, when he'd slipped the tracking device underneath Faith Kelly's car, he'd wondered at what Grant hoped to accomplish. Now that he'd followed Kelly and Miles out onto this lonely trail, a Heckler & Koch SP89 assault pistol in his backpack, the feelings were stronger.

He had yet to understand Faith Kelly's connection to Grant. Theirs was some sort of official relationship—he knew that much. But what her capacity was, he had no idea. As for Eric Miles, he was a total mystery. Grant had told him to focus on Kelly. Drew hadn't even seen Miles up close, yet he was about to take the man's life.

Why?

Grant's strange political machinations, of course. It had begun with Fort Defiance. Grant had had very specific instructions about that, right down to the exact verbiage in the script when he called the media. It was to be as horrifying as possible, guaranteed to make the average American bristle with righteous outrage. With the newfound hero status accorded to police and firefighters since September 11, the strike at law enforcement was guaranteed to inflame the public.

If the media was any true reflection of American life, he'd succeeded on that count. It was a political nightmare, and the president's administration was reeling because of it, and the allegations that had surfaced about his background dealings with the group.

Drew stepped across a boulder, working his way up the face of the mesa. Did it end here? he wondered. From the confluence of the two great rivers at the tip of Illinois, to an isolated trail at the tip of Oklahoma? Would this satisfy Grant?

Of course it wouldn't.

Grant was restless. Drew had known that for a long, long time. Grant could never be in the moment: He was always looking to something else.

Drew sighed. He thought of Sparafucile the assassin, feeling a strange kinship with the character. What if Rigoletto had taken him up on his first offer? How would the story have changed?

Drew squeezed his eyes closed. He was allowing his mind to stray. *Focus, focus!* There is only the job at hand, and nothing else. There will be time for other things later.

Ten more steps. Drew climbed onto the top of the mesa.

The marker was over a mile from the point where the trail reached the top of Black Mesa. The trail ended at the marker, which was rose-colored Oklahoma granite on a concrete base. Eric and Faith stopped a few feet away, shading their eyes against the afternoon sun. They'd approached the marker from the south, and a square cut into the granite at the top of the marker read: TEXAS, 31 MILES DUE SOUTH.

"Texas?" Faith said. "Why does it say Texas?"

Eric thought for a moment. "Look at the other sides."

They walked around to the east side: KANSAS, 53 MILES NORTHEAST. BENEATH IT: NEW YORK CITY, 1,605 MILES.

Faith frowned.

"I read on the Internet that Cimarron County is the only county in the U.S. that touches four other states," Eric said. "I'll just bet—"

He walked around and looked the next side: COLORADO, FIVE MILES DUE NORTH.

"Uh-huh," he said, and Faith followed him.

NEW MEXICO, 1,799 FEET DUE WEST.

Below this, toward the bottom of the marker, was the inscription THIS IS THE HIGHEST POINT IN OKLAHOMA. 4,972.97 FEET ABOVE THE SEA.

Eric swung his gaze back to the north, the direction of Colorado. On a straight line out from the marker he saw the cedar tree.

"Here we go," he said softly.

He and Faith started toward the tree.

Drew was closer to Kelly and Miles than he'd been for the entire hike, and now he had to be very careful. He stopped for a few seconds and, in one smooth motion, had the HK assault pistol out of his backpack.

He slowed his walk. There was no need to rush now. He could be precise.

He watched Kelly and Miles move away from the monument, stop at the tree, and bend down.

Drew stepped off the trail.

Eric and Faith each took out a shovel and began to dig. Helen Harker had said Mattingly buried the documents in a strongbox, but had no idea how far down they were buried or on what side of the tree.

They quickly built up a sweat. The little cedar didn't offer much shade from the high sun. Their digging quickly diverged as they began to work their way around the tree.

Faith stopped suddenly. "Someone's here," she whispered.

Eric had just struck metal. He'd been intent on his digging, searching for Mattingly's box, searching for his own life, buried somewhere out here. He looked up.

A man was approaching, off the trail, coming straight for them.

Eric blinked, took off his glasses, put them on again. The man had something in his hand.

"Oh, shit," Faith muttered, then threw open her backpack and began digging for the Glock.

The man raised his hand. The SP89 took shape in it.

Faith got her hand around the butt of the Glock.

The man's hand stopped in midair. A look of disbelief spread over his face. Eric stood up fully and faced him.

For a moment the image wouldn't form. When it did, Eric's mind couldn't process it at first.

"Edward," he finally said.

27

DREW STARED.

The man was heavier, grayer—although his hair was graying in exactly the same places Drew's was—and wore glasses, but otherwise he was the same: the shape of his face, the eyes, the build, even the way he stood. It was as if someone had held up a strange fun-house mirror beside the cedar tree.

Drew had rarely felt confusion in his life. He'd always seen things with uncommon clarity, with that *focus* that he prized so greatly. And up until a few seconds ago everything had been clear. He had a job to do. He'd been raising the weapon to fire on the two people who stood in front of him, to do his job.

Then Eric Miles had stood up and turned to face him, and everything had changed.

He didn't speak. He kept staring, and his eyes locked onto those of Eric Miles. They were the same as his, and he couldn't look away.

He caught a sliver of movement to the side: Kelly.

The woman had her own gun out and was raising it. Drew finally tore his eyes away and looked at her. Her little automatic was a toy compared to the SP89 in his hand, but she had hers in a rock-steady firing stance, and he'd let the assault pistol dangle loosely.

"Put the weapon down," Faith Kelly said.

Drew looked at her. Eric looked at her at the same moment. *Why is she speaking?* Drew thought. The human voice seemed very out of place up here.

He stood motionless.

"Now!" Faith demanded. "Put the weapon on the ground in front of you and back away."

"Kelly—" Eric said.

"Be quiet! You!" she shouted at Drew. "Put the god-damned weapon on the ground!"

Drew looked at her.

"First in my class in small arms at the academy," Faith said. "I don't miss, especially at this range."

Drew very carefully placed the SP89 on the hard ground in front of him.

"Back up! All the way to the marker!"

Drew stood still, looking at Eric again.

"Back up, I said!"

Drew backed away from the weapon until his back came in contact with the granite monument. Faith lowered herself into a crouch, keeping the Glock trained on him. When she reached the HK on the ground, she used one hiking boot to kick it away, back toward the cedar tree. Drew saw her breathe out very carefully.

"Edward A. Miles," Eric said.

Drew twitched as if he'd been pinched. He shook his head.

Eric was nodding slowly. "Then what's your name?"

Drew twitched again and thrust a hand into his pocket.

"Oh, no," Faith said. "Hands where I can see them."

Drew looked at both of them. He began to feel very strange, as if a cold wind were blowing through his brain.

"Drew," he finally said. "I go by Drew."

"But your name? Your full name?" Eric said.

"Edward Andrew. I don't really use a last name. When I have to, it's usually Worth. Edward Andrew Worth."

Eric took a couple of steps forward, then stopped, as if he didn't know what to do next. "You didn't know. Someone sent you here to kill us, but you didn't know who I was."

"I've never—" Drew stopped. What could he say? His entire life had been a sort of vacuum, an island onto which various people occasionally stepped. Nathan Grant, mostly, a presence in his life for as long as he could remember.

Grant.

Grant had lied to him.

Or had he?

Drew sat down against the monument. It was as if the earth had begun shaking under this mesa, under his feet.

He cleared his throat. "Did you know about me?"

Eric nodded. "I found out a few weeks ago. But I only found out that I had a twin named Edward. I didn't know if you were alive, or where you were." Eric spread out his hands. "Where do you live?" He laughed softly. "Is that a stupid question, or what?"

"I—" Drew's throat felt thick, as if it had been stuffed. "Grant sent me to kill you." He glanced at Faith. "Both of you."

"Stop," Faith said sharply. "Just stop right there."

Eric twisted around to look at her. "Who's Grant? Do you know what he's talking about?"

Faith pointed at Drew with the Glock. "Don't say another word."

"Kelly?" Eric said.

"Why are you protecting him now?" Drew said. "He wants you dead."

"Kelly?" Eric said again. "Grant? What's this? Is Grant C.B.?"

"The son of a bitch," Faith said slowly. "He sent you to kill both of us. He sent you to kill *me*. That arrogant old *bastard!* What's he doing? What's he involved in?"

Drew shook his head. "I don't know. I've never known. I do legwork for him, and I never ask why."

Eric's face crinkled in confusion. "You work for . . ." He looked at Faith again. "Did you—"

"No," Faith said. "Hell, no! Tell me what he's doing!"

"I said I don't know," Drew said. "That's the truth. Go

ahead and shoot me if you want to, but I don't have the answer you want."

"So you work for this man, this Grant?" Eric said. "But if he's C.B., then . . . what? Did he keep you?"

"What do you mean, 'keep' me?"

Eric shook his head. "Tell me your story. Tell me who you are."

Drew did an identical head shake. "Nothing to tell. My mother was a young girl who worked as a housekeeper at Nathan Grant's estate. She got herself pregnant, had the baby—me—and left me with Nathan. She later ran off the road drunk and was killed. Nathan—well, he sort of 'gave' me to his groundskeeper, Darrell Worth. Darrell pretty much raised me, then he died when I was seventeen. Nathan gave me the groundskeeper's cottage on the grounds and started to train me."

The two twins stared at each other.

"It seems Nathan didn't tell me the whole truth," Drew said carefully.

"'Train' you," Faith said.

Drew smiled. "He told me that he'd eventually need someone to do special projects for him. Of course, at seventeen Nathan was all I had, and I worshipped him. I've done everything he asked of me with no questions asked. He told me my mother didn't want me, and no one knew who my father was, and that he was my life. And he was right. He's given me everything."

"Why kill us?" Eric said. "I don't . . . I don't understand."

"I don't question the 'why' of what he asks me to do. I've never questioned him. He took me in when no one would."

They stared at each other a few minutes more, then Eric dropped his eyes. "Forgive me. This isn't how I envisioned meeting you. Since I learned that Edward existed, I've imagined that if he was alive, we'd have a joyful reunion and catch up with each other. I didn't think my twin would be coming up on an isolated mesa in the middle of nowhere, with a big gun to kill me."

"How did you find out about me?"

Eric told him about Colleen's dying words, about the grave markers a few miles away from this spot. He stopped short of mentioning Good Mattingly and Helen Harker and The Center.

"Grave markers," Drew said. "Headstones, with our names on them."

Eric nodded.

The confusion descended back on Drew like a cloud. "Why?"

"I thought you never asked why," Eric said.

"Maybe it's time I started," Drew said.

Faith watched the two men, her guts churning. On the one hand, she'd disarmed a hostile individual who had better firepower than she did. On the other, the situation had just taken a severe left turn. The man she was paid to protect had sent an assassin to kill her, and the assassin was the twin brother of the man Grant had asked her to investigate.

Translation: Nathan Grant was deep in serious shit, and whatever it was, he was terrified of Eric Miles.

The twin, Edward or Drew or whatever the hell his name was, was secondary. Grant had somehow managed to keep one of the babies for himself, "giving" him to his grounds-keeper to raise. Faith had read *Notre-Dame de Paris* in college, and she thought Victor Hugo would have appreciated this. Grant was Frollo to Drew's Quasimodo: Grant had kept the child, thinking that someday Drew might be of use to him. And so he had been.

The arrogant old bastard.

As both Brandon and Grant, the man had corrupted the system so that it was scarcely recognizable. Whatever had been the point of what he had done with Good Mattingly out here, he was somehow still doing something with it. Department Thirty had given him a new life, extracted some information from him, and sent him on his merry way, after which he'd quietly taken up his "important projects."

And we didn't know about it.

Art didn't know about it.

Faith shook her head. It didn't jibe with her mental picture of Art Dorian, that he'd never been curious about it, that he'd never tried to find out.

Grant had twisted everything all to hell. The two men standing a few feet away from her were the proof of it: identical twins with different lives, with different perceptions about who they were and from where they came.

Faith tightened her grip on the Glock. Even though Drew no longer seemed to present a threat, the situation was still far from being under control. She looked from one man to the other, trying to sift through everything she'd learned.

She knew Grant was scared of Eric Miles. She knew Grant was scared of her and what she might find if she and Miles kept digging into his past.

But why?

"I don't believe in coincidence," she said aloud.

Drew and Eric both looked at her.

"Neither do I," Drew said, and she thought she detected a faint smile.

"There's a reason all this is happening." She stared Drew down, green eyes boring in like a drill through bad wood. "There's a reason you were sent to kill us. There's a reason he never told you about Eric being your twin. There's a reason why the two of you have wildly different stories about your mother and your birth."

Drew smiled again. "He's very worried about you. I don't know your role here, Kelly, but I know Nathan thinks you're a little too smart for your own good."

"Tell my father," Faith muttered. She straightened. "We're coming down off this mesa, all three of us. Do you understand me, Edward or Drew or whatever you want to be called?"

"I prefer Drew. I understand you."

"Your weapon is mine now." She stopped. She couldn't threaten him with arrest. Technically she didn't have the authority to make arrests anymore. She would have to get local or other federal law enforcement to take him into custody. And at present she was four miles from her car, another five miles from Kenton, over forty miles from the nearest law enforcement. Her cell phone wouldn't even work out here.

The thought formed deliberately, like a slow storm coming. "I don't want you," Faith said to Drew.

Both men stared at her.

"I don't care about what just happened here. I don't care about the business with the airplane. I want Grant. You're right, I have no reason to protect him anymore. He's stepped outside the boundaries of what I'm supposed to do for him."

Eric stared silently. Drew started to slip a hand into his pocket.

"Hands," Faith said sharply, jiggling the Glock.

"Sorry," Drew said. "Old habit. Trust me, I don't have a concealed derringer or anything. What exactly is it you're proposing?"

"All I need is time. Time to put together what he's doing and put a stop to it."

"Kelly—" Eric said.

"No, listen to this," Faith said. "Both of you."

"I won't do anything to destroy Nathan," Drew said.

"Not even knowing that he's lied to you about your entire life?" Eric said.

"Do I know that?" Drew said. "Do I know who's lying here?"

A fragile silence descended on them. There was no sound but the wind, which seemed to change direction at will on top of the mesa. Faith shuffled her feet, but her grip on the pistol stayed rock-steady.

"Don't do anything, then," she finally said. "Just don't get in my way. Go along with him, but don't—"

"Why should I?" Drew said.

"For your brother?" Faith said.

Drew shook his head. "It's a little more complicated than that. This isn't a movie. If it were, I'd go all to pieces the minute I saw my twin, we'd go off and have a drink together and start making up for lost time. Sorry, but life's no movie. It's more of an opera. Nathan gave me my life. I won't carry out this assignment, but I'm not betraying Nathan, either."

"Just give us some time," Faith said.

Drew waited, then nodded. "I will do that."

Faith exhaled slowly.

"On one condition," Drew said.

Faith raised her eyebrows.

"The stones," Drew said. "These grave markers. I want to see them."

"Yes," Eric said.

Faith nodded. "Nothing personal, but I'm not turning my back on you, Drew. Eric, keep digging."

Eric's eyes widened. "God, I forgot all about it, with everything that's happened. I struck metal just as he walked up."

"What are you digging for? I didn't quite get around to asking what you're doing up here," Drew said.

"Records," Eric said. "Things relating to . . . our parents. Jesus Christ Almighty, I just said *our* parents."

Faith kept the Glock trained on Drew, and Eric worked for another ten minutes to get the rusting metal box out of the shadow of the cedar. He started to work the latch.

"Not now," Faith said. "We need to start down, or we'll be coming off the trail in the dark."

Eric reluctantly left the latch alone.

"Put it in my backpack," she said, and he complied. "Now get his gun. You take it."

"You won't need it," Drew said. "Not now. I want to see those stones. I want to know who's lying too."

"Walk ahead of us," Faith said to him.

"You don't trust me."

"Not even a little."

"Smart move," Drew said. "No wonder Nathan's worried about you."

It was late afternoon when they came off the mesa trail. They still had not seen another soul all day on the trail. Most of the hike was in silence. Eric periodically asked Drew a question. Some Drew answered, others he didn't.

When they reached the parking lot, all three took long

drinks of water. Eric leaned against Faith's Miata to catch his breath.

He watched the other two. Both bodies were coiled with tension. Drew looked to be thirty pounds or so lighter than Eric, and quite muscular. His twin obviously worked out regularly.

His twin.

His twin, the assassin.

Maybe we're the same deep down after all, Eric thought. *After all, I killed Weldon Hawthorne. Maybe we're both killers, just different kinds.*

"Let's go," Faith said. "Eric, you drive my car. You know where these stones are. I'll ride shotgun with Drew. Pun intended."

Ten minutes later they stood at the three-state marker. Again Eric was taken by the vastness of the land, by the incredible openness. A strange place to find all these lies and deceptions, amid this kind of openness.

He walked along the fence line, pointing out stones to Drew. Faith walked behind them, the Glock never wavering. Eric finally knelt by the fence and brushed dirt away from the final marker.

JULY 27, 1965.

EDWARD A. MILES.

ERIC A. MILES.

GONE HOME.

Drew knelt as well. He ran his fingers over the rose-colored granite, tracing the outline of the letters, just as Eric had done the first time he saw the stone.

The two twins squatted next to each other in silence for a long time. Faith stood over them, alternating her gaze between the men and the landscape. She raked a nail across her scar once. She'd managed the crisis well so far—*Too bad the guys at the Marshals Service couldn't see this!*—but the confusion had intensified. She wasn't sure if she was hunter or hunted now.

Drew finally stood up and looked all around at the short-grass prairie, the mesas in the distance. "A strange place," he said.

"Yes," Eric said.

"Who's buried here?"

Eric just shook his head.

"Is the answer in that box you just dug up?"

"I don't know," Eric said. "Maybe, maybe not."

Drew looked at Faith. "I'll do my best to stall Nathan. I'll make up an excuse for not killing you. He'll want me to come after you again. I'll try to buy some time. That's all, that and nothing more. I still won't betray Nathan. But I want to know . . ."

His voice trailed off into the vast distance, where he was studying the point where the three states touched.

"I want to know," he repeated, and he and Eric met each other's eyes.

28

IT WAS ALMOST MIDNIGHT WHEN THE MIATA STOPPED in Eric's driveway. Somewhere west of Oklahoma City, they'd watched Drew's car turn off to the south. It had seemed strange to Eric to just let him drive away, but he also recognized there was little that could be done. Kelly had no jurisdiction to arrest him. Moreover, he'd agreed to let them buy a little time to find out what the man named Nathan Grant was doing.

They had to trust him.

He's my twin. He's a killer. And we have to trust him.

Eric's head pounded so hard, he thought anyone looking in the car window at him would see his temples pulsating, like some sort of demented cartoon character. He'd met his twin, a man who was literally a part of him, a man he'd thought could help him fill in some of the blank spots, the black holes of his life.

But his twin had been carrying a gun.

His twin had been sent to kill him.

"Think you'll be able to sleep?" Faith asked.

Eric looked over at her; it had been easy to forget she was there over the last few silent hours of driving. She was just a dark silhouette, nothing more than a shadow. *In more ways than one?* Eric wondered, then closed his eyes.

"I'm tired and I'm sore and I don't know what to think about anything," he said. "Your guess is as good as mine."

Faith nodded in the dark. "I'm going to call in a protective detail for you."

"You can do that?"

"I can get a couple of federal marshals to watch the house. I'll get a team to your ex-wife's house too. I think"—she cleared her throat—"I think that until this is resolved, she and Patrick may be in danger too." Her tone softened. "I'd hate to see anything happen to that little boy because of all this."

Eric nodded.

"And," Faith said, "I was a deputy U.S. marshal until not long ago, and I still have friends in the local office. I'll get someone to come out tonight."

"Thanks."

Faith waited a long time, until the silence grew uncomfortable between them. "I'm not sure what to say about today, Eric."

"Nothing. You can't say anything. Just let me have the diary, and I'll try to make some sense of it."

Faith paused again. "I can't do that."

Eric turned sharply. "What?"

"I can't let you take the diary."

"What's that supposed to mean? I dug up the box! It's my—"

"Eric, you are technically a material witness in this case," Faith said, her voice weary. "You have even been a subject of investigation in the same case. Whatever is in that box is evidence, and until I see it and evaluate it, I can't let you or anyone else have it."

"Am I hearing this? I can't believe this! Helen Harker told us that my mother kept a diary. *My mother!* My mother wasn't playing your shadow games. She was just used by your pal Grant. There's nothing to—"

Faith shook her head. "No. Not until I've seen it first."

"Look, I don't know what the 'list' is that Helen talked about. That's fine, I don't want that. But the diary—"

"No. I'm sorry, I understand why you want it, but I can't."

Eric slammed a fist down on the dashboard. "Look, this isn't just an investigation for me. It's my life—it's my whole life. Don't you get it? The guy with the gun up there, that was my *twin*, for God's sake. This is not just a *case*."

"I know that, and if it makes you feel any better, my personal feeling is that you should get to read it. But you have to look it at a different way. I mean, you didn't just get a kick out of ruining Weldon Hawthorne. I don't think you're the kind of person that gets off on that sort of thing. But it was your job, your responsibility, to follow it wherever it led. Now I've got to do this, and you need to respect it. I just need a little time to look at it. This is all getting more complicated by the day—by the hour, for that matter. I need to analyze it. I know you understand that."

Eric sat there for a moment. The drumbeat in his head seemed to have receded. Now there was nothing but the sound of the Miata's idling engine and its headlight beams playing over his garage door a few feet away.

"I want the diary," he said.

"No."

"Afraid I'll compromise your security? I've got the man's name: Nathan Grant. I can go in the house, log onto the Internet, and put his name in a search engine and probably find out everything about him."

Faith leaned toward him. "But you won't find out what you really want to know that way. You won't find out about your mother and your twin . . . and you."

"So? I know his name, and I bet I can find his address. I could find him and blow him away, just like that. You mean you're not worried about *that*?"

"No, I'm not."

"Why not?"

Faith leaned closer to him. "I saw the video. I saw you shoot Hawthorne. But see, I watched the whole thing, not just the graphic part where you shot him in the head. I watched it to the end, where you climbed over the hood of the car and grabbed Hawthorne's body. And I saw you look up, right toward the camera, and I saw you crying."

Eric looked away from her, staring out at his driveway.

"Here's the biggest reason of all." She tapped his leg and he looked at her again. "I've seen you with your son. You're not the kind of man who's going to go off and kill Nathan Grant just for the sake of killing him."

Eric bowed his head.

"As soon as I see what's in it," Faith said, "and as soon as I know what it means, we'll talk about it. You have to trust me."

Eric nodded. He felt numb, as if he were encased in a cocoon. He put his hand on the door handle, then turned back for a moment. Faith's features reflected back in the dashboard lights. "Were you really first in your class in small arms?"

She smiled. "No. Fifth, actually. Still not bad out of a class of ninety students. But I didn't think *fifth in my class* sounded very intimidating."

"Good point."

"Try to get some sleep."

Eric nodded, got out, and closed the door. He watched as she pulled back out of the driveway and into the street, then drove to the end of the block. He let himself into the house, flipped on a few lights, then turned them all off again.

The emptiness of the house overpowered him, and he knew why.

Without thinking, he locked the house and went to the garage. He drove the Civic north, and twenty minutes later was at the door of Laura's condo in Edmond.

She came to the door barefoot and wearing a long nightshirt with GEORGETOWN LAW on it and matching sweatpants. She looked tired, but not as though she'd been asleep.

"Eric?" she said. "It's after midnight. What the hell are you doing here?"

"Can I come in? You weren't asleep, were you?"

She shook her head. "Going over a few last-minute briefs." She stepped aside and he walked in.

Her condo mirrored her newfound money and status, all modern, abundant black lacquer and chrome and clunky furniture that looked painfully uncomfortable to Eric's eye. She had a home entertainment system that would probably have cost a year's salary for Eric, and expensive abstract prints on the walls.

"You look terrible," Laura said. "What have you been doing?"

"Got anything to drink around here?"

Laura raised her eyebrows, and it almost took his breath away. She was still indescribably beautiful to him, and he felt like a fool for even having the thought. "Like what?"

"Something stronger than orange juice, I hope."

Laura smiled. "Bad day, huh? It must be, for you to want a drink."

"Interesting day."

He sat in one of the uncomfortable chairs while she went to the kitchen. When she came back, she handed him a glass. "Jim Beam," she said. "Other than an occasional beer, the only alcohol I ever saw you drink."

"And you still keep it around?"

"Don't get any ideas," Laura said quickly. "I keep the bar stocked for entertaining."

Eric raised the glass and took a sip. It had been a long, long time since he'd had a drink of straight whiskey. "Glad we cleared that up." He considered putting his feet up on the glass coffee table, but decided it wasn't worth a fight. "I've traveled more than eight hundred miles today, taken an eight-mile round trip hike to the highest point in Oklahoma, met a twin brother I didn't know existed until a couple of weeks ago, and saw that twin point a gun at me. I dug up a box that may or may not contain answers to who I really am, but I can't look inside the box because it might compromise national security."

Laura furrowed her brow.

"And I still have reports to write," Eric concluded.

"Jesus," Laura said. "You're really not making all this up, are you?"

Eric laughed out loud. "No, my dear, I certainly am not. How's Patrick?"

"He's okay."

"That's it? Just okay. How was his day today?"

"All right. It was a normal day."

Eric restrained himself. "I'd like to look in on him."

"Just don't wake him up. He took forever to go to sleep."

"Different situation, everyone's all tense. That's normal. Did you read him a story before bed?"

Laura shifted uncomfortably.

"That's part of our bedtime routine, Laura. You know that."

"Well, I'm not as good at signing as you are," Laura said. "I can't quite get all the words, and he gets cranky when I don't know the sign for a word."

Eric sighed. "You can take classes."

"When would I take classes?" Laura snapped, then backed down.

Eric held up his hands. They'd had this discussion before. He walked down the hall and turned the knob of Patrick's room. He let in just a tiny sliver of light, so as not to wake the boy.

Patrick's blond hair splayed out on the pillow. A few inches from his left hand was the little green-and-yellow stuffed turtle Eric had given him when he was just a baby. Patrick had never spent a night of his life without it.

Eric watched him sleeping for a long moment, then reached down and fussed with his covers, not so much because they needed adjusting but just to *do* something, to have some connection with Patrick in that moment. The boy stirred, moved an arm, sniffed the air, and was still again.

Eric closed the door but stood in the hallway for a moment. Faith Kelly was right. She had him pegged. No, he wouldn't find this Grant's address and wait for him with a gun. That wasn't the way to handle it. As much as he'd argued with Faith, she was right. He would have done the same thing if he'd been in her position. He would have to wait.

Patrick needed him and Eric couldn't afford to do anything crazy, for the boy's sake. It might chew on him, it might keep him awake nights, it might obliterate his own sense of who he was, but he wouldn't go over the edge. Not as long as Patrick needed him.

Feeling a little better, a little stronger, Eric turned and walked back down the hall, away from his sleeping son.

29

GRANT HAD SEEN DREW RETURN TO THE ESTATE shortly after one A.M. He'd been waiting for a phone call or an e-mail, some sort of sign to know the job was finished. But the sign hadn't come. Ignoring Rachel's ranting and pounding on the door, Grant had locked himself in his study for the entire day. He had even gone to sleep there, finally, sometime after two o'clock.

A little after seven o'clock in the morning, with the sun reflecting off the lake, Grant stood up from the leather couch, raked his fingers through his hair, and stretched. His joints complained. He was in excellent shape for seventy-eight, but age still had its way of catching up. He took a little longer to get going in the morning, a little longer for the body and the mind to get in sync with each other. He promised himself he'd go down into the basement and put in a full hour with the StairMaster. Right after he'd done what he had to do this morning.

He slid open the door that led onto the deck. He walked out into the sun, listening to the birds. He loved Lake Texoma, the pastoral quality of this area, with its earthy people and calm nature. People here got excited over high school football games and homecoming parades and city council elections. It had been a stroke of good fortune that he'd managed to convince Professor Dorian all those years ago to let him settle here. Of course, there had been certain other geographical advantages as well, things Dorian never knew. But the setting had been perfect for him to pursue his plans.

Grant held the rail and walked down the steps from the deck, then took the curving stone path down to the old groundskeeper's cottage, which sat even closer to the lake than the main house. To his surprise, Drew was in the little yard, pruning his rosebushes.

"You never seemed to need much sleep," Grant called as he came down the path.

Drew looked up at him for a moment, then went back to his pruning shears. "The light's better in the mornings for yard work," he said.

Grant came up to the yard and sat on a wrought-iron lawn bench. "I expected some sort of report before you came home last night."

Drew was silent, snipping away.

"I take that to mean you didn't get the job done," Grant said.

"No, I didn't."

"May I ask why?"

Drew waited a moment, the shears open in midair. "There were other people around. I couldn't take the chance of collateral damage."

"Drew, look at me."

The younger man turned around, placing the shears very carefully on the ground beside him. He looked up into Grant's dark eyes. Grant searched his face, studying the set of his jaw, the way his eyes seemed to observe everything at once. But Drew gave away nothing. Nothing at all.

"Tell me," Grant said softly.

"Nathan, why didn't you tell me about Eric Miles?"

So that was it. He'd gotten close enough to see Miles's face. Grant had known he'd have to deal with this issue eventually. "What difference would it make?"

"A twin brother, Nathan? I've always trusted you to tell

me the complete truth. Now, after all these years, I have to discover I have a twin brother when you send me to kill him?"

Grant crossed his legs. "I had hoped it wouldn't come to this. I've been very careful to have you keep your distance from Miles, during the work you've been doing lately."

Drew stood up abruptly. "Christ, Nathan! How can you be so matter-of-fact about it?"

Grant sighed deeply. "Your mother didn't want you, Drew. Eric was born first, and he was healthy. You came second, and you were smaller, less developed. She thought you were sickly, and she didn't want you." He leaned forward, fixing his eyes on Drew's. "Do you get that? *She did not want you.* She wanted the other twin instead. She dumped you here and ran off. What would it have accomplished for me to tell you all this?"

"Why—" Drew stopped. He jammed a hand into the pocket of his jeans and began to palm whatever was in his pocket.

There was a sound behind them, and Grant turned to see Rachel coming down the path. She was still in her nightshirt, her hair disheveled, and she was wearing her glasses: She hadn't put in her contacts yet. "Oh, not now," Grant murmured.

She stopped by Grant, alternating her gaze between the two men.

"Good morning, Rachel," Drew said, when Grant didn't speak.

Rachel nodded to him, then looked back to her husband. "What the hell is the matter with you?"

"Take care in your tone, Rachel," Grant said. "Is there a problem?"

"Is there a *problem? Is there a fucking problem?*"

"Don't be vulgar."

"Vulgar? I'll tell you what's vulgar: throwing things at your wife, locking yourself in that goddamned study of yours and ignoring the world. Now we're going to talk, you and I. Sorry to walk in on you, Drew, but he's mine now."

"Go away, Rachel. I have things to do."

" 'Things to do'! Well, let me tell you something, hotshot. You want to know what I did last night, after I couldn't get you to acknowledge that I exist? Huh? You want to know?"

"I don't care. Go back to the house."

Rachel's blue eyes flashed, equal parts rage and mischief. "I went to the cowboy bar over at Durant, and I drank shots and beers until two in the morning. And then I fucked some redneck in the parking lot. I didn't even get his name, but he thought I was the hottest thing he'd ever seen." She balled up both fists. "How do you like that, old man? I'm not just some trophy, you know! I'm—"

Grant slapped her face.

Rachel staggered backward. "Why, you sorry—"

Drew took a step. "Nathan, I don't think—"

"Stay out of this!" Grant roared. He wheeled back around. "Don't cross me, Rachel. I've sent away better women than you. I will leave you without a penny. No BMW, no designer clothes, no jewelry, nothing! You sleep with all the cowboys you want, but stay out of my way!"

"You bastard," Rachel whispered. "I can't believe I didn't see you for what you really are. You are a chickenshit bastard."

"And *you* are a vulgar, uncouth hick with nothing going for you but your looks. Now leave me alone."

Rachel rubbed her cheek where he'd slapped her. She looked at him, then at Drew, slicing her gaze back and forth between the two men. A strange look came over her face.

She stared for another moment, then turned without another word and walked up the stone path to the main house.

"That was unnecessary," Drew said when she'd gone.

"Don't you cross me, either," Grant said. "Remember, boy, I'm the only one who wanted you. I'm the only one who's ever tried to be anything to you. Without me, you are nothing. You do not exist in the eyes of the world. If you get any crazy ideas about leaving and trying to hook up with Miles, just remember: You don't have an identity. You don't have a

Social Security number, you don't have a birth certificate. You have nothing that will let you fit into the rest of the world. You owe me . . . *your life.* You owe me everything. The fact that you now know you have a twin brother is irrelevant. That twin brother of yours could bring everything I've worked for crashing down, and I'm not going to allow it."

"You shouldn't have slapped Rachel. That was . . . inappropriate."

"She's a stupid wench. She likes my money and my power. Beyond that, she's nothing."

"What is it, Nathan? What is it you're doing?"

"I'm playing the same game others have played, except I'm better at it. I've been patient. That was John Dudley's failing. He wanted everything immediately. That's why he failed, and it's why I'll succeed." He uncrossed his legs. "You understand that you are mine, Drew?"

"Nathan, I—"

"Are your feelings clear on this matter? I have an idea, and it may work better than killing your brother. You should be relieved to know that."

Drew nodded.

"He and the resourceful Officer Kelly must be convinced to keep their noses out of places they don't belong. At least until Monday."

"What's Monday?"

"Memorial Day, Drew."

Drew looked impatient. "I know it's Memorial Day, Nathan. What's the significance to . . . to whatever your project is?"

"Never mind. You keep focused on your individual job. Let me worry about the rest of it. But I have a way to get to Eric Miles, and this time he'll pay attention." Grant stood up. "You'll go to Oklahoma City this afternoon. I have the information all ready for you."

"What's the source?"

"What? You can't possibly think you're my only person in the field. I hate to tell you this, my boy, but I have other resources. Now get yourself together and be ready to leave by noon. Come up to the house and I'll brief you. You may need help with this, and I'll put you in touch with my other people."

Grant started up the stone path.

"Nathan," Drew called after him. "The graves. I saw the grave markers."

Grant stopped. He turned around slowly.

"I saw them," Drew said. "The stones. *Edward A. Miles,* Nathan. Is that my real name?"

Grant shrugged. "Yes. That's what your mother planned to name you."

"But you said she didn't want me. Why would she bother to name me if she didn't want me, Nathan?"

Grant's face hardened. "I asked you if your feelings are clear on this. Are they?"

Drew waited a long moment, standing there on the sidewalk in jeans and a white T-shirt, the pruning shears next to him. He stood very still, and for a crazy moment Grant thought he'd stopped breathing. He was that still.

"My feelings are clear," Drew said.

"Good." Grant started back up the path.

"The graves, Nathan. Who's buried out there?"

Grant stopped again. He turned and smiled.

"No one," he said.

30

FAITH SLEPT PAST EIGHT-THIRTY IN THE MORNING, something she hadn't done since she was an undergraduate. When she jerked awake, with spring sunlight filtering down through the blinds, her first thought was *I'm late for work.*

Then she remembered, blinking away the sleep: *I don't have a boss here. I don't even have to go to the office if I don't want to.*

She got out of bed and stumbled into the kitchen, putting on the coffee. She made a piece of toast and nibbled it indifferently, then drank two cups of coffee, strong and black.

More awake, she thought about the previous day. Her muscles felt a little tight from the long hike over rough terrain, but she wasn't really sore. Physically she felt pretty good. But her mind was already in overdrive, thinking of Eric Miles and his twin.

She showered and dressed, then went into the living room and opened her backpack. She pulled out the rusting metal box, smelling its age. She took it to her dining room table and sat down. The table made her smile: It was a new wooden table to replace the one she'd shot through last year. Her colleagues at the Marshals Service office had bought her the new one. It had been delivered with a note: *Faith—don't try to shoot through this one.*

She started to work on the box's latch, then decided it was much too quiet. She'd had enough quiet the day before, with the hike up Black Mesa and Eric Miles's strange silences. She put on a David Sanborn CD, and as Sanborn's rock-fused sax filled the house, she went back to work.

She'd figured opening the box would be difficult, but it seemed Good Mattingly hadn't bothered to lock it, only fastening the simple outer latch. Faith paused, realizing it made a sort of sense. Why fool around with a fancy lock, when the box was buried on top of a mesa at the end of a rugged four-mile trail? There was a certain logic in it.

She opened the lid and found two large sheets of plastic, just like the ones wrapped around the medical records in Mattingly's freezer. One was small, surrounding only a couple of sheets of paper. The other was more bulky.

Faith unwrapped the bulky one first. Inside was a strange assortment of items. They looked random, as if they'd been scattered on someone's floor by accident. A small gold crucifix on a chain; a couple of unmailed letters on flowery stationery, addressed to a PO box in Cranfills Gap, Texas; a pink baby rattle, broken and crusted with age; a key chain from a car dealership in Wheeling, West Virginia. Just fragments, snippets of the lives of the young women who had been foolish enough or desperate enough or naive enough to get mixed up with Charles Brandon.

At the bottom of the pile was a battered spiral notebook. On the cardboard cover was written: MAGGIE'S JOURNAL.

Logic dictated that Faith look at the other papers first, the "list" Helen Harker had told them about. But she couldn't resist opening the journal Maggie Miles had kept:

June 4, 1964

What a place! Can't believe this is part of Oklahoma. It's sure a lot different from The Landing. Terry says everything will be OK, but it still feels wrong. May the Lord forgive me.

Faith flipped pages. The portrait of Margaret Eleanor Miles that emerged was not what she'd expected. This blue-collar, small-town girl came across as literate and smart, funny and devout. She was absolutely devoted to her husband, yet scared of what was coming.

Faith stopped at the entry for August 28, 1964, where Maggie had written a passage from the Bible, in her own paraphrase:

From Romans 5—suffering makes character, character makes endurance, endurance makes hope, and hope does not disappoint.

I hope. I hope I will someday understand what I've done here. I know I have sinned against God and Man, but I didn't see another way. If only Terry

Faith turned the page. A little flap of paper was in the center of the book, where pages had been torn out. The next entry was October 4, 1964:

I am pregnant now. Dr. Good confirmed today. It's why we came, but why do I feel this way? It is my sin. This is my punishment. I am so mixed up, I can't think straight. I almost feel like

I'm becoming another person. Am I? Does the baby inside me make me lose who I was? Jesus, help me to stand.

More missing pages, then January 10, 1965:

He was here today. Terry was gone for a walk around the grounds and didn't see him. Thank God for that. I don't know why he comes around. He just stares at me and doesn't say anything. Dr. Good came and told him to go away and leave me alone. I don't understand this at all. But we have the money. Terry fixed it just like he said he would. No one will ever know.

May 23, 1965:

Babies are kicking like the devil! They are amazing, and yet I don't know how I am supposed to feel. They are part of me, but in some ways they aren't. Is that crazy?

There were no more entries. Faith saw more flaps of paper where the pages had been ripped. But who'd ripped them? Maggie, or Good Mattingly, or Brandon?

So now Faith had a picture of who Maggie Miles was, but no answers. Only more questions, around and around and around with more questions.

She carefully put the journal aside and unwrapped the other sheet of plastic. In addition to two sheets of paper, there were several photographs clipped to the papers. Faith let the photos—all of young women, she assumed the mothers—fall to the tabletop, and looked at the papers.

Helen Harker had told them that Dr. Mattingly believed as long as this list was safe, the babies were safe. Faith's heart began to match the rhythm of Sanborn's saxophone.

The paper was brittle but was heavy stock. The printing seemed to have been typed on an old-fashioned manual typewriter in pica type. The list was divided into columns. On the left were names Faith recognized: Mary Jane O'Dell, Celia Ramirez, Rhonda Porter, Margaret Miles . . . the mothers. The names and dates of birth of their twins were just below theirs, slightly indented. A line was drawn in red from the name of each twin across to the second column, another list of names.

Faith's pulse quickened again. Her eyes flitted up to the top of the page. She'd been drawn to the names and hadn't read the column headings.

The column on the left was headed SELLER.

The one on the right was BUYER.

"Oh God," Faith muttered.

This was what no one wanted to talk about. This was why Winter had lied. Brandon and Mattingly weren't doing some infertility experiment that went awry: They were selling the babies.

Faith brushed a stray strand of hair back out of her face. She scratched at her scar. She blinked at the page, tracing her finger down the list of the buyer column.

"Jesus, Mary, and Joseph," she whispered, then did something she hadn't done outside of mass in many years: She crossed herself.

She recognized all of the names in the buyer column. No one who was reasonably well informed could live in the United States of America and not know them: They were among the wealthiest, most powerful families in the country—business, entertainment, politics. Especially politics.

And they had all purchased babies from Charles Brandon. Babies born in the isolated Center at the tip of the Oklahoma Panhandle.

But the last entry, the one for Margaret Miles and her sons Eric and Edward, had the buyers' names scratched out. Faith held the paper up close, but she couldn't decipher what was under the heavy markings.

Something had happened. For some reason, Maggie Miles's babies didn't go where they were supposed to go. Eric wound up with his mother's distant cousin, and Edward—"Drew"—had somehow been with Brandon/Grant for all his life.

Faith looked at the list again.

The first two babies on the list belonged to Mary Jane O'Dell of Wheeling, West Virginia. According to this, her first twin, Brenda, had been sold to Warren and Eloise Saunders of Los Angeles. Warren Saunders headed the most powerful media conglomerate in America. The other twin, Linda, went to Hank and Nan Archer of Oklahoma City, Oklahoma.

Linda O'Dell.

Governor of Oklahoma.

Possible presidential contender.

Faith had to get to the office. She needed a secure phone line and the DOJ computer database.

Moving quickly, as if someone were chasing her, she folded all the items back into their plastic sheets, then put the whole thing into a brown paper grocery sack. She had her hand on the doorknob when the phone rang.

"Don't have time," she muttered, and considered not answering it. But she remembered that the office phone was now programmed to roll over, first to her home, then her cell, and she grabbed the phone without looking at the caller ID.

"Yes? Faith Kelly."

"Hi, honey," her mother said.

"Mom, I—"

"I didn't know what time you went to the office," Maire Kelly said, "so I thought I'd try you at home, and here you are."

"Mom, I'm just headed out the door. Can I call you later?"

"Oh, I know. You cops are all alike. Your dad's got this rapist investigation, and Sean's always away undercover now, and you . . . you've got this new thing. Well, I just wanted to know if you were going to be able to get away and come up for Memorial Day."

Faith flexed and unflexed her hands. The Kelly family Memorial Day picnic was a long-standing tradition. There was a mountain of food, gallons of beer, a hundred or more relatives from various branches of the family, and her grandfather, now seventy-five and retired from the Chicago PD, would play Irish tunes like "Scatter the Mud" and "Si Bheag Si Mhor" on his fiddle. She hadn't missed one yet, even when she'd been in the academy—even since she'd moved to Oklahoma.

"I don't think so, Mom. I'm sorry, but I'm working something big right now, and—"

"Oh, honey, your dad will be so disappointed."

"Mom, I can't talk now. I'll talk to you later."

She threw the receiver back in its place, hoping her mother wouldn't get too upset. *Families can be such a pain in the ass,* she thought.

But at least I have a family.

She thought about Eric Miles, and about Drew, and all those mothers and twins.

Faith ran to her car.

Three hours later Faith had barely moved from her computer in the office downtown. Her eyes were strained, her neck and back ached, and her wrist hurt from mouse-clicking and typing.

She sat back, glanced at the catfish on the wall, looked at the computer, then at the notes she'd made. She'd filled nearly half a legal pad.

Her pulse roared in her ears like a plains thunderstorm. She knew who all of the twins had become. She knew where they lived. She knew what they did. They were all powerful people, all highly placed. All had birth certificates with the names of the people who'd bought them listed as their biological parents. All had Social Security cards with their "new" names.

But something was still missing. The link that would tie it all together, that would bring it into the here and now. As it was, it made no sense for Grant to kill Eric Miles and her just to keep this list secret. There was something else. Grant was doing something *now,* something with these people. And how did Eric Miles and the Hawthorne scandal fit into it?

The department . . . Whatever Grant had been doing, he'd been doing it under the protection of Department Thirty.

Faith reached for the phone to call Virginia, then slowly pulled her hand back. Daniel Winter had lied to her. She didn't know why. But she did know she couldn't trust him.

"I think I have a problem," she said to the empty office.

31

SOLOMON AND ASSOCIATES WAS IN ONE BENHAM PLACE, a ten-story office building along Oklahoma City's Broadway Extension, the main corridor from the city proper into the northern suburbs. The agency occupied a modest office suite on the fifth floor, with a small conference room that looked east, providing a startling view of the city's "antenna farm," where all the radio and television broadcast towers for the area were concentrated.

The team working on the Davis for Senate account was gathered around the oval conference table, legal pads and spreadsheets before them. Eric had given his presentation almost on autopilot, without really thinking about it. Now two of the team were arguing about whether transportation or health care issues would play better in the rural areas of the state. Eric tuned out the debate and stared out toward the broadcast towers. His mind was still on top of Black Mesa, facing a man who looked like him.

The debate continued to rage until an intercom clicked and a female voice said, "Is Eric in there?"

"I'm here," he said, sitting up straight.

"Would you come out here, please?"

The rest of the staff stared at him as if he were a child being sent to the principal's office. He shrugged, gathered up his briefcase, and left the room. At the front desk stood his old college friend Jake Solomon, a small man with reddish-brown hair and a confident manner.

"What's up, Jake?" Eric said.

When he saw his friend's face set in a grim line, he was afraid he was about to get reamed for his absences the last few days. But Solomon only said, "In the parking lot."

"What's going on?" Eric said.

They headed out of the suite and took the elevator to the ground floor. "You know the phrase 'When it rains, it pours,' don't you?" Solomon said.

Eric's stomach lurched. "What now?"

"It seems, my friend, that your car's been stolen."

Eric almost laughed out loud. In the midst of the murky pool his life had become, something as mundane as auto theft suddenly seemed funny. Solomon walked in long strides, and even though Eric was taller than he, Eric had to jog to keep up with him, his legs and feet already aching from the eight-mile hike the day before. They reached the area of the Benham parking lot that was reserved for Solomon employees. Eric always parked in the same place, in the far corner, against the fence, pointed toward the street.

The Honda was gone.

Standing in his parking spot was a slim Latino kid in his late teens or early twenties. He wore a T-shirt with the logo of a landscaping service. The name patch on his shirt read *Jose*.

"Jose, tell Mr. Anthony what you told me," Solomon said.

Jose shrugged. "I'd just finished up edging that area by the fence and was sitting down taking a break. I heard a bunch of rattling over here."

"Rattling," Solomon said.

"Yeah, you know, rattling." Jose shrugged. "Like somebody's messing around. And I looked around the corner of the building and here's somebody messing around with the Honda.

"I started to walk over there, thought there might have been trouble and I could help. But I got a few steps closer and saw that the guy's working a coat hanger in the window."

"Go on," Eric said.

"I yelled 'Hey!' but the guy didn't even turn around. He popped the lock and in about one minute he had the car started and just peeled out of here. Just like that. Guy was good. I went in the building and got Security."

"Could you describe the man?" Eric asked.

The kid shrugged again. "I didn't get too close before he was gone, and I never saw his face. White dude, kinda brown hair. Maybe about your age. He had on a blue jacket."

"Well, that narrows it down," Solomon said.

Jose glared at him. "I said I didn't get very close. Sorry."

Solomon sighed. "Come on in, Jose. I've called the police. They'll need your statement. Eric?"

"Coming." They started back toward the building. *Stolen car*, Eric thought. *Something almost ordinary.* It was funny: He almost welcomed it. It was part of real life. He could drive Colleen's old car, the old burgundy Cadillac he'd made fun of so many times.

As soon as he walked back into the office suite, his cell phone rang. "Yes?" he said into it.

"Eric? It's Faith Kelly."

Eric's stomach tightened. "What is it?"

"Can we meet today?"

"Of course. What do you have?"

"Not on the phone. Where are you?"

"I'm at the office, for once. There was a meeting today."

He gave her directions. "Hang on. I'll be there in a few minutes."

Eric hung up the phone and started back down the hall toward the conference room. He wasn't thinking about his stolen car anymore.

Faith had never been patient with traffic, and even though Oklahoma City's jams were nothing compared to Chicago, she found her temperature rising in the noon rush. Trying to get out of downtown, she sat at the interminable light at Northwest Sixth and Classen Boulevard and thumped the Miata's steering wheel.

The legal pad, filled with her looping scribbles, the typewritten "list" Good Mattingly had buried, and Maggie Miles's journal sat on the seat beside her. She'd wrapped the list back in its sheet of plastic. As she sat at the light, she tried to digest everything she'd learned and all the implications. *Good God, what has Grant been doing right under our noses for over thirty years?* She picked up the sheet of plastic and looked through it. The sheet was thick enough that it distorted the printing on the paper underneath. *Appropriate,* Faith thought. Everything about this was distorted, unclear. Something fell out onto her lap.

"Dammit," she said, looking at the scattered photos that had been with the list.

She started to put them back in the plastic, then noticed they all had the names of the mothers written on the backs. When she came to the one with MAGGIE MILES printed on it, she turned it over.

Faith felt like she'd been kicked by a wild horse.

The head shot of Maggie Miles showed a beautiful young woman, with honey hair and wide blue eyes, a hint of playfulness in her open, fresh-scrubbed smile. There was nothing dark or ominous or foreboding about her. She had her entire life ahead of her.

What happened to you, Maggie?

Faith held the picture up close, angling it slightly so the sun wouldn't glare on it.

Behind her a horn honked.

"I know this face," Faith said aloud.

But she didn't. She was certain she'd never seen Maggie Miles before. And yet, she looked familiar.

Faith blinked. A droplet of sweat ran down from her forehead and stung her eye.

The horn honked again.

"Go around," Faith said, and waved the traffic around her. The driver flipped her the finger as he went around and crossed Classen.

What happened to you, Maggie? What happened to you after your babies were born?

Faith looked at the photo for a long time. The traffic light turned from red to green and back to red while she sat there in the street.

Finally she picked up her cell phone. She knew who to call. She'd met Nina Reeves the year before, and Faith had learned quickly that when it came to digital technology, whether sound or video or anything else, that Reeves could work wonders: She was a "consultant" who sometimes contracted with the FBI and other law enforcement agencies in the area to do technical work. She was also an enigma, a gorgeous blue-eyed black woman, originally from Bermuda, who'd lived in England and had hinted that she'd been a private detective in New York. She and Faith had become friends; in fact, she was the only real female friend Faith had in Oklahoma.

When Faith heard Reeves's musical accent on the phone, she said, "Nina, I hope you're not too busy. I may have a job for you."

32

PATRICK LIKED SCHOOL. HE LIKED THE BOOKS, AND HE liked building things in the block center or the Lego center. He liked to play with his friends Mollie and Gabriel and Jordan. He especially loved his teacher, Mrs. S. She was good at signing, and she always smiled.

But as much as he liked school, he loved to be with Daddy. Daddy took care of him, and let him read road maps, and didn't mind if he drank a grape cream slush from Sonic in the backseat of his car. He even took him in his airplane sometimes.

Patrick frowned as he walked in his class line down the hall toward the door. Ever since Daddy's airplane had crashed, he'd been staying with Mama. He liked Mama all right, but she couldn't sign very well. It frustrated him, because he couldn't make her understand things. She always had to look up signs in the big yellow book, and by the time she found it, Patrick usually wanted to tell her something different, and that made *her* frustrated.

He also didn't understand about Daddy and Mama. He could tell Daddy still loved Mama, but she didn't love him back. He tried to ask Daddy about this sometimes, but Daddy always said he didn't want to talk about it.

Patrick's class had a special door that opened out onto the side of the school building. None of the other classes were allowed to use it, which made Patrick feel special. Sometimes he felt strange because he was deaf: Kids who could hear and talk would put their hands over their ears and get down in his face and shake their heads at him, mocking him. When they did, he just looked them right straight in the eye and didn't move. He didn't run away, he didn't cry, he didn't try to hit them or anything. He just stared them down, and after a while they went away.

When Mrs. S. opened the special door and the class filed out, Patrick craned his neck. Mollie was in front of him in line, and she was a lot taller than he was. But he peeked around her. When he did, a huge smile crossed his face. Instead of his mother's fancy silver car, he saw his dad's little blue one with the big scratch along the back door.

Daddy was picking him up today!

Maybe they could go to Sonic and get a slush. Maybe they would wrestle on Daddy's bed when they got home. Or maybe they could go to Will Rogers Park and feed the ducks. The possibilities were endless!

Patrick felt a little guilty for so completely dismissing Mama from his thoughts on seeing Daddy's car, but he couldn't help it. Mama wasn't much fun: She worked all the time, and even though she tried to convince him otherwise, she was always tired and a little sad because she worked so much.

Mollie had just gotten into her mother's car. She waved and signed *Good-bye* to Patrick, and he waved and signed back. Daddy's blue car moved up in the line of parents' cars.

Patrick could see Daddy looking this way. He saw the sun glinting off his glasses and the car's windows.

Okay, Patrick, Mrs. S. signed to him. *See you tomorrow.*

Bye, Patrick signed.

He saw Mrs. S. wave at Daddy, and Daddy waved back.

Shouldering his backpack, Patrick ran to the car and popped open the back door. Once he was in and had his seat belt fastened, he expected Daddy to turn and look at him so he could sign hello.

But Daddy didn't turn.

Patrick furrowed his brow. He could see Daddy's mouth moving, so he was talking. But he wasn't signing.

The car started to move. Daddy took off his glasses.

Patrick's frown deepened. Daddy only took off his glasses at night, when he was getting ready for bed.

Then Patrick sniffed the air. Something was different. Something was *wrong.*

Daddy turned around, smiling.

Except it wasn't Daddy.

It looked like Daddy, except his hair was different somehow. And his eyes. His eyes weren't like Daddy's, soft and kind. This man's eyes were hard, like a stone wall. He said something to Patrick.

Patrick's eyes widened as the man turned back around and pulled the car out into the street.

The man smelled strange. He smelled . . . dangerous. He smelled bad. Patrick didn't know how he knew, but he did.

Patrick turned toward the back windshield and began signing frantically, trying to catch Mrs. S.'s attention. He began beating on the window.

But they were too far away from the school now. No one paid any attention to him.

He opened his mouth and let out a little sound. He knew he could make sounds, even if they weren't words and even if he couldn't hear them. He could feel the sound in his chest when he made it.

The man who wasn't Daddy turned to look at him again, and this time he wasn't smiling.

Patrick had never been so frightened. Not even when the airplane crashed. At least then the nice lady with the red hair, Faith, had held his hand. Now he had no one to help him.

No one at all.

33

ERIC WAS THREE-QUARTERS OF THE WAY THROUGH A chicken salad sandwich, and less than halfway through reviewing one of his colleagues' assessment of voting trends in the suburban areas around Oklahoma City and Tulsa. He was alone in the conference room: The meeting had broken up half an hour earlier.

He heard a tap on the door and looked up to see Faith standing there, looking flushed. They nodded to each other. Eric motioned her to come in and close the door.

She wedged her tall frame into a conference chair and placed the sheet of plastic and the journal on the desk. "How are you?" she asked.

Eric put aside his sandwich and took a drink of Diet Dr Pepper. "I'm sore, I don't know what to think about anything, and, to top it all off, my car was stolen today. You're ready to let me see the book?"

"You can keep it," Faith said. "There's not much in it in the way of real evidence. It's . . ." She waited, tapping a nail on the desktop. "It's good for some insight into who your mother was, but I'll tell you right now that a lot of pages are missing."

"Missing?"

"Torn out. They weren't anywhere in the box. I think the real substance would be in those pages."

"Who tore them out, then?"

"Good question. I don't know yet. I have a theory, but that's all it is right now."

"I'd like to hear it."

She shook her head. "Not yet. It's just a shadow, nothing more than that." She passed him the journal. "Yours to keep."

"Thank you," Eric said.

"I've been over this list," Faith said. "The simple answer is this: Grant—or at the least the person he was before he became Grant—was selling the babies."

She paused to let that sink in, and to think about the fine line she was walking. Eric sat back. In a moment she heard him rattling things in his pocket.

"But he didn't sell me—or my brother," Eric said.

"That's right. I still don't know why. Like Helen Harker said, something happened the night you were born, something that screwed up the whole project. But all of those babies were set to be sold, and they all were, except for you and Edward . . . Drew."

Eric nodded toward the list. "Names?"

"Names. It shows each mother, each baby, and the family each baby was sold to. Each twin was sold to a different family. The families were geographically far apart as well as in different . . . social climates."

"What do you mean, 'social climates'?"

Faith drummed some more. "Eric . . . these babies were sold to some of the most powerful people in this country."

"Let me see."

She hesitated a moment, then handed him the list. She felt in the pocket of her blazer, making sure the photos were safe. She wasn't ready to show them to him . . . not now.

Eric adjusted his glasses and ran a finger over the thick paper. "George McCafferty. He was ambassador to the United Nations. Alexis Bumgarner, the dancer and Broadway producer."

"And heiress to a multibillion-dollar real estate empire."

Eric went on. "Francisco Oliva, Supreme Court justice.

Stephen Holmes, U.S. senator from California. Hank Archer . . ." He looked up at Faith. "My God . . . but . . . why?"

Faith sat back. "The first version of this story I heard said that Good Mattingly had come across an infertility treatment. That part may be true. Remember what Helen said? In those days the medical community was just starting to recognize that infertility could be treated at all."

"So he and your pal Grant, or whoever he was then, lured in young couples and offered them a little money to get pregnant and sell their babies, then they turned around and sold the babies for a big profit to these infertile couples, who just happened to be some of the richest and most powerful people in the country." Eric wadded up a paper napkin and tossed it at his empty drink can, knocking it over on the table. "Nice people you hang out with, Kelly."

Faith ignored the jab. "I spent the morning going over Social Security records and the DOJ database. All of the couples in the buyer column only have one child each."

"The child they bought."

"Right. And those children are now in positions of power themselves. Members of Congress, U.S. attorneys, highly placed leaders in business and media and academia and technology. There's so much power concentrated in that list that it's scary."

Eric stood up so that he could see out the window to the antenna farm. "What are they, all in their forties?"

Faith nodded. "Oldest is forty-nine, the youngest—that's you—is thirty-nine."

"You want to know scary?" Eric said. "In ten years those congressmen will be senators or cabinet members. The U.S. attorneys will be federal judges. The businesspeople will own the big companies by then. They're the up-and-comers, the next generation of power."

"You're right."

Eric leaned back, took off his glasses, and rubbed the bridge of his nose. He closed his eyes. "Think, now. Think about this. Here's all this power, all this money, all on one short list. What if . . ."

Faith's pulse quickened. "What if—"

"What if," Eric said, "a single person or group had control of the people on that list?"

Faith started to see a possible scenario, the shadow starting to take shape, just beyond her reach.

Eric said, "Tell me about Grant. What's he like? You've met him, right? Talked to him? Don't dance around, now. Be honest with me."

Faith rubbed her hands together, beginning to marvel at Eric's perceptive powers. "He's . . . he can be very mannerly, almost . . . courtly, if I can use that word. And then in a matter of seconds it can feel like a cold wind just blew through the room. He can be that menacing."

Eric began to walk around the room. "Go on."

Faith felt the momentum gathering. "He's obsessed with Lady Jane Grey. She was—"

"The 'nine days queen' of England, I know. I've studied a lot of history."

Faith nodded. "Right. Like I said, he's obsessed with her story and that of the duke, the one who manipulated her."

"John Dudley, duke of Northumberland."

"That's the one. He liked the idea of this Dudley pulling the strings. The first time I met him, he said the moral of Jane Grey's story was that if you were going to pull an illegal power grab, to be sure you had the support of the people."

"Dudley didn't, and his scheme failed," Eric said. He was at the back of the room, running his hand along the chalkboard that was set up there, drawing a line in the dust.

"He seemed to think of it as a game," Faith said, turning to follow Eric with her eyes. "Manipulating the aristocracy." She stopped, realizing what she'd said.

Eric slapped the chalkboard. The sound was as loud as a gunshot. Faith jumped.

Eric pointed. "The people on that list. They are all part of the closest thing America has to an aristocracy: the aristocracy of wealth, of power. And your man found a way to manipulate them."

Faith stood up, leaning on the table with both arms. "Grant was adopted. He was an adopted son of an old-money family. But later the family had biological sons."

"And he was squeezed out."

"Yes!" Faith felt flushed. "Crumbs from the family's table."

"Striking at the aristocracy. He's striking at the aristocracy, manipulating them at the most basic level."

Faith moved a few steps. "But how?"

Eric raised an index finger, making a point. "What does aristocracy fear the most?" Eric began to circle the room. He ran his hand along a series of posters of U.S. presidents. "The aristocracy, the rich, the powerful: What are they afraid of?"

Faith circled the other side. They were like two animals, each trying to figure out the other's intentions. "Losing their money. Losing their power."

Eric shook his head. His hand brushed a poster of Jimmy Carter, then Gerald Ford, and came to rest on Richard Nixon. He slapped the poster.

"Scandal. Their money, their power . . . this class of people has been around, and has been in their position, for so long that they're secure . . . as long as they stay clear of scandal. That's what could destroy them."

"And if anyone found out these people had bought their children—much less bought them from poor small-town couples—and then passed the children off as their own, they'd be ruined. The scandal would be enormous. Holy shit, Eric! That's what Grant's doing now. That's what his big 'project' is that's still going on. He's been blackmailing these families for all these years. He keeps them under his thumb by threatening to make it public that they bought these babies and passed them off as theirs. My God—who knows what he's influenced?"

"And all this," Eric said, "from Good Mattingly's little place in the panhandle."

Faith nodded. "But there's something else. It's bothered me ever since I found out you were involved in the Hawthorne business."

Eric flinched.

"No, listen to me," Faith said. "This is no damn coincidence. One of the last two twins, one of the only two twins to not get to their buyers . . . Someone set up Hawthorne, and you were in the wrong place at the wrong time. You were used."

"But I—"

"No, listen! No one could have known who you were until after the fact, after the whole Hawthorne scandal. And then . . . My God, that's it!"

Eric's eyes burned into hers. His face went slack. "That's why they're so afraid of me: They've been afraid I would do just this—put the two together. After Hawthorne was over with, they could leave me alone. . . ."

"As long as you didn't start asking questions."

"Then Colleen died and I started asking."

"Yes," Faith said.

"Who would have that kind of pull? That kind of information, access?"

Faith shook her head. "Winter."

"What?"

Faith nodded slowly. "I've been thinking about this for days. The man who is the director of my department . . . he lied to me about Br—Grant's crimes. He wouldn't even trust his case officer with the information. It's because he was in on it. Most of Grant's paperwork was signed by Winter."

"What does that mean?"

Faith's face turned pensive. "Art Dorian had this job before I did. Winter told me he and Art had grown up together. I don't think Art was in on it, but you know what? I think . . ." She swallowed hard. "I think he trusted his old friend when he shouldn't have." She looked away for a moment. When she spoke again, her voice was lower. "So we have to ask: Who benefited from the Hawthorne scandal? Hawthorne's resignation, his death—who came out ahead?"

"Well, the opposing party loved it, of course."

"But what did they *get* out of it? I'm not a political science person, I'm just a cop."

Eric smiled a little at that. "Careful, Kelly, your cover's slipping a little. Okay, cop: They got political capital out of it. But then again, not that much. They didn't win back the Senate in the next election cycle. In fact, I think they even lost a seat."

"Strike that, then. Hawthorne's family?"

"No. By Senate standards, Hawthorne was downright poor. He'd been a legislator all his life, never made any millions before he ran for office. That's why the whole case made me so suspicious. The money, the offshore accounts—I thought he'd finally just gotten tired of being the poor relation in the Senate."

"Who, then? Who benefited from having Hawthorne out of the Senate?"

Eric thought for a few long moments. He heard someone walking by the conference room, out in the hall.

"Hawthorne was chair of the Judiciary Committee," he said.

"Confirmation of Supreme Court justices, federal judges, jurisdiction over the Justice Department."

"Yes. But that's not . . ." The sentence died.

"What?"

"I'm not sure . . ."

"Tell me! Let's put this damn thing together and nail Grant's ass! Come on!"

"Max Candell."

Faith stood up straight. "Who?"

"Max Candell, senator from Louisiana. He took over as chair of the Judiciary Committee after Hawthorne quit."

"What about him?"

"Oh Jesus, oh God." Eric practically ran to the small table in the corner of the room. He dug out that morning's *Daily Oklahoman* from a pile of papers. On the front page, above the fold, was a color photo of a silver-haired man chopping his hand through the air as if making an important point.

The headline read: CANDELL TO PREZ: TIME TO COME CLEAN.

"The scandal with the President," Eric said, almost out of breath. He waved the paper at Faith. "This Sons of Madison group, and all the attacks on cops. Have you been following it?"

"Not really. I've sort of had other things on my mind, remember?"

"I remember. Candell's now the chair of Judiciary. He's calling for an independent counsel to investigate the President's connections to the Madison people. It's a mess."

Faith strode toward him and took the paper. She scanned the article. "But I don't—"

"Your list." Eric snatched the buyer-seller list off the little desk and shook it at her. "Hank Archer. God, I didn't make the connection before. Hank Archer's only daughter. Angela, the governor."

"I know that, but—"

"How long have you lived in Oklahoma, Faith?"

"Not that long. A little over two years."

"The Archers . . . their tentacles are everywhere. Angela may be an only child, but the old man, Hank, had at least two brothers and a couple of sisters. They've all been in and out of government, both federal and state, for all their lives."

"Get to the point."

"Hank Archer's oldest sister—I think her name was Abigail—married an oilman from Louisiana. His name was John Candell. They had about five or six kids, but only one son: Max."

"Jesus Christ, Eric. You're telling me Senator Candell, the one who's calling for the President's head on a platter, is Angela Archer's cousin?"

Eric let the list drop to the desk. "This whole thing with the President . . . his poll numbers are crashing since the Madison business started. And who's positioning herself for a presidential run? Who looks like the consummate leader? The President's flopping around like a fish onshore, actually linked to cop-killing extremists, and Governor Archer looks cool and calm and like someone you might want to vote for."

Faith resisted the urge to scratch her scar. "Do you think

Winter and Grant somehow engineered the whole Madison thing? My God . . . if they went to those lengths just to get Hawthorne out of the way so Candell would be in a position to pave the way for Angela, wouldn't they do something to light the spark?"

"They might."

"Shit!" Faith finally sat down again. She rubbed her hands across blue-jeaned legs, massaging her calf muscles. "Grant's been manipulating these people for so long, and now he's about to make the ultimate power grab."

Eric nodded vigorously. "Lady Jane Grey. But unlike old John Dudley, he'll have the support of the people. Except the people won't know. They won't know that Angela Archer is really Linda O'Dell from West Virginia, and her parents sold her to Hank Archer like she was so much real estate."

Something kicked at the back of Faith's mind. "If we're going to nail Grant . . ."

Eric leaned forward.

"I'm not sure how this juggernaut could be stopped. It's all been in motion for more than thirty years. All those people . . ." Something urgent, something *dated*, pulled at her. "Memorial Day!" she blurted after a moment.

"What?"

Her grandfather playing fiddle tunes. Food, beer, relatives. *Your dad will be so disappointed.*

The picnic.

Memorial Day.

Faith snatched up the newspaper and smoothed it out. She raced through the article about Candell, then read the sidebar about Angela Archer. The governor had scheduled a news conference for Monday on the steps of the state capitol. Monday at noon.

Monday, Memorial Day.

"She's going to announce for president on Memorial Day," Faith said.

Eric waited a long moment. "Once she's officially in the race, there's no stopping it."

"And the Madison group has threatened to start taking out federal marshals."

Faith thought of her friends in the Marshals Service: Mayfield and Leneski and all the rest. "And Grant's behind it. By God, I am not going to let this happen."

The two stared at each other for a long moment. The tension snapped when Eric's cell phone rang.

Laura's voice scratched through the phone. "Next time you change your mind, I wish you'd let me know in advance."

"What?" Eric said.

"I thought I was supposed to pick Patrick up until further notice. I took my lunch break to come all the way up here and get him. I was running a little late, and then I get here and his teacher says you already picked him up."

The world became quiet around Eric. He almost felt his heart stop beating.

"Eric?" Laura said. "Are you listening to me? This really pisses me off, you know."

Eric understood. His car. Drew. Patrick. *Patrick!*

"He said he'd give us time," Eric muttered.

"What?" Faith said.

Eric put the phone down on his desk. "They've got Patrick," he said.

34

LAURA NORTHRUP-ANTHONY KEPT LOOKING AT THE catfish on the wall, as if she couldn't believe something so ridiculous was actually mounted in a U.S. government office. She stared at it, then back at Faith, then at Eric.

She strode back across the room and leaned across Faith's desk. "I don't know what this is all about, Ms. Kelly, and I don't know who you work for, but let me tell you a thing or two: I am an officer of the court, and I want answers."

Faith wanted to slap the woman. She'd been nothing but officious and obnoxious since she'd arrived. She didn't act much like a woman reacting to her only son's kidnapping.

"Laura, I think—" Eric began.

Laura turned on him. "And you! All this nonsense about a twin, and buried records, and mysterious hikes on mesas. You dump Patrick with me and then allow someone to grab him. I thought you were this incredible father, Mr. Sensitive, the great twenty-first-century dad. Explain this, Eric! Goddammit, I want some answers!"

Both of Eric's hands were flailing away inside his pockets. He rocked back on the balls of his feet. "Listen, Laura, that's not—"

Faith stood up and leaned across her desk. "With all due respect, Mrs. Anthony, will you please just shut up?"

The effect was almost that of a slap in the face. Laura reeled back as if she'd actually been struck, then took a moment to recover. "Number one, it's Northrup-Anthony. Number two, it's Ms., not Mrs. Number three, I want the name and phone number of your supervisor. Your career is finished. Do you understand me?"

"It's not about you!" Eric screamed.

Both Faith and Laura jumped.

"For God's sake, Laura! This isn't about you! Patrick's been kidnapped. Think about him for once, will you? Stop being a high-priced lawyer and just be Laura. Just be Mama for a while."

"How dare you!" Laura hissed. "How dare you talk to me like that! I'll—"

Faith rapped on the desk with her knuckles. "We know who has him, and we know what they want. What we don't know is where he is."

"Then get him back!" Laura shouted. "Call the FBI, get a hostage-rescue team in here, and take care of it."

Faith shook her head. "We can't do that."

"Kidnapping is in the FBI's jurisdiction," Laura said, her voice coming down a notch.

"Not in this case. There are . . . other concerns."

Faith and Eric met each other's eyes. Laura followed the look.

"What's going on here?" Laura said. "Eric?"

"I can't, Laura. It's too—"

Laura raised both hands in the air, then let them fall to her sides.

"If I may," Faith said.

They both looked at her.

"We can get Patrick back. But we need a little time and a lot of calm. Now, would the two of you step outside and wait in the hall for a few minutes?"

"Oh, no you don't, Little Miss Secret Agent," Laura said.

Faith moved around the desk with startling speed. In two strides she towered over Laura. "Don't you ever call me *Little Miss* anything, *Ms.* Northrup-Anthony. I'm the person who's going to get your son back. Now wait in the hall or I'll make a phone call and half a dozen federal marshals will come swarming down that hall and take you into custody for obstruction of justice."

Laura opened her mouth.

"Laura, don't," Eric said. He took her by the shoulder and guided her out the door. With a look backward at Faith, he closed it quietly.

Faith sagged into her chair. She thought of Patrick, the way his beautiful little hands made words and sentences and pictures, the way his huge deep-blue eyes had met hers when they'd clasped hands as the airplane went down.

Now Grant had stepped over the line.

Not only would she no longer protect him, she was going to bring him down. She had to topple everything he'd done, to untwist the system from the way he'd corrupted it. She had an idea, an insane idea, an incredibly simple idea, about how to do it. But first . . .

She flipped open Grant's file, located his phone number, and called it. Rachel Grant answered.

"Mrs. Grant, it's Faith Kelly. I need to speak to your husband."

The woman barked out a laugh. "So do I, honey. So do I."

Faith heard the phone being placed on a hard surface and Rachel's heels clicking away. A moment later another phone extension was lifted.

"Well, Ms. Kelly," Nathan Grant said. He waited. Faith heard the high heels again. "Rachel, hang up the other phone." The other receiver turned off. "And how are you this fine spring day, Officer?"

"Where's the boy?"

"Do not use that tone of voice with me, young woman. I warned you. I warned you and Mr. Miles many times. You made a choice not to listen."

"All bets are off, Grant. Wait . . . I guess I should start calling you Brandon. That'll be your name again before long. Your days under Department Thirty are numbered."

Grant laughed heartily. "Trying to scare me? Sorry, it'll take more than that. Even if you came and personally put a bullet in my head right now, it wouldn't stop me."

"I know what you're doing. I know about the babies, I know about Angela Archer and Hawthorne and Winter and all the rest."

Grant waited a moment. Faith listened to him breathing on the phone.

"Aha," Faith said. "Didn't think we'd get to that, did you? Now where's Patrick?"

Grant's tone changed, and Faith felt the malevolence, the unmerciful hardness, even through the phone line. "The boy is dead. He may still be breathing for now, but he is dead. So is his father. *And so are you.*"

The phone clicked in her ear.

Faith put the phone roughly back in its cradle, then picked it up and put it down three more times, a little harder each time. "That went well," she said aloud. Her stomach knotted, doing a slow burn. She realized there was nothing in it but coffee and the little bit of toast she'd had hours ago.

She opened the door, motioning to Eric and Laura to stay where they were in the hall. She walked the other way to the Marshals Service office at the end of the corridor.

Inside, the usual buzz of activity seemed unusually

muted. She asked the front desk deputy, "Is the chief in?"

The deputy hooked a thumb over his shoulder toward the chief's office.

"Thanks."

The new chief deputy U.S. marshal of the Oklahoma City office was an unassuming man named Mark Raines. He'd been brought in from Connecticut after the scandal with Phillip Clarke the year before. He was in his forties and favored suits instead of boots and jeans, as Clarke had. He was an even-tempered, soft-spoken man, not a great field cop but by all accounts a brilliant administrator. He had also treated Faith fairly and seemed to have no prejudices that she could discern. There was even another female deputy in the office now.

He was in his office, just hanging up the phone, when Faith walked through the open door. "Hello, Chief," she said.

His smile was a thin, worried line. "How are you, Faith? Things all right down in the shadow world?"

"Pretty shadowy, actually." She sat down. "It seems tense around here."

Raines nodded. "Thirty percent absenteeism. Nationally it's close to fifty. Ever since SOMU made the threat against the Marshals, it's been rough."

Faith leaned forward. "Chief, you're not going to believe this."

Raines raised an eyebrow.

"A case I'm working on for Thirty is connected to this whole SOMU mess."

"You're joking. Faith, please tell me you're joking."

"You think I'd joke about this?"

Raines shook his head. "No, I don't."

"Right. And before those SOMU bastards get a single member of this service, I've got a plan to do something about it."

"You sound like you're still one of us."

Faith shrugged. "In a lot of ways, I am."

"I'm sorry, Faith, I didn't have a choice," Raines said. "That Winter has a lot of pull. He said—"

Faith held up a hand. "No apology necessary, Chief. I

understand. I'm having my own problems with the man."

"So what's up?"

"I have a plan. Well, it's more an idea than a plan right now. But I need some support, and I need it right away."

"I don't know, Faith," Raines said. "I don't know if I can get mixed up with you right now."

"Chief, we have to do this. For God's sake, they're threatening to kill marshals! They've already killed more than a hundred law enforcement officers."

"What about the President? The cop community isn't too happy with him right now."

"I'm not worrying about the President. I'm trying to work a little closer to home."

Raines looked doubtful.

"Come on, Chief." Faith's voice turned impatient. "Don't make me invoke a bunch of Department Thirty crap on you. Technically, I can order this office to assist with my investigation."

"I know the rules. You don't screw around with Thirty, and never, never ask questions. Are you sure we're all on the same side?"

Faith looked at him. It wasn't a challenge, but an honest question. Faith remembered her father's words: *If you'll tell a lie, there's nothing you won't do.* "Honestly, sometimes I wonder. But on this, Chief . . . my case is tied up with SOMU. We do this, and we won't hear from SOMU again. That puts us on the same side."

"I'm listening," Raines said.

Five minutes later Faith left the office. Raines hadn't batted the proverbial eye at anything she'd said. Like the consummate administrator he was, he listened, made notes, asked a couple of logistical questions, and said he'd get on it. A couple of the requests were outrageous, but he listened anyway.

Back in the hall, Faith motioned to Eric. "Come back in. Ms. Northrup-Anthony, wait a few more minutes there." Laura glared at her.

Faith smiled. She took one hand, made it flat, and rubbed it in circles against her chest.

Laura's glare intensified, mixed with confusion.

Eric sighed. "She's making the sign for 'Please,' Laura."

Faith and Eric went into the office. "She doesn't sign?" Faith said when the door was closed.

"She does some," Eric said. "She . . . ah . . . she's not, well, comfortable with it."

Faith let it pass. "I talked to Grant." She watched Eric. His eyes were red and his face was flushed with color. His hair was rumpled from repeatedly running his hands through it, and his pants were wrinkled from the way he constantly jammed his hands in his pockets. His entire body looked as if he were carrying heavy lead weights on his shoulders.

"You talked to him."

Faith nodded. "He didn't deny that he has Patrick." She decided to leave out Grant's last threat.

Eric kicked at the air. "And that's it? He didn't deny it?" His voice started to float upward. "That's all you can say?"

"He's—"

"I'm going to get an airplane and I'm going to fly to wherever he is, and I'm going to—"

"No you're not. That won't help Patrick. I have support coming in, and I have a plan to take Grant down."

"I don't care about Grant anymore! Patrick is—"

Faith poked a finger in Eric's chest. "Patrick is alive right now, and let's see that we keep him that way. The reason Grant had Drew kidnap Patrick is to get us to back off the investigation, to keep us at bay until Monday."

Eric was quiet a moment. "Until after Governor Archer announces."

Faith nodded. "Right. He figures, just like we did, that once Archer's officially in the race, nothing stops him. It's the snowball rolling downhill. After that . . ." She shrugged.

"So what's your plan?"

"We do what he wants."

"What?"

"No more investigation. We're finished investigating." She leaned against the desk and folded her arms. "Now we act."

35

FOR THE FIRST TIME IN FIVE YEARS, ERIC AND LAURA spent the night under the same roof. They stayed at Eric's house, closer to the base of operations than Laura's condo in Edmond. Neither slept much, although Laura finally stretched out around one A.M. on Eric's well-worn couch—a couch they'd made love on many times when they were married.

Eric covered her with a sheet and watched her for a while. They had tried to talk. He'd tried to recapture those intense, emotional conversations from when they'd first met, all those years ago back at OSU. But the words wouldn't come for a long time, and when they did, they just sounded silly and overblown. He'd heard of crises bringing people back together; clearly, that wasn't going to happen here.

He wandered the halls, ate a sandwich, read his e-mail, played word games on the Internet, wandered the halls some more. He peeked in on Laura: She seemed to be comfortable under the sheet and was sleeping as well as could be expected.

Eric finally went into Patrick's room. He almost held his breath, looking at the Disney movie posters. There was the framed photo of Patrick last year at Christmas, sitting on the lap of the "Signing Santa" at Northpark Mall. Eric ran his hand over the little bookshelf, with its rows of Dr. Seuss and Jan Brett and Maurice Sendak. Patrick loved *Where the Wild Things Are.*

He sat down on Patrick's bed, then saw a flash of yellow. Poking out from the corner of his pillow was the little stuffed turtle. Patrick had had it since he was a newborn, wedged into a corner of the bassinet in the intensive care unit, where tubes and wires crisscrossed his tiny body. Eric picked up the turtle. This was the first night of his life Patrick hadn't had it with him.

Eric lay down on Patrick's bed, his feet hanging off the end. Still holding the turtle, he slipped into a fitful doze.

The man who wasn't Daddy had driven Patrick around and around, all over the city until Patrick couldn't keep up with where he was. Every now and then he could see the man's mouth moving, and several times Patrick signed back to him, but the man didn't look at him.

Patrick didn't understand how the man could look like daddy, but not *be* Daddy. All he knew was that he was in trouble, and as long as he was in this car, there was no way he could get away from the man.

After driving for a long time, when it was getting dark the man pulled into a parking lot, stopped the car, and got out. He came around to the backseat where Patrick was and pulled open the door.

I won't cry, Patrick told himself. Just like when the kids taunted him on the playground. Look them in the eye and don't move. *I won't cry*.

The man stared down at him, his face with no expression at all. Patrick looked back, unblinking.

Then the man almost smiled. He mouthed a few more words, then beckoned to Patrick.

Patrick sat still, staring up at him, not dropping his eyes.

The smile vanished. More mouthed words.

The man stood there awhile longer, then reached across Patrick, undid his seat belt, and pulled on his arm. Patrick resisted for a moment, but the man was strong. He pulled him out of the car and put his hands on his shoulders, steering him toward one door in a long line of other doors.

The man knocked, and another man opened the door. He was bigger than the man who wasn't Daddy, and looked even meaner. Patrick swallowed fiercely. His stomach started to feel queasy. The second man gave him a little push. There were two beds in the room, a couple of chairs, a TV. There was a sink in the corner.

The second man gave him a bigger push, and the man who wasn't Daddy pointed a finger at him.

Patrick sat down and wrapped both arms around his chest, rocking in the chair. The two men stared at him, especially the man with Daddy's face.

I won't cry, Patrick told himself again.

Eric didn't know how long he slept. But he saw light outside the curtains, and the phone was ringing.

He shot out of Patrick's room and down the hall. Laura was up, barefoot, holding the phone out to him. "It's that woman," she said. "That Kelly."

Eric winced at the way she said that. "Yeah?" he said into the receiver.

"Get any sleep?" Faith said.

"A little. You?"

"A little. I'm meeting the governor at nine o'clock. I think she agreed to it more out of curiosity than anything."

"How'd you manage that?"

"Had the Marshals arrange it. She thinks she's meeting a deputy U.S. marshal to talk about a property seizure that took place on state land."

"What are you going to tell her?"

"I'm going to tell her . . ." Faith cleared her throat. "I'm going to tell her there's someone she needs to meet."

"What?"

"Look, Grant told me yesterday that even if I put a bullet in his head right now, it wouldn't stop what he's started. And he was right. All this has been going on for so long that it'll take something earth-shattering to stop it in its tracks."

Eric thought for a moment. His mind flickered to Black Mesa, to the moment he and Drew saw each other. "Her twin. You're bringing in the governor's twin."

"Her name is Marielle Saunders Brackett. She lives in Seattle, and between her holdings and her husband's, they pretty much own the Pacific Northwest."

"You think she'll come?"

"I'm betting everything on it. Raines is working on the logistics of getting her here."

"What about Patrick?"

"We wait. He'll be—"

"No, I don't want to wait. I want him back."

"We've already been over this. Just be patient. Nothing's going to happen to him."

Eric's voice rose. "Your plan's in place. Now let's find my son."

"I told you last night, I have support coming in. We need to wait a few hours."

"Dammit, no! If you won't do it, I will."

Faith exhaled a frustrated breath into the phone. Eric could tell she was struggling to keep her voice level. "I am handling this, okay? I don't want anything to happen to Patrick. Look, I'm sending over a friend of mine. He's FBI, his name is Scott Hendler. I can't brief him on everything, for the obvious reasons, but I trust him. We have to—"

"No," Eric said. "We don't have to."

"Eric? Listen to me! Eric—"

Eric hung up the phone. He met Laura's eyes—Patrick's eyes. Patrick's features were so much like Laura's that it was heartbreaking.

"What are you doing?" Laura said in a low voice.

"I'm going to get our son back."

Ignoring the rest of her questions, Eric changed clothes, then went into his bedroom and flipped on the computer. Once he was online, he entered *Nathan Grant* in a search box, sat back, and waited. A minute later he had what he wanted. The online directory of the Oklahoma Association of Realtors listed Grant's address. It was a rural route in Kingston. Eric checked his map: It was in the far south, right on Lake Texoma and not far from Kerry's Landing.

He pulled out his address book, flipped pages, and found a number. "Charley, I need to borrow your airplane," he said a moment later.

"Good morning to you too," said his friend.

Within a few minutes they'd made arrangements for Eric to borrow Charley's Cessna Skyhawk. Every pilot who'd trained in the last thirty years had probably spent time in one, and Eric had to admit that it was actually easier to fly than his Cherokee had been. Thinking of his own plane made the anger begin to rise again.

His airplane, then Patrick. The two things in the world that meant the most to him. And all because of the obsessions and machinations of Nathan Grant.

Finally he went out into the garage and pulled a locked metal box off a high shelf. He hadn't opened this box in five years, not since he'd come back to Oklahoma. It had stayed here on this shelf, away from Patrick, away from everything. It was a part of his life he'd stopped trying to understand. But he'd never forgotten. He'd lived with it every day.

You've got it all backwards, Colleen had said as she lay dying. *You remember stuff best forgotten, and won't even consider the things you should be remembering.*

She'd been right, he thought. She'd been right about more things than he gave her credit for.

Eric unlocked the box and gently lifted out the SIG Sauer nine-millimeter automatic pistol, the one he'd used to shoot Weldon Hawthorne. After the board of inquiry ruled self-defense in the shooting, the gun had been released to him. It had gone into the box, and there it had stayed.

Until they took his son.

The Lake Texoma airstrip was only a forty-five-minute flight from Wiley Post. It had begun to spit rain when Eric made his approach and landed. Like Boise City and most other rural airports, Texoma wasn't manned, but Lake Texoma Lodge, one of the most popular resorts in the state, was only a few hundred yards away, and it was the Friday before Memorial Day weekend. He tied down the plane and flagged a passing pickup truck.

A middle-aged man with a few days' growth of beard looked out at him. Eric saw fishing equipment in the bed of the truck.

"What's up?" the man said.

"Does the airport have a courtesy car?"

The man looked at him as if he had two heads. "How do I know? Does this old truck look like an airplane to you?"

Eric leaned in the driver's window. "Do you know a man named Nathan Grant?"

"Nathan? Sure I do. Did some work for him a year or two ago. I did some wiring for one of his—"

"Where does he live?"

"Down at Caney Creek. Say, do you—"

"Give me directions."

The man leaned back. "How about some manners, fella?"

Eric pulled the SIG Sauer out of his belt and pointed it in the man's face. "How about some directions?"

The man hopped in his seat. "Whoa, whoa, now! What's the problem? Put that thing—"

"Grant's house! Now!"

"Okay, okay, settle down. Take the highway here into Kingston. Go left at the light. Stay with that road, and it'll wind around down to Caney Creek. He's got the big house with the fancy gate. You can't miss it. Put that thing—"

"Get out," Eric said. "Get out of the truck!"

"Now, look—"

He motioned with the gun. The man got out and stood in the road. Eric slid into the driver's seat.

"Hey!" the man said.

"Sorry," Eric said, dropped the truck into gear, and roared out of the entrance to Lake Texoma State Park. He turned toward Kingston.

Rachel Grant was alone in the huge house. Drew had left again yesterday, Nathan early this morning, and today was even the housekeeper's day off. Rachel spent some time watching bad television, then wandered through the house, touching expensive things, wondering how she could have become a prisoner like this. A prisoner of this house, of Nathan's money, of his power.

She rubbed her cheek where he'd hit her yesterday. It

didn't still hurt, but the memory stung. The words stung even worse: . . . *you are a vulgar, uncouth hick with nothing going for you but your looks.*

"Asshole," she muttered.

When the gate bell sounded, she went to the front panel and said, "Yes?" into the little squawk box.

"I need to see Nathan Grant," said a man's voice.

"Sorry, he's not here."

"I need to see him *now.*"

"Are you deaf, honey? I said he's gone."

"Mrs. Grant?"

"That's me."

"Let me in, please. Let me talk to you."

"Who are you?"

"It doesn't matter. But you should know . . . your husband isn't the man you think he is."

Rachel jerked, knocking a vase of flowers off the end table. The vase shattered on the floor next to her. She barely noticed. The man at the gate had just said what she'd been thinking about her husband lately.

She pushed the button to let him in, then went to the front door. She stood in the front courtyard and watched the scarred, scratched pickup truck wind up the driveway. When the man stopped and got out, she stopped breathing.

"Drew?" she said. "Not funny, Drew. I don't appreciate—"

"I'm not Drew."

She stepped closer. The man was heavier, grayer, wore glasses, and his shoulders were slightly hunched. But his face . . .

"No, I guess you're not. But you look—"

"Mrs. Grant, let's talk."

Rachel waited a moment, then nodded. She stepped aside to let the stranger into her house.

36

FAITH SMILED WHEN THE DOOR TO HER OFFICE OPENED and Dean Yorkton walked in. "Well, Mr. Yorkton . . . pardon me, *Officer* Yorkton. I didn't know if they'd really get hold of you, or if you'd really come."

The big man settled into a chair. "Oh, yes. I presume you think it would have been dangerous to call me directly, and that's why you had your friends in the Marshals Service relay the message."

"You could say that."

"I caught the early flight this morning. My assignment in Indiana is in a bit of a lull right now, so I'm flexible. Plus, I feel a bit of, shall we say, responsibility for you."

Faith laughed aloud.

"I'm glad you find that amusing," Yorkton said. "I'm guessing that you've thought that since I got you into this department, that I can help you clean up your first mess." He shook his head and began drumming his fingers on the arm of the chair. "I see you haven't changed the decor much. Arthur's catfish is still here. A few new plants is all."

"I think the fish sort of goes with the place," Faith said. "Let me brief you."

She spent half an hour outlining what had already happened, and the plans she'd set in motion yesterday.

"Bold," Yorkton said when she'd finished.

"Grant or me?"

"Both."

"You don't seem surprised at what I said about Winter."

"I'm not surprised by anything." He sighed. "It disappoints me, of course. Somewhere along the way, Daniel decided to work for his own power instead of honoring the mission of the department. But no, I'm afraid I'm not surprised by it. Not at all." Yorkton smiled thinly. "What about the little boy?"

"I'll get him back."

"What about your friend at the Bureau? Your very *close* friend. Hendler, isn't it?"

Faith stared at him. "Yes, it is, and it's none of your business."

"What does he know?"

"Very little. Let's keep this relevant, shall we?" *Damn the man*, she thought. He'd barely been here two minutes and she was starting to talk like him. She never used words like *shall*.

"Indeed. What is your next move?"

Faith winked at him. "I've used a little Department Thirty clout and the Marshals are making some arrangements." He told her about Angela Archer and Marielle Saunders Brackett.

"Brackett was irritated, was she?" Yorkton said. He was still drumming.

Faith wanted to grab his hand and make him sit on it. "You could say that. But she's coming, like it or not. Evidently the chief deputy marshal in Seattle had to threaten to arrest her as a material witness. She'll be on a plane soon, with an escort."

"And you've talked to the governor?"

"Oh, yes. We'll be meeting in the Green Room at the state capitol."

"How exciting. Now, why did you need me?"

Faith held up a finger. She called Eric's home number and got his answering machine. She frowned, calling his cell. Nothing. Solomon and Associates hadn't heard from him all day. After hanging up with Jake Solomon, Faith waited a moment, then called Laura on her cell phone.

"He went *where*?" she shouted a moment later.

After she hung up she muttered, "Oh, Eric, you stupid, courageous, crazy man."

"What?" Yorkton said.

"Our lives have just become more complicated," Faith said.

Rachel Grant went with Eric easily enough. He didn't even have to pull the gun. He gave her a capsulized, edited version of what had happened; she disappeared for a moment, came back with her jacket and purse, and they walked out the door into the misting rain.

Leaving the stolen truck in her driveway, Eric had Rachel drive them back to the Lake Texoma airstrip in her red BMW. There was no sign of the truck's owner, but Eric did notice a couple of lake patrol cars ambling up and down the roads between the lodge and the airstrip.

"You want me to fly in that?" she said when she saw the Cessna.

"That's the only way we're getting there," Eric said.

"I think you're crazy," Rachel said.

"Probably so. But I think your husband's crazier."

She had nothing to say to that.

"Where will he be in the city?" Eric asked as he zipped through the preflight.

"He has an office up there, over on the Northwest Expressway. Or he might be out at one of the job sites."

"Job sites?"

"He's got several development projects going up there. He likes to go out and just walk around them, like he's admiring what he can do."

They climbed into the plane, and Eric gave his cursory passenger brief to her. He started the engine and motioned for her to put on the passenger headset.

Neither of them spoke for a few minutes. "Did he really take your little boy?" Rachel finally asked.

Eric looked at her. "Yes."

Rachel leaned back against the seat and closed her eyes.

"You don't seem surprised," Eric said.

She shook her head without opening her eyes. "We couldn't have kids. I wanted babies so much. I knew he was old, but you know it's different with men. They can still make babies, even when they're old. But he told me he was sterile. Said he'd had a freak case of chicken pox when he was twenty-one, and it left him sterile forever. He told me that two weeks after we got married."

Eric looked at her. She was crying, mascara running straight down her cheeks in little black rivers.

"Help me find him," Eric said.

Rachel didn't answer, and Eric didn't press her. He began to taxi the airplane down the short airstrip. When they were in the air, he looked over at her again. She was still crying.

37

FAITH'S OFFICE HAD BEGUN TO RESEMBLE A WAR ROOM. Laura Northrup-Anthony paced up and down, spending most of her time on the phone. Yorkton had set up camp in a corner and was familiarizing himself with the case file on Brandon/Grant as well as all the other information Faith and Eric had uncovered. Faith alternately worked both her office phone and cell phone.

It was late afternoon, with the rain starting and stopping and starting again, when Faith snatched a call on the cell. She stiffened when she heard the voice.

"This is Drew," he said.

Faith looked quickly around the room. Deputy U.S. Marshal Derek Mayfield had just come in. He'd been one of her friends in the Marshals Service office, tall, lanky, and blond. He was also generally acknowledged as the best marksman of any federal law enforcement officer in the state of Oklahoma. She'd asked the chief deputy to have Mayfield temporarily assigned to her.

"Are you there?" Drew said.

"I'm here."

"Don't try to trace this: I won't be on long enough. Don't record it, because it won't do you any good. Do you want the boy?"

"Yes."

"He's alive. He's being held in the Diamond Motel on I-35 South. Room 108."

"Is he all right?"

"I left him about an hour ago and he was fine. Tell me, is the boy deaf?"

"Yes. Yes, he is."

"Interesting. He's safe now. But he may not be for long. Nathan's hired two other goons. I don't know them. I think they're part of the Oklahoma City underground. They're big and they're armed, but they're stupid."

Faith began to make notes. "Are they both in the room?"

"One stays outside, one's in with the boy."

"Is he tied?"

"No." The voice softened. "He's scared to death, but he's a tough little boy."

"What are you doing now?"

"I have one more thing left to do for Nathan, then I'm gone forever."

"Wait—"

The line went dead.

Faith looked up. Everyone was watching her. "We've found Patrick." She decided not to mention that her source was the man who'd kidnapped the boy in the first place.

"Where?" Laura shouted, rushing forward. "Is he all right?"

Faith nodded. "We're going after him."

Laura put on her jacket. "I'm coming with you."

Faith waited, then realized she couldn't stop the woman from coming. "You'll stay back until everything is clear. But he should have a parent there, and since Eric seems to be out of touch—"

Laura's eyes narrowed.

Faith winced. Open mouth, insert foot. "Sorry, I didn't mean that the way it sounded." She looked around the room. "Yorkton, I need you. Hello, Derek. Glad to see you don't have the 'blue flu.' Welcome to my world. Get your gear and let's roll."

Mayfield grinned. "It'll take more than some nutty home-grown terrorist types to keep me out of action. Nice to see Department Thirty hasn't changed you that much, Faith."

Oh my God, but it has, Faith didn't say. "Let's go."

• • •

Once they were on the ground and Charley was satisfied that his airplane had survived the trip in good order, Eric motioned Rachel Grant to the old burgundy '68 Cadillac, the only car he remembered Colleen ever driving. It was huge and, just like Colleen's house, messy and musty-smelling. Eric made a mental note to clean it out after all this was over.

"This car's almost as big as the airplane," Rachel said. She'd wiped her eyes with Eric's handkerchief. They were rimmed with red now but dry.

"Almost," Eric said. "Where to?"

"The office. It's on Northwest Expressway. I don't know all the cross streets up here, but I can show you the way."

The Oklahoma City office of The Grant Companies, Real Estate Investments was on the sixth floor of an office building near Baptist Medical Center. It was empty but for one lonely desk and a phone.

"Job sites," Eric said. "You mentioned job sites." His guts were firmly knotted, and his skin felt strangely prickly. He felt that if someone even brushed against him he might scream out in pain. Every minute they wasted in office buildings was a minute Patrick needed him.

His cell phone rang. It had rung several times already. Faith Kelly's cell number came up on the caller ID. Eric turned it off. She would be demanding that he come back, that he stick to the plan.

She had her plan, he had his.

He had Rachel drive him around town. A housing development near Yukon, a shopping center in Edmond, another shopping center near Quail Springs Mall. No one had seen Mr. Grant all day.

"They have to be somewhere," Eric insisted.

"I don't know," Rachel said. "I don't know. I don't come with him every trip. I usually just go shopping while he's out doing whatever it is he does, then come back and get him. But—" Her face changed.

"What?"

"He's doing some work down by the river. All that redevelopment. He has some property down there, but there's nothing there yet. They're building a dam, and—"

"Can you get us there?"

"I think so."

"Drive," he said.

Eric's hand closed on the SIG Sauer in the pocket of his jacket.

The Diamond Motel was neither a dump with hourly rates nor top-of-the-line. It was an ordinary interstate motel catering to travelers. Its sign advertised free cable, HBO, and local calls. One wing of the motel faced the interstate service road, the other branched off in an L shape facing a side street.

The team got a break when a quick reconnaissance showed that room 108 faced the side street and not the highway. True to what Drew had said, a single man lounged in front of the room door. He looked to be in his forties, big and muscular, with a graying military-style buzz haircut. He wasn't overly vigilant and seemed to be having trouble staying awake.

"Here's the operation," Faith said. She and Yorkton and Mayfield were crouched behind a dilapidated house just beyond the motel. "Yorkton, you're a drunk who can't find his room. You're loud, you're obnoxious, et cetera."

"Lovely," Yorkton said. "Should be quite a stretch."

Faith smiled. "Derek, once our friend with the bad haircut is distracted, you move in from this side. Do the door. Don't go in firing, because we don't know where in the room Patrick is. I'll be backup, last in the door. I'm not going to be visibly armed. The boy has met me, so I'm the familiar face." She thought of holding his hand on board the doomed airplane. She hoped he remembered that connection as well as she did. "We have to be prepared for the fact that they may try to use Patrick as a shield. If so, there's plan B."

"What is plan B?" Yorkton asked.

"Leave that to me."

"I hate it when she does that," Mayfield said.

"And remember, don't shout out any verbal instructions

to Patrick. He can't hear you, so you're wasting breath and time."

"Well, Jesus, Faith, how do we get him to—"

"Leave that to me." Faith smiled. "Let's rock, gentlemen."

The rain had neither increased nor decreased but was still just a fine spitting mist when Rachel Grant maneuvered the big Cadillac off South Western Avenue, just north of the bridge over the North Canadian River. She followed a dirt path that paralleled the bridge, then turned sharply under it.

The river was now on their right and Eric watched it, reminded of the local joke about the North Canadian being the only river in America that had to be mowed once a month. This stretch, however, meandering south of Interstate 40, was fairly full. Signs of construction were everywhere: truck and heavy equipment tracks. Up ahead he saw a strange structure in the river. He'd seen it from the road many times, the beginnings of a dam. It was all part of Oklahoma City's revitalization of its downtown and surrounding areas. This was one of the last of the projects still under construction.

Rachel drew in her breath, squinting through the misty, fading light. A vehicle was parked ahead. "That's his Range Rover. He's here. Oh God, he's here."

"Stop the car," Eric said.

"What?"

"Stop. You don't need to be in the middle of this. You'll be safer back here. Better yet, take the car and go somewhere else." He stopped, his mind stretching. Faith had said something about having Angela Archer's twin, Marielle Brackett, meet them at the state capitol. That was where the two women would see each other and Grant's manipulations would end. "Go to the state capitol. You know where it is?"

Rachel nodded, eyes wide.

"There's a woman named Faith Kelly. Find her. She can tell you everything. She's tall and has red hair. You can't miss her."

"But—"

Eric opened the car door. "Thank you, Mrs. Grant."

"Call me Rachel," she said, but Eric had already gone.

He crept through the dirt, which was slowly turning into red, brick-colored mud. Ahead in the river the structures began to take shape. There were seven concrete supports spanning the width of the river. Each was shaped like two-thirds of a triangle, and each sported a set of metal stairs bolted to the front. Driving along the Walker Avenue bridge from time to time, watching from the safety of his car, Eric had often thought the supports looked like something out of a surrealist painting. The steps on the front of each support didn't go anywhere: They just led down into the river itself.

Quite a bit of work had been done in recent months on the structure; Eric wasn't quite ready to call it a dam yet. Spillways had been constructed between the supports. Most of the times he'd driven past, two of the spillways had been open, the other five closed, like drawbridges waiting to be lowered.

As he moved closer, Eric looked back over his shoulder. Colleen's Cadillac was still sitting there. Rachel Grant hadn't moved; she hadn't left, but she hadn't tried to come closer, either.

The mist grew a little heavier. It still didn't quite qualify as full-blown rainfall, certainly not by Oklahoma standards, but Eric had to wipe his eyes, and his clothes were beginning to feel damp and thick.

Now he was less than a hundred yards from the Range Rover. It was parked at an angle, facing the field of rocks that surrounded the dam construction. A small building, completely encircled by a high wire fence, was just beyond the Range Rover.

Eric began to circle to the far side of the vehicle. If Grant was sitting in it, he didn't want to be spotted until he was right on top of him. Eric lowered himself into a crouch, his muscles protesting.

He saw the form of a man begin to take shape in the

driver's seat of the Range Rover. He could tell nothing except that the man had white hair.

Eric straightened up at the vehicle's back bumper. The SIG came out of his pocket, pointed at the ground. He wiped rain out of his face.

The driver's door opened.

The man stepped out, and Eric came face-to-face with him.

Grant smiled pleasantly. "Eric Anthony Miles," he said. His voice was calm, even serene. "Congratulations. I wondered if you'd actually find me. I don't know how you did it, but that doesn't matter, does it?"

Eric raised the SIG. "Where's my son?"

Grant cocked his head toward the river, listening to the water rushing through the two open spillways. "In another couple of years, when all this is finished, it's going to make me millions. Oklahoma City will have its new riverfront, and I'll have the most profitable deal I've ever made. Well, at least from a financial standpoint."

"My son, you bastard. I've got you dead to rights. It's all over for your crazy scheme. I want Patrick back."

"Oh, no, Eric," Grant said. The pleasant smile stayed in place. "It's not over by a long shot. It's just entering a new phase."

Eric shook the weapon, and for a crazy moment it was Weldon Hawthorne standing there, not Grant. Eric blinked furiously, but the mist clouded his vision. "Take me to Patrick!"

"The boy is dead," Grant said, with a chilling lack of inflection. "The boy is dead, and you killed him. You refused to heed my warnings. You and your friend Officer Kelly had to keep pushing, and you pushed and you pushed until I was forced to push back. Shameful business, really, being responsible for the death of your own son." A strange look came on his face, almost pensive, thoughtful.

Eric's mind left his body, and he thought he felt it cartwheeling through the misty sky, out over the river, somewhere beyond.

The boy is dead.

Patrick.

He couldn't think. He couldn't remember anything. It was as if Grant's words had wiped his memory clean. In that insane span of seconds he couldn't even recall what Patrick looked like.

"So turn that gun on yourself," Grant said. "Everything you think you know can go to the grave with you. It'll be better if you do it yourself."

Eric raised the SIG. He blinked again. "No," he said. *"No!"*

"Your boy is dead, Eric. Why keep trying? Why go on?" Grant's voice began to lilt.

"You killed my boy. Goddamn you to hell, Grant! All for politics, and *you killed Patrick!* What's to keep me from killing you now? Patrick doesn't need me, so the rest doesn't matter. What's to stop me?"

"Me," said a voice that sounded remarkably like his own.

Drew walked into the clearing holding a nasty-looking assault pistol.

Eric whirled around but he was too slow. In two swift movements Drew had knocked the gun out of his hand and pinned him against the Range Rover.

"Excellent, Drew," Grant said. He looked at Eric. "You know, I questioned Drew's loyalty for a while there. After you and he met, he was, shall we say, a little shaken up. But I helped him to see that you were nothing, and he proved his loyalty to me when he kidnapped your son. When he killed him."

Eric was breathing hard. Drew had knocked the wind out of him when he pressed him against the Range Rover. "You . . ." he said, gasping. "You told us you'd give us some time. You lying—"

"Now, boys," Grant said. "Drew, you're an opera lover. Don't you think this is all very operatic? The two twins confronting each other. The dramatic setting by the river. The rain, the gray sky."

"What now?" Eric muttered.

"Oh, now you die," Grant said. "You've left me no

choices. Your son, you, and then your friend Kelly. She was a bitter disappointment. If only Professor Dorian had lived a little longer."

"We've turned the information over to the government," Eric said. "Kill me if you want, but you're going to fail. Understand that, you son of a bitch?"

Grant looked at Drew. "Kill your brother and be done with it." He leaned against the car. "It really is operatic. I don't like this business of killing family members, but it must be done. The duke of Northumberland sacrificed his own son to his ambitions. I guess it's appropriate that I do the same." He waved a hand dismissively.

Eric stared through the rain. He felt like he was falling. "What?"

"You mean you didn't figure out that part of it? Maybe I gave you too much credit." Grant looked at both twins. "Gentlemen, I'm your father."

38

DEREK MAYFIELD HAD GONE ACROSS THE STREET AND bought a six-pack of beer from the convenience store there. Coming back to the old house, he had Yorkton remove his jacket and proceeded to soak the garment with beer.

"I don't like beer," Yorkton said calmly. "You should know that I prefer gin."

"Sometimes you have to improvise," Faith said.

"So you do."

Faith and Mayfield fanned out to opposite ends of the motel wing. Yorkton, weaving and listing, began to work his way across the parking lot. Halfway there he began to sing.

"*Farewell ye dungeons dark and strong, farewell, farewell to thee,*" he sang in a tenor only slightly off-key. "*MacPherson's life will no be long, on yonder gallows tree. . . .*" He tripped on an imaginary rock just as he reached the edge of the motel. The room 108 watcher looked up.

"Okay, okay, I'm just okay," Yorkton sang. "I've lived a life of grief and strife, I die by treachery . . ."

In position at one end of the wing, Faith peeked around the corner. The Glock was out of sight, tucked into her waistband at her back. She smiled at Yorkton. He was performing flawlessly. She found she even knew the song: It was a setting of a Robert Burns poem. She'd heard her grandmother sing it as a child.

Yorkton stumbled again, only one door away from room 108.

"Oh, there you are, young man," he said, still not quite out of melody. "Could you give me another room key? I seem to have lost mine."

The watcher drew himself up. "Sorry, pal. You'll have to go to the office."

"Office, the office, oh, the office-oh. That's where we are, so I'll take the key, my friend."

The watcher cleared his throat. He shot glances in all directions. "You've had a few too many, mister. Just move along, will you?"

Yorkton broke into song again. "And it breaks my heart, I must depart. . . ."

"Great, a drunk and a lousy singer," the watcher muttered.

"Oh, that's not nice-oh," Yorkton sang, stumbling again. He reached out both arms, and braced himself against the other man.

"Hey, back off!" the watcher said.

"Back off-oh!" Yorkton sang, planting his feet.

The other man tried to back away, and with lightning speed for such a big man, Yorkton knocked his legs out from under him. The man went down with a whoosh of expelled breath, then Yorkton was on his knees beside him, his automatic poking the man in the chest.

"You shouldn't call people names," Yorkton whispered.

Mayfield erupted out of the breezeway, Faith three steps later, coming from the other direction. Using a small Marshals Service battering ram, the door to room 108 splintered open in less than ten seconds.

Mayfield stepped over Yorkton and the watcher, his weapon drawn and ready.

Patrick was sitting in a cheap wooden motel chair, his huge blue eyes round with terror. Another man, about the same age as the other but leaner, with a hungrier look, was holding a gun to the boy's temple.

"You see," the man said, "I'm smarter than Dennis out there. He's a blithering idiot. He mainly strong-arms drug dealers and such. I'm ex–Special Forces. It'll take a hell of a lot more than the singing drunk routine to get to me."

Faith stepped into the room behind Mayfield.

"Oh, it's the tall redhead," said the man with the gun. "Grant said I should expect you. Where's the geek with the glasses?"

"He had another engagement," Faith said. "Who are you?"

"Steele. Now, you"—he nodded at Mayfield—"drop the piece or the kid's brains are all over the wall."

Mayfield hesitated.

"Do you think I don't mean it?" Steele grabbed a handful of Patrick's shirt and twisted it, jamming the gun harder against his ear.

Mayfield carefully placed his weapon on the floor.

"Now back out of the room," Steele said. "Join your pal the singer out there."

Faith didn't move. She looked down at Patrick, saw the terror and the recognition in his eyes. *Get me out of here*, his eyes said.

Plan B, Faith thought.

"So you're the tall redhead," Steele said. "Sexy as hell. Too bad we don't have more time."

"Yeah, too bad," Faith said.

She held eye contact with Patrick and signed to him, *Do you trust me?* She hoped he knew the sign for *trust*.

Patrick waited. He furrowed his brow. Faith had seen the same expression on his mother. With the hand farthest away from Steele, he made a letter *Y* and dipped it forward: *Yes.*

"Hey, what's this?" Steele said. "What's this with the hands? Stop that shit. I don't want to see that."

"This boy is deaf," Faith said, her eyes never leaving Patrick's. "I'm asking in sign language if he's all right."

Step on the man's foot, she signed to Patrick.

His eyes grew wide again.

Step hard on his foot, then close your eyes. Don't open them until I tap you three times on the leg. Okay?

She hoped he'd gotten all that. It was complex, and he was only five. But Eric had said he had an extraordinary vocabulary.

Okay, he signed back.

"I said stop that shit!" Steele said.

Faith smiled at Steele. "Sorry, didn't mean to make you nervous. He says he's okay." *Do it now,* she signed.

Patrick gave a tiny nod. She saw him lift one white Reebok.

Faith reached behind her.

"Don't do it!" Steele screamed.

Patrick's little foot connected with all the force a scared five-year-old could summon.

"Goddammit, you little brat," Steele said. The nose of his automatic slipped a couple of inches away from Patrick's head. Steele lifted his own foot where Patrick had stomped on it.

Faith got her hands on the butt of the Glock. Her peripheral vision saw Patrick tumble out of the chair, his eyes squeezed tightly closed.

Steele's gun hand swung around.

Faith fired.

The shot caught Steele just below the knee, shattering bone. Blood and bone fragments flew. Faith flinched: Some of his blood got on her shirt and jacket. Mayfield stormed back into the room, grabbing his weapon and covering Steele. He kicked the man's gun away from him.

Faith ran to Patrick, scooped the boy into her arms, and tapped him three times on the leg.

His eyes flew open. He saw her, then tried to look back where he had been.

No, Faith signed forcefully. *Don't look at that.*

He nodded, closed his eyes again, and began to sob against her.

Faith called over her shoulder, "Give the signal for his mother."

Sixty seconds later Laura was in the room. Faith handed Patrick over to her and they collapsed onto the bed. Faith saw with some relief that Laura was weeping. So the woman was human after all. She rocked Patrick on her shoulder. He put his arms around his mother's neck and they just stayed that way, rocking back and forth on the motel bed.

After a while Patrick opened his eyes again and looked up at Faith. He touched his fingertips to his lower lip, then dropped his hand down: *Thank you.*

Faith nodded to him. Much to her own surprise, she caught a tear of her own falling. She blinked hard.

Where's Daddy? Patrick signed.

You'll see him later. You rest now.

She walked out of the motel and into the cool of the evening. Local cops were on the scene, called by the motel manager when the commotion started. Yorkton had already put the watcher in the patrol car, and paramedics had been called to treat Steele's wound. Mayfield gave the local police the story Faith had come up with: an interstate child-stealing ring. She appreciated the grain of truth in the story.

She flipped open her cell phone and punched Eric's number. After one ring it went straight to voice mail. "Shit," she said.

She smelled beer. Yorkton had come up behind her. "What?"

"His phone's turned off."

"What do you think he's done?"

"I think," Faith said, "that he went after Patrick himself. And I think he probably found only Grant."

"What are you going to do about it?"

"I'm not sure, at the moment. By the way, where'd you learn 'MacPherson's Lament'?"

"Oh, I've picked up many things in many places over time."

Faith shook her head. The man was more vague than anyone she'd ever met. The phone in her hand rang, and she pressed the Talk button and snapped, "Kelly."

A woman's voice said, "Ms. Kelly, this is Deputy U.S. Marshal Melinda Schipper from Seattle. I'm on the ground at Wiley Post Airport in Oklahoma City with Mrs. Brackett. How do we need to proceed from here?"

Faith smiled. A female deputy. That was good to hear. "How's your passenger, Deputy Schipper?"

"She started out mad as hell, but she's moderated during the trip."

"I should hope so. Stay put, I'm on my way. I should be there in half an hour, then you can head back to Seattle. Good job."

She pressed the End button and started for the car. Halfway there, the phone rang again. She answered without looking at the caller ID. "Eric, is that you?"

"No, Faith, it's Leneski at the Marshals office. Hey, look, we just got this urgent fax here for you."

"A fax?"

"Yeah. What do you want me to do with it?"

"I don't have time to read a fax. I've got nine million things going right now."

"It's from Nina Reeves. Are you working with her?"

Shit! She'd almost forgotten about the photograph, about the work she'd asked Reeves to do for her. "I can't pick it up now. Go slide it under my office door."

"Will do."

"Thanks."

She looked back one more time. The paramedics had arrived, along with a swarm of Oklahoma City police. Mayfield was handling it, per their arrangement: He could snag a little good publicity for the Marshals Service office. She didn't see Yorkton. He'd faded away. He had a talent for that.

Faith got in the car. She had to pick up Governor Archer's twin sister.

The world was spinning around her, too much happening in too short a time. But Patrick was safe, and Grant's manipulations were about to end.

She had one more thought as she headed up the on-ramp to I-35: *Now, where the hell is Eric?*

39

DREW LOWERED HIS GUN. "NATHAN—"

"Let's not get sentimental," Grant said. "It was strictly business."

Eric listened to the roaring of the water, the steadily increasing rain, the sounds of traffic crossing the Walker Avenue bridge half a mile east. His mind felt thick, mushy, as if he'd been dipped in molasses.

His baby boy was dead, and Nathan Grant was his father.

"Terry Miles," he managed to say.

Grant shook his head. "That was the way it was supposed to be. But as you know, things don't always turn out that way."

Drew took a step toward Grant. "Nathan, what the hell are you talking about?"

Grant looked at him. "Sorry, dear boy. I had to lie to you too. I had to make sure you were loyal to me and me alone. The story about your mother dumping you and running off was much better at ensuring that."

"What happened?" Drew shouted.

"Blood means nothing, boys. I've proven that, haven't I? The nobility has always thought that blood was everything. Clearly, it's not."

Eric shuffled his feet, feeling the ground softening beneath his shoes. He thought of something: the day he'd gone to Kerry's Landing, Terry and Maggie Miles's hometown. Curtis, the newspaperman, had thought he looked familiar. He'd wondered if he looked like his mother. But they recognized him because they knew Nathan Grant, a prominent businessman who lived just a few miles away.

"It was all about the money in those days," Grant said. "I had no plans other than to scam some money and to poke the American nobility in the eye while I was doing it. The rest didn't come until . . . later. We paid the sellers a hundred thousand dollars each, half up front and half after they delivered. They came to Mattingly's 'Center,' participated in the 'Mesa Project,' as he called it, and lived for a year. They took Mattingly's little concoction, and they all produced twins."

Eric remembered something Helen Harker had said. "The other side of the building, The Center. That's where the buyers were."

Grant nodded. "Once I identified a buyer, a powerful family who was unable to conceive, I approached them with my foolproof plan. All it would cost them was a year of their time and two million dollars, and they would preserve their family name, their lineage, their *nobility*. They would spread the word to family and friends that they were taking an extended vacation and would come to the center for a year as well. Most of them hated it, hated the remoteness. Of course, that was part of the idea. I wanted them to hate it. I wanted them miserable. I wanted them totally at my mercy."

Eric saw the glint in his eyes, even through the rain. He remembered how Faith had said the man could swing from manners to menace in seconds.

"Mattingly and his old nurse ran the operation, and I gave Mattingly ten percent of the sale price of each baby. After we were sure the babies were stable, I would take them out of the nursery when the nurse was gone, and I would go to the other side and present the families with their newborn sons and daughters. We'd already matched physical characteristics: We got sellers that had the same eye color, hair color, and general appearance as the buyers. These were uneducated young people, the sellers. They were lured by the prospect of more money than they'd ever see in their lives, plus a guarantee that their babies would be well cared for, and that they were free to have other children after they left The Center."

"But none of them were ever heard from again," Eric said. "They all vanished without a trace. Did you kill them, too, after they provided you with what you wanted?"

Grant shook his head. "Don't be rash, Eric. No, all they had to do was take their money and leave the United States forever. That was my one stipulation. Leave the country and never return. Most of them went to Canada, a couple to England or Ireland, one to New Zealand, the English-speaking countries. The one Hispanic couple wound up settling in Argentina. The last I checked, they were all doing quite well. The couple in Argentina went on to have ten more children—and *two* sets of twins. Mattingly's little mixture may have had residual effects."

Grant looked up at the sky. "It's cooling off a bit. I admit, I'm still not used to Oklahoma weather, even after all this time. Up one day, down the next; it's hard to predict. Come on, boys. Let's walk over to the river."

He walked, seemingly unconcerned about Eric and Drew. He ambled around the side of the little building, stopping at the edge of the rock field. A small trail led to an intricate set of concrete and metal catwalks that accessed the dam. A large sign bolted to the front fence read: ABSOLUTELY NO TRESPASSING ON ANY PORTION OF STRUCTURE.

"Our mother," Eric said. "Maggie Miles. What did you—"

Grant waved a hand again, as if he were conjuring something from the rain. "Poor girl couldn't conceive. Mattingly had examined her, she was healthy, but she couldn't get pregnant. She and her husband, the mechanic, were having intercourse twice a day, every day, for two months, but still she wasn't pregnant. We finally got Terry Miles to admit something he hadn't included in his medical history. He'd had a freak adult case of chicken pox the year before. It left him sterile. The idiot didn't even realize it, and I guess no one ever told him of that side effect."

Eric jerked. Rachel had told him that was the reason she and Grant couldn't have children. So he'd borrowed that from Terry Miles. Everything about the man was a lie, convenient fictions adopted from various sources.

"So, what, you raped her?" Drew said.

"Don't be ridiculous. But I will say this: Every day she wasn't pregnant was costing me money. I had to do something. I starting whispering to her, trying to tell her she had to do something. It wasn't her fault, but she had to make it right. 'Think of the money,' I told her. 'Think of what you and your husband can do. Think of where you'll go.' It was a hard sell, I admit. Your mother was a very religious young woman. She was very conflicted about what she was doing in the first place. But she also believed in obeying her husband, and he insisted they keep trying. I've always found it ironic that if her husband hadn't been so adamant, she wouldn't have given in to me." Grant grinned, and it chilled Eric even more than the rain. "By the end, she *wanted* it. By the end, she was *begging* for it."

"You bastard," Eric whispered hoarsely. Nothing had meaning anymore. Everything Eric knew was wrong. This man had killed Patrick. His own grandson—Patrick was his grandson, and he'd killed him. "You murdering bastard."

Grant clucked his tongue. "We're all bastards here, boys." He laughed out loud. "I was adopted, did you know that? Yes, we're all bastards, in the true sense of the word."

"What happened the night we were born, Nathan?" Drew said. He was standing rock-still, steady as the river.

A shadow crossed Grant's face. "Your father—well, Terry Miles—decided to back out of the deal. He and Maggie decided they wanted you, after all."

There was a long moment of silence. Eric thought he heard something move out there in the mud. Then he thought: *Rachel?*

He shook his head. Surely she'd left already. Surely . . .

"Your mother finally convinced your father it was wrong to sell their children. *Their* children. And he came to believe her. I'm sure it was the first time she ever convinced him of anything."

"They wanted us," Drew whispered.

Grant nodded. "It presented me with a new set of challenges. None of the sellers had ever backed out this late before. She was in labor. I was in the hallway, waiting. Terry came up to me from behind and poked me in the back. He was holding a shotgun."

The twins watched him. Something moved out there in the darkness again.

"I don't know where he got it. I still don't know, to this day. No weapons were allowed in The Center, and Mattingly searched the sellers' rooms every week. But he said, 'The babies are ours, and we're taking them.' About that time the old nurse came out with the first baby. You, Drew—Edward Andrew, I should say, since we're being so forthright. I could hear Maggie screaming for her babies in the delivery room. She was hysterical. I tried to calm her down, tried to remind her of what had happened, of *everything*. See, Terry Miles still thought the babies were his. Maggie had begged me not to say anything, and I saw it was in my best interest not to at the time. But Maggie screamed and cried for her babies.

"You'd just been born, Eric, and I was yelling for the nurse to get back and take you. But Terry followed me in with the shotgun. Mattingly was yelling and Maggie was screaming. It was interesting: Terry and I were the only ones who kept our wits about us. He pointed the gun at me, and I honestly thought I was dead. At the last second he swung it around and blew out the window. Then he came after me. We fought, but it was no contest. I was a soft lawyer in those days, and he was a country boy, a hunter. I think he'd been an athlete in high school."

"Track," Eric said, remembering what Curtis had said. "He set school records for track."

"So you've done more homework than I thought," Grant said. "What a pity. But I believe you. The boy was quick. He hit me over the head with the butt of the shotgun, and I went out. When I woke up, they were gone. Everyone was gone, even Mattingly, the old fool. I ran down the hall and found the nurse holding little Edward. I just grabbed him and ran. I took him straight to the buyers, over in the other side of the building. They weren't expecting a newborn, only a few minutes old. I threw you at the mother and left again. I had to catch them: I couldn't let them take Eric out of there."

Grant shuffled along the edge of the rocks, then walked a few steps down the trail to the fence. He leaned over, examining the grid of catwalks below. He raised his voice over the sound of the river. "They didn't do what I expected. They split up."

"What?" Eric said.

"They split up. When I got to the store in Kenton, the man there told me he'd seen them get there in Terry's pickup truck. Then they left in two cars. There had been another one parked around the back of the store, just sitting there for months. But it was dark and he couldn't tell who took what car. One headed west into New Mexico, and the other back toward Boise City.

"I tried to figure who would do what. Maggie had to be weak. I knew that. Good God, the woman had given birth to twins less than an hour before. I knew she wouldn't get far. But I had to think about what I knew of these people, as to what they would do. Maggie, being a woman, should head toward home. Terry was an adventurous sort, anyway: He'd be the one to head off to the unknown."

"So you started toward Boise City," Eric said.

Grant nodded. "The man at the store in Kenton had given me a general description of the car. It was a blue VW Beetle. I caught up to it just below the Oklahoma-Texas border, near the town of Spearman, Texas. I had her and, more important, I had the baby. I had a second family back in The Center, waiting to pay me another million dollars."

Eric smiled suddenly, thinking of a young woman—barely more than a girl and no doubt in excruciating pain from her delivery—and a young man, not well educated but with more common sense than the slick Washington lawyer.

"But it wasn't her. It was Terry in the VW. They fooled you."

Grant's voice rose with sudden vehemence. "Uncouth, hateful people! I was enraged at being outwitted by such people! We struggled, and this time I got the shotgun."

"And you killed him," Drew said.

"One shot was all it took," Grant said. He leaned against the No Trespassing sign. "I took off the VW's license plate, left the car by the road, and bundled the body into my car. I buried him beside The Center, out on the plains. I made Mattingly help me. He was starting to lose his mind even then, but he was afraid of me, so he did what I said."

"And you never saw Maggie or me again," Eric said.

"What about me?" Drew said. "The other family . . . why didn't I go with them?"

Grant waved again. "Damn nobility, they have no courage. They'd heard all the commotion, and they were thrown off when I just came in and unceremoniously gave you to them. They backed out of the deal. I kept the first million and they just left." He focused heavily on Drew. "So I kept you. It wasn't easy, though. I was convicted of federal fraud and conspiracy charges and I went to prison. But I'd worked with the intelligence community, and I had a few assets of my own. I arranged to have you smuggled out of the country. You were kept at a country house in Scotland by a husband-and-wife team of MI6 agents. I'd done a few favors for them, and they wanted out of the field anyway. But before you were five years old I'd become Grant and I was able to get you back. I had the idea to get Department Thirty to settle me in the Lake Texoma area, just in case Maggie ever tried to come home. I hired Darrell Worth to work on the estate, and I gave you to him."

"You lied to me for my whole life," Drew said evenly. "Nothing you told me was the truth."

"Oh, come now, Edward Andrew. Surely you're not having feelings of resentment now. Have I ever denied you anything you needed or even wanted?"

"That's not the point." Eric answered for him. They all looked at him. "Don't you get it, Grant? That was never the point. The point was for us to know who we were."

"Minor details, boys, and I don't deal in minor details. Do I, Edward?"

Drew was thinking. Finally he said, "You said you 'became' Grant."

Grant smiled. "I was Charles Brandon until the government decided to pump me for information and give me a new life."

"Brandon—"

"Oh, yes. Lady Jane's grandfather. It was all fated to be, boys. I met a certain Mr. Winter and we put the plan into motion under the perfect cover of Department Thirty. Very soon, Angela Archer will be President, and I'll be the most powerful man in the country. I will have won the whole game, all the while thumbing my nose at the American nobility. And they're too ignorant to even know it."

"Wait," Eric said. His mind started to fly in a different direction, like a spinning top that was suddenly stopped and spun another way. Colleen had told him . . .

"I need to tend to business," Grant said. He looked at Drew. "Finish this."

Colleen had told him . . . *Think!* Something didn't add up. His father . . . *Terry* . . . the man in front of him . . . his *father* . . .

His mind was shutting down again, fading into some dark recess. Out in the night he heard movement again. Far away an engine started.

Patrick—his boy was dead. The bright smile, the big eyes, part of him. Oh God, part of *himself*. Gone.

He remembered the stones, the grave markers. They had started all this.

Gone Home, it had said on his and Drew's marker.

"The graves," Eric said. "Why the graves?"

"It doesn't matter," Grant said. "Not now. Finish this, Drew."

"Answer him, Nathan," Drew said.

No one spoke for a moment.

"I asked you yesterday if your feelings on this were clear," Grant said. "Are they?"

"They are," Drew said. "Answer him. Why did you make the grave markers?"

"You stupid boys," Grant said.

"Answer us, Nathan!" Drew shouted.

"Don't you ever raise your voice to me again. Not after all I've done for you. The markers were a tangible way . . ." He stopped, wrapping his fingers around the fence at his back. A horn honked over on the Walker Avenue bridge. "I did it to try to help the sellers."

"To help them?" Eric said.

"Yes. If they could view the babies as dead, it would help them to detach. I'm not a monster, boys. After each set of babies was born, I'd take the sellers out and show them the stones. It reinforced the fact that they could never, *would* never, have those babies for their own. They were gone, and they might as well be dead. So I made them dead. There aren't any real graves there, just the markers. I had them made by a company in Nova Scotia and shipped to The Center. No questions asked that way." Grant let go of the railing and folded his hands in front of him. "Your stone, of course, presented some problems. But I went ahead and ordered it. It needed to be there so I could show it to your mother after I took you back." He looked intently at Eric. "I put it in the ground the day before the FBI arrested me."

The stones. It had all started with them, with Colleen's dying words. With the note and the directions from his father, from Terry Miles.

Eric's eyes flew open wide. "Oh my God," he said.

"Finish it," Grant said again.

Drew stood still.

"You're still lying," Eric said. "You still haven't—"

"Now!" Grant shouted into the rain.

Drew didn't move.

"Drew, I have given you everything! Blood is nothing!"

Drew raised the gun and swung it around to Eric.

"Drew . . . Edward," Eric said. "Don't."

"Even with the lies," Drew said, "I owe everything to Nathan. I owe him my life. I can't betray that."

"Don't," Eric said again, but with less vehemence. The lies were still coming, even here at the end, and he was tired of the lies. The lies had killed Patrick.

"Let's go for a walk," Drew said. The gun was leveled at Eric's heart. With his free hand Drew motioned toward the catwalk and the dam. "Out there."

40

MARIELLE SAUNDERS BRACKETT STEPPED OFF THE Learjet and walked to where Faith stood waiting on the tarmac. Brackett looked to Faith's eye to be slightly taller than Angela Archer, her complexion a bit more pale. She wore a business suit, where Archer preferred dresses, at least in public. She also wore dangling earrings, whereas Archer only wore small diamond studs. But the biggest difference was the hair: Although they shared an almost exact color, Brackett wore hers quite a bit longer, almost as long as Faith's.

Otherwise they were the same. They moved in the same fluid manner, both women's hands had the same fluttery quality, and their facial features were almost identical. The only difference: a tiny brown birthmark on Marielle Brackett's left cheek.

"You're the one responsible for all this?" Brackett said without preamble.

Faith extended a hand. "Faith Kelly. Thank you for coming."

"You're not welcome. This is absurd. I'm being treated like a prisoner."

"Mrs. Brackett, I understand you're used to better treatment, but you'll appreciate this visit in just a few hours."

A woman with short sandy hair appeared at the door of the Learjet. Faith assumed it was Deputy U.S. Marshal Melinda Schipper. Faith waved to her. The woman waved back, then disappeared into the airplane again.

"Come on," Faith said.

"Where are we going?"

"Mrs. Brackett, the first place you'll visit in Oklahoma will be our state capitol."

"What exactly is this all about?"

"Trust me. Please just trust me. You'll find out soon enough."

Faith popped the trunk of the Miata and put Brackett's bag in.

"We're riding in that little thing?" Brackett said.

"I didn't have time to arrange a limousine," Faith said. "I had to save a little boy."

Brackett looked at her strangely.

"We'll have to make a stop before we get to the state capitol," Faith said, slamming the trunk closed. "Can't do much about your skin tone, but you can use some darker makeup. We'll cover the birthmark too."

"What!"

"And that hair, Mrs. Brackett. That hair has got to go."

The concrete sloped down to a small break in the fence rail. Drew prodded Eric with the gun. "Climb in," Drew said.

Eric didn't reply. In a way, death would be a blessing. But he would die with lies still swirling around him, like the waters pouring over the spillways of this unfinished dam.

He stepped from concrete up onto the metal gridwork of the catwalk. He followed it to where it intersected the first dam support.

"Forward," Drew said.

Eric walked until he faced the concrete wall of the first support.

"This is a strange place," Drew said. "All these little twists and curves, walkways that don't lead anywhere, staircases down into the river . . ." He shook his head. "Sort of like our lives, yours and mine, don't you think?"

Eric shook his head, almost mimicking what Drew had done. "I don't understand why you're still so devoted to him."

Drew shrugged. "Neither do I. But it's . . . different now. He's our father . . . *my* father."

"And I'm your brother. So what? You heard him: 'Blood is nothing,' remember? What difference does that make?"

"None, really." Drew gestured with the gun. His eyes seemed to flicker away, then met Eric's. "Start climbing."

Grant strained to hear what was going on below him but finally gave up. Slightly hard of hearing in the first place, the sounds of the river and the rain made it even more difficult for him to hear. He would have to trust that Drew would handle it. He walked back to the Range Rover, pulled out his cell phone, and started punching buttons. He had an evening meeting with the governor and her father, to help them put the finishing touches on her announcement speech for Monday.

He called Angela Archer's private line. When she answered, he said, "Hello, Angela. I should be there soon. I've gotten tied up at one of my job sites, but I'm on my way."

The governor was silent.

"Angela? Governor, are you there?"

"I'm here, Nathan."

"Is everything all right?"

"See you when you get here, Nathan. Let's meet in the Green Room. Security will clear you and you can come straight up."

"Angela—"

The governor hung up. Grant frowned. It wasn't like her to be so abrupt. But then, he reminded himself, she was about to launch her presidential campaign. The woman no doubt had a lot on her mind.

There was no easy way to climb the support. The only hand-hold was a rectangular metal protrusion from the concrete. Eric clawed at the metal, got his hands around it, and pulled himself up. Behind him Drew seemed to move effortlessly, even holding on to the gun.

The rage boiled up inside Eric. "Go ahead, dammit! Why don't you just go ahead and do it!"

"Keep going!" Drew said, shouting above the roar of the river. "This isn't finished yet!"

Eric reached the top of the concrete, then dropped to the other side, splashing waist-deep into the river, the water tugging at him. He braced himself against the spillway gate.

"All the way to the staircase," Drew said, dropping down behind him.

"No, dammit!" Eric said, facing him. "This *is* finished!"

"Don't you get it?" Drew shouted.

"What do you mean, don't I *get* it? Almighty God, just get it over with. I'm not going to beg you not to, if that's what you're waiting for! This is what he turned you into: You've got to live with it! Just do it! *Do it!*"

Drew extended his gun arm, the nose of it even with Eric's heart.

Eric closed his eyes, waiting for the pain, then the blackness. Maybe it was justice. This was what Weldon Hawthorne felt, after all.

The gun roared.

Eric's eyes flew open.

Drew had moved the gun off target and fired off into the night.

"What are you doing?" Eric screamed.

Drew turned the pistol around, butt first, and extended it to Eric.

"What?"

"Take it," Drew said.

"What? I don't—"

"Take the gun, Eric. Do it now. We don't have much time."

"What are you talking about?"

"Right now," Drew said. "Here, now, this is the chance for both of us."

Eric took the gun, backing away until he came in contact with the metal staircase. "I don't—"

"You want to destroy Nathan for what he's done." Drew

inclined his head toward the bank. "He said he wasn't a monster. But he is. I can't destroy him, though. I just can't. I guess that makes me a monster too. But you—you can do it."

"What do you mean?"

"You take care of him and I disappear. He'll think I killed you down here. That was the whole idea. But I'll just float away. I'll find a new life. Life after Nathan Grant. I need time to digest who I am, what I am. I'll become someone else."

Eric shook his head violently. He started to open his mouth, then he saw it. "We'll exchange clothes."

Drew nodded. "You'll go back there and tell him it's finished. Then do whatever you have to do. If he thinks you're me, it'll buy you time, or access, or whatever."

"But—" Eric gripped the gun tightly, his mind raging. "I'm heavier than you. I have more gray hair. He won't—"

"Yes he will. Remember what Nathan said up there? He's a big-picture person, not a details person. *I* always took care of his details. Plus, it's dark. He won't notice, not until it's too late."

Eric lowered his voice. "What if he heard us?"

Drew shook his head slowly. "Nathan's hard of hearing. All he will have heard is the gunshot. Tell him you had to chase me—or you, I guess that would be." He smiled in the darkness. "Tell him you got me over here, and the body's in the river."

"And what do you do?"

"I work across to the other side of the river. Should be fun getting through the open spillways. I have a car on the other side. It's untraceable. So's my airplane. I'll fade away into oblivion." His voice turned bitter. "Since I don't really exist anyway, it won't be too hard to become someone new."

"Your airplane. You're a pilot?"

Drew smiled again. "How do you think I knew about putting the pencils in the fuel tank vents? That's not exactly common knowledge."

Eric waited, then said, "I wonder how else we're alike."

"Are you sure you want to know that?"

"Maybe not. I suppose that's best."

Neither spoke for a long moment; they listened to the rush of the river. Thunder rumbled in the distance, far to the west.

"You should know something," Drew said slowly. His tone made Eric look hard at his face. "I did all the things that have been attributed to the Sons of Madison United. I killed the people at Fort Defiance, the officers in Maryland, made all the calls. It was part of Nathan's grand design."

Eric breathed quietly for a moment. "Didn't you feel anything?"

Drew waited, then said, "I don't feel for people. I just don't. I can't explain it. Maybe it's Nathan, maybe it's something within me. They weren't people to me. They were jobs to be done. And because Nathan said they had to be done, I did them."

"He's had that kind of power over you?"

Drew shrugged. "I don't know how to answer that. It's just who I am." Eric saw his head move in the darkness. "The old man, Mattingly. I killed him. I followed him down that country road. I underestimated him, though. He was onto me and turned it into a real chase, then he drove right into that church. I think he had a heart attack, but I killed him all the same. Just before he died, lying there in his wrecked truck, he looked up at me, and he recognized me. *He recognized me!* He said, 'You.' And I didn't understand it. It haunted me. I'd never seen him before. Then after I met you up on the mesa, I understood."

"He thought I'd killed him," Eric said.

"Yes," Drew said. "I'm sorry for that." He waited, looking off downriver. "I don't know what else to say."

"Tell me one more thing, and please make it the truth. I have to know. Did you kill my son, or did he have someone else do it?"

Drew looked him in the eye. "I didn't kill your son."

Eric nodded. "Let's change clothes."

Holding on to the stair rail and the gate, they awkwardly

switched clothing. Neither of them spoke. They traded places.

"Go on," Drew said. Without another word he turned his back on Eric and began to crawl onto the second gate.

Eric watched him go. He grew smaller in the distance until Eric could barely see him in the rain. Then he turned and started to work his way back to the other bank, where Grant waited.

41

GRANT HELPED ERIC CLIMB UP ONTO THE ROCKS. "TOOK you long enough," the older man said.

"He was tougher than I expected," Eric said. "His body will wash up somewhere downstream in a day or two."

Grant squeezed his shoulder. Eric felt his skin crawl. "Your loyalty will be rewarded," Grant said.

"I know."

They climbed into the Range Rover. "Now," Grant said, "I have to get to the capitol. Where do you want me to drop you? Where did you leave your car?"

"Over by your office."

"Fine, I'll drop you there. You're free to go home."

Gone home, Eric thought.

Grant maneuvered the Range Rover through the mud and away from the river. They passed the spot where Rachel had parked the Cadillac. *Thank God she finally got out of here,* Eric thought.

When Grant had the vehicle back on Western Avenue, Eric raised the pistol.

"I don't want to go to your office."

"What?" Grant glanced at him and saw the gun. "What are you doing?"

"We're both going to the capitol."

"Are you insane? You can't—" All the animation drained

out of Grant's face. He pulled the car into a parking lot and stared at Eric. "Dear God. Dear God, it's you. What did you do with Drew? I can't believe—Drew. Where's Drew?"

Eric leaned forward and pressed the pistol against the old man's temple. "Don't you have a meeting with the governor?"

"Is Drew dead? Did you kill him?"

"Drive," Eric said.

Faith had been calling Eric's cell phone at five-minute intervals all evening long. For the moment she was alone in the Green Room of the Oklahoma state capitol. It was immediately adjacent to the governor's office and served as a functional conference room, unlike the more ceremonial Blue Room around the corner.

Portraits of former governors adorned the dark-green walls, and a wooden conference table commanded the center of the room. Somehow Faith had expected something more from the conference room of the state's chief executive. But then, this room was where real things were done. The trappings of office weren't needed here.

Scott Hendler came into the room from the side door, the one that led into the governor's actual office.

"How is everyone?" Faith asked, clutching her phone.

"Cranky. Impatient. Nervous. Mad as hell. Any other questions?" Hendler smiled at her. He came to her, put his hands on her shoulders, and began to knead the muscles there. "God, you're tense."

In spite of herself, Faith leaned into him. She had to admit, he had nice hands. She closed her eyes, and for sixty seconds or so lost herself to the touch of someone for whom she was beginning to care. For one minute she didn't have be tough, didn't have to be smarter and stronger and quicker than everyone else. She didn't have to think about the blood on her jacket, or Patrick's eyes, or all those mothers and babies, or Eric Miles, somewhere beyond her reach.

"Feels nice," she murmured. "But I think you'd better stop now."

He stopped instantly. "Am I pushing too much?"

"Yes," Faith said after a moment.

Hendler sighed.

Faith touched his arm. "You're a good man, Scott. Don't give up."

"Never."

Faith laughed a little, then sobered quickly. "Scott, you know you can't talk about any of this."

"Faith, I don't even know what's going on, other than what I've seen with my own eyeballs. Besides, I'm off duty. This is my own time."

"Yeah, but you're an FBI agent. You're like me: You're never *really* off duty."

He smiled.

A capitol patrol officer, a young blond man named Pfeiffer, rushed into the Green Room. "Officer Kelly?"

Faith and Hendler separated themselves from each other. "Yes?"

"There are two men at the east entrance, downstairs. One of the men is holding a gun on the other. I believe one of them is Mr. Grant."

"Holy shit," Hendler said.

Faith smiled. "Eric, you clever dog. Clear them up, Sergeant Pfeiffer."

"But the gun? I should call the response team—"

"I'll take responsibility for it."

Pfeiffer was struggling. "A gun in the state capitol. Ma'am, I just don't think—"

"Escort them if you like, Sergeant. Just let them come." She trotted to the side door and said, "It's showtime, ladies."

Eric kept the gun jammed in Grant's back all the way through the security checkpoint. They climbed a set of marble stairs, then another, into the capitol rotunda. They passed the sculpture of "The Guardian," a replica of the statue that stood atop the new capitol dome. It was a Native American warrior looking purposefully to the southeast, toward the ancestral home from which his people were "removed" to Oklahoma.

"I don't know what you think's about to happen," Grant said as they passed the statue. "You'll die, whether it's here or somewhere else. You'll join your little boy soon."

Eric didn't respond, jamming the gun against the old man's back. The lighting in the rotunda was dimmed for the evening, but he saw light spilling out of the Green Room. When they walked in, the room was empty except for one person.

Governor Angela Archer sat at the head of the table, examining a sheaf of papers. She looked up at them, then tugged her ear, that characteristic gesture that the cartoonists liked so much.

"Angela, thank God," Grant said. "Now that we're here, call your security team. Do you see what this man—"

Archer stood up, appraising the two men coldly. She didn't speak.

"Angela?"

"Over here, Nathan," said a hidden voice.

An identical woman walked into the Green Room from behind them.

Grant staggered against a chair.

The woman behind them said, "You must be mixed up, Nathan. That's my twin sister, Brenda." Her hand fell on Grant's shoulder. "My name's Linda. Linda O'Dell."

Grant looked wildly at both women. They were identical. But the last time he saw a photo of Marielle Brackett, her hair was longer. She had the birthmark, and her skin tone . . .

Faith walked into the room and stood next to Brackett.

"You," Grant said.

"Glad you could make it, Mr. Brandon," Faith said.

Grant jerked at the sound of his original name.

"Oh, yes," Faith said. "Nathan Grant doesn't exist anymore. His assets all are frozen, and everything about him is null and void. See, he didn't follow the rules of the game, so he doesn't get to play anymore." She looked at Eric. "Are you all right? Eric?"

Eric nodded numbly, looking at the two twins, thinking of Drew, thinking of his mother, and the *lies*.

"Your father—" Grant said, looking at the real Angela Archer.

"I've spoken to my father. He's not feeling well right now."

"The campaign. The President and Hawthorne . . . the Sons of Madison . . ."

"No," Archer said, with a terrifying finality.

"My colleague Mr. Yorkton has gone to Washington to visit Mr. Winter," Faith said. "I'm guessing that Winter approached you once you'd been, ah, reassigned, Mr. Brandon. He hatched the idea of the blackmail, the manipulation, and you did all the heavy lifting. He provided you with intelligence, like the gathering of the police officers in Illinois, the SOMU agenda, and you put it all in motion." She moved around the table. "I knew something bothered me about you the first time we met. I only figured out what it was a little while ago. That first time, when you were posturing and throwing your weight around, you threatened me. You told me to do my job or you'd have to go a little higher up the food chain. But see, there is no food chain. Your only contact is supposed to be your case officer: first Art Dorian, then me. You shouldn't have known of the existence of anyone else in the department. I knew something had to be wrong."

"Angela?" Grant said. "Marielle? How—"

"It's a shame we've never met in person before," Brackett said. "But you know my parents well. They're retired and living on the coast of France these days. I think I'll visit them this weekend."

Grant recoiled. "No." She looked pleadingly at Archer again. "Angela, please!"

"You never learned the lessons of Henry VIII, did you, Nathan? He played at all the games of intrigue and manipulated people around like chess pawns, had people executed when they didn't satisfy him—but his reign was a failure. Style over substance. He left his country in a terrible mess."

"But I could have—"

"No, you couldn't," Faith said. "When attempting an illegal power grab, have the support of the people: You told me that was the moral of Jane Grey's story. But see, here's what you didn't understand: The people find out. They always find out."

Eric had been standing silently, dripping onto the carpet. He raised the gun and placed it against Grant's temple again. The man had to die. For all he had done, he had to die. There was no other choice.

"Eric, there's no need for that now," Faith said, as gently as she could. "He's done. Put it down. We finished him."

"No," Eric whispered. "It's not finished. He killed Patrick. For all this, for power. He killed Patrick. He and Winter . . ." Eric's vision started to blur. "All those mothers, all those babies . . . and Patrick. Don't you understand?"

Faith nodded. "Yes, I do." She turned toward the door and made a sign with her hands.

Patrick ran into the room.

Eric let out a little cry. The gun tumbled from his fingers as if it had burned him. He fell to his knees. The little boy ran to him, nearly bowling him over with the strength of his embrace.

Grant stumbled back even farther, collapsing into one of the chairs against the conference room wall. "He lied to me," he said.

Faith looked at him questioningly.

"Drew," Grant said. "He told me the boy was dead. *He lied to me!*"

Faith didn't respond. The irony, she thought, was eloquent enough.

Eric clutched his son to him tightly, hugging him, rocking him. He didn't even see Laura come into the room, didn't see her begin to cry. He didn't see the governor of Oklahoma begin to cry silently as well.

He just held Patrick, and the two of them clung to each other as if they were drowning.

42

DEPUTY U.S. MARSHALS MAYFIELD AND LENESKI TOOK Charles Brandon/Nathan Grant into official custody. He was searched and handcuffed and led out of the Green Room into the rotunda.

He stopped in the center of the huge open space, staring at the marble, the paintings and sculptures by Oklahoma artists. "I paid for two of these paintings to be hung here," he said. He looked at Faith, trying to focus. "You have no idea of everything I've done. My influence has been felt in every area of American society. I . . ." His voice trailed off, and his eyes shifted again, deep in their sockets. He watched the movement in the Green Room. "What's Angela going to do?"

"I think she's going to rewrite her speech for Monday," Faith said. "And then I believe she wants to get to know her sister."

Grant shook his head. "You people have no idea."

"Sure we do." She nodded at Mayfield and Leneski. "Guys, why don't you bring the car around? I'll walk the prisoner down to the exit." The two deputies walked on ahead. Faith pushed Grant along with her hand. "Let's move it."

The old man—Faith thought, finally, that Grant looked his age—shook his head again and slumped his shoulders. They walked slowly down the stairs and out the east door of the capitol into a pouring rain.

When they turned the corner toward the south parking lot, Grant stopped short and Faith nearly ran into him.

"Hey!" Faith said, then looked up.

Rachel Grant stood ten feet in front of them. Her blond hair was like a fallen flower, plastered against her skull. Her Western-cut shirt was molded against her body. Faith looked past her; parked at the foot of the capitol steps was the big old Cadillac, the one that had belonged to Colleen Cunningham.

Faith understood. She raised her hands.

"Rachel," Grant breathed.

"Chicken pox," she said.

"Excuse me?"

"The goddamned chicken pox. You've never told me the truth about anything, you chickenshit son of a bitch!"

Faith noticed her Little Dixie drawl was even more pronounced as she grew angrier. "Mrs. Grant," she said, and took a step forward.

"Oh, honey, leave it to me," Rachel said. "That chicken pox story was what happened to the man who should've been those boys' real father. You decided it suited your purpose and used it on me. 'Oh, Rachel, honey, I'm so sorry, I'm sterile. We can't have babies.' "

Grant raised his cuffed hands. "Rachel, you have to understand—"

"No, no, *no!* See, I heard it all, every damn word of it. How did you think Eric knew where to go to find you?"

Grant seemed to stumble. His white hair was beginning to mold to the shape of his skull. He raised his hands higher. "No, Rachel—"

"Oh, yes, you chickenshit. You're sterile, are you? But there they were: your *sons. Your* sons, you asshole. I heard it all!" Hands shaking, she reached into her black leather purse. She drew out a gun, a small revolver.

"Here, now, Mrs. Grant," Faith said. "Put that down, now. He can't hurt anyone else. It's all over." She started to edge toward the woman.

"I've got no quarrel with you," Rachel said. "You and Eric helped to uncover what this piece of chickenshit really is. But he's *mine.*"

She lifted the revolver. Her hands weren't shaking anymore.

Faith edged closer. Grant took a step backward. "No, Rachel! You don't understand—"

"I sure do," Rachel said. "For the first time I do."

Faith lunged. Rachel fired.

The shot went wild as Faith tackled Rachel around the

waist, dragging her to the wet pavement. The little revolver clattered away, skittering into the rain.

Faith put her mouth next to Rachel's ear. "Stop," she whispered. "Just stop. He's going to pay many times over for what he did. Just let it go."

Rachel was crying, her head against the concrete. Faith heard shouts from the direction of the capitol steps. That would be Leneski and Mayfield, wondering about the gunshot. Faith heard the sound of their feet running, splashing, and other footsteps as well. She jerked away from Rachel.

"Well, ladies," said the man who'd lately been Nathan Grant. He was a few feet away from the spot where he'd stood, in a crouch, holding Rachel's revolver in his shackled hands.

Faith straightened slowly. "You can't possibly think you have a way out of this. You don't exist anymore. You're a nonperson."

"You're going to clear a path for me, unlock these shackles, and get me a car, Officer Kelly."

"No I'm not," Faith said.

More running and splashing behind them, closer now.

"You do not have a way out of this," Faith said. "Let me repeat that: You do *not* have a way out. Put the gun on the ground."

Here were Leneski and Mayfield, pulling up a few feet from them. "Faith?" Leneski said.

"Hang on, guys," Faith said, feeling the rain drip down the back of her neck. Her eyes never left Grant's. "See what I mean, Mr. Brandon? No way out."

Grant's eyes flickered to Rachel, coiled on the ground like a spring, to the two deputies behind Faith, back to Faith herself. A small smile came over his face. He raised the revolver, wrapping both shackled hands around it.

"Don't do that," Faith said, struggling to keep her voice even.

"Faith?" Leneski said again. Without looking she knew both he and Mayfield had their weapons drawn. She felt her heart beating in her ears. Thunder cracked. Grant jumped.

"Stop me," Grant said. He swung the revolver toward his wife. "Still think I'm a . . . what was the word you used? A *chickenshit* . . . Rachel?"

Rachel rolled over onto her back. She wasn't crying any longer. She spat in Grant's direction. "You don't have the balls to shoot me, asshole."

Fumbling with the gun and the handcuffs, he pulled back the hammer. The snub nose of the revolver zeroed in between Rachel Grant's eyes.

One of his fingers nudged onto the trigger.

Faith's hand went behind her back and all conscious thought was gone. Pure instinct ruled her. In less than a second the Glock was out of its holster and in her hand.

Thunder rolled again. Grant jumped again, the nose of the revolver wavered, and he squeezed the trigger.

His shot thudded into the granite of the state capitol building, chunks of stone flying. Two seconds later he was cut down in a hail of gunfire, Faith's first shot ripping into his chest. Mayfield and Leneski's supporting shots exploded the arteries around the heart. The fourth shattered his left collarbone; the fifth hit the jugular in his neck.

Grant, amazingly, was still standing, spinning in place like a marionette with a crazed puppeteer, holding the revolver. His mouth was working, blood pouring out of it, out of all his wounds, making rivers on the sidewalk of the Oklahoma state capitol. He managed a couple of bloody steps, then toppled off the sidewalk, over a low chain, and into the wet grass.

Sirens sounded. Capitol patrol cars and officers appeared out of nowhere. One of Governor Archer's aides appeared at the east door, then covered his mouth and ran back inside.

This was no disabling shot, as with Phillip Clarke, or even with the thug who'd been holding little Patrick. From the time she'd seen him holding his wife's gun, Faith had known she was going to have to kill Nathan Grant. She shuddered into the rain.

Rachel was suddenly at her side. "Down at the river," she whispered, loud enough for only Faith to hear, "he kept saying 'Finish it, finish it' to Drew. *Drew.* My God, I never knew it. They didn't really look alike, but then again, I never really saw them together much. But their eyes—their eyes were sort of alike."

Faith was silent, feeling the rain.

" 'Finish it, finish it,' he kept saying. Well, I guess it's finished. He shouldn't have slapped me. He shouldn't have ignored me. But most of all, he shouldn't have lied to me."

"No," Faith said. "He shouldn't have."

EPILOGUE

Memorial Day

Drew stayed in the same motel in Clayton, New Mexico, where he'd stayed before he began following Good Mattingly, before the day he chased the old man's truck onto the little country road between Clayton and Kenton.

He got up at dawn and put *Rigoletto* on his little boom box. He used the headphones and listened to the entire opera, uninterrupted, barely moving from one spot on the motel floor. Sparafucile still offered his services, Rigoletto still refused, and Gilda still eventually wound up dead. Drew found himself almost weeping at the end, the first time he'd ever done that.

A little before noon he wandered around town on foot. He bought some bottled water from the town's only grocery store, then walked back to the motel. He turned on CNN while packing, then came back into the room to watch the news conference.

Angela Archer looked tired, as though she hadn't slept much, but she was still marvelously charismatic. Without even saying a word, she could communicate power and empathy and intelligence and experience, all at once.

"My friends," she began, looking sincerely into the camera, "we live in troubled times. The current presidential administration is in crisis, due to a combination of circumstances. Some of those circumstances were brought about by bad choices on the part of some of the people involved. Some were not." She paused, looking directly into the camera.

"You know of my tradition of public service to the people

of Oklahoma, and to this great nation. You also know I've been mulling over my next race."

A buzz swept through the crowd. This was what they'd been waiting for.

"But my next race will not be a political one. . . ."

Eric stopped packing boxes in Colleen's musty living room for a few minutes and watched the speech. He straightened up, wiping his brow, listening to his entire body complain. He glanced down at Patrick, playing Game Boy on the bean bag chair, then looked at CNN again.

"Recent events have convinced me that I need to reexamine my priorities," Governor Archer said.

A collective gasp went up from the assembled media.

Eric smiled.

"Therefore, I am today announcing . . ."

An entire nation held its breath.

". . . my resignation from the office of governor of the great state of Oklahoma."

Shouts went up. Archer held up her hands like Moses at the edge of the Red Sea, and the group quieted.

"I will not comment further, except to say that I'll be spending more time with family." A tiny smile played on Archer's lips. "I've worked very closely with Lieutenant Governor Fields, and he'll do an excellent job for the people of Oklahoma. He'll help us educate our children and create jobs and make Oklahoma an even greater place to live than it is today. Thank you for your patience, and for the opportunity you've given me to serve you."

Archer turned, oblivious to the shouts, and walked back up the capitol steps.

"She's good," Eric said aloud, then went back to packing boxes.

Drew drove slowly up New Mexico 406 until it dead-ended, then turned east. Less than two miles later he crossed back into Oklahoma at Kenton. He turned at the Black Mesa sign and went north until he ran out of road.

Parking at the little turnout in front of the three-state marker, he walked around to the trunk of the car. He took a bulky, canvas-covered bundle out and began to walk along the fence line between New Mexico and Colorado, leaving Oklahoma at his back. *Borders and boundaries,* he thought, just as he had when he'd stood at the confluence of the Ohio and Mississippi rivers and prepared to destroy hundreds of lives. Borders and boundaries, real and imagined, had shaped his life.

He kept his eyes on the ground, finally seeing the stones begin to appear. When he reached the final marker, he climbed over the fence and brushed the dirt and grass off it.

Eric A. Miles.
Edward A. Miles.
July 27, 1965.
Gone Home.

He unwrapped the bundle and took out a large sledgehammer. Without hesitating, he swung it up over his shoulder and down into the center of the rose-colored stone. He swung again and again and again, and when he was finished, he had beaten the stone into dust.

"There," he said aloud, wiping sweat off his forehead. "Now Edward A. Miles can really go home."

He gathered up the hammer and turned to walk back toward the car.

When the tap came on the storm door, Eric looked up from taping a box and smiled. He motioned Faith in. She was wearing a plain white T-shirt and blue jeans, and the gray "newsboy" hat. When Patrick caught sight of her, he jumped up and hugged her hard.

Are you okay? she signed.

Great! he signed back to her. Then, almost shyly: *I like you, Faith.*

I like you, too, Patrick.

He beamed, sitting back in his bean bag.

"Hey," Faith said.

"Hey, yourself," Eric said. "Nice hat."

"Wore it just for you." She pretended to tip the hat to him. "I thought you'd be here."

Eric nodded. "Still a lot to do. Colleen amassed a lot of junk."

Faith glanced around. "So she did."

"Did you see the speech?"

"Most of it. Archer's a gutsy woman. Might make a good president someday."

"Someday," Eric agreed. He finished taping the box, wrote *knickknacks* on it with a black marker, and piled it on the couch. "What happens to Rachel?"

"I'm not sure yet. We're still sorting it all out. Yorkton's been working overtime. She heard an awful lot of things she shouldn't have heard. Most likely she'll be offered a deal to get her into Witness Security."

"Is that who you work for?"

Faith waited a moment. "Not quite."

Eric let it drop. "What about your man Winter?"

Faith sighed. "You know, I really don't like the way we do things in my agency. It's all this need-to-know stuff. We're so compartmentalized."

"What are you trying to say?"

"I asked Yorkton. He said Winter has been handled, and very politely but firmly told me not to press it. So I didn't. But it seems Winter has gone on a leave of absence—medical leave, I believe is the official line."

"And the President? How much of that SOMU stuff was true?"

"There were grains of truth in it. The President did give five thousand dollars to Wayne Devine. But he thought Devine was doing an educational program on the Constitution."

"So he really didn't know SOMU was violent?"

"That's what it seems. The whole business of the President getting Devine off on the weapons charges seems to have been fabricated."

"So they took a tiny truth and twisted every which way to fit what they wanted to do. Sounds familiar."

Faith said nothing.

"And as for you, Faith Kelly? How are you holding up?"

Faith shrugged.

"Come on," Eric said. "You can do better than that."

Faith shifted her feet. "Grant . . . he perverted what we do—what I do. He made a mockery of the system. And whatever flaws it has, I have to believe in the system. He . . . I don't know. There at the end, I think he wanted me to shoot him. I think part of it may have been his little fantasy about Lady Jane Grey and the duke of Northumberland."

Eric looked at her questioningly.

"The duke, the manipulator . . . he was executed. Queen Mary had him beheaded. Who knows? When Grant saw that it really was over, standing there in the rain, he decided to play out the role to the end. That's why he shot at Rachel: He knew we'd cut him down."

"And maybe he was just insane," Eric said.

"That too. I've seen a lot of blood in the last year and a half or so." Faith started to say more, then stopped.

Eric nodded. "I guess Grant got what he deserved. God knows, I was almost ready to kill him myself, when I thought he'd murdered Patrick. But . . ." He looked out a window at the tree-lined street. "But I wish I'd gotten to talk to him again. He was still lying, even at the end."

"Oh?"

"He said he killed Terry Miles on a road outside of a little town in Texas. Shot him with Terry's own shotgun. But Colleen told me that Terry had shown up in L.A. with me in his arms. That's how I came to be with Colleen."

Faith held up an envelope. "Someone was lying, but it wasn't Grant. Not about that, anyway."

Eric stared.

"Sorry to say it that way," Faith said. "Colleen lied to you."

"She was on her deathbed, Faith. That doesn't make sense."

"She still lied."

Eric felt anger rising. "Look, this whole thing is over. I don't see why you came in here and—"

Faith tossed him the envelope. He caught it awkwardly. She found space on the floor in front of the couch and propped her back against it. Patrick looked at her. She winked at him.

Eric opened the envelope. It was a fax page showing a photo of smiling young blond woman, an all-American girl type.

"Maggie?" he breathed.

He shook out the next page. It was a photo of Colleen, her most popular publicity photo, one that still sometimes circulated. In fact, he'd used it for her obituary. It had been taken right before *Angels Cry* was released, a looking-back-over-the-shoulder head shot, her dark hair falling across her face, eyes smoldering, looking dangerous.

"I don't get it," Eric said.

The third page was also Colleen, though he didn't recognize the picture itself. It was Colleen at around age fifty, a few years before the cancer struck. The hair was still raven-black, but her face was hardened, and she no longer looked dangerous but formidable, experienced. That face had seen it all.

"I don't recognize this shot," he said. "Where did you get this?"

"The photo of Maggie was in that box of stuff we dug up from the mesa. You'd never seen her picture before, had you?"

"No, never. I—"

"I have a good friend who's a computer wizard. Sound, photography, anything digital, and she can do it. When I saw that photo, I knew."

Eric looked at the pictures again. He felt as if someone had hit him in the stomach with a sledgehammer.

"They're different enough that the average person wouldn't notice," Faith said. "But in the context of everything that had happened, it just struck me. There were enough similarities that it made me wonder. I think I've said before that I don't believe in coincidence. I'd seen *Angels Cry* on TV not long ago, and then I saw the poster that first time I came over here."

Eric very slowly took his eyes off the pages and looked up at Faith. Her eyes were soft, concerned.

"I had my friend Nina take the picture of young Maggie, and then she downloaded that shot of Colleen Fox off the Internet. I asked her to change the hair, raise the cheekbones, change the nose, the shape of the jawline, and give her dark eyes. Then I asked her to make her fifty years old. Digital computer aging is a wonder. Lots of missing persons, especially kids, are found every day because of it."

Eric dropped the three pages and backed onto the dusty love seat, knocking off a large box. Patrick felt the vibration and looked up at him.

It's okay, Eric signed. He looked at Faith. "How?"

"It seems, my friend, that your mother was a remarkable woman. Just after giving birth to twins, she took you and drove off across New Mexico. She didn't sleep, only stopping long enough to nurse you, until she got to Los Angeles three days later. She was so weak she could barely stand by then, but she made it to the home of a friend who'd gone out there to pursue an acting career a couple of years earlier.

"The friend took her in and took care of both of you until Maggie was stronger. You see, Maggie and Terry had known all along they wanted to keep their babies. They knew Brandon's scam was illegal, and it seems they were both smarter than he gave them credit for. Terry came up with the plan to turn the tables on him. After all, what could Brandon do? Go to the police? Don't think so. Sue for breach of contract? Nope. So they took the first half of the money, fifty thousand dollars, and wired it to a bank in Los Angeles."

"They'd already planned to go to L.A.," Eric said. Everything was murky, as if he were seeing it underwater, as if he were back at the dam across the North Canadian.

Faith nodded. "Terry knew they'd have to take the babies and run as soon as they were born. He also knew they'd have to split up. That's why he'd bought the VW and paid someone to drive it out and park it behind the store in Kenton, so it would be there when they needed to escape." She put her hands in her pockets in unconscious imitation of Eric's nervous habit. "It's strange. For a while Maggie was severely depressed—right up until you were born, as a matter of fact. So depressed she almost hoped she would die in childbirth. She was feeling regret for having let Brandon get her pregnant, feeling that she'd betrayed Terry, betrayed her own soul, everything she stood for. In all the commotion after the delivery, she passed out for a few minutes. When she woke up, it was like she'd already become another person. She knew she had to do whatever she could for you. I think I would have liked her. She had enough sense to ask hard questions, to look at deeper issues; but when she needed to be, she was tough as nails."

Eric smiled vaguely.

"Maggie never knew Brandon had killed Terry on that road in Texas. She just knew that he didn't meet her at the rendezvous in L.A. She never saw her husband again. And he never knew that the babies weren't his. She knew something had gone wrong, and she knew that to protect the one baby she'd been able to take, she had to disappear. So Margaret Eleanor Hendrickson Miles ceased to exist."

"And Colleen Cunningham was born," Eric said.

Faith nodded. "She used almost every bit of the fifty thousand and went to a plastic surgeon in Beverly Hills. She changed her face, changed her hair, and wore dark contact lenses for the rest of her life."

"But it doesn't make sense," Eric said. "Maggie was a devout Christian, she was gentle, she never swore. I've read the journal over and over. Colleen drank, and took dope, and cursed like a sailor, and brought home strange men, and ignored me, and did things Maggie Miles would never have done."

"Did you ever actually *see* Colleen drinking or using dope? Did you ever actually catch her *in the act* with any of the men?"

Eric stopped. It couldn't be. The liquor bottles, Colleen stumbling around drunk in the middle of the night, all those men . . .

"And as for the cursing . . ." Faith smiled. "The one thing

she said she would never, ever do was to take the Lord's name in vain."

"But I—" he started, then broke off. She was right. For all Colleen's salty language, he couldn't remember her ever once saying *God* in anger, as a curse.

Faith nodded again. "See? Colleen Cunningham was an actress. So was Colleen Fox. Cunningham acted for you; Fox acted for the public."

Eric pressed his hands to his head. "Curtis."

"What?"

"Curtis, the newspaperman in Kerry's Landing. He said Maggie was in the drama club in high school."

"Oh, yes, she had always wanted to be an actress. You see, Eric, Maggie had to become something so totally different from what she really was that no one could find her. If someone came around looking for Maggie Miles, mild-mannered, churchgoing blonde with an Oklahoma drawl, they wouldn't find her. They'd see Colleen, the tough-talking, sometimes crude, sometimes inappropriate, dark-haired mystery woman who'd gotten stuck raising a distant relative's kid." Faith shifted on the floor. "She did it for you, just like changing your name. She did it so you'd be safe. She couldn't be your mother, so she was something else. At least she was there. She tried, Eric. She spent her life trying. In her mind the further she was from Maggie Miles, the better for Eric Miles."

"How—" Eric choked. "How do you know all this? How did you—"

She pointed at the envelope.

He dug into it again and came out with a handful of slightly yellowed notebook paper. "Her journal. The missing pages. Where—"

"Here," Faith said. "This house."

"What?"

"Remember Saturday, when I locked you in my office downtown and had you write your statement on my computer? Writing a statement that will disappear into Department Thirty's information archives, never to see the light?"

"Of course I remember. It was just two days ago."

"I'd picked up the fax from Nina by then and seen the pictures. It was then I knew Maggie was Colleen. I figured she'd torn the pages out herself and hidden them somewhere."

"How did you get in here?"

Faith smiled warmly. "You said it yourself. This is the worst house on the block. One of the back window screens was totally off. I cut a hole in the glass and opened the window. I'll pay to have it fixed, by the way. I climbed into her bedroom. It took over an hour, but the pages were wrapped up in her Bible, on the top shelf of her closet."

"I never saw Colleen with a Bible."

"You weren't meant to. Tucked into the Book of Romans, chapter five, were these pages. That passage in Romans seems to have been one of her favorites. The one about suffering and endurance and character and hope."

"Do you have the Bible?"

"I put it back on the shelf. I guess you haven't gotten that far in cleaning yet."

"No, I—" He choked again.

Faith stood up. "Don't be too hard on her. Read the pages. She wanted to be a mother to you, but she thought they'd find both of you and that they'd kill her and take you away."

"One thing I still don't understand," Eric said. "Colleen knew she was dying. Why didn't she just tell me the truth then, instead of sending me chasing off looking for those stones?"

Faith crossed her legs at the ankle. "That's where I run out of answers. Maybe she was really more Colleen than Maggie by then anyway. Maybe she wanted you to look for yourself. Maybe . . . maybe she was afraid of what you'd think of her."

"And yet, she said she would have told me about it if I'd ever asked about my parents. Would it have been the truth or the lie?" He began to feel an icy numbness. "But I never asked."

"Like I said, don't be too hard on her."

Eric waited a moment. "You want to stay for lunch? I was going to make some hot dogs for Patrick and me."

"No, but thanks for asking. I'm going on a picnic with a friend." She gestured to the window.

Eric peeked out. A dark four-door sat at the curb. He saw Scott Hendler's bald spot in the driver's seat. He smiled. "Have a good time."

They were both silent for a long, long time. Patrick noticed the two of them just standing there, and he got out of the bean bag chair and went to his father.

Daddy? he signed.

Eric gave him a thumbs-up. *Go clean up for lunch. Wash your hands. Use soap.*

Patrick rolled his eyes and went off down the hall.

The silence fell again. The two stared at each other.

Finally, Eric looked away and walked around the love seat toward the mantel.

"What are you doing?" Faith asked.

"Just a minute." He began to dig through piles of framed pictures, scrapbooks, old magazines, paperbacks. At the back, against the window, he found what he wanted and dragged it out into the light.

"Will you help me with this?" Eric asked Faith.

Faith touched a fingernail to her scar, very lightly. "Sure."

He dragged in a chair from the dining room and put it in front of the mantel, then climbed up on it. "Okay, hand it up."

She turned it so that it faced outward, then hefted it up to him. In a moment Eric had hung the *Angels Cry* poster on the wall over the fireplace, back where it belonged.

AUTHOR'S NOTE

The twins' cemetery is real. It is not in the place I described it in these pages, and in real life it is one small section of a larger cemetery, but rest assured that it does exist. The name of the town where it actually lies is mentioned in passing within the book. I do not know what really happened to the infant twins who are buried there. I leave that search to my journalist friends.

Black Mesa, the Three State Marker, and the towns of Kenton, Boise City, and Clayton, are real. The town of Kerry's Landing is fictional. I have my reasons.

D.K.

The mystery never ends.

The biggest names in crime fiction from Pocket Books.

DENISE HAMILTON
Sugar Skull
With murders marked by intricate
Sugar Skulls, the Mexican Day of the Dead celebration
takes on a horrifying new significance.

MICHAEL MCCLELLAND
Oyster Blues
Shell' em. Shuck' em. Shoot' em.

S.W. HUBBARD
Swallow the Hook
In a small Adirondacks town, a big-time scam can be lethal.

ETHAN BLACK
Dead for Life
A tragic mistake from the past holds the key
to stopping a killer bent on revenge.

ERIN HART
Haunted Ground
The truth never rests in peace...

M.G. KINCAID
Last Seen in Aberdeen
In a Scottish village, murder is just the beginning.

Wherever books are sold.

POCKET BOOKS
A Division of Simon & Schuster
A VIACOM COMPANY

POCKET
STAR BOOKS
A Division of Simon & Schuster
A VIACOM COMPANY